Cassie's Blessings

by
Yvette Blake

SKINNY BROWN DOG
MEDIA
EST. 2013
ATLANTA | PUNTA DEL ESTE

Published by Skinny Brown Dog Media Atlanta, GA
www.skinnybrowndogmedia.com

Distributed by Skinny Brown Dog Media
Developmental Editing and Design by Eric G. Reid
Content Editing by Timothy Swiney
Cover Design by Skinny Brown Dog Media
Publisher's Cataloging-in-Publication Data Print

Cover Photo by Yvette Blake, Moonlit Dreams, LLC
Copyright 2023 All Rights Reserved.
Cover Model: Melanie Gallup

Book ISBN: 978-1-957506-75-3
Hardback ISBN: 978-1-957506-73-9
Paperback ISBN: 978-1-957506-72-2
Case Laminate: 978-1-957506-74-6

Cassie's Blessings

WHAT OTHERS ARE SAYING

Even better than the debut, *Cassie's Blessings* envelopes you in a tale of love, gratitude, and self-lessness. Right when you think the story is becoming a little too cozy, the unexpected happens and gets your heart racing! Another beautiful and enriching story. Can't wait for the next journey in Cassie's life.

~ Nicole Waters

My family has always enjoyed reading aloud stories with each other. It's a tradition that carries on, even now that my children are young adults. Yvette Blake's growing series has become one that we excitedly wait for each new release with anticipation! We especially enjoy historical fiction, and the added element of clean, family friendly romance has made it all the better! Her latest edition, *Cassie's Blessings*, continues to endear our hearts to the beloved, and thoughtfully developed characters. Any family can confidently know that this entertaining series not only invites the reader into the world of those who lived in the late 19th century, with rich and historically accurate details, but they offer wonderful role models for the values and community spirit that have been the foundation of our country. This is much needed in the quickly changing and turbulent times we're living in. Indeed, Yvette has the gift of making fiction become reality! Her attention to detail is superb and helps draw vivid pictures as you read.

~ Rebekah Bishop

I would give *Cassie's Blessings* a solid five stars. Very well written. The story is so interesting that it feels as if you are right there. You get so engrossed in the story that you are unaware of the real world around you. When you are reading you just have to keep going even if it's well past midnight. Having personally explored the locations described in the book, Yvette Blake's descriptions are absolutely accurate. Love the book, one of the best I've ever read.

~ Richard Crawford

Jesus said, "And now these three remain: faith, hope and love. But the greatest of these is love." 1 Corinthians 13:13

Once again, Yvette Blake gives us an excellent view of the many attributes for the folks who lived in an era specific time period in *Cassie's Blessings.* The outstanding qualities gained by Cassie, Ed and all the rest of the people you meet in this book show a journey that is blessed by the relationships that are formed. Yvette Blake has indeed given the reader an excellent historical backdrop but also the ultimate appreciation of love and its awe-inspiring place in all of our hearts.

~ Marvin Levi James

Dedication

Dedicated to all those who have faced profound trauma, sorrow, and heartbreak, *Cassie's Blessings* honors your strength. Despite pain and adversity, you've embraced life's many blessings, clung to hope, and maintained unwavering faith. Your positive perspective, selflessness, and capacity to forgive, even those who've caused harm, serve as an inspiration to us all. Through the power of forgiveness, like Cassie, you have discovered the ultimate blessing– profound joy and peace, a gift from the Almighty, a true miracle.

Acknowledgement

First and foremost, I must give thanks to my Heavenly Father who blessed me with a gift–a talent that I am striving to grow and share with others. He has inspired me to tell these stories, and I hope and pray that they will bring you joy and peace as you read about the characters I have fallen in love with.

A very special thanks to Peggy Jefferson, my wonderful friend, kindred spirit, and line editor who has been there for me through every page of every novel I have written so far. She has read and reread every word over and over to make sure it's not only grammatically correct, but also beautiful to read. I appreciate the overwhelming support she gives me through every step of the book writing and publishing process. Peggy, you deserve an award for supporting a writer!

My overwhelming appreciation goes to my family and friends on and offline, who have given me support over the past few years as I have embarked on this writing journey. Your positive encouragement has kept me motivated to continue even when it gets discouraging at times.

A special thank you to Melanie Gallup for being my Cassie on the cover of *Cassie's Blessings.* You are a good sport and I appreciate you humoring a writer in her vision.

And last but not least, a heartfelt thank you to Eric G. Reid and his team at Skinny Brown Dog Media. Your skills as a writing coach, editor, and publisher have helped me grow to become better than I could have imagined. I know God put you in my path and has helped us create a story that will bring enjoyment for many, many years. My passion for writing my favorite stories and having them published have become a reality because of your guidance and expertise. It's a dream come true. Thank you for your patience while working with me over the past two years. I hope to continue our writing journey together, until my stories reach the whole world, spreading the good message of peace and joy in spite of the hardships we face.

Contents

Chapter 1

Mr. and Mrs. Havoc

Cassie awoke to the birds chirping in the trees outside the open window above the bed. The room was bright with the sun's first rays as an early morning breeze blew in, caressing her skin with its cool, comfortable touch. A small, pleased smile spread across her face as she stretched and reached out to softly touch Ed's pillow. *He's already up,* she thought. The delicious aroma of frying bacon filled the house and her smile widened as she inhaled deeply. *And he's cooking.* Climbing out of bed, she slipped on her robe and sat at the dressing table. Cassie silently chuckled as she looked in the mirror at the mop of unkempt curls around her face. Her reflection gave her pause as she pushed back the dark curls. She leaned forward and looked closer, trying to see what was different, and noticed an inner glow to her skin and a brightness in her eyes this morning. Her expression was one of pure joy and she knew what had put it there. It was love, and every part of her radiated it. *This must be what they call wedded bliss,* she thought as she touched her lips, remembering his tender kisses. Closing her eyes, she recalled his words of endearment and the intimacy they had shared on their wedding night.

A sound from the kitchen brought her mind back to the present. She should have brushed and braided her hair before going to bed last night. But nothing would have drawn her away from his arms. So, as best she could, she brushed through her hair, trying to tame her massive black mane. Cassie finally gave up as her stomach growled and the smells from the kitchen called to her. *I'll work on it later,* she thought, shrugging her shoulders. *Ed awaits.*

Setting the brush down, Cassie got up and quietly opened the bedroom door, to see Ed standing over the cast-iron stove, pouring pancake batter into a sizzling skillet. When he didn't turn around, a mischievous smile crossed her lips and she decided to sneak up on him. Quiet as a mouse, she tiptoed across the room and slipped her arms around his waist and rested her head against his back.

"Oh, good morning, darling." Ed, surprised by her touch, carefully turned around, remaining in her arms, and wrapped his arms around her. Pulling her close, he kissed the top of her head, loving the feel of her as she fit perfectly against him.

"Good morning, love," Cassie sighed, soaking in his affection. "Did you sleep well?" she asked as she listened to his steady beating heart.

"Like a baby. And how did you sleep, my dear?" Ed stroked her soft curly hair, noticing she was shorter in her bare feet, fitting right under his chin.

"Mm, wonderfully." Cassie closed her eyes and took a deep breath of his scent. "You smell delicious. Like coffee, hay, and soap, and maybe a little like…" Her brow furrowed as she sniffed, "…burnt pancakes? OH! Your pancakes are burning!" she exclaimed, finally realizing what she was smelling.

Ed released her suddenly as she began to laugh.

"Darn it!" he cursed, as he quickly flipped the pancakes over. Ed chuckled as he turned back and wrapped his arms around her again. "I got distracted by something more interesting," he said, and kissed her forehead as she tipped her head up.

Cassie smiled at his good-naturedness. It was wonderful to wake up to her sweetheart. *What a glorious morning,* she thought, looking up into his sea-green eyes. "Good morning, husband," she said sweetly.

Ed was overwhelmed by her beauty. He noticed she was still wearing her nightdress and had allowed her wavy hair to flow freely down her back. "Good morning, wife." Ed kissed her and completely forgot about his cooking again. He withdrew abruptly as the smell of burning batter assaulted his nose. "Oops again!" And they both began laughing hysterically as he took the pan off the stove. "These are getting thrown out, there's no hope for them," he said, and dropped the burnt pancakes into the rubbish bin. "I think I'll make eggs," he concluded, and she laughed.

"Maybe I should help you," Cassie offered, looking at the dirty kitchen counter dusted in flour, splattered milk, and broken eggshells. "You go get the eggs while I clean this up."

Ed kissed her quickly on the cheek. "Yes ma'am. I'm on it." He grabbed the egg basket and hurried out the front door.

Cassie scraped out the rest of the burnt pancake and wiped out the skillet, letting it cool for the eggs. She set the kitchen table that looked so pretty with its new blue and white checkered tablecloth. She loved having her own kitchen, bright and cheery with the morning sun shining through the window.

Cassie had a thought and went to her bedroom and opened her trunk, taking out the carefully wrapped Bluebird of Happiness. She had forgotten all about it until now, saving it for her own home one day. And that day was today. It was one of the only things that had survived the fire. It had been her mother's and had sat in her kitchen window for as long as Cassie could remember. The clear blue-glass figurine was in the shape of a simple bluebird, meant to bring the owner happiness when set in a sunny windowsill. Cassie tenderly cradled the egg-sized bird, as she took it to the kitchen window and set it on the sill and smiled. *Perfect, just like Mama had it,* she thought as the sun's light cast a blue shadow as it passed through the sky-blue glass. Pushing back the white curtains, she opened the window wide to let in the cool fresh air, hoping to clear out some of the burnt odor.

Cassie's stomach churned; she was starting to feel queasy. Pouring herself some milk, she drank it down and began wiping up the counter. Soon the cool air and milk eased the nausea and she moved on with her breakfast preparations. Slicing the bread thick, she placed the slices on the stove to toast as Ed came in with the eggs.

"Here you are. Eggs for my pretty." Ed set the basket of brown eggs he'd gathered from the henhouse on the cupboard.

"Thank you, darling. Breakfast will be ready in just a few minutes." Cassie slid the black skillet back onto the heat. "Could you get me some butter from the cellar, Ed?" Cassie asked, noticing the empty butter dish.

"Would be my pleasure." Ed pulled back the rug from the cellar's trap door and lifted it open, feeling a wave of chilly air as it entered the kitchen. At the bottom of the stairs, he found the crock of butter on a nearby shelf and brought it back up. "I sure love having a cellar," he said, setting the butter on the counter; then he closed the trap door, and replaced the rug.

"I'll say! It will come in handy in the fall once the garden is gathered. We'll have vegetables all winter long," Cassie said, dreaming of a full cellar, as she took four brown eggs from the basket.

"It's a great place to cool people quickly, as well," he said, alluding to her harrowing experience with heat exhaustion just a few days ago. "As we discovered," Ed teased, leaning over her shoulder and kissing her pink cheek.

Cassie knew he was referring to her and was glad he was able to joke about it now. She gave him a sideways glance and a tender smile. "Yes—it has many uses."

Ed watched as she scooped a slab of butter from the crock, melted the butter in the warm skillet until it sizzled, then cracked four eggs into the pan. It felt almost like a lovely dream; Cassie standing in her bare feet and nightdress, cooking him breakfast in the kitchen of their cottage. He had imagined it when they had bought the place, and now it was real. Cassie was his wife, and he could hardly believe it.

"Now, how do you like your eggs, darling?" Cassie asked, realizing there were still things to learn about her new husband.

"Any way you cook them, will be my favorite." Ed honestly didn't care, as long as she was there with him. He loved her so much, he would have eaten the egg whole, shells and all, if that's how she served them.

Cassie smiled at him over her shoulder and shook her head in disbelief. "Well, if I leave the yolks runny you can soak them up with the toast I made. Would that be OK?" she asked as she flipped the eggs, careful not to break the yolks.

"That sounds wonderful." Ed took the kettle off the stove and poured himself some coffee. "Would you like some?" he asked, ready to fill her cup at the table. When she declined, he returned the kettle to the stove.

Cassie brought the skillet to the table and slid the over-easy eggs onto their plates.

Ed stared at the two fried eggs on his plate and his stomach growled. "It looks delicious, Cass."

"Thank you, Ed." Cassie set the skillet in the sink

and brought the pitcher of milk to the table with the plate of toasted bread. Remembering the preserves that Aunt Mabel had given them, she brought that to the table too. Cassie's heart swelled with pride as she served her first meal to her husband in her own kitchen.

"Let's eat," Ed announced as he pulled out her chair. Once she was seated, he took his place at the head of the table. Taking her hands in his, he bowed his head and said the blessing. "Dear Lord in Heaven, we thank thee this Sabbath day, for thy bounteous blessings. For this home and food and especially for Cass, for becoming my wife. I love her so much. Please bless this holy union, and our precious baby, and keep it safe. In the holy name of Jesus Christ. Amen." He finished and gave her hands a gentle squeeze.

Cassie opened her eyes and a tear rolled down her cheek. She leaned forward and kissed him soundly. "I love you, darling, I'm so happy you're my husband. Every day I thank the Lord for you," she said, smiling as he kissed the back of her hands one at a time before releasing them. "Now eat your breakfast before it gets cold," she chided with a wink, and wiped away the joyful tears.

"Yes, dear," Ed said sweetly, smiling as he took the thick toast and slathered butter over it, breaking the yolk with the corner, coating the crust in bright yellow goodness, and took a bite. "Mm, perfect. Just the way I like 'em," he said, with his mustache lifting at the corners.

Cassie smiled; she had never tasted such a delicious breakfast either. It was truly a glorious day. *My first full day as Cassandra Havoc,* she thought contentedly as she ate with her favorite person. *I wonder if this is how Ma and Pa started out?* she asked herself, wanting her marriage to be as happy as theirs. Cassie was determined to try her best, to be a good helpmate for Ed.

***

Being the Sabbath, Cassie knew she would need to get dressed for church soon. Once she had cleaned up breakfast, she retired to the bedroom to make the bed and dress in her Sunday clothes while Ed went out to finish up the morning chores. When Ed came back inside, he found Cassie sitting at the dressing table, twisting and pinning up her hair.

"Done already?" Cassie asked, surprised to see him back from chores so soon.

"Almost—I saw this and thought of you." Ed held a little white flower between his thumb and forefinger and presented it to her, then leaned over and kissed her on the cheek. "A woman should be given flowers—not just on special occasions."

"Oh, how pretty," she said, admiring the dainty petals. "Thank you, darling." Cassie placed the flower in her hair just above her ear. "There—beautiful," she said, admiring the snowy white petals against her upswept curls in the mirror.

"Yes, you are," Ed said, watching her look at her reflection.

Cassie blushed and smiled up at him. "Oh Ed. You're too kind." Lovingly, she took his hand and kissed the back of it with a gracious, "Thank you."

"You keep that up, you'll have a bouquet by the end of the day," he said chuckling, loving every second of her tender kisses.

"You keep this up," Cassie said, pointing to the flower, "and I'll marry you again and again." And she laughed at the thought.

"It's a deal. How soon can you be ready?" Ed's quick retort made her smile spread across her face. And just as quick, he took her hand and kissed the ring on her finger. "I do!"

"Oh, Ed. You big tease." Cassie touched the handsome cleft in his chin and tipped her head back to kiss him. "We have to get ready for church. I'll marry you again later today," Cassie said, laughing at the game they were playing.

Ed let her hand go. "Fine, you promised. And I'm holding you to it." He pointed at her as he chuckled and backed away. "I'll be back to change for church once I've finished the chores," Ed said, and he hurried out the door.

Cassie watched him go, thinking how much she loved being married. It was a wonderful feeling to be with someone you loved and adored and who felt the same way about you. With Ed, she never knew what to expect next, he was such a tease. She was happier than she had ever been and hoped he was as happy as she was. More and more she was learning what a generous and loving man Ed was. Already he had done so much for her. Writing her a special song and singing it to her on their wedding day had been the best gift she'd ever gotten, and she wanted to give him something just as special to let him know how much she loved him. *But what can I give him?* she wondered as she finished dressing for church in her blue Sunday dress. Sadly, nothing came to her mind immediately and she continued to think of all the things a man would appreciate.

Ed finished the chores and came inside, heading straight to the bedroom to change. He paused in the open bedroom doorway as he saw Cassie dressed in the dusty blue flower print dress with white lace edging. It reminded him of the first time he saw her in that dress at the church picnic. He remembered how different she looked then, so pale and somber, yet so beautiful. His heart was drawn to her, aching to help her somehow.

Through the open bedroom door, Cassie heard Ed come into the house. With her back to the door, she turned her head, wondering why he hadn't come into the bedroom to change into his Sunday suit.

Ed smiled as she looked back at him. "You look lovely, dear. Even more lovely than the day I first saw you."

Cassie blushed and brushed self-consciously at the non-existent wrinkles in the skirt and straightened the front of the fitted bodice, checking in the mirror to make sure all the buttons were done up.

"I'll never forget that day. You looked so beautiful, sleeping so peacefully under that tree. Of course,

I had to check and make sure you were all right," he said with a dreamy look in his eyes, leaning against the doorframe, appreciating the way the dress accentuated her feminine curves.

Cassie smiled lovingly at her handsome husband. "You know, I feel like you pulled me out of my slumber that day and brought me back to life again." She went to Ed and hugged him, resting her head on his broad chest. "I have so much to thank you for. And I have no idea how to go about doing it. I don't know what to give you to show you how much I love you. You showed me by giving me a song and so much more. But what can I give you?" she asked, honestly wanting to know how to show him her gratitude and love.

Ed squeezed her, then loosened his embrace to look into her green eyes. "Cass, you have given me more than anyone. Every day you give me hope, and joy, and love beyond my wildest dreams. I don't have need for anything else, except you," he said softly, then kissed her deeply, to show her he meant it.

Cassie didn't know how he did it, but he always did. Ed had a way of making her feel special and loved beyond any doubt. He slowly released her lips as her heart swelled with love for him. Looking into his soft green eyes she whispered, "Darling, you are all I need. And all I want and all I love…and then some," and returned his passionate kiss with one of her own.

Blushing from her forwardness, Cassie made a quick excuse and left the room, saying she needed to read the Bible before church and would give Ed some privacy to change. Ed smiled after her, loving her spontaneous show of affection, and chuckled to himself at her modesty.

Cassie sat reading the Bible in the front room, when suddenly she remembered what day it was. She jumped up and rushed into the bedroom, banging open the door and startling Ed as she entered.

"Ed, we forgot! It's the 4th of July! It's Independence Day. There's a church picnic today and I haven't got a thing to bring," Cassie said franticly. All her growing up years, Cassie's mother had taught her that one never attended a church picnic empty-handed.

"Cass, it will be OK," Ed calmly responded as he finished buttoning his white shirt and tucked it into his brown Sunday pants. "I think we can rustle up something. Let's just think a moment." Suddenly an idea popped into his head. "Do we have time to bake some pies?"

"Yes—but with what? I have nothing to fill them with," she said, trying to figure out what he was thinking.

"Yes! You do! Peaches!" Ed exclaimed, his eyes beaming with excitement. "Remember the jars of peaches down in the cellar? They'll be perfect. If you started on the crusts right now, I could help, and we could have two hot pies out of the oven just in time to take with us," he said, quickly pulling on his vest and stringing his pocket watch through the buttonhole. "I'll go get the jars and you get started." Ed gave her arm a reassuring squeeze as he rushed past her to the cellar's trap door.

Cassie hurried to put her apron on over her Sunday dress and took out the ingredients for the pie crusts. She stoked the fire in the stove and set out a pot to get the filling ready as Ed came back up the cellar steps with two jars of peaches. Cassie worked quickly, pouring the syrup off the peaches into the pan on the hot stove and adding sugar, corn starch, butter, and cinnamon. As she worked, she had Ed cut the peaches into slices. Cassie rolled out the crusts and had them pressed into the pie tins by the time the oven was hot enough to bake the pies. Adding the sliced peaches to the bubbling orange syrup, she continued to stir as it thickened. The vibrant orange peaches made their mouths water from the heavenly scent as Cassie poured the filling into the crust-lined tins. Carefully placing the top crusts on, she trimmed and pinched the edges together, then cut a few slits across the tops. Lastly, she whipped up an egg white and brushed it over the top and edges to keep the crusts from burning.

"There, that should do it," Cassie said as she carefully placed the two pies in the oven. "I hope they have enough time to bake before we have to leave," she said, feeling panicked. She'd never been late for church before.

Ed checked his pocket watch. "We have almost an hour before we have to leave," he said as he filled a pan with water to boil for the dishes.

"Oh, thank goodness. That should be just enough time for them to bake. Thank you for the great idea,

Ed. You're a life saver. Everyone will love the pies… as long as they turn out." Cassie now fretted over how they would taste as they started cleaning up.

"We make a pretty good team, I think," Ed said proudly as he swept the floor.

"I couldn't have done it without you. I didn't even remember we had the peaches in the cellar," Cassie said, setting the pans in the sink and adding soap shavings and a few pumps of water from the spigot.

"Oh, I did. Ever since I saw them in the cellar I've been wondering when we would get to eat them. I love peaches." He poured the hot water from the stove over the dishes, making the soap shavings dissolve and bubble.

Cassie swished the soap around and began washing the dishes. "I love them too but forgot all about them. I just hope they taste good." She'd never made peach pie with bottled peaches before and wondered how they would turn out. "You'd better finish getting ready. We'll have to leave as soon as the pies come out."

"You're right. I'll go hitch up the team. It's getting hot out there, so you'd better bring your fan with you," Ed said as he hurried outside.

Cassie finished the dishes and put them away as she thought about Madeline. Her new-found friend would have already left on the early morning train to make the trip home to her husband and children. Cassie would miss her good friend that was so much like an older sister. It had been a godsend having her there on her wedding day. Having Madeline, as well as Aunt Mabel and Uncle George there on her most important day had helped her not miss her family as much.

When it came down to it, she had felt her family there with her, at least in spirit. Cassie knew Ma and Pa and her brothers and sisters were happy for her; she felt it. But if they had been there, surely her little sister Mary Jane would have been the flower girl, dressed in a pretty pink dress, leading the wedding march down the aisle. And her sister Charlotte would have stayed awake with her late into the night, talking and giggling—until their Pa got after them, that is. Ma would have helped her get ready, curling her hair, and helping her get dressed in the wedding gown she would have insisted on making for her. Her brothers Mark and Nathan would have helped set up the tables and decorations for the reception. And Pa would have walked her down the aisle to Ed.

Her family would have wholeheartedly welcomed Ed, loving how hard-working, fair-minded, and generous Ed was with his time and affection for her. His teasing and cheerful disposition were so like her brothers'. Pa would be happy, knowing his daughter was loved and cared for, as he had done for all those years. Her mother would have cried a few tears, but they would have been tears of joy. Ma would have been so excited to see her daughter become a wife and mother. It had been Ma's one desire for her children to find the same joy she had found in building a family. Even still, her wedding had been beautiful and special all the same. And she was certain she felt them there as she and Ed took their vows. Cassie had felt such peace and joy surrounding her that day.

Ed came back inside, and her daydreaming ended as her lovely reality continued.

"Those pies smell wonderful," he said as he passed, kissing her on the cheek. "I'll just be a minute."

"That's about all they need." Cassie checked the pies. "Just a few more minutes to brown the top," she said as she closed the metal door. From the pantry, she got a large basket and set it on the table, lining it with towels, ready to set the pies in and cover them.

Loaded in the buggy with their hot pies, they headed to town. Cassie held the basket on her lap to guard them from being jostled to pieces as Ed drove as carefully as he could. It was a warm July morning. The sky was blue with a few high clouds and a nice breeze blowing across the prairie. Cassie slipped her arm through Ed's and enjoyed the ride in the shade of the canopy. They arrived at church just in time. Walking in together holding hands, they sat on the pew next to Uncle George and Aunt Mabel, who greeted them with smiles.

Chapter 2

Church Picnic

It was a nice church service but by the end, everyone was very warm, and Cassie was glad she had listened to Ed and brought her fan.

As they were leaving, Cassie paused to talk to her aunt. "Aunt Mabel, thank you for the beautiful wedding quilt and the curtains and tablecloth. Our home looks amazing now." Cassie gave Aunt Mabel a quick hug.

"Well, I had help. With the fabric from a few of my old dresses, the ladies of our Sewing Bee Circle were able to piece it together and did most of the quilting as well. It turned out beautiful, I think," Mabel said, pleased that Cassie had liked it. "And the curtains, Madeline and I sewed up and hung while you were busy."

"Oh, how kind of you and Madeline and the ladies. I'll be sure and write Madeline and thank her too. I would also like to thank the Sewing Bee ladies," said Cassie, looking around at the emptying church. It was clear everyone was excited to get to the picnic and hadn't wasted any time leaving.

"Well, maybe you can. Are you going to the church picnic now?" asked George.

"As a matter of fact, we are. We happened to remember it was the Independence Day church picnic just in the nick of time," Ed explained, joining in the conversation.

"Yes, thank heavens, Ed had a great idea and saved the day, again," Cassie said, smiling up at Ed with adoring eyes.

Ed put his arm around Cassie's shoulders and gave her a squeeze. "I had the idea, but Cassie was the one that made it happen. Peach pie. I can hardly wait to taste it. Makes my mouth water just thinking about it," said Ed.

"That sounds delicious. I haven't had peach pie in years. We'd better be first in line for desserts," said George, licking his lips. "I was going to suggest thanking the sewing ladies when you get to the picnic, since they will all be there. We also have all your presents at the house. When you come over for supper tonight you can take some of them home. There are quite a few. The people were very generous with the gifts," George said as they began walking down the aisle to leave.

"Oh, we should thank the Pastor as well," Cassie said looking around, and saw him outside, shaking hands with the members as they were leaving the church.

Ed led Cassie to the Pastor. "Reverend Gather, we wanted to thank you for doing such a nice job on the ceremony yesterday. It was perfectly beautiful," Ed said graciously as he shook his hand.

"Yes, thank you, Reverend Gather," said Cassie as she shook his hand.

Reverend Gather smiled and held Cassie's hand and placed his other hand over hers. "I want to thank you, for asking me. It was a pleasure to marry such a wonderful couple. You both really are blessed to have each other. God will be with you if you keep your covenants. I know this to be true," he said. "Congratulations, you two."

Joining the church members at the picnic, Ed and Cassie helped set up as quickly as they could. Cassie helped the women with the food and dishes as Ed and the men put up the make-shift tables and brought out the chairs. It reminded Cassie of the first church picnic she attended in Cheyenne. That day she had felt lonely and apprehensive. So much had changed in such a short time. Now she was part of a community of worshipers, feeling their support and fellowship as they worked together. The women chatted excitedly with her about the wedding, complimenting her on how beautiful she was and how handsome Ed had looked. Cassie spent the afternoon thanking the many women who had helped with the quilt, being sure to mention how beautiful it was. She also thanked those who had given other gifts. Although she hadn't had a chance to open any of them, she made sure they knew how much she appreciated it. Often, they would make apologies: "Oh, it was nothing, just a set of pillowcases." An older woman remarked, "It wasn't anything fancy, just something practical." "I figured you could use them," said a young mother about some dish towels she had given Cassie. To each humble woman, Cassie expressed her gratitude for their thoughtful generosity and well wishes.

"When we heard your story and what had happened to your dowry, we all pulled together and gathered up what we thought you could use," mentioned a kindhearted woman.

It touched Cassie to think how blessed she was because of their good hearts. Ed came over to the ladies and announced the tables were ready and asked if he could carry some food to the tables for them. The ladies handed Ed a large dish to carry and then whispered to each other how sweet he was. Cassie smiled as she overheard them and agreed completely.

As the members bowed their heads for the blessing, it was clear how tight the community was. With the blessings said, everyone lined up at the tables filled with the food they had all brought to share. Cassie's pies had been placed on a separate table with the other desserts. Cassie silently pointed out the pies to Uncle George so he would be sure to get a piece. George and Mabel found a place at the end of one table while Ed and Cassie sat at another, visiting with those around them. With a grin, Ed arose, being the first one to finish eating, and went to the dessert table and dished up a slice of the peach pie. He proudly walked back with his prize, grinning like a little boy who had caught a whopper of a fish.

"I got some of the peach pie! I can't wait!" Ed sat down and cut a bite with his fork and offered it to

Cassie. Holding the fork out for her, he waited for her to take a bite. Cassie smiled and opened her mouth. She closed her lips and Ed slid off the flaky crust and sweet juicy peach pie into her mouth.

"Mm, it is delicious!" Cassie said, with her mouth still full. "Now you try some," she said smiling, and cut him a piece with her fork and fed him. Ed opened his mouth to accept the pie, smiling as she fed him, and thought what an endearing thing it was to be fed by your love.

"Oh, it is delicious. It really is the best peach pie I think I've ever tasted," Ed said, enjoying the sweet peach flavor and flaky crust. "Cassie, you work wonders with food."

Cassie knew Ed had helped her, and felt he was being very generous with the compliment, but accepted it graciously. "Thank you, my dear. I couldn't have done it without your help," Cassie said, smiling as others around the table remarked how good it looked. Oh, how she loved her husband.

The couple across from Ed and Cassie finished eating and left the table. Moments later, to Cassie and Ed's surprise, Bart and Bea came over and sat down.

"Hi Ed! Hi Cassie! How are the newlyweds today?" Bart asked, grinning ear to ear.

Ed responded with gusto, "Perfect!" then looked back and forth from Bart to Bea, trying to figure out why the two of them looked like the cat that swallowed the canary. Ed was good at reading people, and it was obvious to him that the two of them had something they were hiding. "And how are you two?

Got any news to share?" asked Ed with a mischievous grin, wagging his eyebrows.

"Ed, don't pressure them," Cassie said, gently scolding him for teasing the couple, seeing them both grin and blush at his question.

"We will let you know as soon as it's official," said Bart quietly, and reached under the table and squeezed Bea's hand.

Bea smiled and blushed even deeper, looking around to see where her sisters and parents were. Her sisters would never let her live it down, if they knew she had a beau and was showing public affection.

Cassie understood what they weren't saying and smiled at them both. "I'm so happy to hear that. And thank you both again, for helping us with our wedding. Ed looked perfectly dashing. It was a good thing I was marrying him. At least now everyone knows he's taken," Cassie said, teasing him a little.

"Why do you think I married you so quick, my dear?" Ed quipped, squeezing Cassie around the shoulders. "I wanted to marry the prettiest girl in town before someone else did. And I think my plan worked out pretty well," Ed teased back.

Bart watched them bantering, and thought, *I think I'll do the same. I'll marry the most beautiful girl in town just as soon as possible.*

Bea must have read Bart's thoughts, for she smiled at him, looking at him as if he had said the words out loud. Bart squeezed her hand in secret, letting her know he understood.

Bea turned to Ed. "I would love to get the music

for the song you sang last night. Would you be willing to lend it to me? I would love to play it on the piano. I thought it was very beautiful," she said kindly. "You have a very nice singing voice."

"Well, thank you, that's nice of you to say so. I would have to write it down for you. But I could do that. I think it would be great to play it together some time," Ed said looking at Cassie. "I would love to sing it to you again, my dear…with accompaniment."

"How about we get together some time, and I can play my violin as well," suggested Bart. "I think it would sound amazing, all of us playing and singing together." Bart could imagine singing the words to Bea as he played his violin. He silently thanked his mother for making him take violin lessons.

"Oh, that would be wonderful," said Cassie, looking to Ed with a knowing look. He nodded, and she proceeded. "How about you both come to our house this Friday for supper? I'm sure Ed can get you the music by then," Cassie said, as Ed nodded again. "We don't have a piano, but Bart could still bring his violin and play along with Ed while we sing." Cassie clasped her hands to her chest in excitement. This would be their first real company.

"Sure thing, if that works for you, Bea?" asked Bart, looking hopefully into her blue eyes.

"I would love to. It will have to be after six o'clock, that's when we get off work." Bea was excited by the invitation, and to get to spend more time with Bart. "I would need to pick up Bart and drive out to your place. Would seven o'clock be all right?" Bea asked.

Cassie looked at Ed who smiled his reply. "I think that will work just fine. I can hardly wait." Cassie's eyes sparkled with excitement.

"Looks like I'd better get practicing if I'm to be the entertainment," Ed said, grinning. He loved the idea of having guests in their new home. Showing off his wife and her talents made Ed proud.

As they continued to visit, Cassie noticed how easily they got along. There was no awkwardness between them, all issues had been resolved, and seemed in the distant past.

"Did you try the peach pie?" asked Ed. "It's amazing, Cass made it," he said, smiling as he finished the last bite.

"It looked wonderful. I'll go get us each a piece," Bart said to Bea, and he stood to go.

"I'll come with you. I'll show you where it is," Ed said, as he came around and put his hand on Bart's shoulder. "You don't want to miss it," he said, chuckling.

Bea looked at Cassie as soon as the men were gone and whispered, "I about died of embarrassment last night when I caught the bouquet. But it was all worth it. Bart says he wants to marry me. I can hardly believe it," she said with astonishment, her eyes shining.

Cassie reached across the table and patted Bea's hand. "I'm so happy for you. Bart's a good man. He just wasn't right for me." Cassie smiled. "He's lucky to have found you. You seem so good together."

"Thank you for saying that. You are the only

person that knows. Bart says he will ask for my hand when he has something to offer. But I don't care about that; he has everything I need right now. I think he feels like he has something to prove," Bea said.

"Why would he feel like that?" Cassie asked, and then remembered what Ed had told her. "Oh, because of his father."

"Yes, his father wrote to him and told him he was on his own, essentially disowning him for coming to Cheyenne. Bart read me the letter. It was heart-breaking to hear," Bea whispered, and looked over at Bart standing at the dessert table with Ed. "But I think Bart's doing what's right for him. He'll be a better man because he's had to make his own way. I love him more for it." Bea's cheeks turned as red as her hair as she said the words.

"You're right. I can already see a wonderful change in him since he came here. This is good for him, and you are great for him, too," Cassie added. "Bart seems more sure of himself than I've ever seen him. He can be himself—the man *he* wants to be." Cassie was truly happy for Bart. He was going to be a good husband to Bea.

"Oh, here they come. Shh," Bea whispered, not wanting Bart to know they had been talking about him.

"We come bearing gifts," proclaimed Ed, handing Cassie her own piece of pie, now that she had finished her dinner.

Bart had brought back two pieces, one for Bea and one for himself. "We got the last of the pie. I feel bad, so many people are missing out," Bart said grinning. "But not that bad," he said as he took a bite. "Mm. It is perfectly delicious. It makes me miss…" Bart stopped before he said the word "home" and looked away, feeling an overwhelming sadness.

Bea tenderly touched his arm. "It's OK to miss home. You can't deny that you miss them. They're your family. Of course you miss them. They'll come around eventually, give them time. And when they see how good you're doing, they'll be proud of you," said Bea. "*I'm* proud of you," she said softly.

Bart registered her words and turned to look at her. "Thank you, Bea. That means so much to me," he said with a small smile.

"I'm proud of you, too," announced Ed cheerfully. "You have become a model citizen in such a short time," he said chuckling, and they all started laughing, remembering not that long ago, Bart had spent the night in jail for fighting. Ed had such a way of brightening the mood of the conversation.

"Ed, dear. You are quite the character. What would we do without your teasing?" asked Cassie, leaning over to hug him.

"Lead a peaceful, but boring life, probably," Ed teased. And they all laughed again.

"OH Ed! You're incorrigible," exclaimed Cassie as she tried to stop laughing.

On and on they talked and laughed as they told stories about their lives. Before they realized it, people were beginning to put away tables and pack up. It had grown late, and they stood to help clean up. They were all looking forward to Friday's get-together. It seemed they were becoming great friends.

Everyone packed up their empty food dishes and took down the tables and began to leave for home. Ed and Cassie were some of the last ones to pull away. With their buggy packed, they headed out, waving goodbye to Bart and Bea as they drove off.

***

Later that afternoon they went to Aunt Mabel and Uncle George's house to unwrap their presents and have Sunday supper together. As evening set in, they headed home with their buggy loaded with wedding presents and talked happily about their first day together as husband and wife. It felt glorious to be married. Ed expressed how nice it was to be going home to their own place and Cassie smiled in agreement. She loved having her own home with Ed. And soon they would be a family of three, as she suddenly remembered; she was already two months along. It was funny how she'd forgotten for a moment, being so busy with the wedding. Cassie sat quietly and smiled. Her dream of having a family was coming sooner than most.

Ed sensed a change when he saw her become thoughtful and asked, "What are you thinking, my dear?"

Cassie turned and looked at him as he focused on the dark road ahead. "I was just thinking how wonderful it is to be married, and then I remembered I'm pregnant. I had forgotten for a while. I was so busy with the wedding and all. I was thinking how truly happy I am. And that we'll have a baby soon. Our family has already started," she said contentedly. "I just wish it was yours," she sadly remarked.

Ed stopped the buggy on the road and secured the reins. He turned to her and took her face gently in his hands, pausing before he spoke. "Cass, my dear. It is mine. Do you hear me? I made you mine. You and this baby are mine. Never doubt that. I love you and the baby more than life itself." Ed looked down at her moonlit face and continued. "You two are a complete package. You are giving me what I want most in life. A chance to be a husband *and* a father. *You*, my dear Cass, are the greatest gift to me. Do you hear me?" he asked with passion that made tears roll down her cheeks and her heart overflow with love.

"Yes, dear. I hear you. It's just so hard to believe sometimes, it's such a miracle. I have to remind myself, and maybe sometimes you will have to remind me of that too, OK?" Her chin quivered as she tried to explain. "Sometimes my mind plays tricks on me, and tells me it's too good to be true, but my heart tells me otherwise. I just have to stop doubting my heart. I feel so completely loved by you that it aches sometimes." Cassie reached her hands up and placed them on his cheeks. "I love you so much. You *are* my greatest gift. Thank you, my love, for being *you*," she said, and kissed him softly as tears of joy streamed down her cheeks.

Ed pulled her closer and kissed her until the tears stopped. Gently, he stroked her hair and cheek. "Let's go home, my love," he said.

Cassie's spirit was soaring with joy. *This must be what heaven is like,* she thought. *To be with the ones you love forever and ever. To be so full of love for eternity, would definitely be worth striving for.* Cassie was determined do her very best, to be the wife Ed deserved, and the best mother she could be.

Chapter 3

Making a Home

Monday morning began before sunrise on the Havoc Ranch. The milk cow mooed from the barnyard and the birds began chirping in the peaceful darkness, heralding the approaching dawn.

Cassie awoke to Ed beside her, gazing at her in the faint lamplight, and reached out and touched his stubbled cheek and smiled sleepily. "Good morning, sweetheart."

Ed wrapped his arm around her waist and pulled her close. "Good morning, darlin'," he said, kissing her on the forehead. "Did you sleep well?"

"Mm, yes I did." Cassie wrapped her arms around him and rested her head on his chest. "I could stay like this forever."

"Me too." Ed breathed in the sweet scent of her hair as he stroked its length. "It's too bad the animals need fed and the cow milked, or I would."

"It's OK, we have forever to spend together." Cassie came up on her elbow and kissed him on the lips. "And I'll enjoy every second of it. Meanwhile,

30

Mr. Havoc, we have a ranch to run. I don't want people thinking we are neglectful of our home and animals. How about I make breakfast while you feed the stock and milk the cow?" And kissed him again.

"But Mrs. Havoc. I want to stay in bed today," he whined, teasing her.

"That's enough out of you, Mr. Havoc! Up and at 'em. There's work to be done." Cassie pretended to scold him, then laughed as he snuggled closer and kissed her.

"What if I decide to never let you go. What will you do then?" His voice was playful as he held her securely in his arms.

"Hmm," she sighed, laying her head against his chest again. "I hope you never let me go." Ed relaxed his hold to rub her back. Then seeing her chance, Cassie tickled his ribs until he burst out laughing.

"Hey, no fair. You're playing dirty." Ed laughed, trying to keep her away from him. "OK, OK! I'll let you free if you promise no more tickling."

"OK, I'll stop." Cassie relented and relaxed her arms, rolled over, still laughing, thinking she'd won.

Unexpectedly, Ed rolled on his side and tickled her.

"Ed!" Cassie protested with a giggle. "What happened to, 'No tickling'?"

Ed laughed while he continued to gently tickle her sides, careful to not hurt her. "I said, 'You promise no more tickling'. *You* promised, but *I* didn't." Encouraged by her continued laughter, he rolled closer to tickle her neck with his mustache as he kissed her.

"Ed! We have work to do!" scolding him as she laughed.

Reluctantly, he rolled back over on his side of the bed, chuckling, leaving her breathless and grinning.

"Ok, I'll behave. But only because I have work to do." Ed smiled and rolled out of bed to get dressed. "But this isn't finished." Oh, how he loved her. Waking up to her angelic face was a dream come true.

Cassie eased from under the covers, took the robe off the end of the bed and slipped it on. "I'll get your coffee going. Wouldn't want you falling asleep on the job." Cassie smiled back at him as he pulled on his shirt. Oh, how she loved him and all his playful spontaneity.

"That would be very much appreciated, darlin'. And I'm sure the cows thank you too," Ed teased as she left the room to start the fire for the coffee.

***

Even in the early morning hours, the day promised to be hot. No clouds in the sky or breeze to cool, signaled that working under the blazing sun would be the order of the day. Monday was washing day, and it began with setting up a large cauldron of water to boil over a fire in the yard. Cassie worked while seeking shade on the north side of the house. Placing two wash tubs on a bench alongside the house, she filled them with cold well water, and set the washboard inside the first tub. Pulling the clothes from the boiling water with a long paddle, she carefully placed them in the tub of cold water so she could begin to soap them up with the lye soap, scrubbing and rinsing the clothes against the corrugated washboard. Once washed, she placed each article of clothes in the rinse tub. When rinsed clean, she pulled them out and twisted the fabric and wrung out as much water as possible. Untwisting the articles of clothing, she snapped them to get the wrinkles out and hung them on the clothesline. It was a long process, but thankfully there weren't too many clothes to be washed that day.

As Cassie worked, she noticed the carpet of weeds that covered the garden. She knew she would have to clean out the weeds before the day got too hot.

Ed had fed the animals, milked the cow, then moved the animals out to pasture, all before breakfast, then headed back to the barn to muck the stalls and chop some firewood. With all he had to do, he still found time to help Cassie set up her wash kettle over the fire. Now with the morning chores done, he decided to ride out to check the cattle.

Ed yelled across the yard as he brought Major out of the barn, "I'm going for a ride to check the herd. I'll be back in an hour or so. Will you be all right here alone?" He was a bit concerned about leaving her alone for the first time since their wedding. *Who knows what kind of trouble she could get into while I'm gone?*

Cassie had her hands in the tub and turned, wiping the perspiration from her forehead with her sleeve. "I'll be fine, Ed. I just have some laundry to finish and then I'll weed the garden. You can go. I promise, I'll be just fine," she said reassuringly.

"OK, but if you have an emergency and need some help, go to your aunt's first. I don't want you riding out on the range to find me." As he led Major through the gate of the corral, he added as a gentle reminder, "And for heaven sakes, take the buggy."

"Sure, sure!" and waved him off as she bent over the tub again, intent on getting her work done before the day got too hot.

Ed snuck up behind Cassie, as she dunked and swished in the rinse water, and wrapped his arms around her waist. "No more horse riding for you. You hear?" he teased, as he held her and kissed her bare neck beneath her bonnet.

Cassie giggled and squirmed until he loosened his grip, and she turned around. "Oh, all right," she said mischievously, putting her soaking wet hands on his cheeks and rubbing them all over his face as she laughed.

"Oh, you think that's funny, do you?" he asked, trying to hold back his smile, his moustache twitching at the edges.-

"Yes," she managed through her laughter.

He leaned down and rubbed his wet face all over hers as he held her securely. Cassie giggled and tried to get free, when suddenly, he picked her up and headed across the yard. "You feel hot, I think you need a little cooling off."

"No! Ed! You wouldn't!" She giggled and tried to get out of his arms. "Not the trough!"

Ed reached the trough, and held her over it, as she wrapped her arms around his neck. "Are you sure? You would be much cooler," he teased as she protested. "Are you going to behave if I put you down?" he asked, lowering her over the water.

"I'll be good, I promise," holding tightly around his neck. "Now, go check the cattle, you silly man," trying to scold him as she chuckled.

Ed stepped back and set her down. "Ok, I'll let you have your way. But I really think you could use some cooling down," he suggested with a smile.

"Maybe later I'll go to the creek and soak my feet, but right now, I have work to do and so do you," trying to further dissuade him from dipping her into the stagnant trough water.

"OK, I'll hold you to it. As soon as I get back, you're going to go get cooled off one way or another." Ed smiled and winked at her as she turned and headed back to her work. "I'd love to see my water baby playing in the creek again," he suggested after her. Cassie looked back and smiled, shaking her head.

As he watched her walk away, Ed remembered the day he found her wading in the creek. *She looked so peaceful and happy that day, like she belonged there, at one with nature. The stream is so much like her, bubbling as it goes, bringing life wherever it flows. She brought me back to life, and she's all I thirst for still,* he thought as he watched her dip her hands into the rinse water.

Whew. That was a close one. Not a dull moment with Ed around, Cassie thought as she returned to her washing.

Ed called out a farewell and waved one last good-bye to Cassie as he rode out of the yard, hoping she would be all right.

***

Cassie finished hanging the last bit of laundry on the line and after some searching, she found some gloves in the barn and went to the garden to pull weeds. She quickly realized what a big chore it would be, as she knelt and pulled the stubborn weeds with their long roots. Looking through the garden she could see the weeds were thick everywhere. It had been over a week since the last weeding, and that clearly was too long.

As she worked, she examined each plant. Small thin string beans were just beginning to form, and the corn was as high as her shoulders, with small ears emerging. The carrots, with their fuzzy tops, and onions, with tall thin stems, were also doing well. Little green tomatoes loaded the few tomato plants along the sunniest side of the garden. The broad leaves and vines of the cucumbers, pumpkins, squash, and zucchini were spreading across the open space they'd been given. It was glorious to see what God's world could do, from such a tiny seed.

It took over an hour to clear out all the weeds, but the garden looked so much better when Cassie was through. Rich brown dirt lay beneath the dark green vegetable plants, waiting for the next watering.

She was dripping with sweat; even with her hair

off her neck and her bonnet on, she was feeling the heat. Cassie wished she had started earlier in the day. While picking weeds, she noticed the first peas were ready, so she went to the house and got a basket to pick them as well.

As Cassie plucked the long green pods of crisp sweet peas off their vines, she had an idea. Once she finished picking the peas, she moved to the row of red potatoes. Digging around beneath the mounds of potato plants, she found some smaller potatoes, about the size of eggs, and pulled them out, leaving the rest of the plant and roots intact. These, along with the shelled peas would make delicious, creamed peas and potatoes for supper.

She loved the first pickings from the garden, especially when it was her garden, and it could provide such delicious meals for the two of them. Maybe she would even add some ham from the smoke house to the menu, she thought. The garden was hard work, but it was so rewarding. Not only did she enjoy watching the seeds grow into their various plants, but she also found strength and healing in the feel of the dirt in her hands and the smell of freshly turned soil.

Mr. Crowley had done a good job caring for the garden, and she had promised to take good care of it too. Cassie stood with her hands on her hips, her basket full of new potatoes and peas, and wiped her brow, feeling the perspiration running down her cheeks and neck. The garden plants looked healthy and strong, but she noticed they too were beginning to wilt in the heat.

Cassie decided she would water the garden as soon as she took the freshly picked vegetables into the house. Remembering what Mr. Crowley had mentioned, she went to find the water gate. She followed the small ditch, lined with wooden planks that began at the garden and led toward the stream. She thought it would be fun to see how the water gate worked.

As Cassie walked along the dry path to the water headgate, she wondered why they called it Crow Creek, since it was much larger than a creek and she hadn't seen a crow once while in Cheyenne. Maybe it was just easier to say creek. Either way, it was one of her favorite parts about their homestead. That day, the stream was running clear and cold, bringing life wherever it flowed.

Examining the headgate, Cassie could see how it worked. The board between the side walls lifted with some effort as she eased it up an inch or two. Slowly at first, the water seeped out a little from the bottom and began running down the ditch, then more quickly as she lifted the board higher. Cassie watched the water run down the narrow ditch and walked alongside it as it flowed, picking out debris that had fallen in the water's path along the way. When the water reached the garden it slowly ran down the rows, soaking the roots of each plant as it passed.

Smiling, Cassie thought how beautiful it was to watch the water move down each row, turning the dry dusty dirt to a rich dark brown. The tiny stream that filled the garden looked so cool and refreshing, she was tempted to go back to the creek and rinse off.

Realizing just how dirty and sweaty she had become from the morning work, she decided to take a break and wash off in the cool creek.

Cassie hurried back into the house, grabbed some soap and a towel, and headed to a spot in the creek where it was deepest and most secluded. She arrived at the shady deep pool and looked around to make sure she was alone. Confident that there was nothing around her except the birds and the trees, she sat on a fallen log, and removed her bonnet, shoes, and stockings and then her skirt and blouse. Lastly, making sure she was alone, she removed her petticoat and tossed it over the log with her other clothes. Deciding to leave on her camisole and bloomers, she stepped toward the pool of running water.

The damp sandy creekbank felt good on her bare feet. Gingerly, she stepped in and gasped as the cold water ran over her hot feet. Pausing for a moment, allowing her body to become accustomed to the cold water, she then proceeded in a bit deeper. Gritting her teeth, she sat down in the deepest part of the creek and let out a squeal as the water came over her chest. Cassie quickly splashed water on her neck and face, rinsing off the sweat, realizing the creek was colder than she expected. Standing, she used the soap on her arms, body, and finally legs and feet, which turned out to be trickier in the moving water. Covered completely in soap, she tossed the soap bar back to the shore and sat down in the rushing water to rinse off. The water was starting to make her shiver, but it felt wonderful.

Cassie walked back to the shore and grabbed the soap again, took the comb out of her hair, set it aside, and let her hair unwind and fall down her back. Cassie waded into the middle of the creek again and lay back into the water. The cool water rushed over her head, taking her breath away as her hair was caught up in the current. She scrubbed her hair clean and threw the soap to shore and lay back again to let it rinse with the current. As she sat up, she caught a movement out of the corner of her eye. Cassie whipped her head around and gasped as she saw Ed walking towards her.

"Oh, look what I found, a mermaid." Ed reached the bank of the stream and smiled broadly.

"Ed, you startled me." Cassie's teeth chattered, as she sat in the rushing water, getting colder by the minute.

"Sorry, darling, I didn't mean to. I got back and came looking for you. When I found the water running down into the garden, I wondered if you'd come here. I'm happy to see you're getting cooled down. It's a scorcher today." Ed watched as Cassie stood up in the middle of the stream, crossing her arms in front of her as she shivered. Words escaped him seeing how perfect she looked in that moment. He grabbed the towel on the bank and brought it to the edge of the water. He couldn't take his eyes off of her. Cassie truly was a mermaid, and she was putting a spell on him.

Cassie blushed as she realized her wet underthings were now see-through. She snatched the towel and wrapped it around her. "Thank you, dear," she said, feeling self-conscious. *Good thing I kept my underthings on; I can't imagine if he'd caught me completely naked. I'd have never gotten out.*

"You know, you have a great idea here. I think I'll take a bath as well." Saying that, he removed his hat and sat to remove his boots and socks, then removed his shirt and trousers.

Cassie looked away as she handed him the soap and he waded into the water with just his drawers on. Ed gasped as his bare chest hit the water when he sat down. "Oh! It's cold! But it feels great."

Standing on the bank, Cassie smiled as he soaped up his arms, chest, neck, and hair. Soon his teeth began to chatter, and he let out an exuberant whoop. Cassie laughed at his enthusiasm as she appreciated his lean muscular physique; even the scar across his chest was attractive. Cassie blushed as he smiled back at her, realizing she'd been caught watching him.

"Here, catch!" Ed tossed her the soap. When she caught the slippery soap with both hands, her towel fell to the ground and Ed laughed at her. "You know it's cute that you're so modest. But we're married now...," he said letting the sentence trail off as his smile widened.

"Oh?" she asked teasing him, then suddenly had an idea. *Cute, eh?* she thought. She would teach him; he was just as modest as her. Cassie hastily pulled on her shoes, skirt, and blouse, not bothering to button her shoes or her blouse. Then slyly, she picked up his clothes and started backing up. *I'll let him walk back to the house, half naked, and see who's modest now,* she thought with an impish grin.

Ed saw her moving away with his clothes. "Oh no you don't!" Ed said smiling. Quickly he stood up and came running towards her, as fast as he could, splashing up water as he came.

Cassie squealed and turned to run, realizing she was in over her head. She only made it about ten feet, when he caught her around the waist.

"Never tease a weasel." Ed laughed and swiftly picked her up as she dropped his clothes. Her arms wrapped around his bare neck as he turned around and headed back towards the creek.

Cassie kicked and squealed as she tried to get out of his arms, but he was determined to hold on. Her shoes went flying as she kicked to break free. He waded into the creek laughing as she protested. "NO! Ed! I was just kidding. I would have brought them back," trying to convince him. But it was too late. Ed lowered her, holding her just above the water, as she held onto his neck for dear life. *If I'm going in, then so are you.*

When Ed realized she wasn't going to go easily, he thought, *What the heck. Guess I have to do this the hard way.* He attempted to sit down in the water while holding her, but lost his balance and ended up falling backwards, releasing her as they both splashed under water. Cassie came up gasping from the cold, in her now soaking wet hair and clothes. Ed came out of the water coughing and sputtering. Cassie started laughing, finding it comical that he had dunked himself too.

Laughing with her, Ed wiped the water from his face and smoothed back his hair. He had won but had paid a price for it.

Cassie pushed her soaked hair out of her face as she laughed hysterically. "Will you hand me the soap, Ed?" Cassie asked between bursts of uncontrollable laughter. "I think I'll wash this dress while I'm in here!" Her wet blouse and skirt now clung to her body.

Ed was hysterically laughing now. "Sure, sweetheart." Leaning forward, he kissed her. "You're the best."

"So are you." Cassie drew closer as if to kiss him but instead pushed him backwards under the water again. She laughed as he came up sputtering and squealed as he caught her in a bear hug and kissed her as he laughed.

Ed was breathless. "OK. I see I've met my match. I call a truce. I'll let you go if you promise no more dunking." He loved to hold her and could do it all day. But at some point he wanted dinner, too. So, he called a truce.

Cassie relaxed in his arms and rested her head on his shoulder, breathing hard from all the excitement. "OK, but only if you promise as well." She'd been fooled once before by this trick.

"You're learning fast, Cass. OK, I'll promise, no more dunking today," and kissed her on the cheek. "I'm starved. Let's go get some dinner." Ed stood up and helped her to her feet. "My little mermaid," he whispered as he wrapped his arm around her and together they walked out of the creek, breathless from the cold.

The hot air felt good as they walked back to the cottage, holding hands. Cassie's blouse and skirt were still dripping wet as they stepped up onto the porch.

"Wait here." Ed went inside and grabbed another towel. "I'll hold a towel up around you while you take off those wet clothes. I promise not to look. Then you can go in and get dressed while I hang your clothes on the line," Ed offered sweetly.

Cassie reluctantly complied. She didn't want to track water through their house. "OK. But no peeking."

Once her clothes were off and laying on the porch, she took the towel out of his hands and wrapped it around herself.

"Thank you," Cassie said, and ducked quickly inside the cottage and hurried to their bedroom.

"Any time, darling." Ed smiled, watching her slip away with only a towel covering her.

Ed came into the house after hanging Cassie's clothes on the line and saw her now dressed, brushing through her long black hair. "I'll start us some dinner while you finish your hair." Ed really wanted to help since he was the one that let things get a little out of hand in the first place. Cassie was such a good-natured woman. Some women would have thrown a fit at having their hair and dress soaked in a creek. Ed knew how lucky he was for marrying such a fine woman as Cass. He fixed sandwiches and set them on the table just as Cassie emerged with her hair brushed smooth and sleek falling down her back to finish drying.

"Mm, that looks great. I'm starved," Cassie said as Ed pulled out her chair for her.

Ed poured them each some milk and blessed the food before they began eating.

"The cattle are doing well. Seem to be fattening up nicely and sticking close to the water. We should see a good profit come fall," Ed said between mouthfuls.

"That's wonderful," Cassie said excitedly, then motioned towards her basket full of vegetables. "Did you see? I got some peas and potatoes from the garden."

"I did see. That's wonderful," he said, mimicking her enthusiasm.

"I can make us some creamed peas and potatoes for supper. Maybe we could even have Aunt Mabel and Uncle George over."

"That sounds delicious. I can ride over and ask them after we finish eating. Unless you want to come with me?"

"No, that's OK. I'll stay and shell the peas and take down the laundry. I have some things to get ready if we're to have company for supper," Cassie said, loving the sound of having company in her own home.

"All right, I'll go as soon as I'm done eating."

"Oh, I just thought of something." Cassie had an idea. "Wouldn't it be nice to have some iced tea with supper tonight? Maybe there's some ice in the ice-house. And I can check the smoke house to see what's in there." Cassie's meal plans began forming in her head. "Some meat with the peas and potatoes would be nice."

"There's a large ham shank and ribs, a slab of bacon, and plenty of smoked beef." Ed ran through the list of what he could remember from when Mr. Crowley showed him the smokehouse. "I can get you whatever you'd like to use."

"Oh, that sounds wonderful. Would you bring back a chunk of the ham? We can get the ice when it's closer to suppertime. I think I'll mix up the tea now and put it in the creek to cool." Cassie smiled. Thinking about the evening ahead made her excited.

After Ed retrieved the ham, he left her and headed to the Hartford's. Cassie took down the clean clothes and placed them in a basket for ironing tomorrow. Passing by the garden, she noticed Ed had closed the water gate on his way to the smokehouse. Now that the garden was well watered, she smiled at how good it looked. She had accomplished a good day's work and it was a wonderful feeling.

Sitting on the porch she began shelling peas into a large bowl in her lap. It felt nice sitting in the shade of the porch as her hair dried in the afternoon heat. She had daydreamed about a day like today not that long ago. Humming softly, she thought about her daydream that had now become her reality. Oh, how she loved being married to Ed, and having this time alone to just sit on the porch surrounded by trees and flowers, and listen to the birds calling and the farm animals making occasional noises in the barnyard. A breeze rustled the branches in the trees, carrying the smell of nature with it. With the orange cat rubbing against Cassie's bare feet, everything seemed just perfect. *I am so blessed.*

Chapter 4

Dinner Guests

That evening when Aunt Mabel and Uncle George joined them for supper, they brought the rest of the wedding gifts with them and stacked them in the spare bedroom for Cassie and Ed to sort through later.

"Oh, Cassie. This meal is delicious," raved Mabel. "You're a very fine cook," taking another bite of the ham, peas, and potatoes in the thick white cream-sauce. "And the biscuits are just perfect," she added, taking another.

"Thank you, Aunt Mabel." Cassie felt pleased with how everything had turned out.

Uncle George and Ed were ready for seconds, and Cassie rose to refill their bowls.

"Cassie, I can't believe we let you get married. We should have insisted you stay with us forever. I don't know how we can go back to eating just regular food now, having been spoiled with this treat," George teased. "And this iced tea, it's so refreshing. It sure hits the spot on a hot day like today," he said, taking another long drink. "Glad you invited us over."

"We're always happy to have you for dinner, Uncle George." Cassie appreciated his compliment and she smiled at Ed, who beamed back at her proudly.

Together they all gathered on the porch for the apple dumplings that Aunt Mabel had brought.

"It was so nice of you to have us to supper, Cassie." Mabel walked with Cassie to their rig. "I know it's only been a day since we saw each other, but I miss you," Mabel said and hugged Cassie, before she climbed into the rig to go home.

"I miss you too, Aunt Mabel," Cassie said sincerely. "Come on over anytime for a visit. I'm still trying to get things organized, but would welcome a break to chat with you any time. We'll see you soon." Cassie squeezed her hand one last time and waved goodbye.

***

The rest of the week flew by as everyday life went on. Cassie cleaned, cooked, ironed, weeded, and watered, as Ed worked on the ranch with the animals and repairs that constantly needed done.

Finally, Friday arrived, with Bart and Bea on their way over for supper. It had been a lot of work getting everything ready, but Cassie was excited to have company. Cassie prepared a roast beef and more creamed peas and potatoes, biscuits and iced tea for the meal. The table was set with only minutes to spare, as Cassie hurried to the bedroom to change into a clean dress before Bart and Bea arrived.

"You've really outdone yourself, Cass," Ed voiced as he entered the kitchen, smelling the food cooking and seeing the table set with a vase of flowers in the center. As he washed up at the sink, he called out to Cass, "Is there something I can help with before they get here?"

"I would love it if you could bring up bottles of pickles and peaches from the cellar," Cassie instructed from the bedroom, doing up the last of the buttons on her dress. "Then we'll be ready."

Ed retrieved the bottles and set them on the counter, then went to change out of his work clothes, finishing just as Bart and Bea drove up.

"They're here!" Ed announced as Bart and Bea pulled into the yard.

Cassie's heart leapt with excitement as she pulled the last of the food out of the oven and set it on the stove top, ready to be dished up.

Ed opened the front door and greeted the couple as they climbed out of the buggy. "Great to see you both. How're you doing?" Ed asked cheerfully from the top of the porch steps.

"Hello, Ed! We're doing very well, thank you." Bart stepped down and turned to help Bea out of the buggy.

Cassie came out onto the porch and wrapped her arm around Ed's waist as he hugged her around the shoulders. "I'm so happy to see you both. And right on time; supper's ready." Cassie gave Bea a hug and shook Bart's hand. "Come on inside."

"Thanks for inviting us. It smells wonderful," said Bea as she looked around the living space. "You have a lovely home."

"Thank you, Bea, we sure enjoy it," Cassie said proudly.

"We could smell the food all the way down the lane. I'm starving." Bart smiled as he rubbed his stomach.

"Bea, you can sit here and Bart, you sit there," Cassie offered, pointing to the chairs. "Ed, will you please set on the roast, and I'll get the biscuits and vegetables?" she asked as she placed the bowl of pickles and the bowl of peas and potatoes on the table. The iced tea sat on the table along with ice in the glasses. As Cassie prepared to sit down, she placed the plate of hot biscuits on the table beside the butter and preserves. "OK, I believe we're ready for the blessing."

Ed began by blessing the food and thanked the Lord for their good friends. Closing the prayer, Ed began dishing up the food and passing it around the table. The dinner conversation was lively with shared news about the ranch, the weather, the local news, and other pleasantries.

"So, how's the dress shop going?" asked Ed as they ate.

"Very well," said Bart with a grin. "We've been so busy, it's hard to keep up." Bart took another bite of biscuit. "This is delicious, Cassie," he said, dishing up another helping of roast beef.

"Thank you very much," Cassie said graciously. "I'm glad to hear you're doing so well. When do you open the men's clothing shop?" Cassie passed Bea the bowl of pickles.

"In a few weeks. We already have some orders

coming in, thanks to Ed for modeling for us," Bart said graciously, smiling at Ed.

"It was my pleasure. I still feel like I got the better end of that deal. But I really appreciated it." Ed still couldn't believe they'd given him a suit to wear to his wedding just so they could advertise the new men's clothing shop.

"We need to find some more seamstresses that can start before we open," said Bart. "Ed, can you pass me the biscuits, please?"

"You know, Cass here has a sewing machine." Ed handed the plate of biscuits to Bart. "Mr. Crowley left it here when he sold us the homestead." Ed looked from Cassie to Bart.

"Yes, it's practically new, but I've never used it before. I would be happy to help take in some sewing if only I knew how to use it."

"I can show you how to use it, Cassie," Bea offered with a smile. "It's really simple. You'll love how it works." Bea finished and wiped her mouth with a napkin.

"I would love that. Can you show me something tonight?"

"I would love to. Let me help you get the dishes done first, then I'll show you." Bea folded her napkin and stacked her utensils on her plate. "That was delicious, Cassie, thank you." Bea stood, taking her plate to the sink.

"Forget about the dishes." Ed was excited, more than once Cassie had voiced her desire to learn how to use the wonderous machine. "Cass, you go and learn how to use the sewing machine. Bart and I'll do the dishes. Besides, you did all the work making this wonderful meal. You shouldn't have to do the dishes too." Ed stood up and began taking the dirty dishes to the sink.

"Yes, you both run along, and we'll take care of this," Bart offered, and began helping Ed clear the table. "Bea can show you everything you need to know; she's the best," Bart praised, smiling at Bea.

"I know enough, and I can show you that." Bea modestly smiled back at Bart.

Cassie lit the lamp in the spare bedroom and uncovered the machine. The black Singer sewing machine with the gold scrolling on the arm and roses on the base of the machine was very pretty sitting in the dark wood cabinet with the black legs and treadle.

"Mr. Crowley told Ed it's a Singer 'New Family,' made a couple years back," Cassie said proudly.

"I use the same one at work. I've heard that they're coming out with a new one next year. I can't wait to see what it'll do." Bea sat down in front of the sewing machine. "So, Cassie, here is where the spool of thread is loaded and then strung through the machine like this." Bea hooked the string through the parts along the arm and through the needle. "The bobbin is loaded down here," she said pointing to the bobbin casing. "It's going to catch the thread above and make a lockstitch. If you have a piece of scrap fabric, I can show you how it works."

"Yes, I'll get you one." Cassie pulled a piece of cloth from a bag. "Here, this'll work." She handed the fabric to Bea.

Bea folded the fabric in half and let the presser foot down and moved the treadle up and down with her foot. The oscillating shuttle moved the fabric forward with even stitches being made across the fabric. At the end of the seam Bea lifted up the fabric and asked Cassie for scissors to clip it away from the long thread. Bea used the scissors Cassie handed to her from a drawer in the cabinet.

"Do you see how straight and even the stitches are on both sides?" Bea opened up the two pieces of fabric, pulling against the seam, showing Cassie how tight they held without a gap. "And see how strong it holds?"

"That's beautiful. And look how fast and easy that was!" Cassie was impressed. "I want to try." Bea stood and let Cassie sit in front of the machine.

"OK, here is where you let the presser foot down. And now put your foot here," Bea said pointing to the treadle. "Be sure and keep your fingers away from the needle as you guide the fabric through, as you move your foot slowly." Bea watched as Cassie moved her foot up and down. "Yes, just like that," encouraged Bea, as Cassie fed the fabric through the presser foot and needle, making a perfectly straight seam. Bea showed her another stitch and then a corner.

They worked together, trying different techniques, until Cassie felt confident to do it on her own.

"I love it!" Cassie lifted the fabric she had been working on, examining the front and back that looked identical. "I can't wait to make something."

"You're a quick study. I'm sure you'll be able to sew anything you want with a little more practice." Bea was impressed with how well Cassie was doing on her first try.

"Thanks, I'll keep practicing. Maybe you can come back sometime and show me more. If I'm going to be any help, I need to know how to do it all."

"Better yet, why don't you come to the shop a few times next week and we'll show you there? You can practice on some easier pieces and then we can teach you more as you get comfortable." Bea was excited to have Cassie coming to work with them. "I think you'll really like it."

Cassie couldn't believe what an opportunity this was. "I would love that. Let me talk to Ed, but I think that I can manage it easy enough. Let's go tell them." Cassie blew out the lamp and walked back into the kitchen with Bea.

"You fellows look like you're doing a very nice job. Cassie is going to come into town for some sewing lessons at the dress shop, if that's OK with you, Ed?" asked Bea as she came into the room.

Bart was drying the dishes as Ed finished washing and rinsing the last ones.

"That sounds great to me. If Cass wants to learn, then by all means she should go." Ed smiled proudly at Cassie.

Cassie's eyes twinkled as she clasped her hands to her chest, feeling the excitement nearly bubbling out of her. "I really want to learn. It's so much fun. And just think of all the things I could make for our family. And the extra money I could make for us!"

"We could really use the help," Bart added, becoming excited as well. "We'll let you work as much as you'd like!"

"But before we go to work, let's have some fun!" Bea gave Bart an amused smile as the men hung up their towels. "I want to hear some music before we have to go."

"I'm ready! I'll get my guitar. Bart, did you bring your violin?" Ed strode across the room to the corner where he kept his guitar.

"I'll be right back. It's in the buggy." Bart hurried out the door.

"Shall we go sit on the porch and enjoy the cool air?" suggested Cassie.

Moments later Bart came back up the steps holding his violin case. Ed brought out two more chairs, and everyone sat at the small table on the porch. The evening breeze had picked up as the long shadows spread across the yard. Dusk was soon approaching.

"Bea, here's the music for the song I sang to Cass." Ed placed the sheet music he had written, titled *Be My Wife*, on the table.

"Will you play it for us again?" Bea asked Ed.

"Sure." Ed took his guitar and began singing as he strummed, while staring into Cassie's eyes.

The words brought Cassie to tears again just as it had on their wedding day. *Together forever and ever as husband and wife.* That's what she believed they would be.

After Ed finished, Bart stood and looked over the

music. As soon as Bart was ready with his violin, he played with Ed, as Cassie and Bea sang along.

"I can't wait to play this on the piano." Bea softly clapped, delighted with the beautiful music.

Cassie leaned over and kissed Ed on the cheek. "I love you," Cassie whispered, wiping away another tear.

Ed took her hand and squeezed it as he whispered, "I love you too, Cass."

Bea and Bart looked at each other and warmly smiled.

"You play so beautifully, Bart. I love the violin," Bea said with a sparkle in her eyes. "Can you play us something else?" she asked, amazed by his skill as a musician.

Bart blushed, feeling the heat rise in his cheeks.

"Yes Bart, please play us something else," Cassie encouraged with a smile. She was having the best time and already couldn't wait to do it again.

"Humor us, Bart," Ed softly nudged Bart until he relented.

Bart chuckled. "All right, all right. Let me think of something. Hmm." Bart rubbed his chin trying to think of a good song. "Oh, I have one!"

Bart picked up his violin and began to play a song. It was a hauntingly beautiful, soulful tune. Feeling the emotion of the song, he moved his bow, sliding it across the strings gracefully as if he was dancing a waltz. Even the evening songbirds seemed to stop and listen.

"I love that song. What's it called?" Cassie already

wanted to hear it again.

"It's called *Fur Elise*; it's Beethoven. I've loved it ever since I heard it. It's said that Beethoven wrote it for a student he loved, making the beginning of it simple enough so she could play it. But then he found out she loved another. So, he made the last part harder so she would never be able to finish playing it."

"Wow, how sad, and very interesting. It's so beautiful. And you played it so well," said Ed, impressed with Bart's knowledge and his talent.

"I would love to learn that song on the piano." Bea smiled as she imagined her fingers gliding over the ivory keys. "I'm sure I can find the sheet music and then we could play a duet." Bea looked up at Bart, hoping he took the hint.

Bart was silently thanking his mother for making him learn the violin. Anything that made Bea smile was definitely something he was happy to keep doing. "I think that would be lovely. I could come over some time and we could practice," suggested Bart, hoped he didn't sound too presumptuous.

"Yes, most definitely!" Bea's heart was pounding with anticipation.

"I wish I could play the piano, or any instrument for that matter," Cassie wished.

Bea turned to Cassie. "I could teach you how to play the piano. It's very easy, it just takes practice."

"Yes, I would love to learn to play the piano. But first I should learn to use the sewing machine, then you can teach me the piano," Cassie added with a grin. "Is everyone ready for some peaches and cream?"

"I'll help you bring it out." Ed stood and followed Cassie inside.

Bea turned to Bart and whispered, "What luck that Cassie has a sewing machine."

"I know, it would be great having her help. She could be a good seamstress. Back in Missouri I know she helped make her own clothes. She'll pick up how to use the sewing machine quickly. Especially with your help." Bart spoke in hushed tones, taking Bea's hand that was resting on the table. He couldn't wait to ask for her hand in marriage. Seeing her every day at work was wonderful, but also torture. He wanted to take her in his arms and kiss her all the time. But he would be patient. He pushed back his red curls from off his forehead; it was so hot tonight. Or was it just being close to Bea? His heart always picked up when he touched her.

"I'll do everything I can to help her. She really is a sweet person. It would be fun to work with her." Bea was trying to keep her words straight as Bart gently stroked her fingers with his thumb. She wished she had a fan to cool her face; she was blushing and hot under her high collar. "Do you think she would work in town sometimes?" Bea asked, trying to make conversation.

"I think she might. I'll ask her. But first, Bea, I have something to ask you." Bart spoke each word carefully.

Bea's heart jumped at his words. "Sure, what is it?" Her face flushed deeper and her hands shook. *He's finally going to ask me,* she thought.

Bart looked down at their clasped hands and asked, "Would you come and work with me in the men's clothing store?" The question had been on his mind for some time, but he'd wanted to ask her first before suggesting it to Mr. Holden.

Feeling a little disappointed, she smiled weakly. "I would like that very much." It wasn't what she had thought he was going to ask her, but it was a step in the right direction. Recovering a little, Bea put her chin up. "And I think my father would approve as well. I'm his top seamstress, and I know he wants to get off on the right foot with the men's shop. Besides, I would love to spend more time with you," Bea added, blushing as she confessed her true feelings.

"Oh, Bea. I was hoping you would want to. I can't bear to think of not seeing you every day." Bart looked into her blue eyes and leaned forward and kissed her.

"Sorry to keep you waiting." Ed grinned. "But I see you made good use of the time," he teased, having caught them pulling apart from a kiss.

Bart and Bea looked at Ed and then at each other and burst out laughing.

"What's so funny?" Cassie asked. Her question only made them laugh harder. "What? What did I miss?" Cassie smiled, looking back and forth at the three of them.

"I'll tell you later, OK Cass?" Ed didn't want to embarrass Bart and Bea any further and set the bowls of peaches and cream in front of them.

"OK." Cassie relented, giving them all puzzled looks as she set the other two bowls of peaches and cream down and handed them each a spoon.

Moving past the embarrassment, they began eating and chatting. As they finished, Bart suggested there was time for one last song before they had to go, and asked Ed if he would play *Beautiful Dreamer* with him. Ed picked up his guitar. Together the four of them sang, Ed in his deep bass, Bart tenor, Cassie alto, and Bea soprano. When they finished, Cassie and Bea clapped while Ed and Bart theatrically bowed and laughed.

"We sound amazing together. We should sing together again soon," said Cassie.

"How about next Friday at my house?" suggested Bea. "I could make you all supper and I could play the piano as we sing," said Bea excitedly.

"That would be great," Bart and Ed echoed.

"Wonderful idea. I can bring the dessert, Bea," Cassie offered. "Shall we say seven o'clock?"

"Yes, that should give me enough time to get things ready after work. I may be able to get off a little earlier; I know the owner really well," Bea joked.

"Maybe I can get off early too, I know the owner's daughter really well," Bart added, and they all laughed.

Once they'd settled, Cassie stood to gather the dishes. "I can come into the shop a few times next week, if that works for you, Bea?"

"Sure, you come whenever it's convenient. I'll be there every day," said Bea as she and Bart stood to leave. "Thank you for dinner and the wonderful entertainment."

Bart shook Ed's hand and Cassie gave Bea a hug goodbye.

"Thanks again for a wonderful supper, Cassie. It was delicious." Bart tipped his hat to Cassie then turned to assist Bea into the buggy.

"You're welcome, any time. We'll see you both at church. Have a good evening." Cassie waved goodbye as they pulled away.

"Keep your eyes on the road Bart," Ed hollered with a chuckle as they drove out of the yard. Ed wrapped his arm around Cassie and kissed her on the forehead.

Cassie smiled and looked up at Ed. "Now, what was everyone laughing at earlier?"

"Oh, that." Ed smiled broadly. "I caught Bart and Bea kissing. That's all." He smiled down at his beautiful wife. "Like this." Then kissed her softly on the lips.

"Ed, you are such a tease, and I love it. You know just how to make me feel wonderful." Cassie wrapped her arms around his waist and hugged him tightly.

"Poor Bart, he has to sneak in a kiss here and there. At least I get to kiss you any time I want and thank heavens." Ed pulled her close and kissed her again. "You really are amazing, Cassandra Havoc. I could never get enough of you." He picked her up and carried her inside and shut the door.

***

Bart and Bea broke out laughing at Ed's parting comment about keeping Bart's eyes on the road.

"Little does he know how hard that is." Bart

chucked as he drove down the lane. He could hardly take his eyes off of Bea long enough to even work, lately.

"Bart…!" Bea was at a loss for words and blushed as she looked down at her hands.

Bart held the reins in one hand and reached out to take hers. "Bea, I need to tell you something. I want to ask for your hand in marriage. But first I need to find us a place to live and to know that I can support you as you deserve."

Bea's heart ached for him to say the words. "Bart, I don't need a fancy home or lots of money. I just need *you*. We don't need to wait. I'm ready *now*. I already told you that I've been waiting for you all my life. What more can I tell you?" asked Bea, her eyes pleading.

Bart pulled the buggy to a stop. The moon was rising in the east and the stars began to appear above them.

"You would risk marrying a man with no family to back him and an unsure future? You deserve more than that." Bart looked down, wishing he had more to offer her.

"Bart, you are everything I need. You love me, don't you?" Bea lifted his chin, forcing him to look at her.

"Bea, I never knew I could love someone this much. You're all I think about and the only person I want to be with for the rest of my life. I want to start a family with you," Bart said, fighting to keep the tears from coming.

Bea swallowed. "And I love you, Bart—so ask me. Ask me to be your wife. So we can start our lives together," she said, looked into his green eyes, searching for a way to help convince him.

Bart took her soft face in his hands and kissed her sweetly. He released her lips and looked into her eyes. "Bea, I will love you forever and ever if you will just be my wife."

"I will, Bart! I will! It's all I dream about." Bea wrapped her arms around his neck and cried tears of joy as they embraced.

Bart held her tightly. "I will ask for your hand in marriage on Sunday then. I'll make it official. You'll be mine and I'll be yours."

"Can we get married right away?" Bea asked in excitement. "I don't want a fancy wedding. Just something simple." Then an idea came to her. "We can live upstairs at the men's clothing store—if that suits you. Just so we are together, Bart." Bea wanted what Cassie and Ed had; to be married to the one you love.

"If that will make you happy. I have nothing holding me back now. I will marry you tomorrow if you wish," Bart said, smiling as he released her a little to look at her.

"How about the Friday—before we open the new shop? I want to have a few days to get our new home settled before the grand opening." Bea smiled as she thought about making a home with Bart.

"I'll ask your father this Sunday and if he says yes, I'll leave the planning to you. You just tell me where and when to be there and I'll be there." Bart hugged her again in excitement. "I'd better get you home before your father decides I'm not the gentleman fit for his daughter."

"Oh, he'll be plenty happy when you ask him. Don't you worry." Bea slipped her arm through his and rested her head on his shoulder.

Bart took the reins in both hands and snapped them over the horse's rump, his smile broadening as he thought about how soon they would be married. Within two weeks, Bea would be Mrs. Bartholomew Clark.

Chapter 5

More New Beginnings

Sunday after church, sitting together with Mr. Holden in the private office of his home, Bart summoned up the courage to finally speak. Working with Mr. Holden every day sure didn't make it any easier for Bart to ask for Bea's hand in marriage. Bart breathed a sigh of relief once he finally got the words out, not even sure what he'd said in the end.

"Well, Bart, I think it's about time you asked," Mr. Holden said, smiling and shaking Bart's hand. "Congratulations, son. I couldn't be happier for the both of you. I probably don't have to tell you, but Bea is a very special gal. And the fact that she picked you, says a lot about you. So, again, congratulations," said Mr. Holden, getting a little choked up and patting Bart on the back as a look of relief crossed Bart's face.

"Thank you, Mr. Holden. I couldn't be happier. I want you to know I love Bea with all my heart and will treat her with all the love, honor, and respect she deserves," said Bart, getting a little emotional as well.

"Son, I know you will. In the short time I've gotten to know you, I'm proud of you and what you've accomplished so far. I know your pa would be proud of you too if he could just see you. Welcome to the family, Bart." Mr. Holden pulled Bart in for a big hug, both of them shedding a few tears and wiping them away before the other could see.

"Thanks again, Mr. Holden," Bart said, grateful to have his blessing. "Ever since my pa told me not to come home, you've made me feel very welcome here and I appreciate it." Bart smiled, then sped on to the next part. "I know this will come as a shock to you, but Bea wants to be married in two weeks, on Friday the 23rd, to be exact. She doesn't want a big wedding; she just wants it to be a simple church wedding and luncheon. I know I gave you a lot to think about. I was worried about where we would live, but Bea suggested we live in the apartment above the men's clothing store for a while. I'm not sure how you feel about all this."

Mr. Holden pressed his lips together and rubbed his chin as he thought. "Hmm, that is quick. I guess when you're ready, you're ready. As far as the apartment goes, I think it's a splendid idea. It would be nice to have someone that close, to keep an eye on it. Let's go break the good news to the family," said Mr. Holden, smiling and walking with Bart back into the parlor.

"Thank you, Sir," Bart said, in hushed tones as they came into the parlor where Bea and her mother and sisters were sitting.

"We have some good news!" announced Mr. Holden to his family as he walked into the room.

"Bea and Bart are engaged!" His smile spread further across his face with the happy news.

The girls all squealed and hugged their sister, and Mrs. Holden gave Bart a big hug and a kiss on the cheek.

"Oh, me, oh my! What a wonderful surprise! Congratulations, both of you," Mrs. Holden's voice raised with glee.

Bea came up to Bart and put her arm through his. Bea was brimming with joy now that it was official.

"When, when!" shouted Bea's youngest sister, May, still clapping her hands in excitement.

"In two weeks, Friday the 23rd," said Bea, looking at Bart and then her mother.

"Oh, that soon?" Mrs. Holden's mouth dropped open in awe. Recovering quickly, she went on. "Well, I guess we'd better get planning. It doesn't leave us very much time to get things ready. But we can do it with everyone's help," she said smiling finally, looking at her husband and shrugging her shoulders.

"Yay! I can help!" shouted eight-year-old May. "I know just the dress she can wear, too!" May jumped up and down, clapping her hands.

"I think we should leave the dress decision up to Bea, May. After all, it's her wedding. You can help with something else. Ok?" Mrs. Holden patted her little May on the head.

"Ok, but I get to help with everything else, then," May offered, then suddenly realizing something, she ran up to Bart and gave him a big hug around the waist. "You're going to be my big brother now!

I've never had one. And you have red hair too!" she exclaimed, and everyone burst out laughing. "What?" May looked around the room in confusion, waiting for someone to tell her. "Well, he does," she retorted, not sure exactly why they were laughing.

"Yup, I'm going to be your brother-in-law. And I love your red hair; it's very pretty, just like Bea's," Bart said, ruffling up her hair a little.

"See! He loves red hair. He thinks it's pretty," May said, beaming up at him, dreaming he was going to marry her instead of Bea.

"That's right, dear. Your hair is pretty," said Mr. Holden, picking May up in his arms and giving her a hug. "Now let's get planning this wedding. We have lots to do," he said, sitting down on the couch with her.

As a family, they spent the rest of the evening planning the arrangements for the wedding. Sitting at the table surrounded by the Holdens, Bart couldn't believe how at home he felt. Christy, Bea's eighteen-year-old sister, offered to be in charge of the wedding luncheon. And Heather, just sixteen, asked if she could help with the flowers and cake, leaving Mrs. Holden to make the wedding dress. The wedding was planned for ten o'clock on Friday, July 23rd at the church. Bart wanted to ask Clancy to be his best man, since he was his closest friend here and the one who introduced him to Bea. And Bea would ask her sister Christy to be the Maid of Honor.

Monday morning Bart sent a letter to his family explaining the past week's happenings.

July 12, 1869

Dear Father, Mother, and Family,

Although you've made yourself very clear, Father, that I am not to come home, I want you to know I bear no hard feelings towards you. I hope one day you can understand my decision. Although it saddens me deeply, I don't blame you for feeling as you do. I know you feel I have betrayed you. I'm sorry for that.

I have good news. The woman I told you about has agreed to marry me, and her father has given us his blessing. Her name is Beatrice Holden. I pray you will one day forgive me and come meet my bride, Bea. She is a beautiful woman, elegant and talented. She's a schoolteacher and a seamstress at her father's dress shop. She sings beautifully and plays the piano as well.

Mother, Bea has red hair just like yours and reminds me so much of you. She's proper and intelligent, very much a lady. Interestingly, Bea's family is all redheads. Her parents are both from Ireland and have beautiful accents. I know you would love them as I do.

We are going to be married in the church on July 23rd at 10:00 am. It would mean so much to both of us if you could come. But I understand if you are still angry with me.

I've been working for Bea's father at his dress shop as a bookkeeper. Together, we are opening a new Men's Clothing Shop here on the 26th, the Monday after the wedding. I've learned a new kind of business, the clothing business. I'll be the general manager and part owner, running daily operations, as Mr. Holden will be running the dress shop. Thank you, Father, for the years of training you have given me. I haven't forgotten where I got my business sense. You taught me well. I'm forever grateful for the good man you've helped me become.

I wish you the best and miss you all very much.

With Love, Your Son
Bart

Bart hoped his letter would soften his father's heart and his parents would come to the wedding. He wanted them to share in the happiest moment of his life. He prayed for it. But he also wasn't going to put too much stock in it. He knew his father was stubborn and very old fashioned.

After posting the letter, Bart headed to work and tried to focus on the business. There was a lot to get done in a very short time. Maybe it wasn't a good idea to have the wedding so close to the opening of the new shop. *Oh well, the plans have already been set in motion, and I can't wait to be married. As soon as we're married, we can focus on the business,* he thought, as he walked into the dress shop.

***

Tuesday morning after chores, Cassie headed to town in the buggy for sewing lessons, blowing Ed a parting kiss as she drove out of the yard.

Cassie entered the dress shop all smiles as she saw Bea behind the counter, adjusting some hats on display. Cassie had been looking forward to this day ever since Bea had first shown her how to use the sewing machine. "Good morning, Bea. How are you today?"

Bea's smile widened as she saw who had entered the shop. "Good morning, Cassie. I'm wonderful. How are you?"

"I'm doing very well. Just came into town for some training on the sewing machine—if you have time?" Cassie paused as she saw the wider-than-usual smile on Bea's face. "What's up? You're smiling like you have something to tell." Cassie gave her a quizzical look.

Bea's eyes twinkled as she leaned forward, resting her forearms on the counter, ready to spill the news. "Cassie, you'll never guess what happened. Bart asked me to marry him!" Bea announced with glee, wanting to shout it out into the street but instead letting out a little squeal only loud enough for Cassie to hear.

Cassie was stunned at first. "Oh, my goodness." And then the reality sank in. Bart and Bea were getting married. "That's wonderful news, Bea! Congratulations! I'm so happy for you and Bart." Cassie clasped Bea's hands and gave them a squeeze, sharing in the excitement.

"I can't believe it's finally happening. He asked me right after we left your place on Friday. And then asked my Father on Sunday for his blessing. We've been planning the wedding ever since. We're getting married next Friday," Bea added quickly; there was no time to waste. There was so much to do.

"What can I do to help?" Cassie would happily do anything to help her new friend.

"I'm sure I'll think of something. But first, I need to ask. Do you think Ed would sing, *Be My Wife,* with Bart at the luncheon? I just love that song." Bea hesitated and a look of genuine concern crossed her face. "That is, unless you don't want them to; after all, it is your song."

"It's fine with me. And I'm sure Ed would love to sing it again. But you'll have to ask Bart and see what he says. If I remember correctly, he doesn't like to perform in public. Oh, Bea, you'll love being married," Cassie bubbled, coming around the counter and giving her a big hug.

"I know I will, I can't wait." Bea squeezed Cassie in joy. "Come into the back, let's get you started. We'll need all the help we can get. And if you know of any other seamstresses, let me know." Bea led Cassie through the curtained door to the back of the shop.

"As a matter of fact, I know of three others, but they live in Kansas. Ed's mother and two sisters are seamstresses. I don't know if they have ever used a sewing machine. I wonder if they would consider moving here?" Cassie wondered out loud as she glanced around the sewing room full of fabric, dress forms, and sewing machines with seamstresses working intently on their projects.

"That would be wonderful if they would. You should have Ed write and ask them," Bea suggested. Bea paused and took a moment to introduce Cassie to the other seamstresses and then showed Cassie her workstation. "Ok, let's sit here and go over the basics again." Bea pulled up another chair beside her sewing machine, as Cassie took the chair directly in front of it.

They spent the next few hours going over different stitches and techniques used on the sewing machine. When Bea felt confident, she assigned Cassie a simple skirt to work on over the next few days.

Mr. Holden offered to pay Cassie for her training time and any clothing she finished. Cassie felt that was very generous of Mr. Holden, but he insisted that he would have had to train someone anyways.

On Thursday, Cassie went back into town for more sewing lessons and to show Bea the skirt she completed.

Before she headed home, Cassie stopped at the post office to post a letter she had written to Madeline.

> *July 15, 1869*
> *Dearest Madeline,*
> *What a wonderful surprise it was that you could come to the wedding. It meant so much to me. You're a wonderful friend and kindred spirit. I appreciated your help with my hair*

and everything else while you were here. You truly are my Fairy Godmother. Thank you again for the beautiful fan, I will continue to use it at church and special occasions.

I've been feeling much better. Married life suits me. I love being a wife. I love having my own place. Making a home and becoming a family has always been my fondest wish since I was a little girl.

I've been learning how to sew on a sewing machine. I'll soon be taking in work from the dress shop and men's clothing shop. It's fun and exciting to learn a new skill. Learning to sew should also come in handy sewing baby clothes as the time approaches.

Exciting news, Bart and Bea are going to be married next Friday. Ed and I have become fast friends with them.

I miss you and love you, sweet sister of mine.

Love,
Cassie Havoc

***

Friday, Ed and Cassie drove into town to Bea's home for supper. The rest of Bea's family had gone to a fancy restaurant and to a play that night, giving the two couples the home to themselves.

Bart helped Bea as much as he could, to get the supper ready by setting the table and filling glasses with ice for the tea. Bea was very organized and had supper ready when Ed and Cassie arrived.

"Welcome," said Bea opening the door. "We're so glad you could come." Bea gave Cassie a hug.

"Come on in," said Bart, shaking Ed's hand and moving to let them in. "Supper is ready," Bart said, giving Cassie a quick hug.

"Let's go sit down. I'm sure you're hungry, I know I am," said Bea, leading everyone through the parlor and into the dining room. The dining room was ornately decorated with carpeted flooring, heavy draperies, and a crystal chandelier hanging over a beautiful hardwood table that was covered with a lace tablecloth.

Bart pulled an intricately carved chair out from the table for Cassie. "Cassie, you sit here. And Ed, you are next to her," he said, motioning to the other chair. "Bea, I'll go get the dinner out of the oven. You sit down, you've had a long day," he said as he pulled her chair out and helped her sit down.

"Thank you so much, Bart," she said, watching him go through the swinging door and into the kitchen. "He's such a gentleman. So considerate of me," remarked Bea to Cassie. "It's one of the first things that I noticed about Bart when I met him," she said with a sparkle in her eye as she smiled.

"I know what you mean. Ed is the same with me. I can hardly do a thing without him helping, and I love it," said Cassie, smiling at Ed.

"Who, me? I don't know what you're talking about."

"Ed," said Cassie, smiling at him. "You know I

love you and how you dote on me," she said, patting and squeezing his hand.

"Supper is served," announced Bart, holding a large dish. "Chicken pot pie. Hot out of the oven." Bart set the dish down on the table. "Let's have the blessing and then I can dish everyone up," Bart said, sitting down beside Bea and taking her hand and Cassie's. Ed took Cassie and Bea's hands, as Bart bowed his head and said the blessing.

The supper was delicious and talk of the upcoming wedding filled the conversation. Bea asked Ed and Bart if they would sing for her at the luncheon reception. They weren't planning on a formal reception, just a potluck-style luncheon after the wedding. Ed immediately agreed to play and sing, but only if Bart agreed to as well. Bart was reluctant. He didn't like to play in front of large groups of people, but agreed with pressure from everyone. Dessert was fresh strawberries and cream.

After supper they all gathered around the piano and sang. Ed's song *Be My Wife* sounded even better with the piano accompanying. Listening to Bea play the piano made Cassie wish even more that she could play. Bea would pick a tune she knew and Ed would pick up the chords on the guitar, as did Bart on his violin. Cassie suddenly realized it was getting late and hinted to Ed they should be heading home, and not overstay their welcome.

"We should do this every week. Except maybe next Friday; we'll be pretty occupied that night," teased Bart, causing Bea to blush as they all laughed at the joke.

"But for sure the next week," said Ed. "You know we could become quite a famous singing quartet," he joked.

"Yes, we will sing at weddings for a small fee," joked Bart. "The Clark and Havoc Harmonizers," Bart smiled, and then laughed.

"I think you're on to something," said Ed. "But maybe they will have to pay us NOT to sing."

"Oh, Ed," said Cassie. "We sound great. Just you wait, they'll be begging us soon," she said laughing.

Turning to leave, Ed shook Bart and Bea's hands. "Thank you again for the invitation. Supper was delicious. And we had a great time," said Ed, as they walked out the door toward their buggy. "Bart, we can practice together once more on the morning of the wedding if you want," offered Ed.

"Yes, let's meet at the church Friday at 9:30 for a quick run through. And Cassie, can we expect to see you on Tuesday at the shop?" asked Bart.

"Yes, I'll be there. And we'll see you both at church on Sunday," said Cassie as she waved goodbye to her friends.

Ed helped Cassie into the buggy and climbed in beside her and clucked to Major as they drove off toward home.

"That was a lovely time. I really enjoy spending time with them," said Cassie, resting her head on Ed's shoulder.

"Me too, they're so much fun. I've never had the opportunity to play and sing with anyone but family before. It was wonderful," Ed said contentedly as he put his arm around Cassie. "Who would have ever thought this is how things would have turned out a month ago?"

"It's interesting how things worked out," said Cassie. "And I'm so happy they did, too," she said, thinking about the events of the past month.

"Me too, you're the best thing to ever happen to me." Ed turned and kissed her on the forehead.

"Bart really is a good man, and Bea is a wonderful woman. We're lucky to have such good friends." Cassie thought a prayer of gratitude for the good people in her life. She felt blessed to be surrounded with love and friendship.

"Yes, we are" Ed echoed, hugging her tight while he started humming and singing, *Be My Wife,* to her.

"I love you, Ed." Cassie relaxed into her sweetheart, listening to her favorite song sung in his smooth deep voice.

***

Bart and Bea worked together cleaning up the supper dishes and putting away the food. It was late as Bart stood in front of the door saying goodnight to Bea before he left.

"I'll miss you until tomorrow," Bart said, taking Bea in his arms and kissing her softly.

Surprised, both of them jumped as Bea's sisters burst through the door, excitedly talking about the play as they entered. Bart and Bea quickly stepped back from each other, blushing as they did so.

"Good night Bea, good night everyone. See you tomorrow," Bart confirmed as he passed them on his way out the door, blushing.

"Did we scare him off?" Mr. Holden asked, smiling as he and Mrs. Holden came inside.

***

Cassie went into town three days that following week and learned more about being a seamstress. By the end of the week, Cassie felt like she would be able to take a pattern home and bring back a completed garment. Cassie even spent a few afternoons that week helping the Sewing Bee Circle make a wedding quilt for Bea and Bart. Getting to know the sisters of the congregation and making something for the wedding was pleasant. The ladies of the Sewing Bee Circle were the same ladies who'd made her own Wedding Ring quilt.

The men's shop was nearly ready for the grand opening, and with the addition of a few new local seamstresses that Bart had hired including Cassie, the shop preparation seemed to be moving along smoothly.

A sign had been painted on the store front just below the second story windows. It said "C&H Men's Shop." For now, it was covered with a tarp to remain hidden until the grand opening. Mr. Holden had insisted that C&H sounded better than H&C. Bart was very appreciative; he knew Mr. Holden was just being nice. The store windows were also covered in newspaper to keep what was happening inside a secret from the public for as long as possible. A small sign on the front door announced that Monday, July 26th at 8:00 am, would be the big grand opening.

Bea and Bart spent the week setting up the shop for the big day. They dressed the mannequins in various suit styles similar to the ones back East and in Europe, and placed them around the store and in the display window. The dark wood counter was polished to a high shine, and the glass display case filled with tie pins and tacks, as well as cuff links and various ties. At the front of the shop was a fitting room with two full-length mirrors where Bart would be taking measurements.

The back room was furnished with new sewing machines, a cutting table, and male dress forms. Bolts of fabric were already lined up on shelves, and spools of thread, buttons, and other notions were nicely organized in boxes for quick access.

Bart's office was a small room in the very back. He had learned quite a bit over the past four weeks. The business experience he had learned at his father's mercantile made him feel confident that he could handle being in charge of the new shop. He knew Mr. Holden would be available to answer any questions.

All the work Bea and Bart were doing for the wedding and the shop, left little time to work on organizing their apartment. Seeing the need, Clancy and the seamstresses volunteered after work to get the apartment clean and livable for the newlyweds. They even moved in the furnishings that Mr. Holden had so graciously provided as a wedding gift. Bart and Bea were touched by the support from their friends and family, and by the generosity of Bea's parents. Bea's dowry would furnish some of the essentials, like pillowcases, towels, a blanket, and a few small doilies. Thursday was their last day of preparations, and it seemed as if everything was as ready as it could be.

That evening Bart moved into the apartment above the shop. Moving in was quick as he only had his trunk with his few belongings. He hung his clothes in the bureau, making sure his black suit was freshly pressed for the wedding, and polished his boots. As evening approached, the more nervous Bart became, and wondered if he would be able to sleep that night.

Clancy, figuring it was his job as the Best Man, stopped in to check on Bart that evening to make sure the wedding jitters did not get the best of him.

"Hey, do you want to go to the saloon and have a few drinks to calm the nerves?" asked Clancy, smiling as he stood at the top of the stairs leading up to the apartment. "It's your last chance to do whatever you want before you get married," he said, teasing Bart.

"Clancy, this is why I'm getting married and you're not. When you fall in love you'll understand. It's not like that. I'm doing what I want. I want to do what makes Bea happy. That's all I care about now," said Bart, patting Clancy on the back. "Come on in," he said, opening the door wide. "I guess I could use some company for a minute."

"Will you at least have one drink with me?" Clancy asked, patting the breast pocket of his vest. "I want to toast your good taste in women," teased

Clancy, referring to his cousin Bea. He pulled out a small metal flask from his pocket and smiled.

"Fine, I'll have one drink with you. And then I need to try and get some sleep before it gets too late." Bart took out two glasses from the cupboard and placed them on a small table in the kitchen area.

The two friends sat down for a drink and shared stories about growing up, marveling at the contrasts and similarities in their lives. Laughter and jokes filled the air, gradually giving way to more serious conversation as the evening progressed.

"You know, Bart, I envy you. You're being your own man. Good for you. To turn your back on your father's wishes and walk away from a life of ease would be hard to do for some men, I think," said Clancy pensively.

"I'm not exactly turning my back on him. It's just that I don't want to go back and take over my father's mercantile. I'm here because I love Bea and I want to run my own business. Make my own way. I still love my family and wish they understood," mused Bart, deep in contemplation. "Being the oldest, I suppose he just assumed that I'd naturally take over what he'd started," Bart added, beginning to understand how his father must feel.

"Well, if you're successful here, don't you want your son to take over the business when you get old?" asked Clancy, making more sense than he realized.

"You have a good point. I guess maybe I would. I would be proud of my business and would want him to have the opportunity to keep it growing. I definitely would want to make sure that's what he wanted, though. I see what you're saying. Because of my love for my business and my son I would want to share that with him. Like leaving him my legacy," said Bart in deep thought.

"You see, your father just loves you so much, Bart, that he thinks he's giving you his legacy. He probably feels like you're rejecting him and his gift. But what he doesn't realize is that you're his biggest accomplishment—the man you grew up to be, because of him." Clancy took another swig from the flask.

Bart was impressed by the wisdom of this rough around the edges cowboy. "How did you get so wise, Clancy?" asked Bart. "I had no idea you were such a deep thinker," he said with a quizzical look.

"It's all those years on cattle drives, it gives a man lots of time to think about life. I figured that one out a while back, when my pa was upset that I didn't stay on the farm and grow corn with him. I needed the great outdoors, to see the world and have adventures. I couldn't stand in one place to watch vegetables grow. As soon as I came to visit Aunt and Uncle Holden, I knew this is where I fit in. I left my father's farm years ago, and finally he's proud of me for doing what makes me happy. I reckon that's because he loves me. Love is wanting the other person's happiness above your own. Isn't that what you were just telling me?" Clancy smiled knowingly at his friend.

"Clancy, you're wise beyond your years. That makes perfect sense. You're right. I just wish my father would come to that realization sooner than later. I would love for him to be here for my wedding, and to meet Bea and her family. And you too, good friend." Bart smiled broadly, patting him on the back.

"All right, before you get all mushy, I should go." Clancy chuckled. "You save all your lovin' for Bea," joked Clancy, lightening the mood. It had been a long time since he'd had a good respectable friend. Most of the men he hung around were derelicts and got him into trouble more times than not. He never felt like he could trust them with his deep thoughts. But he felt Bart was one of those men that you could trust and talk to about anything, a true friend.

"That's right. I plan on it. And you had better get yourself home, so you're here bright and early to get me to the church on time. That's your job, remember." Bart stood and walked Clancy to the door.

"I'll be here, dressed up in my Sunday best. You know, I'm sure glad you decided to stay here in Cheyenne, and especially glad you're marrying Bea. You both are very lucky to have found each other. One day I hope to be as lucky." Clancy waved good-bye and walked down the back steps behind the shop.

Chapter 6

Bart and Bea's Wedding

Bart awoke to gentle sunlight streaming through the apartment window above the men's clothing store. The open window welcomed a refreshing breeze that played with the curtains, delighting his senses. He stretched and let out a satisfying yawn in the cozy bed, then pushed the sheet aside as he sat up, dangling his long legs off the edge. A radiant smile spread across his face as he realized that in mere hours, Bea would officially be his wife and this space would transform into their shared home.

Bart swiftly arranged the covers and plumped the pillows. He carefully laid out his new black double-breasted suit and the gold vest that he had sported at Ed and Cassie's wedding. With a systematic approach, he bathed, shaved, and applied a touch of pomade into his curly red hair, combing it until his reflection pleased him. While he was halfway into putting on his pants, a knock echoed at the door. Bart hastened to fasten up his pants and swung open the door, revealing Clancy, adorned in his finest Sunday attire, smiling broadly.

"Morning, my friend! It's wedding day!" Clancy beamed, playfully wagging his eyebrows.

Bart brushed off the banter, more focused on Clancy's remarkably polished outfit—a departure from his usual cowboy attire. "Clancy, you're looking sharp today," Bart commented, taken aback by the unexpected sight of Clancy in a crisply ironed shirt, tie, and suit jacket. Stepping back, Bart gestured for Clancy to come in, genuinely impressed by the transformation.

"I can scrub up pretty good when I've got to," Clancy boasted, his finger hooked into the collar of his white shirt as he stepped into the apartment, fidgeting with it uncomfortably. He couldn't recall the last time he'd worn the suit jacket and tie, which now felt a tad snug around his arms and neck. A few years back, upon his arrival in Cheyenne, he'd purchased the trousers along with the matching suit jacket and tie, with the intention of accompanying Aunt and Uncle Holden to church. However, once he left on the cattle drives, those clothes were stashed away. Now, back in Cheyenne, the chance to attend church regularly existed, yet he consistently found an excuse not to. If he was being honest with himself, he often attributed it to a bit too much time spent at the saloon the night before.

"Why not join us this Sunday? Who knows, you might catch the eye of a lovely young lady. When you spruce up this good, just think of the pretty gals you could charm," Bart playfully suggested, his smile carrying a hint of teasing. Now that their friendship had grown, Bart wished for Clancy to experience the happiness of finding a good woman much like he himself had. Bart genuinely hoped that Clancy would discover love and walk down the aisle someday.

"Yah, maybe. But only if you plan on feeding me supper afterwards. I'm not getting all dressed up to sit in a hot church unless there's food involved at some point," teased Clancy, fishing for the invitation to supper on Sunday.

"We're eating at the Holden's this Sunday, but I'm sure they would gladly welcome you. You are their nephew, after all. Maybe Bea could invite one of her seamstress friends from the men's clothing shop to join us as well." Bart sat on the edge of the bed, sliding on his newly polished boots.

Clancy unexpectedly felt a surge of nervousness for Sunday supper. "I'm not sure I'm up to snuff for those elegant ladies. They're all fine Christian women. I reckon they'd steer clear of someone like me. They've most likely already heard about me and would turn me down regardless." Clancy's gaze dropped to his scuffed boots, pondering if he'd ever have the chance to meet a nice young lady.

"Nonsense, Clancy. Don't be so hard on yourself. A bit of polishing is all you need, and you'll fit right in," Bart encouraged, donning his freshly pressed white shirt.

"You really think so? Could you help me?" Clancy felt a glimmer of hope. "You seem to have a knack for knowing how to treat a lady. I couldn't help but notice the way Bea reacted whenever you were near. I've never seen her turn so red." Clancy paced around the one room apartment, wondering how he could capture the attention of someone who would blush in his presence.

"Sure, I can help you. It's not complicated. Women are a bit like flowers, you know. They thrive when treated with care. Compliments about their beauty and affection go a long way. They love feeling cherished and unique. A man who's hardworking yet knows how to clean up after is a plus. They desire strength intertwined with tenderness. Above all, they want to be recognized for who they are. And in return, they'll give you the same. Well, at least that's what I've come to understand," Bart said with a shrug and a smile. He turned to the small mirror hanging over the wash basin stand, deftly tying his puffy tie around the shirt's high collar and securing it with a pearl tiepin.

"Hmm, who's sounding wise now?" Clancy chuckled, parting the curtains to peer out of the upstairs apartment window onto the street below. The early sun cast long shadows across the dusty street that was beginning to bustle with men and women on the move. Letting the curtains cascade shut, Clancy allowed Bart's words to sink in. "You've got a point there. I reckon I can give it a shot. But for now, I'm whipping up some eggs and coffee. I'm absolutely famished," Clancy said, busying himself by rummaging through the kitchen cupboards, gathering what he needed to prepare breakfast for them both.

***

Bea rose with the sun, her home bustling with the final wedding preparations. After her sisters expertly styled her hair, she slipped into her dress. The gown was a vision in white, its V-neck collar adorned with delicate lace edging and a lace yoke. Satin-covered buttons graced the fitted bodice, culminating in a V-shape at the waist. A satin bow adorned the fitted back, resting above the gathered mock bustle that cascaded gracefully over her hips. The skirt featured white ribbon accents above the ruffled hem, flowing elegantly to the floor, buoyed by her crinoline. Sleeves embraced her wrist, secured by a neat line of tiny satin buttons, and trimmed with lace at the cuffs. Her veil was attached to a dainty white hat that she pinned atop her head, keeping her skillfully woven red hair in place beneath the airy netting. Bea spun before the mirror, ensuring every detail was perfectly arranged. Content, she donned her white gloves and made her way to the parlor.

May clapped her hands together in delight as she caught sight of Bea entering the room. "Bea! You're like a princess!"

"Do you really think so?" Bea inquired humbly. Her mother and sisters entered the parlor, and she executed a slow spin to reveal her finished appearance.

Bea's mother placed her hands on her heart and began to tear up as she beheld her oldest daughter in her wedding dress. "Oh, Bea, you're a vision of perfection, simply beautiful!"

"Mother, it's a bit early for tears," Heather said,

quickly fetching a handkerchief as she noticed tears rolling down her mother's cheeks.

Bea's father entered the parlor and overcome with emotion, took Bea in a loving embrace. "My dear daughter. You are a picture of elegance. I'm overjoyed for you and Bart. What a glorious day of celebration this will be," he said kissing her on the cheek as tears escaped.

"Father, we ought to head to the church now. It's already 9:30," Christy said urgently, tugging on her gloves and adjusting her hat. She then seized the bouquet meant for Bea and prepared to take it to the church.

***

Cassie and Ed reached the church right on time at 9:30. Bart kept an eye out for their arrival, exhaling a sigh of relief when he spotted them approaching. There was just enough time to rehearse their duet before the wedding attendees started to arrive.

"Morning, Havocs!" Bart rushed down the church steps to welcome them, waving as they halted. "Hurry, come on in and let's get started." Bart's smile was a mix of excitement and nerves.

Ed greeted Bart with a comforting smile, while assisting Cassie out of the buggy. "I'm all set. Just need to grab my guitar."

"You're looking quite dapper, Bart," Cassie commented sincerely, looping her arm through Ed's, and joining Bart as they entered the church.

"I appreciate that, Cassie," Bart replied with a

smile. "You two are looking sharp as well." He was eager to finally get a glimpse of Bea and could only imagine how radiant she would appear in her wedding gown and veil.

As they entered the hushed chapel, Cassie released Ed's arm and trailed behind both him and Bart, their footsteps echoing up the aisle past the vacant pews towards the front. Selecting a pew two rows back, Cassie settled in, aware that the foremost row was reserved for immediate family. Bart and Ed promptly set about tuning the violin and guitar in harmony with the piano, their voices aligning to begin their rendition of the duet, *Be My Wife*. The fusion of their bass and tenor voices, entwined with the guitar and violin, created a heavenly resonance. The music swelled, enveloping the lofty chapel walls and soaring ceiling. Time raced toward the impending wedding ceremony. Cassie detected the initial guests' arrival; the chapel door swished open and shut gently as they discreetly took their seats on the very back row. Her attention returned to Ed and Bart as they restarted the song, aiming to perfect it before the rest of the attendees filed in. Movement caught Cassie's eye. Through a side entrance, Reverend Gather entered, dressed in his black suit and clerical collar. Observing his journey to the rear of the chapel to welcome the guests. Cassie's hand shot to her mouth, a quiet gasp escaping as she marveled. In that instant, her eyes brimmed with tears, recognizing the exquisitely attired couple in the back.

In a subdued tone, Reverend Gather greeted the

couple. "Welcome to the wedding ceremony. Are you a friend or family of the bride or groom?" As he neared the couple, Reverend Gather extended his hand, warmly clasping theirs.

With tears glistening in her eyes, the red-headed woman responded with pride, "Bart is our son."

Reverend Gather's smile broadened upon meeting the groom's parents. "I'm pleased to make your acquaintance. Allow me to guide you to your seats," he suggested, as he led them up the aisle, gracefully gesturing for them to occupy the front row.

Upon reaching the front, the couple's arrival caught Bart's attention. Bart stopped singing, gradually lowering his violin and bow, his gaze locked with his father's in astonishment. Ed's voice trailed and his strumming ceased as he observed the two men, noting their striking resemblance. A hush enveloped the room, punctuated only by the delicate sound of muffled sniffs as the two women quietly dried their tears.

"Father," Bart murmured softly, his voice trembling, words escaping him.

Suddenly, Bart's mother sidestepped her motionless husband and enveloped Bart in a motherly embrace. Tears streamed down as she held him close. "We had to come. Your letter…," her words gave way to sobs.

Bart's father moved forward, focusing on his son, and inquired, "Bartholomew, may we talk to you in private?"

Bart nodded, a lump forming in his throat, and gently let go of his mother. "Sure." With a mixture of anticipation and apprehension, he cast an anxious glance around the chapel. Noticing the side door, he indicated it with a gesture.

Cassie and Ed exchanged quizzical glances. As Bart and his parents exited through the side door, Ed joined Cassie on the pew. Observing her tears, he drew her close with an arm around her shoulders, leaning in and inquiring softly, "Do you know those people?"

Her voice quivering, she nodded and whispered in his ear, "They're Bart's parents." A surge of emotions swelled within her heart and mind. The last encounter she'd had with them was at her family's funeral. She never thought she would see Mr. and Mrs. Clark again or anyone else from Missouri, for that matter. Yet there they stood. Neither of them looked very happy and Cassie wondered if their presence indicated an attempt to persuade Bart to return home, or to support him in his decisions. Cassie hoped and prayed that Mr. Clark would be understanding. She recalled his firmness at times when running his mercantile back in Jackson County, Missouri.

Bart swung open the door to the hallway that led to Reverend Gather's office, ushering them in before gently shutting the door. Inhaling deeply, he turned to face them, a hopeful smile gracing his face. "Mother, Father, I'm pleased you made the choice to come."

His father's tone dripped with bitterness, "Your mother was insistent. According to her, we would regret it for the rest of our lives if we didn't come."

"I'm sorry to have disappointed you both." Bart's

gaze dropped with dejection, then forced himself to meet his father's eyes. "But I felt an undeniable pull to come here and bring Cassie back with me. I didn't know she'd become engaged already. I felt I was meant to be here. Now I understand it was for a different purpose. Finding Bea has shown me what true love is. I'm more excited and determined than I've ever been. Building my own business is hard work, yet deeply fulfilling. Father, I regret this isn't what you wished for me. I never intended to let you down. Your dream was for me to take over the business, and I went along without knowing my own desires. Now I know. I aspire to build my own business from the ground up, much like you did. Please understand, I'm not trying to be ungrateful. Your desire for me to take the reins of the mercantile is an honor. I see now how much you care for me, and wanted me to inherit your hard-earned legacy. But, Father, you've imparted more than a business, you've molded a man—me. I want you to be proud of the man I've become. You're the reason I know who I should be. You're a wonderful role model, Father." Bart felt tears tracing down his cheeks and wiped them away. *There, I've laid out my heart. Now, it's up to you, Father, to take the next step.*

"Son." His father's voice quivered, stepping forward to enfold him in a fatherly embrace. He held Bart tightly while time stretched out, searching for the right words. "I'll always love you and I am proud of you, Bart. I admit, there was initial disappointment—I had such dreams. But you're correct, those were my dreams. You're your own man, and I now see what a remarkable man you've become. The change I see in you is palpable. Your happiness and peace are evident. If your dream is to stay here and run your own business, then I will support you. And we stand with you in your decision to marry Bea," he affirmed, giving Bart a hearty pat on the back before releasing him and cupping Bart's face in his hands. "I'm genuinely proud of you, my son," he declared, locking eyes with Bart, and offering a sincere smile.

"We love you, son." Bart's mother beamed through tears of joy, drawing him into a loving embrace. Her once unyielding husband had finally softened; the transformation was an answer to her prayers. Her heart was rejoicing. "Let's head inside so you can get married. Your bride might get worried if you keep her waiting." She linked her arm with Bart's and guided him tenderly back to the chapel door.

Sniffing and hastily wiping his tears, Bart readied himself before they re-entered the chapel. His father followed suit, discreetly drying his own tears and clearing his throat.

"Take a seat here," Bart directed, leading them to the front row of pews adjacent to where he'd stand. Behind them, guests took their seats, a hushed anticipation filling the air. Bart's gaze shifted to the other side, where Bea's mother and sisters had found their places.

Approaching Bea's mother, Bart greeted her with a soft smile and a gentle handshake. "Mrs. Holden, let me introduce my parents, Mr. and Mrs. Clark." Bart gestured across the aisle to his parents.

Mrs. Holden extended her hand across the aisle, meeting Mrs. Clark's halfway. "Delighted you could join us," Mrs. Holden whispered, giving Mrs. Clark's hand a gentle squeeze, her smile encompassing both of Bart's parents.

"Wouldn't have missed it for the world," Mrs. Clark whispered, returning the smile to the charming red-haired woman. She was grateful everything had turned out as well as she had hoped and prayed.

All at once, the chapel doors swung open at the back, revealing Bea and her father. The sunlight framed her, casting an angelic glow around her figure. To Bart, it felt as if an angel had descended from heaven. His heart was pounding out of his chest.

Beside Bart, Clancy had positioned himself ready to offer support if needed. The guests stood as Bea embarked on her journey down the aisle, the organ playing the wedding march. Bea paused and turned to face her father. He raised her veil and placed a kiss on her cheek before presenting her hand to Bart.

Excitement painted Bea's cheeks a rosy hue as she bestowed a sweet smile upon Bart. Her vivid blue eyes sparkled, radiant with happiness, as she intertwined her hands with his. She had never felt so happy in all her life.

For Bart, reality felt softened, almost dreamlike. Everything seemed to blur at the edges, leaving only Bea, standing like an angel before him at the center of his vision. He swallowed hard, determined to hold back tears of joy. His loved ones congregated around him, uniting to celebrate the happiest day of his life. The people he loved the most were all in the same room on the happiest day of his life. Silently he offered gratitude to the Almighty for his abundant blessings.

Reverend Gather concluded the ceremony, his voice ringing out, "You may now kiss the bride."

Bart's heart soared with elation as he took Bea in his arms, pressing a tender kiss upon her lips. It was their first kiss as husband and wife, a symbol of their newfound union.

Reverend Gather happily announced, "I present to you, Mr. and Mrs. Bartholomew Clark."

Bart and Bea's faces radiated joy as they stood side by side, united as husband and wife. With linked arms, they strolled down the aisle, their smiles wide and infectious. Beyond the chapel doors, guests playfully tossed wheat, a gesture of fertility and prosperity. As the newlyweds boarded the adorned buggy, a sign proclaiming "Just Married" displayed proudly. Ribbon and streamers danced in the breeze, creating a festive atmosphere. The buggy set off toward Bea's parents' home, where the luncheon awaited, beginning the next chapter of their journey.

Outside the church, Cassie and Ed joined the other guests, observing the newlyweds as they departed. Cassie put her arm around Ed's waist and leaned her head against him. "That was truly beautiful," Cassie murmured, wiping away a tear.

"It was indeed, though it pales in comparison to the day I married you, Cass," Ed replied, draping his arm over her shoulders, drawing her close for a kiss.

"Ed, I love you," Cassie professed as their lips parted. "Marrying you is one of the best decisions I've ever made." She nestled her head against his chest, finding comfort in their bond.

"I'm yours for all time, my love. And you're mine," he murmured, his embrace unwavering. Unaware of the bustling guests making their way to their carriages or towards the Holden's residence, he held her close.

"Shall we head out to the celebration?" Cassie asked, scanning the area and realizing they were alone for the moment.

"Sure, I guess we should get going. I have to perform soon." Ed replied, clasping Cassie's hand as they reentered the church to retrieve the instruments.

"Mr. and Mrs. Clark, so good to see you." Cassie smiled when she saw them standing just inside the chapel doors.

"Cassie, it's wonderful to see you," Mrs. Clark greeted, embracing Cassie warmly. "You seem to be doing splendidly." She couldn't help but notice how radiant and healthy Cassie looked, a stark contrast to the last time she'd seen her.

"Thank you. It means a lot that you could be here for the wedding. I know Bart must be very pleased; he values your support immensely," Cassie replied with heartfelt emotion, relieved that the situation with his parents had resolved positively.

"We're pleased we came. And this must be your husband. Bart mentioned you two were engaged," Mrs. Clark remarked, her attention drawn to Ed's ring and his joyful countenance fixed on Cassie.

"Oh, yes. Ed, these are Bart's parents from Missouri, Mr. and Mrs. Clark. Mr. and Mrs. Clark, I'd like you to meet my husband, Edward Havoc," Cassie introduced with pride.

Ed stepped forward, his hand resting on Cassie's back as he extended the other to shake hands with Mr. and Mrs. Clark. "It's a pleasure to meet you both. I'd be more than happy to show you to the Holden's place. I'm sure everyone would be delighted to meet you," he offered warmly.

"I don't know if we're invited," Mr. Clark admitted, feeling out of place.

"Of course you're invited. Bea's parents would be disappointed if you didn't show up. You're esteemed guests. Come on, it's just a few blocks away," Ed assured, motioning them towards the door.

"So, Bart mentioned he's opening a men's clothing shop. Where's the shop located?" Mr. Clark inquired, his gaze sweeping down Main Street once they stepped outside.

"It's just three blocks down Main Street. And the dress shop is another two blocks further," Cassie clarified, pointing down the street.

"We walked from the hotel to the church and noticed the sign for Holden's Dress Shop—it looked quite lovely from what we could see. However, we couldn't quite identify the building for the men's clothing shop," Mr. Holden explained, wondering how they had overlooked it.

"That's because the sign and windows are

concealed until the ribbon-cutting on Monday. When you head back to the hotel, you'll be able to spot it now that you know the building. It might appear deserted from the outside, but inside, it's quite impressive. They've put in a lot of effort to get it ready for business," Cassie informed them.

"I'm intrigued to see what it looks like," Mr. Clark remarked, his eyes squinting against the sun as he surveyed the buildings along the street. "I'm eager to see what my son is so enthused about," he added, a smile gracing his lips.

"I'm sure he'll give you a tour during your stay. I really hope you'll be here for the grand opening." Cassie said, knowing how happy it would make Bart.

Mrs. Clark felt a surge of excitement at the prospect of being involved in her son's life once more. "I believe we can arrange that. Our train isn't departing until Monday afternoon."

Cassie and Ed led the way to the Holden home, introducing Mr. and Mrs. Clark to friends and neighbors as they made their way to the parlor. There, Bart, Bea, and her parents were greeting guests.

Bart stepped forward, his grin radiating joy. "Mother, Father, I'd like to introduce you to Mr. and Mrs. Holden," he said as they exchanged warm handshakes and hugs. "And this is my wife, Beatrice. Bea, these are my parents." Bart placed his hand gently on Bea's back, guiding her forward as he made the introductions, his smile stretching from ear to ear. He couldn't have dreamed of a better day.

"So delighted to meet you both. Your presence

means so much to us. Thank you for coming," Bea added, stepping forward to give each of them a heart-felt hug.

"And we're absolutely delighted to meet you, my dear. You're simply lovely, Beatrice," Mrs. Clark said, her pride evident as she gushed. She had noticed Bea's light red hair, something Bart had mentioned in his letter, noting its resemblance to her own.

"Bart, I can see now why you've chosen to stay in Cheyenne. She bears a striking resemblance to your mother when I married her," Mr. Clark chimed in, his arm around his wife as he fondly reminisced about their own wedding day. He felt a sense of pride for his son and gratitude for his wife's wisdom, always more inclined towards forgiveness.

Reverend Gather offered a blessing upon the food, and the attendees formed a line to fill their plates with the delectable potluck luncheon offerings. After the luncheon concluded, everyone convened in the parlor, where Bea occupied the seat front and center while Ed and Bart readied themselves for their duet. Bart poised his violin on his shoulder, bow at the ready, while Ed adjusted his guitar strap and struck the first chord of the song he had composed for Cassie on their own wedding day. The audience watched and listened intently as Ed and Bart delivered the heartfelt verses of enduring love and commitment through a lifetime. As the performance drew to a close, Bart felt a mixture of relief and satisfaction. Bea's eyes shimmered with tears as she gazed affectionately at him. He approached her and kissed her lips, while the guests broke into applause.Bottom of Form

Bart's parents were thrilled to witness Bart's musical talents on display, and they showered both him and Ed with praise for their captivating performance.

"Thank you, Mother. Thank you for convincing Father to come. It means the world to me," Bart expressed, his voice tinged with emotion and unshed tears.

"I'm glad we made the journey. I knew that once your father heard your heart, he'd come around to understanding how you felt," Bart's mother shared, her eyes welling up with gratitude as she hugged him tightly and placed a tender kiss on his cheek. "I only wish we had more time to spend with you and to get to know your wonderful wife and her parents before we have to return home. Having you back in our lives is an incredible gift, and I want to cherish every moment we have together."

Mrs. Holden overheard the conversation and joined them, offering her warm hospitality. "Mrs. Clark, it would be our pleasure to have you join us for supper each evening during your stay here. And, of course, Bart and Bea will be joining us as well once they return from their honeymoon."

Bart's father chimed in, curious about their honeymoon plans. "And where are you two headed for your honeymoon?"

"We actually haven't made any plans," Bart replied with a fond smile directed at Bea, who blushed at his words. "With all the wedding arrangements and preparations for the opening of the men's clothing shop, we haven't had the chance to organize anything. We'll simply head back to our apartment above the shop, after this."

"Oh, I see. Mrs. Holden, we appreciate the invitation for supper. We'd be delighted to join you." Bart's father replied graciously.

Amidst the gathering of friends and family, Bart and Bea started opening their wedding gifts, followed by cutting the cake. In a quiet moment, Bart's father leaned in to his wife and shared a whisper, then discreetly slipped out the front door, and headed back the way they had come. He felt a sense of responsibility for not having brought a wedding gift for Bart and Bea and wanted to rectify the situation right away.

As soon as Bart's father returned, he sought them out. "Bart, Bea, I've got a surprise for you. Go get your bags ready. I've arranged a room for you at the Cheyenne Hotel for the next couple of nights," he announced, his smile wide as he handed Bart an envelope containing cash. "This is for meals during your stay. We want you to know how happy we are for you both, and we wish we could do more." He held back his emotions, giving them each a warm hug and offering congratulations once again.

"Father, thank you," Bart's voice quivered, his eyes shining with tears of gratitude. "And thank you for this thoughtful gift."

Bart and Bea exchanged gleeful glances, and Bea chimed in with her gratitude. "We're truly thankful for this." Bea gently squeezed Bart's hand.

"It's our pleasure," Bart's father responded.

Excusing himself from the festivities, Bart gathered his belongings for the upcoming days, as did Bea. With their bags ready, they decided to bid farewell to the party to head to the hotel for their honeymoon.

On their way out, the guests cheered for Bea to toss the bouquet. Bea's laughter echoed as she playfully hurled the flowers over her head. Watching the lively scene, Cassie shared a laugh with Ed. Among the onlookers, Shirley, one of Bea's colleagues, unexpectedly caught the bouquet. Blushing, and casting a shy glance, Shirley's eyes met Clancy's. A nervous smile played on Clancy's lips, and he felt his heart skip a beat as Shirley smiled back, creating a heartwarming connection between them.

Chapter 7

Love is in the Air

The black-suited porter swung open the door to Bart and Bea's honeymoon suite at the Cheyenne Hotel. "Wait here. I'll be just a moment," he said, carrying their luggage inside, making his way through the large room with the help of the muted light filtering through the heavily draped windows.

Bart and Bea stood waiting outside the doorway, not knowing what to expect, exchanging looks of anticipation, with eyes twinkling and special smiles only meant for each other.

The porter set their luggage down and went to the far side of the room and lit the painted lamps, one on each of the bedside tables and the one on the small table between the two parlor chairs.

Bea's eyes were immediately drawn to the tall four-poster canopy bed, covered with deep-red and gold brocade and matching curtains draped over each post, tied back with golden ropes with tassels. Her heart beat faster as Bart squeezed her hand, following her gaze to the bed. She returned his squeeze, as a trembling started inside her. Both felt excited and slightly nervous for their first night together.

Bart felt his heart pounding against his chest, near to bursting with love for Bea. He couldn't believe he was married to this elegant lady in white standing beside him, and gave her hand a reassuring squeeze as he felt her trembling.

The porter went to the tall windows on one side of the room and unhooked the golden ropes and drew the thick red and gold curtains closed, for privacy. "Sir, madam, your room is ready," the porter said with a slight bow and sweep of his arm, inviting them into the grand room.

Bart and Bea felt like royalty about to step inside their castle bedchamber. Everywhere they looked were the colors of rich deep-red and gold. Even the walls illuminated by the romantic lamplight glinted off the gold paisley of the red wallpaper. Dark chestnut furniture, ornately carved, and covered in lacy doilies, filled the corners of the room. Every detail conveyed opulence; even the plush ornamental rug covering the room's dark polished floor. It was a room like no other they had ever seen and only imagined from the books they read.

Before he said a word, Bart swept Bea up into his arms and carried her over the threshold of their elegantly furnished room. Bart set Bea down on one of the deep-red velvet chairs in front of a small carved table that held a bottle of champagne and two champagne glasses. Bart turned to the porter and handed him a tip and thanked him as the porter slipped out and closed the thick door quietly behind him.

"Bea, you have made me the happiest man alive," said Bart, pulling Bea up and holding her close to him as he stared into her bright blue eyes. "I feel as if I could conquer the world with you by my side."

"Oh Bart, you're such a wonderful man. You've made my dreams come true," Bea said with her arms around his neck, looking longingly into his shining eyes.

Bart leaned in and kissed her softly on her perfectly pink lips, then whispered, "I felt like I was dreaming today when you came through the chapel doors. You looked like an angel descending from heaven. I'll never forget it," he said as a warmth grew from his middle and coursed throughout his body.

Bea blushed, feeling the heat build in her. "I love you so much, Bart. I'll never forget today either, you're so handsome," Bea said sweetly, daring to touch his smooth cheek with her hand. She chuckled to herself as she thought of her walk up the aisle. "It was all I could do not to run up the aisle to you. Good thing my upbringing kept me in check. And it didn't hurt that my father was walking with me, so I didn't fall over." She moved her hands to the back of his neck and gently stroked his soft red hair.

"It was a good thing you came to me. I was stunned and could hardly breathe, let alone move when I saw you," he said, laughing lightly, then became serious as her soft touch transfixed him. All he could think about was how wonderful her fingers felt running through his hair.

Gently, she pressed the back of his head closer to hers, looking longingly at him. With her unspoken message, he pulled his wife closer, no longer holding back, and kissed her long and sweet.

***

Later, dressed in their formal wear, Bart and Bea sat in the Cheyenne's formal dining room, eating by candlelight in a secluded corner. The room around them glowed with crystal chandeliers hanging over thick carpeting, drapery, and papered walls. Lamp-lit sconces, framed art, and greenery decorated every wall and corner. Each white linen-covered table was set with tall crystal glasses, fine bone china, and polished silverware. Waiters in black ties and tails moved gracefully around the room, serving the elegantly dressed patrons. Having heard that it was their wedding day, musicians serenaded the couple at their table. After finishing dinner, they moved to the dance floor. A small orchestra played romantic music for the newlyweds, as Bart and Bea moved gracefully around the polished floor under the sparkling candlelit chandelier. Their wedding night felt magical, just like something out of a fairytale. Oblivious to those watching, Bart and Bea stared lovingly into each other's eyes, sending warm signals back and forth until Bart leaned close and whispered something into her ear and with a nod, they retired to their room for the night.

***

The next two days were spent getting the last-minute things ready for the grand opening of the shop, but every other minute, Bart and Bea rejoiced in the time they got to spend together with their families. Right away, Bea could tell that Mr. and Mrs. Clark fit right in with the Holdens. Saturday afternoon Bea and her mother gave Mrs. Clark a tour of the Holden home. More than once, Bea heard Mrs. Clark compliment her mother for her fine taste in decorating, going on and on about the lovely furniture and wallpapers she'd chosen for each room. The women and girls gathered in the kitchen sharing tea and cake, with Mrs. Clark and Bea's mother excitedly talking about their similar hobbies, their homes, and raising children, while the three men congregated in the parlor and had coffee and cake as they discussed work. To Bart's delight, Mr. Holden and his father had a lot in common, both having started their own businesses from nothing, and sat sharing stories of their similar struggles and successes. When they had both exhausted their past stories, Mr. Holden moved on to his most recent endeavor.

"Mr. Clark, I want you to know how lucky I was to have Bart come along when he did. Your son is quite talented. Right away I could tell what a hard worker he was. Bart has picked up the clothing business very quickly," Mr. Holden commented as he set down his empty teacup and forked a bite of his favorite spice cake into his mouth.

Not wanting to interrupt the conversation, Bea quietly entered the parlor and silently offered to refresh their cups with the pot of coffee she brought with her. Her father held up his teacup as she filled it, and smiled his thanks. She turned to Mr. Clark and filled his after a nod of his head and received a quick thank you.

Bart smiled proudly as he watched Bea move smoothly around the small parlor table and chairs, looking elegantly dressed in her pink satin frock, with her long hair held perfectly in place with pins he'd watched her situate earlier that morning. Bea was every bit a graceful lady and hostess. Bart forced his attention back to Mr. Holden to respond to his compliment. "Thank you, Mr. Holden, that's very generous of you." Bart nodded and smiled graciously, then turned his attention back to Bea. His loving smile said more than words could as he held up his cup and thanked her.

Bart's father took a sip of the hot coffee from the fine china, and set it down as he swallowed, then added to Mr. Holden's observation, "Bart's always been a quick study. When he wants something, he goes after it. I guess I shouldn't have been surprised when he made up his mind to stay here and start a new business. I'm really proud of what he's accomplished in such a short amount of time." He looked across the table at Bart and gave him a nod as he raised his cup, congratulating him. The others joined in, and raised their cups, and took a swallow.

That is, Bart *tried* to swallow. He smiled at his father as tears gathered in his eyes. He bowed his head and forced the liquid past the lump in his throat.

Staring at his full cup of coffee, he picked up his spoon and stirred absently as he fought back the tears of joy, thinking this was one of the best moments of his life. His father had never praised him so highly before, let alone in front of anyone, and it touched him deeply. To receive his father's approval was something he didn't realize he wanted so badly.

Bea saw Bart's eyes glisten at the compliment, knowing what it meant to Bart, and put a gentle hand on his shoulder and gave it a squeeze before she turned and silently slipped out of the room.

***

That last evening all together, the family's conversation was especially lively as they shared stories of Bart and Bea's childhood. With the supper dishes left on the table for the maid to clean up, they moved into the parlor to continue reminiscing as laughter filled the room from the stories they told. The parents gathered around the lace-covered table and were served tea while the three girls sat on the floral-print settee, and Bart and Bea shared the cushioned sofa, forming a semi-circle around the empty fireplace of the extravagantly furnished room.

May, Bea's youngest sister, could hardly sit still in her seat, swinging her short legs and nearly bouncing with excitement as she listened. She loved hearing stories about Bart and Bea when they were little. And especially about Bart, and tried to imagine him as a shy skinny boy her age, getting into fights at school for being called "Red." May knew what it was like to be teased for having red hair and thought he was brave for standing up to the bullies.

"Next time someone says something about my hair, I'm going to give them what for, just like Bart," May declared and jumped up with her fists held in tight balls, and squinted her eyes, glaring at the imaginary bullies in front of her, challenging them to a fight. "I dare you to say it again," she hunched over, moving her fists in small circles as she had seen the older boys do when they fought in the schoolyard.

Mrs. Holden's two teenage daughters laughed at their spunky little sister. Mrs. Holden shared an understanding look with Mrs. Clark before she shushed her daughters' snickering. "Shh, you two. That's enough."

Bart blushed, and feeling obliged, warned May, "Believe me, May, it's not good to resolve problems with your fists. I learned that the hard way." He subconsciously rubbed his jaw and thought back to a month or so ago when he'd gotten into a fight at the saloon.

Mrs. Holden waved her youngest daughter over to her. "Come here. Now May, we will have no fighting here or anywhere else. Do you hear me? It's not ladylike for a girl to fight." She pulled her little girl to her side and gave her a tight hug. "Remember what Jesus taught. It's better to turn the other cheek and to love your enemies."

"I know, but why does it have to be so hard?" May asked, her little red braids almost matching her fiery cheeks of indignation as everyone hid their smiles and muffled their laughter behind their hands.

"Now you do as you're told." Mrs. Holden gave her daughter a little pat on the bottom before she retreated back to her spot between Heather and Christy on the settee.

Heather suddenly thought of a memory about Bea and turned to Christy and asked, "Do you remember when we were little, how Bea made us play school and pretended to be our teacher and we were her students?" asked Heather.

Bea's sisters told all about the lessons they were taught in reading, writing, and arithmetic.

"Because of me, you were reading and writing long before you even started school," Bea said, defending herself from her sisters' teasing.

Heather and Christy grinned and bowed, "Thank you, Ms. Holden," they echoed and giggled.

Christy added her memories of young Bea. "Do you remember how Bea used to write plays for us to perform for Mother and Father?" she asked laughing. "Heather, do you remember the one about the Founding Fathers?"

"Yes!" Heather admitted. "How could I forget? You at least got to play Martha Washington. I had to play George Washington and dress up in Father's trousers," she recalled as she wrinkled her nose, reaching over and poking Christy and May in the ribs, eliciting giggles.

"Girls!" Mrs. Holden looked heavenward for strength, shook her head, and gave Mrs. Clark a knowing smile as she thought, *Oh, these girls of mine! Will they ever learn to act like ladies?* She took a deep breath to calm herself and turned her attention back to Mr. and Mrs. Clark. "You know, even as a little girl Bea was a talented teacher and pianist." She wanted them to know what a wonderful daughter-in-law they were getting. "She wrote songs to go with all her plays and accompanied them while the girls sang and danced for us. All written and choreographed by Bea." Mrs. Holden looked at her oldest daughter, and felt a tear gathering. Her daughter had grown into such a lovely young lady and now a beautiful married woman.

Bea smiled back at her mother and looked away as the others stared at her, making her blush.

"She is as beautiful as she is talented, and cultured as well," Mrs. Clark assured Mrs. Holden as she took a sip of her tea and smiled over at Bart and Bea on the sofa, thinking they made a handsome couple. She was so proud of Bart for finding a worthy helpmate.

Bea graciously thanked Mrs. Clark, feeling her love growing for her new mother-in-law.

Mr. Holden cleared his throat. "I can remember one of Bea's first productions. One that *she* performed in." Mr. Holden settled back into his leather chair and hooked his thumbs into his vest pockets while everyone waited for him to tell the story. "She was maybe, six or seven, and was playing the part of a tree in a school program. Do you remember?" He looked over to his wife sitting across from him in her red velvet chair.

Mrs. Holden smiled and nodded, "Yes, I

remember the little sprig of a girl with bright red braids, wearing the little green dress I'd made for her, just for that part."

Mr. Holden continued, "Bea was so shy—back then," he said with a grin and a wink, receiving a few chuckles in response. "She didn't want to hold up the two leafy branches that we'd cut from our tree as part of her costume. It took quite some convincing for her to get the courage to walk up the aisle to the stage to say her part. Finally, she started up the aisle. Halfway up, she decided to lift her branches and in the process knocked off a man's hat as she walked by. Everyone in the audience started laughing, and poor Bea started crying, and would have bolted out of the school if it hadn't been for the man's quick actions. The man picked up his hat, smiled, and put it back on his head, then crouched down beside her and said loud enough for everyone to hear, 'I like your branches and love it when trees as pretty as you grow tall and beautiful.' He took her hand and walked her up the aisle to take her place on the stage with the others. Once everyone settled down, and with his encouragement, she lifted up her branches and recited the poem about trees."

Bart gave Bea a hug around the shoulders as she tipped her head close to his. "That's my Bea. Tall and beautiful." He gave her a quick peck on the cheek and Bea's sisters giggled to see him kiss her.

Bea blushed and slowly joined in the laughter, still remembering how devastated she was at the time and how silly it all seemed now.

It was so much fun reminiscing that no one

wanted it to end. But when the clock on the mantel struck nine, Bart stood up. "We hate to say goodnight, but it's getting late, and tomorrow is going to be a big day," Bart said, helping Bea up from the sofa.

"We should be going as well," Mr. Clark said, looking at his wife, who agreed.

Mrs. Clark reached over the table and squeezed Mrs. Holden's hand. "We've enjoyed your family so much and hope we haven't overstayed our welcome," Mrs. Clark said as she stood with the help of her husband.

"Nonsense. We've loved having you here and hope we can do this again someday," Mrs. Holden smiled, standing and leading their guests out of the parlor with the girls and Mr. Holden following behind.

At the door, Mr. and Mrs. Clark paused to say goodnight to everyone with handshakes and hugs before they thanked Bea's parents once more and hurried out the door down the front steps to the walk that led to their hotel in the center of town. Bart and Bea called out and waved a final goodbye to Bart's parents, then turned to say goodnight to Bea's parents and sisters, promising to meet at the shop bright and early the next morning, with the refreshments for the grand opening. As Bart and Bea walked silently back to their apartment, hand in hand, each was deep in their own thoughts, replaying the events of the last two days. The summer night was full of stars and promise. Bart looked up and took a deep breath of the fresh night air. They were nearly home to their apartment when Bart could no longer hold in his thoughts, wanting to share them with his wife.

Bart paused on the boardwalk and waited for her to stop and look at him.

"What is it, Bart?" Bea asked with concern, searching his glistening eyes in the yellow lamplight of Main Street.

"I'm so happy, Bea. I can hardly believe these past few days have been real. They've been filled with so many wonderful blessings. I can't believe my parents came all this way and forgave me and even support me in my dream now." His chin trembled as he tried to contain his emotions. "These have been the best days of my life."

"Mine too." Tears gathered in her eyes as she smiled.

Bart returned her joyful smile and took both of her hands in his. "And the best part of all—was marrying you," and sealed his words with a promise of his own.

***

Monday, the grand opening of the men's clothing shop went off without a hitch. C&H Men's Shop had a nice ring to it and gave Mr. Clark a new sense of pride in his son and hope for his future. After the grand opening, Bart saw his parents off at the train station. As happy as he was to see them come, he was equally sad to see them go. With tears of joy and sadness, Bart promised to write weekly and keep his father up to date on his progress and made a special promise to his mother to try to come for visits before the year ended. She knew that with the business being so new, it would be hard for Bart and Bea to get away, but she was sure they would try. The unspoken reality was that they might never see each other again.

Chapter 8

Fall Blessings

The summer of 1869 continued to be hot and dry until mid-September. Then suddenly, the nights turned colder, taking half the day to warm again. Bea decided not to return to teaching that fall. She was happy spending her days working with her husband in their new business. Bart was equally happy to have her by his side and found her more and more invaluable as the orders came pouring in. Soon they would need to look for additional help.

Each week, Cassie took in sewing from the C&H Men's Shop. On Mondays she would pick up the pattern, cloth, and notions, and on Friday mornings she would bring back the finished article of clothing. Cassie found it enjoyable, creating the stylish suits from start to finish and it was an added blessing to be able to work on her own sewing machine at home and fit the work in between chores and canning. As fall approached, the bountiful garden kept Cassie busy gathering, drying, pickling and preserving the vegetables. The cellar and pantry shelves were filling up nicely with beautiful bottles of fruits and vegetables and preserves. Her favorite were the bottles of dill pickles. With the colder nights and shorter days, she felt a sense of urgency to get as much put away as fast as possible in preparation for the long winter ahead. Nearly every day the cottage was filled with wonderful smells as Cassie was busy preserving everything she could.

"Land sakes, I can smell your delicious preserves and baking bread clear out to the barn! My mouth is watering so bad I had to come in and have some!" Ed announced as he came up behind her at the stove, wrapped his arms around her waist, and kissed her on the cheek. "You actually are more delicious than that jam, but I'll take what I can get right now," he said kissing her, then dipping a freshly baked piece of bread into the still warm jam Cassie was preparing.

"You will have to settle for that bread and jam for now. I need to get this cleaned up and start supper," she said, leaning back against him, cherishing his embrace. She had never felt so content. Having her own home and seeing the results of her hard work was her idea of heaven. Every bottle that lined the shelves and bushel basket full in the cellar gave her a sense of satisfaction and peace. She had accomplished so much for her family's survival and was proud of the home she was working so hard to create. After all, this was for her and Ed and their future family.

Later that week, after church let out, Cassie and Ed stood holding hands talking to Bart and Bea when Cassie wondered if she should let them in on their secret.

"Ed, do you think we should tell them?" Cassie asked with a twinkle in her eye and a squeeze of her hand.

"Tell us what?" Bea asked, looking back and forth from Cassie to Ed, who both looked as if they were about to burst with excitement.

Ed grinned and wrapped his arm around Cassie's shoulders.

Bart thought he knew but waited to see if he was right.

Cassie blurted out, "I'm going to have a baby!"

"Oh my goodness! That's wonderful!" Bea exclaimed, taking Cassie into a quick hug. "When?" Bea asked, releasing her and smiling broadly, rejoicing in the good news.

"Around the first of April I think," Cassie said placing her hand on her small belly.

"Congratulations!" Bart exclaimed, shaking Ed's hand and slapping him on the back, then giving Cassie's hand a squeeze. "Really, I'm so happy for you both."

One of the ladies at church who'd walked by, overheard them, and stopped. "What's this? Did you just announce you're expecting?" she asked Cassie and Ed with excitement, loud enough for almost everyone in town to hear.

Cassie and Ed laughed and blushed as heads turned to look their way.

"Well, I guess the cat's out of the bag now!" Ed declared with a grin and soon the word spread through the group of worshipers still milling around the carriages and wagons, saying their goodbyes.

In minutes, women were buzzing around Cassie excitedly as they congratulated the expectant parents. Only Ed, George, Mabel, and Madeline knew it would actually be the first of February. Cassie was five months into the pregnancy and was feeling healthy and strong. Her morning sickness had dissipated, and her appetite was ravenous. With each passing day she became more and more attached to the tiny baby growing inside her, feeling its little fluttery kicks and movements that made her heart swell with love. Cassie had already finished crocheting the pink baby blanket and had completed a few clothes for the infant. Aunt Mabel was also working on a small patchwork quilt for the crib, sewing every stitch with love and care.

A few weeks later, during one of their customary Friday evening gatherings at the Havoc's, Bea burst out, "We have some exciting news! I know it's early, but I couldn't wait to share it." She gave Cassie's hand a gentle squeeze. "I kept watching you and wondering what being pregnant felt like, and now I'll get to experience it myself," she exclaimed joyfully.

Springing up from her chair, Cassie enveloped her friend in a hug. "Oh Bea, that's fantastic news! Congratulations to both of you," Cassie exclaimed, her gaze shifting to Bart, who stood by Bea's side, his face radiant with pride.

Ed warmly shook Bart's hand and gave him a hearty pat on the back. "Congratulations, my good man! I'm thrilled for you both. When are you expecting the baby?" Ed's grin was infectious, reflecting his genuine happiness for the couple.

"We believe it will be in June, so just a couple months after you," Bea shared with a joyful smile.

"That's wonderful," Ed responded, exchanging a knowing glance with Cassie.

Bart grinned. "I can hardly wait. In fact, we've decided to move out of the apartment before the baby arrives. We're planning to buy us a place in town. If you happen to know of anyone interested in renting the apartment, please let us know. We're aiming for someone who's quiet and trustworthy."

"You know, I should write to my ma and see if she'd consider coming out here with my sisters to work in the shop for you. They're highly skilled seamstresses and would be ideal tenants for your apartment," Ed mused.

Bart eagerly clasped his hands together and pleaded, "Yes, please tell them to come as soon as possible. We are in dire need. We'd even be willing to offer the first few months rent-free, to assist with their travel expenses," Bart proposed, hopeful that it would prove enticing.

***

Ed didn't waste any time and immediately penned a letter to his mother. He shared the exciting new about the job openings at the men's clothing shop, emphasizing Bart's exceptional qualities as an employer as well as describing the cozy upstairs apartment available for rent. He hoped this would entice his mother and sisters to move to Cheyenne. But if that didn't, the joyful news of Cassie being expectant with his ma's first grandchild, may.

As Ed's mother read the letter, her heart swelled with joy. She couldn't wait to be a grandma and was determined to be there for the birth of her first grandchild. The prospect of steady work and a peaceful life away from the demands of running a farm was also appealing. And being near her son, daughter-in-law, and grandbaby was icing on the cake.

But not everyone was as excited as Ed and his mother. His oldest sister, Beth, had declined the offer, announcing her upcoming marriage in a few months. Ed and Cassie were disappointed but understood. And yet they were overjoyed to learn that his mother and youngest sister, Joy, were finally going to move to Cheyenne.

For Ed and Cassie this was the start of a new chapter in their lives. They welcomed the prospect of having family nearby and looked forward to the arrival of their little one. As they sat together, dreaming about the future, they knew that no matter what lay ahead, they would face it with faith, love, and the support of their family.

It was a whirlwind, starting from the moment they made the decision to move, to the day Ed's mother and Joy set out on the train journey to Cheyenne. The sale of their homestead was completed within mere weeks, and with their belongings packed and train tickets purchased, they embarked on their new chapter.

September 18th, Ed and Cassie stood on the
bustling platform of the train station watching for
the afternoon train to arrive. They heard the train
whistle blow while it was a ways off and their hearts
leapt as it neared the station. The train approached,
slowing with each billowing cloud of steam from the
engine's pistons. Ed and Cassie felt the warm steam as
it passed them like dragon's breath, blowing out along
the platform.

The screeching of the metal wheels on the steel
tracks filled their ears until the engine halted and
its cars came to rest with a ring of the bell from the
engine, signaling to travelers of their arrival. Their
eyes scanned the crowd for the first signs of Ed's ma
and sister stepping off the train. Amidst the flurry of
passengers stepping down and rushing to their next
destination, Ed and Cassie watched and waited with
hearts racing in anticipation. Ed had waited two long
years to see his family again. They were both filled
with excitement and joy at the thought of his family's
arrival.

With his arm over Cassie's shoulder, he looked up
and down the cars, this way and that, trying to see any
sign of them over the crowd. Suddenly out of the corner of his eye, he caught a glimpse of his ma stepping
off the train. Without hesitation he released Cassie
and ran to her, his heart leaping with joy. He wrapped
his arms tightly around his mother, hugging her with

all his might. Then without warning, picked her up and swung her around before setting her down again.

"Oh Eddie, my son," Ed's ma cried, as she clung to him and wept as they rocked back and forth, muttering affectionate words to one another.

"Ma. How I've missed you," he said, kissing her on the cheek as he held her tightly. A flood of emotions came back to him. He hadn't realized how much he had missed his mother and tried to hold back the tears. "I'm so glad you're finally here." Suddenly seeing his sister, as she stood there with tears running down her cheeks, he released his mother and opened his arms and took her into a tight hug as well. "Sis!" he exclaimed in excitement.

Cassie couldn't help but smile as she watched the joyful reunion of Ed greeting his family, and fought back the tears, feeling the warmth of the family's love radiating around her. As they all embraced, she knew that this was the start of a new beginning, one filled with hope, love, and the promise of a brighter future.

Standing quietly back, she observed Ed's ma, appreciating the beautiful petite woman who had taken Ed in when he was an orphan. Her dark brown hair and pretty green eyes were complimented by her stylish burgundy skirt and jacket with matching hat. She had a warm friendly smile that eased Cassie's apprehension, and she finally stepped forward to introduce herself. "Mrs. Havoc, I'm Cassie," she said, extending her hand.

"Cassie!" exclaimed Mrs. Havoc with a smile. "Aren't you a beauty. I shouldn't be surprised that

Ed picked the prettiest woman in the West for his wife," she said, sincerely. "Come here and give me a hug. We're family now. You can call me Kathy, Ma Havoc, or Mother Havoc, if you wish," she said as she stepped forward and took Cassie in a warm motherly embrace.

Cassie felt her heart melt under her words and affection. "It's a pleasure to finally meet you, Mother Havoc. Ed's told me so much about you," Cassie said, trying to speak past the lump in her throat.

"And I'm Joy," said Ed's youngest sister, as she stood beside Ed with her arm wrapped around his waist.

Joy was a striking young woman with light blonde hair that fell in soft waves around her shoulders. Her emerald green eyes sparkled with joy and curiosity as she surveyed her new surroundings. Dressed in a flattering light green skirt and white blouse, with a delicate cameo at her neck, she looked more mature than her eighteen years.

"Welcome to Cheyenne, Joy. I hope you learn to love it here as much as I have," said Cassie, recalling all too well what it was like to step off the train in the wild west town of Cheyenne. "We're so happy you decided to come," she said, with a quivering voice, and suddenly tears spilled down her cheeks as Joy stepped forward and embraced her. Watching the happy reunion between Ed and his family made her heart ache for her own, but she felt an instant love for Ed's mother and sister, like a part of her had come home.

The two women were touched by Cassie's emotions and brought fresh tears of their own.

"Cassie, my dear," Kathy said, taking her hands in hers. "We're so happy to have you join our family. It brings me great comfort and joy to see how happy you make Ed. And soon a baby, too. It's a wonderful thing."

Kathy's heart was still heavy with grief for the loss of her daughter-in-law, Mary, and her grandchild. But she understood why Ed had to leave Kansas and start anew. Losing Mary had left him heartbroken, and it was only through Cassie's love and care that he had found happiness again. Seeing Ed with Cassie, so happy and in love, filled her with a sense of hope and gratitude.

As they visited, Kathy watched Ed and Cassie talking and laughing, their eyes filled with promise. She could see the love he had for Cassie written all over his face, and she knew that the baby would only deepen that love. For in her heart, she knew that this new family was destined for great things, and that they would face whatever challenges lay ahead with love, faith, and the unbreakable bond of family.

Ed felt deep emotions of joy and love bubbling up as he saw his family embrace and accept Cassie as one of their own, and cleared his throat. "We should take you to the apartment so you can leave your trunks there, before we head out to our place for supper," suggested Ed, brushing away something from his eyes.

Kathy looked around quickly, seeing new

passengers loading, and knew the train would be pulling out soon. "Yes, we should get our trunks off before the train leaves," she said smiling. "We're excited to see your homestead," she said, taking Cassie's arm.

Ed gathered their trunks from the freight car as Cassie led the women to the wagon. Kathy climbed in the front at Cassie's insistence, and she and Joy sat in back. Ed returned with the trunks and climbed in beside his mother. They all chatted excitedly as they drove down the busy Main Street, and finally pulled over and stopped at the C&H Men's Shop.

"We're here! Your new home!" announced Ed, as he jumped down and helped them out of the wagon. "I'll go get the keys."

Ed hurried into the shop to get the keys from Bart, eager to get his mother and sister settled into their new home. Meanwhile, the women gathered their bags as Cassie led the way to the back of the building, and up the stairs to the apartment.

Ed met them at the top of the stairs and unlocked the door and went back for their trunks. The three women carried in the bags, chatting excitedly as they looked around the space. Kathy and Joy were delighted with the apartment, finding it cozy, with all the amenities they needed to live comfortably.

As they freshened up and changed their clothes, Kathy couldn't help but feel a sense of gratitude, knowing that this was a blessing from God, and she was determined to make the most of it.

As soon as they were ready, they headed back

downstairs to the shop to meet their new employers. With a smile on her face and a heart full of hope, Kathy knew that this was only the beginning of a new adventure, with the promise of a brighter future.

Chapter 9

Kathy and Joy

"Ma, this is Bart and Bea Clark," said Ed proudly, still beaming from the knowledge that his mother and sister were finally here. "And this is Joy, my youngest sister," he said with a broad smile as they stood in the front of the shop.

"It's so nice to meet you, Mr. Clark," Kathy said with a smile, enclosing both her hands around her employer's, feeling gratitude for the generosity he had extended to her and her daughter. With the offer of free rent for the next two months, they had been able to purchase to the two train tickets for the trip.

"We're so glad you made it safe and sound. We hope your journey wasn't too hard," Bart said politely, releasing her hand and placing his arm around Bea, and smiled at her, excited to soon have the much-needed help in their shop.

"It was a very long journey, but we are relieved to have made it," Kathy said, sharing an understanding look with Joy, remembering the three days and nights they spent sitting on the hard benches of the stuffy passenger cars in coach. Both day and night they were jostled to and fro, feeling every bu-bump of the tracks in the crowded train car. The nights seemed the longest part of the journey. It was difficult to sleep sitting upright, resting their heads against the wall of the car or taking turns, resting on the other's shoulder. The days passed more quickly as they looked out the windows at the mountains, valleys, rivers and open plains, and looked forward to the short stops in the small towns along the tracks. It was their only opportunity to stretch their legs as they disembarked to use the necessary and purchase food at the eating houses before they reboarded, continuing their journey until they finally reached Cheyenne. "Seeing the beautiful countryside along the way was amazing, but we're happy to finally be here," she smiled in relief, knowing those days were behind them. Looking around, she was impressed with the beautiful shop filled with handsome suits hanging in the display window, and the friendly faces of her new employers. She felt grateful for the new opportunity and hoped it would be a good place for Joy to start a new life as well. Even though Kathy would miss her daughter Beth dearly, she knew she had made the right decision. Beth was sad to see them leave, but Kansas was where John was able to make a living and provide for Beth, and they hoped to start their family there. Beth understood that her mother needed to be where she could work and have an easier life, even if it meant missing out on her oldest daughter's wedding.

"I think we can get you both trained pretty

quickly, so take a few days to recover. In the mean-time, I would be happy to show you around town after work. And when you're ready, just come down the stairs; the work will be waiting," Bart said kindly.

Kathy and Joy thanked him and politely excused themselves, saying they needed to get going. They were excited to see what Ed had been writing them about all those years.

Ed drove them through town, eagerly pointing out each building along the way like a child show-ing off his favorite collection. As they passed his old Sheriff's Office, Ed pointed it out and waved at Sheriff O'Malley as he came out. Ed slowed the wagon and stopped, so the sheriff could approach them.

"Ed! How are you?" hollered Sheriff O'Malley, waving as he walked up to the wagon.

The first thing Kathy noticed about the handsome sheriff was his tall stature, broad shoulders, dark hair, and mustache.

"Sheriff O'Malley, it's great to see you," Ed said eagerly. "I would like to introduce you to my mother, Kathy Havoc, and this is my sister, Joy."

The sheriff tipped his hat and greeted them warmly, his Scottish accent adding a touch of charm. As he shook Kathy's hand, he couldn't help but feel a sense of familiarity, like a dream he couldn't quite remember. She was a beautiful woman, looking much younger than her years, as he quickly calculated.

"Nice to meet you," said Kathy, smiling down at the ruggedly handsome Sheriff.

"I hope you find Cheyenne to your liking. If you

need anything, don't hesitate to stop in and ask," Sheriff O'Malley said, finally releasing her hand.

Kathy blushed, realizing she had held eye contact a little too long with such a good-looking man. It had been years since a man had made her blush. *What's happening to me? I'm too old to feel like this. I'm forty-five, and almost a grandma,* she thought. *I wonder if he has this effect on all the women he meets?* she asked herself. "Thank you for the offer. I'm sure we'll be seeing you around at the C&H Men's Shop. We'll be working there and living in the apartment above it," she said nervously, realizing she had offered more information than he probably wanted to know, and blushed again.

"Oh, yes, I know. Ed said you'd be moving here," Sheriff O'Malley said, remembering she was also a widow.

Ed could see that Sheriff O'Malley had not taken his eyes off his ma. It made him smile to see he wasn't the only one who thought his mother was one of the prettiest women around.

Kathy looked down at her hands as she explained their situation. "My husband and sons were killed in the war, and my daughters and I have had to work to make ends meet. Ed's been paying for the hired help to run the farm, but we decided it was easier to sell it and simplify our lives," she said, her voice tinged with sadness.

Sheriff O'Malley felt a deep sense of sympathy for this kind woman. "I'm so sorry to hear that," he said, his heart breaking for her. "The war took so many wonderful men."

Kathy looked up at him, her eyes filled with determination. "Yes, it did. But we still have each other, and it's made us stronger because of it."

The sheriff could only imagine the years of hardship and loneliness she had endured, but he was struk by her optimism and strength. "If you need anything, I'm here to help," he said, tipping his hat as he backed away. "Goodbye, Mrs. Havoc, and it was nice to meet you too, Joy," he added with a warm smile.

"Goodbye, Sheriff O'Malley," said Kathy, feeling his concern and giving him a smile that finally reached her eyes.

"See you later, Sheriff," said Ed, smiling as he clucked to the horses to start heading home.

"What a nice sheriff. It appears they found a good replacement for you," Kathy said, smiling at her son.

"Yes, Mayor Hook has known Patrick O'Malley for a while; he's a good man. He was a deputy in Laramie, about fifty miles west of here. He's been wanting to move up to Sheriff for some time. Lucky for him, I resigned so he could have the job. It was not hard for him to move—he's a bachelor," Ed said, smiling at his mother as she looked over when he mentioned the word 'bachelor'.

Kathy smiled at Ed and then changed the subject quickly. "So, how far away is your homestead?" she asked, looking around at the prairie that spanned out for miles, hiding her blushing face.

"We live about four miles out of town," said Cassie from the back of the wagon. "My aunt and uncle live a bit closer than we do. I can't wait to introduce you to them on Sunday at church."

Supper was in the oven keeping warm and would be ready as soon as they got there. Cassie was excited to show them around their home.

Ed beamed with pride as he gave his mother and sister a tour of the homestead. They took a quick walk around the property and then went into the cottage.

"My, what a lovely home you have here, Cassie," said Kathy as she looked around the cozy kitchen and living area.

"Thank you. We love it," said Cassie as she set on the last of the bowls of food on the set table.

Ed came up beside Cassie and put his arm around her shoulders. "Cassie has made this a beautiful place for us," he said with pride, and kissed her on the forehead as she smiled up at him.

"You have done a wonderful job. I can see you both work very hard taking care of it," said Joy, wishing she could have a home of her own someday.

They spent the rest of the evening visiting and catching up on events as they ate the delicious meal Cassie had made. Before they knew it, it was very late, and Ed needed to take them back to town.

***

As September came to a close, the hot summer days were replaced by pleasant, crisp fall mornings. Ed built fires in the stove and fireplace each morning, taking the chill out of the air inside the cottage. After their daily scripture study, Ed and Cassie shared a hot breakfast before starting their busy day.

While Ed tended to the chores outside, Cassie worked on cleaning, baking, and sewing inside. By noon, it was warm enough to hang clothes on the line or work in the garden to gather the last of its bounty.

During the first weeks of October, Cassie bottled or dried the last of the garden produce and put it on shelves or in barrels in the cellar. After the first hard freeze in mid-October, she dug up the root vegetables such as carrots, potatoes, onions, and more. She hung braided bunches of onions and garlic from the rafters in the cellar and packed the other root vegetables loosely in crates with sand.

Cassie had always loved fall, and loved it even more now, working on her own land, surrounded by the trees with their leaves turning brilliant orange, red, and yellow. As she progressed further in her pregnancy, the more Ed insisted she wait for his help with the heavier chores. Waiting for Ed tested her patience. She was not one to put off chores and rely on someone else to help complete what she felt was her responsibility. But she complied with his wishes and tried to do something else with her time while she waited. Some days were harder than others, when Ed spent most of the day out on the range. As the time for roundup neared, Ed spent long days counting and recounting the herd, trying to get an estimate of how many cattle he would be sending to market. On those days, Cassie was sure to have a hot meal waiting when he returned. While Uncle George and

Ed were out with the herd, occasionally Aunt Mabel would come over for a visit and they would sit in front of the fire in the fireplace, having tea and cookies while they crocheted and talked.

As the end of October neared, Cassie looked forward to the cattle roundup and butchering season. She knew the colder days ahead would keep the meat fresh, allowing it to hang overnight without spoiling. The next day, they would cut and cure the meat, and hang it in the smoke house for smoking. With the help of family and neighbors, they butchered a cow at the Hartford ranch and a hog at the Havoc ranch over two Saturdays, and divided up the meat as thanks for the assistance.

Ed and Cassie loved the harvest season; despite the hard work that left them exhausted each night, they felt blessed beyond measure. They enjoyed filling their cellar shelves, smokehouse, and cupboards with food that would sustain them through winter and into the spring. As they lay in bed at night, Ed would place his hand on Cassie's stomach and feel the baby kick. Cassie felt her love for the baby growing as she felt the increasingly frequent movements within her. As the weeks passed, their excitement grew as she began to show more and more that she was pregnant.

***

Bart and Bea were excited to move into their new framed home, located just a few blocks from Bea's parents' home and the shop. Decorating their new home was something Bea had always looked forward to, and soon they would be completing the baby's room as well.

***

Kathy and Joy quickly adjusted to life in Cheyenne and adapted well to the sewing machines that simplified their work as seamstresses. They were able to keep up with their coworkers and even made some new friends. Sheriff O'Malley's frequent visits and genuine interest in Kathy's well-being made her feel flattered and appreciated. Joy also made friends with the seamstresses and began to feel more at home in the new city. Despite the differences from their hometown in Kansas, they both felt like Cheyenne was becoming their new home, especially since they could visit Ed and Cassie often.

***

Clancy had been attending church services regularly, ever since Bart's invitation, and for the past few weeks he had noticed a beautiful young woman with golden hair styled in ringlets, sitting with Mr. and Mrs. Havoc. That Sunday, as he was leaving church, Clancy lingered a bit longer outside and greeted Ed as he came down the church steps, wanting to know more about the mysterious young woman. "Mr. Havoc, how are you this fine day?" asked Clancy, reaching out to shake his hand as Ed reached the bottom step.

"I'm very well, thank you, Clancy. I'm very glad

to see you. I've been meaning to talk to you. I was wondering if you would be able to help me with the roundup this year?" Ed asked, moving aside to let people pass as they exited the white church.

Clancy was distracted, as the young woman with the golden hair caught his eye as she stepped out of the chapel doors and into the sunlight, making her way down the front steps. She was laughing with Cassie about something, and he heard her light laughter over the crowd's friendly chatter.

Ed repeated his question when Clancy didn't answer.

"What's that you say?" Clancy asked, trying to focus on what Mr. Havoc was saying, while still keeping his eyes on the beautiful blonde in the pale green skirt and jacket.

Ed looked over his shoulder, following Clancy's gaze, realizing Clancy was staring at his sister, Joy. With a grin Ed repeated what he'd said, nice and slow, "I was asking if you would like to help me with the roundup this year?"

Clancy finally registered the question and formed an answer. "Uh huh, yes. I could do that. When do you want me to start?" he asked, keeping his gaze fixed upon her, not wanting to miss his chance to speak to her if he could find the right moment.

"Why don't you come on out to my place, say around five o'clock, and join us for supper? We can discuss the particulars then." Ed turned and greeted Cassie and Joy as they joined them, putting his arm over Cassie's shoulders, giving her a squeeze.

He loved how radiant she looked today in her blue Sunday dress and shawl. "Oh, Cassie, I hope you don't mind. I've invited Clancy to supper. He's agreed to help us with the roundup next week, and I need to go over a few things with him before then," said Ed, winking at Cassie.

Cassie smiled back at Ed, giving him a squeeze around the waist. Then, addressing Clancy, "We'd be happy to have you join us. Everyone will be there; my Aunt and Uncle Hartford, Joy, and Mother Havoc." Cassie suddenly realized introductions needed to be made. "Oh, I'm sorry. Clancy, I don't think you've met Joy."

Joy and Clancy stood grinning at each other with beaming eyes.

"No, I haven't had the pleasure," Joy said, reaching out her gloved hand to Clancy. "Pleased to meet you, Clancy," she said in her slight southern lilt.

Clancy took her delicate hand in his. Hearing her say his name sounded sweet as honey. "Pleased to meet you, Miss Joy." He slowly released her hand with a tip of his hat. *She's a pretty little thing,* he thought, hardly able to breathe or even think, for that matter.

"Joy's my sister, she moved here with my ma from Kansas," said Ed, looking for his mother so he could introduce her as well. He could see her talking with Aunt Mabel and some of the other church ladies and decided he could wait for another time.

Joy smiled at the handsome cowboy, admiring his rugged appearance. She had heard stories of cowboys in the Wild West and seen some of them around town. But now she was about to meet the real thing standing right in front of her. He wore brown pants with a white button-up shirt, black vest, and a black string tie. His tan cowboy hat and boots with spurs completed the look. Although not tall, he had a strong, broad-shouldered stance that made it seem like he could handle anything. Joy's heart was all a-flutter at the sight of him.

"Well, Miss Joy, welcome to Cheyenne. I hope you find it to your liking," said Clancy politely, hoping she was going to stay permanently.

"Thank you, I think I'm going to like it here," Joy said smiling, liking it better since meeting Clancy.

Ed smiled, watching Clancy and Joy watching each other. "OK, it's settled then. Clancy, we'll see you at five o'clock tonight," said Ed definitively. "And Joy, I'll come and gather you and Ma at four o'clock and bring you out."

"That's just fine, Ed," said Joy, not taking her eyes off of Clancy.

"Until then, Miss Joy. It's been a pleasure meeting you," said Clancy, tipping his hat and turning away from her.

"It's been a pleasure meeting you too, Clancy," said Joy sweetly, watching him walk away.

Chapter 10

Clancy

That afternoon, Ed brought his mother and sister to the cottage for supper, where Aunt Mabel and Uncle George were already helping with the cooking. As they waited for the meal to finish cooking, they chatted about the upcoming roundup and work at the ranch and shop.

Joy stepped out onto the front porch to sit and enjoy the cool fall day. The sun was low in the sky, casting long shadows across the yard as the golden leaves in the trees were rustling in the light breeze. She watched the occasional leaf break free and drift to the ground as she sighed contentedly, the orange cat circling her legs until she reached down and scratched behind her ears and stroked her back.

Clancy breathed in deeply the smell of fall and cooking that filled the air as he rode down the lane toward the cottage. To his delight, he saw Joy sitting on the porch, her blonde curls falling over her shoulders as she leaned over, petting the orange cat. Clancy waved when she looked up at him.

"Hello there!" Clancy called out, as he approached.

Joy waved at him and blushed. *Wow, he's even more handsome on his horse,* she thought as she smiled at him.

Clancy pulled his horse to a halt and jumped down easily, took the reins, and tied them to the hitching post, then strutted up to the cottage as easily as if on a morning stroll. A huge grin spread across his face.

"Hello, Miss Joy," he said, coming up the steps of the porch, removing his cowboy hat and taking her hand, noticing how warm and soft it was.

"Good afternoon, Clancy," Joy said, blushing again as she felt his strong thick hand around hers. He held it gently, and finally released it. "You're right on time. Supper is just about ready. Would you sit outside with me until they call us?" Joy asked, trying to keep eye contact, but became self-conscious under his gaze and finally looked away.

Clancy sat down on the chair opposite Joy. "Thank you, that sounds right nice. And how are you finding Cheyenne?" he asked. His mouth felt dry as dust as he gazed at her rosy cheeks and green eyes, finding it hard to swallow.

"Oh, it's definitely different than Kansas. But I'm liking it more and more all the time," Joy said truthfully. "Cheyenne has an energy about it. It never seems to sleep. There's constant music coming from the saloons, with people laughing and shouting as they come out. But overall, I find there are good hard-working people here, just like back home. Just with a bit more adventure and excitement going on here," she said. *And now Cheyenne seems even more interesting,* she thought.

Clancy nodded, listening intently to Joy. "Yes, there's definitely some excitement to be had in Cheyenne. It's a bustling place, for sure. But I'm glad to hear you're finding it to your liking," he said, smiling at her. He had to admit, he was finding Joy to be quite charming, and he was enjoying their conversation.

Clancy understood that Joy might be finding it hard to adjust to life in Cheyenne. He could relate to her struggles, as he too had left his hometown to pursue his dreams. "I can understand what you're going through. I grew up in a small town in Iowa and came to Cheyenne a few years ago to escape the monotony of farming. I was looking for something more adventurous and that's when I discovered my passion for being a cowboy. I went on cattle drives, and it was everything I was looking for," Clancy said, his eyes fixed on hers, looking at him in awe.

Joy listened intently to Clancy, intrigued by his words. "That must have been so exciting! How long were you usually gone for?" she asked, her eyes sparkling with interest.

Clancy noticed Joy's eyes light up as he spoke about his time as a cowboy. He continued to recount his adventures. "We're usually gone over three months. On the trail, we had to deal with thunderstorms, stampedes, and bandits. I even had a run-in with a mountain lion once." Clancy chuckled, remembering the close encounter. "It's a hard life, but there's nothing like it. The freedom, the adventure, and the bond you form with your fellow cowboys. It's like nothing else."

Joy listened with wide-eyed wonder. Clancy's stories were thrilling and captivating, and she couldn't help but admire him. He was unlike anyone she had ever met before. "It sounds incredible," she said, "I've always wanted to go on an adventure like that."

Clancy smiled at her genuine enthusiasm. It was a refreshing change from the women he typically met who saw cowboys as rough, smelly, and uncouth. "Yes, it can be quite an adventure," he said. "Sometimes, we encountered Indians on the trail. Luckily, we were able to avoid any major conflicts, and we never lost any cattle. During those times, we spent the night in the saddle, watching the herd. And when we slept, we did so with our guns close at hand," he said, reminiscing about his time on the trail. But he didn't want to alarm her with the reality of how dangerous those situations could be, so he left that part out.

"My goodness, how frightening!" she exclaimed. "How many men were out there with you?" she asked, getting more impressed with Clancy by the minute.

"There were about fifteen of us cowboys on the drive. A cook and a foreman as well. It's hard work but we all loved it. Nothing like it in the world. Open plains, rivers, streams, mountains, valleys, deserts; I've seen it all. Some not so pretty, like the days we had to push the cattle fifteen miles through the night, across a desert because there was no water. We were all pretty worn out after riding twenty-four hours in the saddle that day," he said with a chuckle, remembering how he could hardly stand when he did get off his horse.

"Really, and what happens when you have really bad weather or when wild animals come around?" she asked, imagining being in a desert riding a horse all night, hoping your horse didn't step in a hole or something worse, or a coyote or wolf attacking your horse.

Clancy was thoroughly enjoying the conversation with Joy. He could talk to her for hours on end about his adventures. "In bad weather, it gets a lot trickier," he continued. "Cattle move in herds, so if one gets spooked, they can stampede. Let me tell you, that's the scariest thing ever. Longhorn cattle stampeding across the plains sound like a locomotive train, and the ground shakes like an earthquake. The dust is blinding and chokes the breath right out of you. We have to use our pistols and whips to keep them from going over dangerous gullies, or they will blindly kill half the herd. I've only seen one stampede, but I'll never forget it." Clancy animatedly described the experience, hoping to impress Joy with his bravery.

"Is that the only time you've been scared?" Joy asked, so interested now, she completely forgot she should be inside, helping put supper on.

"I remember one night, it was very hot, and we were close to a river, when a thunderstorm came rolling toward us. The cattle produce a lot of heat in that big of a herd and must have had some strange reaction with the weather, because lightning struck, and we watched as a blue light bounced from the tips of the horns all around the herd. It had a buzzing sound and was quite unsettling; it spooked the cattle and us cowboys, too. You could hear the cattle bawling in fear as they huddled together. We were later telling another group of cowboys about it, and they said they'd seen it once before as well. They called it 'Foxfire,' or 'St. Elmo's Fire,' as the sailors call it. It's some phenomenon, rarely seen since the conditions must be perfect. But it still leaves me with a funny feeling every time I think about it," explained Clancy, almost shuddering at the memory.

"My goodness, I could listen to you tell me about your adventures all night. It's just so fascinating!" she exclaimed in awe.

Just then, Ed stepped outside the cottage door. "I thought I heard talking out here. Welcome, Clancy. I see Joy's been keeping you company," he said, walking over and shaking Clancy's hand.

"Yes, she has. And great company at that," Clancy said, winking at her, causing her to blush. He had no idea why he'd just done that; perhaps he wanted to see her blush. It did cause his heart to race as she did so.

"I should excuse myself; I need to go in and help with supper," she said, still red-faced. "Thank you, Clancy, for telling me all about your experiences. We'll have to continue later," Joy said, standing and hurrying into the cottage.

"Sis, they're almost done. Clancy, shall we go inside? I'll introduce you to everyone," Ed said, following behind Clancy as they entered the cottage.

The group made introductions and offered a

blessing of gratitude for the food. Everyone dished up their plates with roast beef and potatoes, rolls and vegetables and found places to sit and eat. Clancy was pleased when Joy suggested they enjoy their meal outside on the porch away from the crowded interior. As they sat down, Clancy took the opportunity to continue his conversation with her.

"May I ask what brought you out here to Cheyenne?" he inquired, genuinely curious about her story. He couldn't help but wonder what a young woman like Joy was doing so far from home in the middle of the Wild West.

Joy thought back to all the things that had led her to Cheyenne and didn't know how to explain. "Well, it's kind-of a long story."

"I'd like to hear it, please."

"I guess it all it started back when my father and brothers were killed in the war. Ed was the only one to come back to help with the farm. Shortly after, he married and moved to a farm of his own. Sadly, Ed was married only about a year when his pregnant wife died after an Indian attack. It devastated him. We understood when he couldn't stay around, being reminded of her and their baby's death. So, he moved out here to Cheyenne and took the job as Sheriff, looking for some solace, I think."

Clancy felt a wave of emotion for the man he respected and looked up to. "I had no idea about Sheriff Havoc, I mean Mr. Havoc. That must have been so hard on all of you. I don't blame him for wanting to escape." His heart broke as he imagined how he would feel if he lost his wife and infant.

"Yes, but that left just me, my sister, and Ma to take care of the farm. We had such a big place that even with a hired hand it was difficult to keep up with the property and all the animals. It took all three of us taking in sewing just to keep the place from being taken over by the bank. So, when we heard that the Men's Shop needed seamstresses, it just made sense to sell and move here and be near Ed and Cassie. My older sister, Beth, stayed back in Kansas and is engaged to be married next month. It's sad that we will miss the wedding," Joy explained, realizing what a strain the past four or five years had been on them all.

"It sounds like you've been through a lot," he said, his voice soft with sympathy. "I'm sorry for your losses, but I'm glad you found your way here." He couldn't help but feel a sense of admiration for her resilience and strength.

"I'm glad too. It's been hard, but recently things have been looking better." Joy had seen his concerned look as she talked about her family's tragedies and was baffled at Clancy's thoughtfulness. He was not only strong and fearless; he was tender and thoughtful.

Clancy couldn't help but feel drawn to her, admiring her strength and beauty. He was determined to get to know her better and see where their friendship might lead. "It's wonderful that you and your mother were able to find work at the shop. How do you like working there?"

Joy smiled, her green eyes lighting up. "I love it.

It's been such a blessing to have steady work and be able to use our sewing skills to contribute to the community. And the people there are so kind and friendly. We feel very welcomed."

"And I'm sure Ed and Cassie are happy to have you close by too," Clancy added, especially happy that Joy had come to Cheyenne.

"I've missed my brother for a long time. Now I've got my oldest brother back, and I've gained a sister-in-law as well," Joy said with a smile.

"It's interesting how things worked out," Clancy pondered out loud, thinking of what he now knew about Ed, and remembered when Cassie come to town and how quickly the two fell in love. "As if it was meant to be," he said thoughtfully.

"Cassie has been an answer to our prayers. She's been a real blessing for Ed and our family," Joy said, adding a silent prayer of thanks.

"I remember when she first came to Cheyenne after the Indians wiped out her family," he said sadly, thinking of Cassie, the frail, grief stricken young lady who'd lost everything. Then thought of the way she'd changed and brightened when Ed came around. "They made each other so happy. It's a blessing. I guess that's what love does," he said with a sincere smile.

"It's true. I've not seen Ed this happy in years. I'm so overjoyed for both of them, and now they're going to have a baby. What a blessing. It's such a miracle how it all happened," she said, feeling a little envious.

Clancy could see that Joy was clearly in love with

the idea of having a family of her own. And who wouldn't want that? His thoughts drifted to just how wonderful it would be to have his own place and a beautiful wife and children. Especially if it was with Joy. "You know, you'll be having a family of your own before you know it. As pretty as you are," he said, teasing her just a little, and yet also very serious. He could imagine it all so easily.

Joy blushed at his words. "Well, so far there's really only one man I would even consider allowing to sweep me off my feet," she said, looking down shyly at her plate of food she had hardly touched. She had never been so bold to even hint at such a thing. But Clancy was wonderful; she couldn't imagine anything more exciting than having him court her.

Clancy felt a little rattled. He wondered if he had misunderstood her, perhaps she already had a beau. "Well, I hope he's worthy of your attention, because if I find out that he is anything but a gentleman, then I'll have to teach him a lesson on how to treat a woman," he said, feeling like he had to defend her honor. If she wasn't interested in him, then he would make sure it was at least some other worthy man.

"Oh, I believe he's a respectable man, from what I've seen and heard. He seems very polite and gentlemanly. I actually feel very safe and comfortable with him," she said, trying to hint that it was him she was talking about. She looked up at Clancy as he looked away a little disheartened.

Clancy's mood seemed to sour further upon thinking that Joy was already taken, and he could feel his heart sinking. He tried his best to hide his disappointment, but it was evident in his tone. "Well, I'm glad you've found someone. You deserve to be happy, and I hope it all works out for the best," he said, trying to sound sincere, but sadness crept into his voice. He then fell silent, feeling like he was wasting his time and thinking about leaving.

"I appreciate that. You don't know how hard it's been to find someone you can trust and feel safe with," she said, reaching across the table and putting her hand on his. Joy couldn't bring herself to be more direct, but she had to do something. He was getting it all wrong. Couldn't he see she was interested in him?

Clancy gently held Joy's hand, wondering what was going on. Could she possibly be interested in him? He couldn't help but wonder, especially as she smiled sweetly at him with cheeks blushing and her eyes twinkling. "Do you mean me?" he finally asked, breaking the silence.

"Yes, Clancy. I mean you. I think you're trustworthy and a perfect gentleman," said Joy, looking down at their hands still together on the table.

Clancy could hardly breathe. "Joy, may I have the pleasure of courting you?" he finally mustered.

Joy smiled up at him and answered, "Yes, you may, Clancy." And blushed again as she looked at him, hardly able to catch her breath as her heart raced.

The front door began to open, and they pulled their hands away from each other, as Cassie's aunt and uncle and all the rest emerged.

"Oh, yes, it's much cooler out here. Who's ready

for dessert?" asked Mabel.

Ed joined the two at the table and looked at his sister, who seemed to be avoiding his glances and appeared to be blushing, then looked at Clancy who was grinning broadly. Ed had noticed the growing connection between his sister and Clancy, and he smiled knowingly.

The evening continued pleasantly as they talked about the upcoming roundup, and enlisted Clancy to help George's herd as well. As the night drew to a close, Ed offered to take his mother and Joy home, with Clancy following behind to ensure their safety in the dark. He bid them goodbye and turned off towards his employer's place, feeling happier than ever. Clancy had found himself a sweetheart, and she was a true beauty. Joy said goodbye to Clancy and wished she could say more, but her ma and Ed were there, so she just waved and watched as he rode away, just like a knight in shining armor.

Chapter 11

Roundup, Day One, October 1869

Ed awoke long before dawn and rolled over to look at Cassie in the moonlight. He hated to wake her, seeing her sleeping so peacefully. Watching her each day, it was clear that she was having a harder time getting up in the morning, now that she was six months along. He'd let her sleep until the sun came up, if he could. But that wasn't a possibility today. Today was one of the biggest days of the year for the Havoc and Hartford ranches. It was the last weekend of the month, fall roundup time, and they needed every available hand to help, including hers.

"Time to get up, Cass," Ed said softly as he smoothed the hair away from her angelic face and kissed her cheek.

"Good morning, dear," she said with sleep in her voice as she slowly reached out to pat his cheek.

He turned his head and kissed her palm and held it there for a second. Cassie was the best part of his day. As he laid beside her, he breathed in the familiar scent of her hair and felt the softness of her skin against his. He loved everything about her; her laughter that always seemed to echo in his ears, a sound that never failed to lift his spirits. He loved to watch her as she worked, humming as she went and marveled at her ability to find joy even in the seemingly mundane. He loved that, despite the hardships she had endured, she still saw beauty in the world, a quality that he found both admirable and inspiring. He marveled at the enthusiasm she had for anything she was interested in, and recently, the roundup had her bubbling with excitement. "I love you, darling," he said as he kissed her again, then reluctantly withdrew from her warmth to get out of bed.

"I love you too, sweetheart," Cassie said, already missing his warm lips. She would never tire of waking up next to her husband. Mornings always looked brighter with his good morning kisses. Cassie pushed herself out of bed and stretched her arms over her head, fighting the urge to crawl back under the covers. With a yawn she rubbed the sleep from her eyes, eager to start the day. The chill in the room made her shiver as she slipped her feet into her slippers and wrapped her robe tightly around her ever-growing belly. Despite the cold, a burst of energy spread through her as she anticipated the adventure that lay ahead and instantly she was wide awake. She hurried to the dressing table, lit the lamp and sat down to unbraid and brush her hair. As she thought of all the hard work that lay ahead, she smiled to herself as she untied the ribbon holding her thick hair in place. It was going to be a great day and she was determined to enjoy every bit of it.

Ed sat on the edge of the bed, pulled on his thick wool socks and boots and finished dressing, lifting the suspenders of his wool pants over the shoulders of his flannel shirt and put on his leather vest. He stopped at the dressing table to take his pocket watch from where it lay on the crocheted doily and strung it through the button hole of his vest and placed it safely in the pocket. Stooping down, he gave Cassie a parting kiss as she paused her brushing to gaze up at him.

"I'll be back with Clancy after we've finished the morning chores," Ed said as he hurried out and pulled the bedroom door softly closed behind him.

***

The cottage seemed quiet in the dark morning compared to the previous night when the house had been filled with the hustle and bustle of preparations. Ed and Cassie were grateful that Clancy, Mother Havoc, and Joy had joined them that evening to finalize the baking and planning for their two-day excursion. As they packed their bags, the group worked together seamlessly, sharing stories and laughter late into the night. Despite the long hours, their spirits were high, and they couldn't wait to embark on their adventure.

Clancy's expertise in running roundups came in handy. Even Ed, who'd been on a few roundups before, found Clancy's knowledge of great value.

A final count of the number joining them was made, and Clancy shook his head. "I'm worried that there won't be enough. I'd hoped there would be more hired hands coming," said Clancy, as he ran his hand through his thick dark-blond hair.

Ed apologized for the oversight. "I should have checked around for more hired help. There might be more neighbors showing up, but I can't be one-hundred percent sure."

"We're going to be stretched pretty thin," Clancy said, deep in thought. "We can round up the cattle on the first day with the people we have, but keeping them rounded up overnight will be a challenge. And when it's time to drive them to the train station, we'll need every able-bodied person we can find. It would be best if two could ride point, two flank, two swing, and two drag. It'll take at least eight riders to get them to town."

Joy listened to what he was saying as she closed the oven door, deciding the pie needed another few minutes to bake. She turned from the stove to give Clancy a puzzled look, trying to understand him and asked, "What does that mean—point, flank, swing, and drag?"

Clancy forgot that not everyone had been on a roundup before and appreciated her interest. "It means we will need two to ride up front or point, two in back at the flank of the herd, two on the sides to swing the herd, and two pushing from behind, for the cattle who drag behind." He smiled when Joy's face lit up with understanding. "With George and his hired help and a few more neighbors on Saturday, we might make it work, but we could definitely use a few more hands to ensure everything goes smoothly." Clancy paused, racking his brain for a solution.

While normally the men did the rounding up and driving, and the women stayed in camp and cooked, there *now* seemed to be a greater need for *all* of them out on the range.

"I wish there was at least *one* more rider," Clancy said, as he glanced at Joy, who was busy bending over the open oven door, taking out the bubbling hot apple pie.

Using the hot pads, Joy set the steaming pie on the counter and turned to meet Clancy's gaze, then smiled, and wondered if he meant her.

Joy looked at her ma who was sorting through some dishes in a crate. When she looked up, Joy raised her eyebrows and smiled hopefully, as if to ask if it was all right to volunteer. Her ma returned the smile, feeling the young woman's excitement and shrugged her shoulders with a quick reply to her unspoken question, "I don't see why Joy couldn't help."

With that, Joy cheerfully announced, "I can ride!" Suddenly she realized what that meant and timidly admitted to Clancy, "I've never herded cattle on a horse before. Will that be all right?"

Clancy's heart leapt at the prospect of riding with Joy for two days. "More than all right. I guarantee, you'll learn fast. I'm just happy to have your help."

"Then you have one more rider!" Joy's cheeks reddened a shade deeper than the heat from the kitchen had turned them. Clancy's smile widened, sending a fluttering of butterflies in her stomach.

The smell of the hot apple pie had drawn Ed over to the counter where it sat cooling. He was inspecting the golden-brown lattice, his mouth watering, when he heard his sister volunteer to ride. Picking off the tiniest piece of crust, he shoved it into his mouth before he could get caught and turned his head just in time to receive his sister's disapproving look as she put her hands on her hips to scold him. With a sheepish smile he put his arm around her shoulders and kissed her on the cheek. "Thanks, Sis. You've saved the day!" She gave him a nudge in the ribs with her elbow and chuckled.

"You rascal." She couldn't stay mad at him. It seemed she was the hero for once and too excited to be angry.

Joy began peppering Clancy with questions about what she would be doing as she helped clean up the last of the pots and pans they'd used to make the pies. It wasn't long before she was wondering out loud which horse she could ride.

"You could ride Midnight," Cassie offered as she placed the last apple pie into the oven and closed the door.

"Are you sure?" Joy knew how much Cassie loved her black stallion and searched her eyes for any apprehension. With a vigorous nod and smile from Cassie, Joy rushed over and gave her sister-in-law a quick hug. "Oh, thank you, Cassie. I can't wait. It's going to be so much fun!"

"It's the least I can do," Cassie replied with a hint of sadness as she looked down at her round belly. "I just wish I could ride along too." She glanced over at Ed who had stopped packing and now stood with his hands on his hips as he lowered his gaze and stared at her in mock disapproval. It was Cassie's turn to look sheepish. "But I have to follow the doctor's orders. No more riding until after the baby comes," she parroted the doctor's words, frowning and sticking out her bottom lip just a bit. Although she teased about it, she couldn't help feeling a twinge of real disappointment. These were her and Ed's cattle, and her first roundup, and she wanted to be a part of it so badly. It didn't seem fair.

Ed gave her an understanding smile and in two long strides met her at the stove, wrapped his arms around her and kissed the top of her head, trying to console her in her pretended and real disappointment. "One day my dear, you will get to ride. For the sake of the baby and you— you need to sit this one out," he said softly against her hair. She hugged him back and tried not to cry as she felt his sincere concern for her and the baby.

Clancy put his hands in his pockets and looked down at the tip of his dusty boots, then studied the wide planked floor, as he politely averted his eyes while Ed showed his open affection for his wife.

"I know, I promise. I'll be good," she said half-heartedly, her eyes shimmering.

"I'm sure we'll be fine now with Joy riding. No need for you to worry, Mrs. Havoc." Clancy cleared his throat and tried to think of something that would cheer her up. "You know, you and the other women

162

will be just as valuable to the group of riders, if you have the coffee hot and meals ready when we come into camp." Clancy finally looked up when Ed left her and headed to the corner cupboard and returned to the kitchen table, handing Clancy the box of extra ammunition to be placed in the saddle bag he was packing. Clancy tucked the ammunition deep into the bag and strapped the flap closed. "It's what'll keep us going for those long forty-eight hours. Just ask any cowboy who's been on a cattle drive—we live on coffee and beans for a full three months straight. The chuckwagon is the backbone of any cowboy." Clancy grinned, knowing the importance of a well-fed group of riders.

They all chuckled at the thought, and imagined it was almost true.

As they packed the rest of the saddle bags, Clancy enthusiastically shared stories of his adventures as a cowboy on the cattle drives. Something he said gave Cassie an idea, and she excitedly drew Joy by the hand, away from the kitchen to her bedroom, offering to let her borrow her riding clothes.

The bedroom door closed behind them, and the two women giggled as if they were young schoolmates picking out a gown for the ball. As Joy tried on the clothes in the bedroom, the others in the front room could hear the sounds of her and Cassie's laughter. Clancy couldn't help but smile to himself— he was grateful for the extra help, for more than one reason. He had been eagerly anticipating this day for a week now, and even more, once he found out that

Joy would be joining the roundup. He couldn't wait for Joy to witness firsthand what he did best.

The two young women rejoined the group and finished what they could as they continued to visit excitedly. All the pies were now baked and cooling on the counter, the beans had boiled and were slid to the back of the stove to soak overnight, and the saddle bags and boxes were packed and sitting by the door. There wasn't much more they could do until morning.

"Well, I guess it's time to hit the hay," Ed announced as he surveyed the room of readied supplies.

"I guess that's my cue to say goodnight." Clancy hated for all the fun to end, but politely excused himself and left to go to the barn to bed down for the night.

Joy and Mother Havoc removed their aprons and hung them up. "Goodnight Ed, goodnight Cassie." Joy and Mother Havoc hugged Ed and Cassie, then excused themselves and went to the spare bedroom where two small beds had been set up.

It was hard to settle down, the excitement coursing through their veins made it difficult, but they all knew they needed to try. The next morning would start hours before dawn, and they knew they needed to be well-rested for the two-day adventure ahead.

***

Cassie dressed for the cold autumn day as she pulled her flannel petticoats over her long wool underwear and thick wool socks, then slipped on her green cotton dress and grey knitted vest overtop. She took a final look in the mirror, turning her head side to side, checking the bun at the back of her head, making sure the pins would hold in place for the long day ahead, and hurried to the kitchen.

Cassie was greeted by the warm glow from the kerosene lamp Ed had lit in the middle of the table in the cold kitchen. Taking her apron off the hook by the pantry door, she tied the seemingly shorter ties behind her ever-growing waist. She removed the stove's metal plate with the lid lifter and rattled the grate in the fire box to expose the red coals she had banked the night before. Taking an old newspaper from the wood box, she crumpled a piece and stuffed it into the hole and added a few slivers of kindling. Orange flames caught on the edge of the printed paper and then the kindling. She added larger sticks before she replaced the heavy metal plate that clanked as it fell into place. She filled the coffee kettle with water and coffee grounds and set it to the front of the stove where the fire was hottest. As she dumped a measure of flour, salt, and soda, into her largest bowl, and cracked an egg into the well of ingredients, she heard Ed's mother and sister stirring in the guestroom.

"Good morning, Cassie," Joy said brightly, emerging from the bedroom dressed in Cassie's riding outfit, complete with borrowed riding boots.

"Good morning, Joy." Cassie smiled and set the cast-iron skillet on the stove to heat and returned to the bowl on the counter. "I hope you slept well."

Joy yawned. "Yes, I did, and thank you for lending

me your riding clothes. They fit so nicely," she said, admiring the soft leather of the split skirt as she finished buttoning the last button of the suede vest.

"You look lovely in them," Cassie said, admiring Joy's thick, honey-blonde hair, plaited down her back, complementing the light-brown deerskin clothes. Joy graciously thanked her for the kind words as she tied on an apron to protect the beautiful skirt and vest while she worked. As Cassie finished mixing up the pancake batter, she couldn't help but think about how grateful she was for Joy's help with the roundup, although she still wished it was her riding Midnight across the prairie, chasing cattle with the others. As she waited for the black pan to heat, she rested her hand on her rounded belly, and gently reminded herself that she needed to think of the baby and do what was best for her unborn child.

Cassie took the wooden bowl to begin pouring pancake batter into the now hot skillet and glanced up as Kathy emerged from the bedroom. "Good morning, Mother Havoc." The batter sizzled in the grease as she poured out four, six-inch pancakes that immediately began to bubble and raise with the heat.

"Good morning, Cassie. Don't you look radiant this morning," Kathy said, thinking that Cassie had a certain glow about her that seemed to increase every day. "What can we do to help?" She tied on her apron and pulled the bedroom door closed behind her, helping to keep the heat in the kitchen. She came to stand beside Cassie at the big black stove where the fragrance of boiling coffee and cooking pancakes made her stomach growl. A smile spread across her face as she breathed in the heavenly aroma.

"Let's see…" Cassie looked around the room, thinking of the breakfast that needed cooking, the table that needed setting, the soaking beans that needed finishing, the bedding that needed gathering, and all the other things they needed to do before they left, and began feeling a little panicked. "Could you fry the bacon and scramble the eggs while I finish cooking the pancakes? Joy, if you could set the table and put the butter and syrup on, that would be great. Oh! I almost forgot! I'll need some vegetables from the cellar for the stew. Could you get those for me too, Joy?" she asked, hoping she wasn't asking too much of her guests. "Thank you both for helping me. I really appreciate it. There doesn't seem to be enough time to do everything we still need to do, and I think Ed and Clancy will be in from chores soon." She looked at the front door then hurried to grab a plate from the cupboard to lift out the pancakes she'd just flipped, before they burned. She stacked the golden-brown pancakes onto the plate and set them on the warming shelf on top of the stove. Joy and Mother Havoc rushed to do their assigned tasks as Cassie added another dab of animal fat from the crock to the skillet and spread it around, greasing the pan for the next batch of pancakes. There was a thump in the firebox as a big stick dropped as it burned through, reminding her that she should add more wood to the stove. With more wood added, she then went back to pouring pancake batter into the skillet. Kathy worked at the counter cracking eggs into a bowl, and Joy lifted the rug and the hatch and headed down into the root cellar with a lantern she'd found hanging in the pantry.

The kitchen became filled with a myriad of sounds of breakfast cooking; eggs being beaten in a metal bowl with a whisk, the scraping of a wooden spatula against the pan of scrambled eggs that hissed as they cooked. In another pan, bacon popped and sizzled as it fried, splattering grease onto the hot surface of the shiny black stove. The strong smell of coffee boiling and bacon frying filled the room and seeped out the cracks around the front door and were carried with the autumn breeze toward the barn, calling the men in for breakfast. As the food was speedily cooked, the three women chatted excitedly while weaving around each other, stepping quickly from the stove to the counter and back again, piling food on platters and placing them on the table. Joy began taking dishes and utensils from the cupboards and drawers and placing them on the kitchen table that was becoming crowded with bowls and plates of food. She had brought over a small jug of syrup and a bottle of strawberry preserves; and in the cellar she had found cool crocks of milk and butter and brought them up with the vegetables. With a sense of nervous anticipation, they filled the baskets and wooden crates with enough food that would last for two days and brought out bedding to be packed out to the wagon for the next two nights. Although it was frosty outside, they were plenty warm in the cottage as they worked frantically around the hot stove to get everything ready in time.

Just as the last of breakfast was set on the table, they heard Clancy's footsteps come up the porch landing and approach the door.

"Good morning, Clancy," said Joy, looking up from the table she had just finished setting as he entered. There was something about him that made her heart race as he tipped his hat and smiled at her in the dim light. Maybe it was how his unruly dark-blond hair flipped out from under his hat and over his shirt collar and red bandana. Or maybe it was the way his shirt and vest stretched over his brawny arms and shoulders as he turned and removed his coat that made her become flustered. As she watched him hang his coat up on the peg by the door, Joy couldn't help but admire the way he carried himself. He looked like a man who worked hard every day, and it showed in his rugged appearance. Like the way his cowboy boots and well-worn pants fit his trim waist and clung to his stocky frame that exuded masculinity. He turned around unexpectedly, catching her off guard, and tipped his hat to her again. Unprepared for the appraising look he gave her; Joy felt her cheeks flush with embarrassment.

"And good morning to you, Joy," Clancy said as he took his hat off and hung it on the peg beside his coat. Hastily, he ran his fingers through his uncombed hair, trying to smooth it down. He groaned inside, wishing he'd gotten it cut weeks ago. Clancy wasn't sure what he looked like. He hadn't had a chance to shave or comb his hair but could feel the stubble of a day's growth as he self-consciously rubbed his jaw.

Oh well, it will have to wait another couple of days, he thought, trying to reassure himself. He hoped Joy didn't mind seeing him this way, but the anxious feeling in his gut wouldn't go away.

"You look like you're ready for a roundup," he said, appreciating how pretty she looked in the borrowed riding clothes. He wished he could tell her how attractive she looked but wouldn't dare, not in front of her mother and Mrs. Havoc. Not sure what to do and at a loss for words, he hooked his thumbs through his suspenders at his waist, shifted his weight and smiled, waiting to be invited to the table.

Joy could feel the warmth of his approving gaze as he barely blinked, still standing by the doorway. Never flinching, she held his gaze, as she struggled to gather her thoughts and find something to say. When nothing brilliant came, she responded with the first thing that came to her mind, "Thank you, Clancy. So do you." Inside, she kicked herself, *He says, 'You look ready for a roundup.' And you respond with, 'Thank you, Clancy. So do you.' Clever Joy, real clever.*

His smile widened at the sound of his name and she blushed, looking down as she rearranged a fork on a plate, trying to hide her embarrassment.

Cassie decided to rescue the couple's awkward moment and cleared her throat. "Good morning, Clancy. Why don't you wash up at the sink and then come sit down? Breakfast is ready." Cassie set the last platter stacked with fluffy pancakes on the table.

Clancy went to the sink, pumped the water and washed his hands and face, then ran his wet hands through his hair for good measure.

Ed came through the door cheerfully exclaiming, "Good morning, everyone!" He set the bucket of fresh milk on the counter then took off his coat and hung it up with his hat, then went to Cassie and kissed her on the cheek. "It smells heavenly," he said, and went to the sink to wash up.

Once he was cleaned up, Ed helped Cassie with her chair and then his mother as they talked of the activities of the day ahead.

Clancy, seeing Ed's gentlemanly behavior, quickly pulled out a chair. "Joy, you can sit here," he said as she came over, and he helped her scoot in as she smiled up at him.

"Thank you, Clancy." *He's such a gentleman,* she thought.

Joy's sweet southern accent made his heart skip a beat, as he heard her say his name again. He could never tire of hearing her speak his name.

"Are y'all ready for an exciting day?" Clancy asked as he took his place at the table. His mouth watered and his stomach grumbled as he viewed the feast in front of him. As huge as his appetite was this morning, his enthusiasm for the day ahead was even greater.

"I can't wait to see what it's like," Joy gleefully said in anticipation. Ever since she had volunteered she had wondered what a real roundup would be like. And now she was going to find out. Riding with the men, rounding up all the cattle on the wide-open prairie, and herding them all the way to town, would be an adventure she would never forget. She hoped she would be able to prove she was worthy of the task, especially to Clancy.

"Me too," said Cassie and Kathy at the same time, and then giggled at each other. Their excitement was building, as if children looking forward to Christmas morning.

"Let's have the blessing so we can eat, and you can find out," said Ed, chuckling as he took Cassie's hand and his mother's on his other side and paused momentarily to compose himself.

Clancy took Mrs. Havoc's hand and reached for Joy's. As their hands met they felt a warm buzzing flowing between them and sat transfixed, smiling at each other across the table, their eyes twinkling, completely unaware of the three older folks sitting at the table watching the exchange. Ed cleared his throat and the spell was broken, and the two younger folks blushed before bowing their heads for the prayer.

"Our gracious Lord, we thank Thee this day, for the bounteous harvest we've received and for this food before us. We ask Thee to bless this food for our health and strength. And we thank Thee, dear Lord, for the blessing of our family and friends, who are gathered with us today." Ed was still overjoyed at having his mother and sister living so close after being separated all these years.

Clancy gave Joy's hand a gentle squeeze at the words "family and friends," and she returned the squeeze, causing him to smile as he kept his head bowed and eyes closed for the rest of the blessing. In his heart he thanked the Lord for Joy and the Havoc's.

"And we ask Thy blessings to be upon us this day, that we will be protected, and no harm will befall us and those who are coming to help with the roundup. In the holy name of Thy son, Jesus Christ. Amen." Ed lifted his head and smiled.

"Amen," they echoed, and Clancy slowly released Joy's soft warm hand.

Breakfast was a rushed affair as they reviewed the plan for the day. Aunt Mabel and Uncle George were due to arrive soon. And with more preparations to be completed before the rest of the neighbors arrived at six o'clock, the conversation was light. Together, today they would set out to gather the herds. The next day, they would separate the old Crowley herd and brand them with the Havoc ranch brand, carefully selecting the ones destined for the market. These cattle would be driven to the train station, a task that required skill and endurance. As they ate, Clancy's thoughts drifted to Joy, and he couldn't help but feel a sense of admiration for her courage and determination to join them on this challenging journey.

After breakfast, Kathy and Joy took care of clearing and washing the dishes while Cassie was busy preparing the ingredients for a hearty stew. She filled a large Dutch oven with meat and vegetables and in the other Dutch oven of soaked beans, she added fresh water and onions, butter and a ham hock. Once everything was on the stove she added more wood to the firebox and let it all come to a boil.

Kathy finished the dishes and started gathering

the ingredients for biscuits that would be baked on top of the stew later as it finished cooking over the campfire. Meanwhile, the four apple pies they had made the night before were sitting on a shelf ready to be packed in the wagon as soon as it was time to leave. The now clean dishes and utensils were added to the rest of the kitchenware and were placed in a basket, which they would pack in the wagon to use as their chuck wagon out on the range. It felt as if they were embarking on a long journey, even though it was only a five-mile ride out onto the prairie. They had a lot of work to do over the next two days, and this required plenty of food and supplies for the meals and overnight stay, so they packed accordingly.

Chapter 12

Heading Out

C assie heard the first arrivals approaching and went out to greet them along with the others.

"Good morning!" hollered George and Mabel as they pulled into the yard seeing Cassie coming down the porch steps.

"Good morning, Aunt Mabel and Uncle George." Cassie hurried out to their wagon as fast as she could in her condition and hugged each of them as they stepped down. "I'm so excited. It's going to be a wonderful adventure," Cassie said, bubbling with excitement.

"It should be. Fall roundup is one of the best weekends of the year," said Mabel. "It's lots of work, but great fun to be a part of and a wonderful time to get to know your neighbors better. Working together and eating around the campfires builds a bond as strong as family."

Cassie loved the sound of that and put her arm around her aunt as they headed into the house to finish packing. Kathy and Joy welcomed Aunt Mabel as they entered the cottage and exchanged quick hugs.

George, dressed in his chaps and riding gear, went to the back of the wagon where his horse was tied and checked the cinch on the saddle, making sure everything was ready to go. He reached up into the back of the wagon and gave his cattle dog a quick pat on the head and told Sally to stay. Obediently she crouched down and waited inside the wagon bed, resting her head between her paws. George caught sight of Ed coming around the house, his arms loaded with a pile of split wood and called out as he waved, "Good morning, Ed." George made himself useful and went to the woodpile at the side of the house and loaded his arms with a load of firewood and followed Ed to his wagon. "The neighbors should be here soon, and then we can head out to the range," George surmised, as he helped stack enough wood in the back of Ed's wagon for what they would need for the campfires.

"I'm glad you came over early. You can help me make sure we have everything before the others arrive. I don't want to forget anything." Ed looked over the pile of things he had already loaded in the back of his wagon, checking off his mental list.

George rested his gloved hands on the rough sides of the wagon and surveyed the supplies Ed had already packed. "Looks like you've got the feed for the horses, tarps, ropes and poles for the tents, a grate for the cookfire, an ax, a shovel, a water barrel, and a tripod to cook with." He held his chin between his thumb and forefinger and squinted, searching for one of the most important things they would need. "Did you pack your new branding iron?" he asked, lifting a coil of rope to see if it was hiding under it.

"Oh, right. Thank you, George. I almost forgot. It's in the barn. I'll be right back." Ed jogged back to the barn to grab his new branding iron. He'd designed the new brand and had it forged at the smithy and even got it registered. Cleverly, he had changed the capital C of the Crowley brand into a circle and added an H in the center to form the Circle H brand for the Havoc cattle. It was a proud moment for him as he thought about marking his cattle with his very own brand.

Ed passed Clancy coming out of the barn carrying his saddle to his copper mare, Penny. When Clancy saw George had arrived, he shouted his welcome to the older man.

George waved and hollered back, "Hello Clancy. Great to see you. So glad you're comin' along today."

"Me too!" Clancy effortlessly swung the saddle up onto his horse, who seemed just as excited as him. "I wouldn't miss it for the world," he said as he situated the saddle and cinched it nice and snug. Penny had been with him for the past four years on every cattle drive and every roundup, and he believed she loved it just as much as he did. Since taking the steady job on Mr. Brook's ranch, he and Penny had missed the excitement of the cattle drive, and he wondered if he had made the right choice in taking the job. However, since meeting Joy, he knew he'd made the right decision. He buckled on his leather chaps and looped his lasso and swung it over the saddle horn, which got Penny prancing around the corral fencepost where she was tied.

"I think your horse is excited." George walked up to the corral and rested his arms on the top rail. "She's a beauty," he said, watching her breath form clouds of smoke in the cold air as she whinnied and shook her head, her ears twitching back and forth as if she knew what the day would hold.

Clancy ran his hand down her neck and patted her on the shoulder. "That she is. No other like her. We make a great team, Penny and I." He scratched under her chin and rubbed her muzzle. "Don't we, Penny?" She blew and bobbed her head up and down, then nudged his shoulder signaling it was time to go.

Ed emerged from the barn carrying the branding iron. "I think we're nearly ready. I just need to saddle Major and load up the food and bedding from inside." Ed placed the branding iron behind the seat in the wagon bed and headed to the cottage as the first rays of sunlight brightened the Eastern horizon.

Clancy called out to Ed, "I can saddle up Major for you Ed, and Joy's horse as well."

"Thanks, Clancy. I'll be back in a minute," Ed hollered over his shoulder as he went inside to help the women, and Clancy headed into the barn to get the saddles. Major and Midnight were enjoying the hay Clancy had pitched out to them in the corral.

Cassie was stirring and salting the beans when Ed entered the cottage. "Is it time?" she asked, feeling frantic as time was running out and still having so many things to do.

"Yup. I think we're about ready to go. The rest

will arrive in just a few minutes. I'll help you carry out everything."

Cassie smiled up at his handsome face. "That would be much appreciated, dear. These two pots are very heavy and very hot." Cassie placed the heavy cast iron lids on the two steaming Dutch ovens.

"I'll take them both," he said. Using potholders and his leather gloves, he lifted each Dutch oven by the handle and took them off the stove. Cassie hurried ahead of him and opened the front door. Steam rose from the heat of the pots in the cold October air as Ed's boots crunched through the frosty grass that sparkled in the first rays of sunlight. Cassie followed with an old blanket that she wrapped around the pots to keep them warm in the wooden box Ed set them in. The four women carried out the rest of the food, dishes, and bedding, and placed them in the back of the wagons while Ed adjusted things, making room as needed, then threw a tarp over it all and announced everything was ready to go.

They pulled on their long wool coats and grabbed the last items as the neighbors entered the yard on horseback and in wagons. Excitement filled the air as the friends and neighbors greeted each other. Cassie climbed into their rig with Ed's help, followed by his mother who offered to drive their wagon. Mabel climbed into her heavy loaded wagon, packed with food, bedding, and camping supplies, as well as a fifty-gallon water barrel that was tied securely to the side of the wagon.

Joy emerged from the cottage, taking one last look

around inside, then closed the door behind her. She shivered in the cold, even though she had buttoned up her long over-coat, and wore Cassie's cowboy hat, and a pair of leather gloves to keep her warm. Approaching Clancy with the saddled horses, she felt a twist of nervousness in her stomach but pushed it aside as he smiled approvingly at her. Clancy assisted her up onto Midnight with ease, feeling a thrill of excitement mixed with a hint of uncertainty as he handed her the reins. She felt the powerful stallion pull against the reins, wanting a little slack on the bit. Grinning down at Clancy, she relaxed her arms and thanked him for his help, feeling a greater sense of admiration for the rugged cowboy standing close beside her.

Clancy, Ed, and George also climbed onto their horses and the four of them followed the neighbors down the Havoc's lane, heading out to the main road and toward the open range.

Cassie's heavy loaded wagon was the last to leave the yard, with Mother Havoc driving the team, while Cassie sat beside her taking in the long procession in front of them. Cowboys and cowgirls of all ages rode various steeds, following the two wheel-worn tracks. Cassie couldn't help but admire the long overcoats, chaps, bandanas, and cowboy hats that they all wore, prepared for the challenging work ahead. The horses walked with heads held high and proud, as if carrying noble knights on a valiant quest, with their heavy breaths creating silvery clouds around their snouts, adding to the magnificent scene set before her. Cassie loved crisp autumn mornings, but this one especially. With the group leaving, the homestead seemed quiet, until the rooster crowed, and the milk cow called out mournfully, seeming to bid them farewell. Leaves crunched under the horses' hooves and wagon wheels, as they traveled over the road strewn with bits of red, brown and yellow. She looked up through the bare branches of the trees, when she heard geese honking and watched them cross the clear blue sky flying south in their V formation. She smiled contentedly and inhaled deeply the rich scent of damp earth, pine needles, and decaying leaves. Today was a perfect day and she wished Bart and Bea could be there to enjoy it with them as well, but unfortunately they couldn't.

As Mother Havoc turned the team onto the main road and headed north following the trek of ranchers, Cassie noticed two more wagons and a group of riders coming up the road from town.

One of the men on horseback shouted, "Hello!" and waved to them as he kicked his horse into a trot.

Cassie recognized him—it was Sheriff O'Malley, dressed in chaps and a long overcoat. She smiled as Sheriff O'Malley slowed his horse to walk beside their wagon.

"Good morning, Sheriff," said the two women in unison.

Kathy smiled brightly at the surprise and felt her cheeks flush and her heart race at the sight of him.

"Good morning, ladies!" Sheriff O'Malley said, tipping his hat to greet them, noticing Kathy's sparkling eyes and joyful smile and hoped he had been the one to put it there. *What a beautiful woman, Kathy is.* Calling her Kathy in his mind instead of Mrs. Havoc had become a habit of his, these past few months.

Kathy tried to focus on where she was driving, but the way he smiled at her made her insides feel like butter melting over hot pancakes and had to keep adjusting the horse's reins to keep the wagon on the road. "What brings you out this way so early in the morning?" Kathy asked, feeling almost as flustered as a young woman being greeted by her old school crush.

"I came out to help," he announced with pleasure. *And to spend time with you, Kathy. Isn't it obvious?* he wondered. Sheriff O'Malley had always been happy to help with the local roundups, but today he was particularly excited because he knew she would be there. He had decided to join them as soon as she had told him she was taking the days off to help with the roundup. That very day, he'd made arrangements with his deputies and let them know where they could find him in case of an emergency.

Kathy smiled gratefully at Sheriff O'Malley, feeling the warm buttery feeling spread clear to her toes. "That's very nice of you," she said sweetly, grateful for the help and thankful for the growing friendship they shared. Since her husband's death, she never thought she'd feel this way again—excited and hopeful for the future. And now every day seemed brighter. Sheriff O'Malley made her feel alive and young again and she treasured every moment she spent with him. She knew deep down it was just a fantasy but couldn't help but wonder what it would be like to be kissed again.

"It's the least I could do for my good friends," he said, winking at her and nudging his horse into a trot.

Kathy watched breathlessly as he rode off, feeling the cold morning air cool her cheeks that burned like hot coals. Had he really just winked at her or was her mind playing tricks? Maybe he was just teasing her, she told herself. But deep down inside she hoped it was a sign of something more. The thought of it made her heart pound harder, and her stomach flutter with butterflies. *How ridiculous, I'm a mature woman,* she told herself. *I'm too old for feelings like this.* But she couldn't help but smile, watching the handsome Sheriff slow to chat with her son.

Cassie glimpsed the increased color in Mother Havoc's cheeks as Sheriff O'Malley rode off, and it pleased her to see how happy he made her. Since the day Mother Havoc had arrived in Cheyenne, Cassie had noticed the special attention Sheriff O'Malley showed her, and hoped someday the two would realize they were more than just friends.

It took only a few hours or so for the group to reach the campsite. They found a spot near a small stream and an old firepit with rocks where they could cook their meals. Cassie, Mabel, and the others pulled up their wagons and began unloading supplies. Further away from camp another fire pit was prepared for branding the cattle.

After arriving, the riders were given their instructions for the day. Groups of two or three were assigned to drive in the cattle to the campsite from different directions. Once the herd was gathered, the bulls would be separated from heifers and calves and more assignments would be made.

Clancy and Joy paired up to cover the far west, while Ed and George went north, and Sheriff O'Malley joined a younger couple to head east. The other neighbors went northeast and south, each covering their assigned area to drive the cattle back to camp.

As the sun rose above the hills and cast long shadows across the plains, Joy and Clancy rode westward away from camp. The birds chirped as they flew above the tall blonde grass, searching for insects as the sun warmed the earth and vegetation. Joy felt her heart swell with the beauty around her. She suddenly realized, since coming to Cheyenne, she had missed this time of day outside of town. The sunrise on the prairie was stunning.

"I understand why they named you Joy. I see it on your face all the time," Clancy said, watching Joy stare out over the wide-open range of dry grass spotted with grazing cattle.

Joy blushed at the compliment. "I feel it all the time when I'm with you."

"So do I," Clancy admitted, and she blushed further.

They rode for a few miles until they came to a little gully. Clancy knew the places where cattle liked to congregate. He found a group of cattle and their yearlings grazing on the dry stubble next to a small stream and a wallow where buffalo had gathered in the past. He signaled to Joy to circle around the opposite direction from him, so they could guide the small herd back to camp, and picked up his lasso and gave it a snap against his chaps, catching the attention of the cattle. With a loud "whoop, whoop," he spurred his horse into motion. The cattle began moving and Joy swiftly turned her horse and drove the cattle in the right direction. Clancy was impressed with her natural talent and quick grasp of the task at hand, despite her lack of experience in cattle drives and roundups.

Joy smiled at Clancy's approving hat tip as they walked the cattle back toward camp. Together they adjusted the direction of the cattle whenever necessary to prevent them from straying off. Joy even let out a few "whoops" to get their attention when a yearling tried to bolt in the opposite direction. Clancy felt proud of her and mentioned it as they headed back out, leaving the cattle in camp for the other riders to keep herd on them as they grazed.

Ed and George made their way north and found a small herd of cattle near Horse Creek. It would take them well over an hour to drive them back to camp even for such experienced cattlemen. They did have one advantage with George's cattle dog. George would whistle and point, and Sally would go after the rogue cow. The more Ed watched, the more convinced he was that he needed a good cattle dog, like the black and white collie.

Meanwhile, Sheriff O'Malley and the young couple arrived back at camp by mid-morning with thirty or so cattle. As Sheriff O'Malley rode through camp, he stopped just long enough to tip his hat to Kathy, thinking she looked lovely in her bonnet and overcoat as she worked over the campfire.

Kathy smiled and waved, realizing he only acknowledged her in the group of women in camp. It made her feel flattered that of all the single women he could have noticed, he had sought her out. He jumped down with ease and led his horse over to the wagons.

Kathy went to join him to see if she could help him with anything. "Are you doing OK? Can I get you anything—food—coffee?"

Sheriff O'Malley untied his saddle bag and took out his canteen. "I just need to fill this." He shook the round metal flask. "In my haste to get here, I completely forgot," he said with a chuckle.

"I can fill that for you," she said, taking the canteen from him, and went to the back of the wagon holding the water barrel.

Sheriff O'Malley flipped the horse's reins over the wagon wheel and followed her to the end of the wagon where a wooden crate served as a step. As Kathy stepped onto the crate, it tilted and she started to lose her balance. In an instant the Sheriff's hands quickly wrapped around her waist, stabilizing her. Kathy gasped and blushed at the unexpected contact. With his help, she easily stepped up into the back of the wagon.

"There you go," he said.

"Thank you." Her cheeks flamed as she went to fill the canteen from the barrel. Her hands shook as she lifted the lid and dipped the canteen in, filling it. She replaced the lid on the barrel and turned to walk back to the end of the wagon. She felt her stomach flip. There he was, smiling up at her with his hands lifted to put around her waist. Her cheeks burned even hotter as she rested her free hand on his shoulder while he took her around the waist, and helped ease her down.

Once she was safely on the ground, Sheriff O'Malley momentarily forgot what he was doing, standing only inches from her, gazing into her green eyes. Kathy smiled shyly, looking down at his hands still around her waist, feeling self-conscious. Sheriff O'Malley finally remembered where he was and quickly dropped his hands and stepped back.

Kathy remembered she was holding the dripping wet canteen and held it out to him. "Here you go," she said in a shaky voice.

Sheriff O'Malley cleared his dry throat and smiled. "Thank you, Mrs. Havoc." His mind was spinning with thoughts as he took the canteen and placed it in his saddle bag. He was feeling giddy, like some young schoolboy with a crush on the prettiest girl in class. At this point he was determined to do anything, just to have a chance to talk to her and see her smile at him again.

"You know, Mrs. Havoc, now that camp is set up, would you like to come out with me, to look for more strays? We'll only be gone a couple hours. It'll give you a chance to see some of the countryside," he said, hoping he could spend more time with her. "You could ride with me."

"Well…," Kathy hesitated for a moment, glancing at the other women chatting by the campfire. Finally she made up her mind and turned to the Sheriff saying, "I could come with you, I suppose." She quickly walked over to Cassie, whispered something in her ear, then hurried back to the Sheriff, feeling a mixture of excitement and nervousness at the thought of riding with him.

"Here, you ride up front in the saddle and I'll get on behind you," he said, walking with her to his horse by the wagon. He helped her place her foot in the stirrup and lifted her up as she swung her leg over the other side. Kathy adjusted her skirts that had come up a little on her legs. He smiled and helped her with it. Then putting his foot in the stirrup and holding onto the saddle horn, he pulled himself up behind her. Sheriff O'Malley wrapped his arms around her to hold onto the reins as she held onto the saddle horn, and they started off, joined by the young couple who were smiling at each other as they followed.

Chapter 13

Love at any Age

Kathy felt the warmth of Sheriff O'Malley's body through her coat and felt both comforted and excited to be riding so closely with him. They rode in silence for the first mile or so, their horse moving quietly along. The sun was warming up the day, painting the sky a bright blue with wispy white clouds drifting by. Kathy tried to calm her racing heart as she got used to the closeness of the Sheriff.

Sheriff O'Malley could feel his heart pounding almost out of his chest, she was so close and wondered if she could hear it.

Kathy broke the silence when she slipped off her bonnet so she could see him better and asked, "Have you done this often?"

Sheriff O'Malley was confused. "What do you mean?" he asked. Hoping she didn't think he did this with other women?

"I mean—do you help out all the ranchers in town?" she asked, realizing how she must have sounded.

Sheriff O'Malley chuckled. "Well, yes, some I have," he replied with a laugh.

Kathy joined in, feeling relieved.

And then he laughed as he admitted, "I thought you were asking if I rode around with other women."

Kathy laughed. "Oh, goodness no! I would never ask that of anyone," she said, blushing.

"Well, if you were wondering, the answer is no. You're the only woman I've ever ridden double with. Except my sister, and that doesn't really count," he said, chuckling, and then he blushed. She was making him flustered.

Kathy smiled, as she thought of herself as the only one he'd ever invited to ride with him. "Then, I feel honored, Sheriff O'Malley."

"Would it be all right if we called each other by our first names?" Patrick asked, his heart beating a little faster at the thought of calling her Kathy. He had always liked the sound of her name and wanted to use it for a while now.

"I would like that very much, Patrick," Kathy said a little breathlessly, as her mind reeled at the direction their conversation was heading.

His heart skipped a beat as she said his given name. It had been so long since anyone had called him Patrick, he'd almost forgotten how wonderful it sounded. "Thank you, Kathy," he said, trying to focus on the terrain ahead as the horse continued walking east. He kept stealing glances at her profile, trying to memorize every detail. She turned around and he caught a whiff of her hair. It smelled wonderful and her chocolate-brown hair looked so soft and shiny. He longed to touch it but knew he had to hold onto the reins.

Moments later, they came upon a small brook with large bushes growing along it, perfect places for stray cattle to hide. They followed it as it meandered along, heading northeast.

She finally decided now was as good a time as any to ask the question she had wondered since she first met him. "Patrick, why have you never married?" she asked, and immediately regretted it. "Never-mind, it's none of my business. I shouldn't have asked that," she said, feeling a little ashamed for prying.

"It's okay. I don't mind. Believe it or not, I did want to get married at one time. I had a sweetheart when I was about nineteen. I even asked her to marry me," he said, pausing as his thoughts drifted to the past.

Kathy gently encouraged him to continue. "What happened?"

"She said I didn't have high enough aspirations. She said she couldn't be happy with a lowly cowboy. She wanted someone who was going somewhere, and who would make a difference in the world. So, I set out to convince her that I could do just that. I took a job as a deputy in Laramie and worked hard so I could be elected Sheriff someday. I actually really liked the job as deputy. But before I could become Sheriff and ask her to marry me again, she met a lawyer from back East and married him." Patrick looked away from her, feeling vulnerable as he shared his past heartbreak. "Once she was engaged to him, I wanted nothing more to do with women. That was twenty-five years ago. I figured one heartbreak was enough to last a lifetime. I haven't had any interest in women since then." The hurt he'd felt for all those years seemed like a distant memory now. His heart was full of hope as he glanced at her profile. "Well… until you came along, that is," he admitted, feeling his heart pounding hard up into his throat.

Kathy was at a loss for words and could hardly believe what she was hearing. Her head felt fuzzy as her heart raced. Slowly, she finally found her voice. "I don't quite understand why you would be interested in me. There are many young women who would happily welcome your attention," she said, trying to reason with him and herself why this didn't make sense. "I'm forty-five. I'm old. Don't you want children of your own? I'm nearly a grandma," she said, adding more reasons to the list.

Patrick smiled at her attempt to dissuade him, finding it endearing that she thought she was old. For all he could see was a beautiful mature woman with charm and experience. "Kathy, age is just a number. It's who a person is on the inside that matters to me," his voice gentle and sincere. "And as for children, I've never been one to focus on that. If it's meant to be, it will happen, but if not, that's okay too. What's important to me is finding someone I can share my life with, someone I can love and be loved by. And that person, Kathy, is you," he said, gaining courage as he realized how much he really did want to be with her. For the first time in twenty-five years he really wanted to be married. He was astounded by his own boldness.

Kathy was shocked. They rode in silence for a minute as she tried to gather her thoughts.

"I'm sorry. I should've never said that," said Patrick, feeling foolish for being so forward. It wasn't like she didn't have options. Maybe she wasn't interested. All sorts of things were going through his mind at once, as he tried to figure out how to get out of this mess he'd made.

Kathy spoke up, "No, don't say that. I'm flattered, really, I am. I can't think of anyone else I've met, since my husband, that's made me feel this way. I'm still trying to convince myself that this is real. You don't understand. I never thought this would happen again, especially at my age," she said slowly, still processing his words.

Patrick pulled the horse to a halt in the shade beside the small brook they'd been following. He jumped off the back and reached his hands up and took her around the waist. "Come on down here for a minute. I need to talk to you face to face," he said as she complied and swung her leg over the horse, and he eased her down.

Kathy turned to face him. Patrick was still standing so close, and she kept her eyes on his chest, trying to not let the tears that were collecting spill over. She made the mistake of blinking, and they rolled down her cheeks as she looked down.

Patrick kept his hands around her waist until he saw her tears. He took her face in his hands and gently wiped the tears away. "Kathy, you don't see what I see. I see who you are, a lovely vivacious woman, who's raised her children all these years alone to be independent, strong women, just like you. You're humble, hardworking, and gracious. Any man would be a fool not to want a wife like you, young or old. You're like a fine wine; to me you are refined and every bit as beautiful as I imagine you were twenty years ago. I would be honored to be by your side for the rest of my life. Do you believe me yet?" he asked, as he looked into her sparkling green eyes.

Kathy tried to form the words but instead shocked herself by reaching up to pull his face down and kissed him. Her heart nearly burst out of her chest with exhilaration. It was better than she'd ever imagined. It had been so long ago since she'd kissed a man. They lingered there for a moment.

Patrick couldn't have been more shocked by Kathy's kiss. His arms instinctively pulled her closer. When they parted, they were both breathless and smiling.

"I guess I believe you," Kathy said laughing lightly, feeling a little embarrassed by her actions.

Patrick began laughing. "I guess you do!" he said, as they hugged each other and continued to laugh.

They finally calmed down as Patrick released her slightly. He looked down into her eyes and asked her seriously, "So, will you? Will you marry me, Kathy?"

Kathy shocked herself again and followed her heart since her head was still in a daze. "Yes, Patrick, I will," she said lovingly.

Patrick smiled and kissed her softly again. "I love you, Kathy," he said, when he released her lips.

"I love you, Patrick," Kathy said, as tears rolled down her cheeks at his words.

This time he let them go and pulled her to his chest and held her tight. He had longed to hear those words for a lifetime. Finally, he had what he had wanted over twenty-five years ago, a woman whom he loved would be with him for the rest of his life.

***

The rest of the day was a whirlwind of activities. Around dinner time, Patrick and Kathy returned to camp grinning from ear to ear. They had successfully brought in a group of cattle with the help of the young couple they met up with after their heart-to-heart conversation.

Cassie could tell from the look on Mother Havoc's face that something had happened but kept her questions to herself. She figured she would share with her when the time was right.

The rest of the herd was brought in by supper time and kept close for sorting and branding in the morning. Supper was shared around the campfire as they told stories about the roundup. The food was delicious, having cooked over the fires all day. They watched the sun set, noting brilliant orange and yellows with pink around the cloud's edges, until the sun dipped below the horizon and dusk set in. The cattle were settled in for the night and lowing in the distance. Tents were pitched and the remaining food and dishes were stored away.

Ed brought out his guitar and began strumming a very soulful song about the lonesome days and nights of a cowboy's life, and Clancy joined in. Joy sat beside Clancy and gazed into the campfire watching the flames as she listened to the two deep voices harmonize. She glanced over at her mother and Sheriff O'Malley sitting next to her. Joy knew her mother and Sheriff O'Malley were good friends, but it seemed something had changed between them. They seemed more at ease and comfortable with each other, sitting particularly close. She decided she would ask her mother about it later.

As the song ended, Patrick stood up, taking Kathy by the hand and asked her to stand with him as he put his arm around her shoulders. "I have an announcement to make. I've asked Kathy to marry me, and she's said yes," he said, smiling down at Kathy, who beamed up at him as she wrapped her arm around his waist.

"Ma!" Joy shouted in excitement. She jumped up and wrapped her arms around her mother tightly. "I'm so happy for you!" she said, tears welling up in her eyes. All these years she'd been concerned about her mother's happiness and now seeing her in love brought her so much joy.

Ed and Cassie shook Sheriff O'Malley's hand and congratulated them, then hugged his mother. "I'm so pleased. You deserve to be happy and loved again, Ma," he said, and kissed her on the cheek.

Kathy had tears of joy rolling down her cheeks at

the happiness she felt. She'd worried what her children would think of her marrying again and her worries were put to rest.

Cassie hugged her tightly. "Mother Havoc, I am so happy for you. Maybe I should just call you Kathy once you're married so I don't get mixed up and call you the wrong name. Although Mother O'Malley has a nice ring to it," she said laughing.

Kathy found the name "Mrs. Kathy O'Malley" to be wonderful as well, considering she'd been called Kathy Havoc for over half of her life.

The brilliant stars twinkled brightly in the dark sky as the harvest moon came up huge in the eastern horizon with a halo around it. It was a beautiful night. The tents had been set up and everyone retired to their respective tents and sleeping spots. Patrick walked with Kathy to her tent and kissed her quickly before he left to roll his bed out by the fire.

Clancy said goodnight to Joy and went to get his horse to take the first watch over the herd. He planned to take the third watch as well, as he was used to staying up late when he needed to.

Joy joined her mother in their tent and settled beside her and together they talked excitedly about the happenings of the day.

Ed and Cassie snuggled in their tent together, hearing Joy and Kathy mumbling in the other tent nearby. Cassie and Ed whispered for a little while before they fell asleep in each other's arms. It had been a wonderful but long day, and sleep overtook them quickly.

Chapter 14

Roundup, Day Two

Patrick stowed away his bedroll and turned towards the fire, moving the pot of coffee closer to the flames. He stood and stretched his arms over his head, arching his back, trying to work the stiffness out of his muscles. He was feeling his age more and more and was feeling it especially today. It had been a while since he had slept on the ground and wondered if he'd actually slept at all. His mind had kept him awake most of the night, thinking about Kathy, how she'd agreed to become his wife, and imagined what life would be like by her side.

Kathy emerged from her tent into the dark, frigid morning and shivered as the cold seeped through her wool coat and her breath came out in little white clouds. She tucked a stray hair under her bonnet and attempted to smooth out the dress she'd slept in overnight, then headed towards the campfire to warm herself. Kathy's heart gave a little leap of excitement as she recognized Patrick tending to the fire.

Patrick caught a movement out of the corner of his eye and smiled with delight as he recognized her and opened his arms to welcome his future wife. "Good morning, Kathy." Patrick enclosed her in his arms and glanced around the quiet camp, grateful for a moment alone with her, and kissed her on the forehead.

"Good morning, Patrick." Kathy snuggled close, wrapping her arms around his waist. It was hard to believe she was his fiancé, and she smiled contentedly. Laying her head against his chest and breathing in his scent, she heard his heart beat strong and steady. She didn't want to move. Patrick's arms made her feel safe and secure. She tipped her head up to study his face in the twinkling starlight and dancing flames and closed her eyes as he bent down and kissed her sweetly. His gentle kiss caused a warmth to fill her body, flowing from the center of her being down to her toes.

"Did you sleep well?" Patrick whispered, inches from her lips, looking down into her dreamy eyes.

It took a moment for the question to get to the starry sky, where her mind was soaring. "I think I'm too old for sleeping on the ground." With a light self-conscious chuckle, she smiled at him. Kathy had tossed and turned in her tent all night thinking about Patrick and their promising future together.

"I know what you mean." He reached around to knead his lower back with his fist. "I feel like I slept on a pile of rocks." He motioned to the ground in front of the fire. "Oh, look, I did," he chuckled.

Kathy looked down at the rocky ground surrounding the campfire. "That would do it!" She chuckled with him. "I think I did too. I'm getting too old for this."

Patrick rested his arm over her shoulders and gave her a squeeze. "Maybe *we* are."

He grinned as they turned to face the fire, feeling the combined warmth of the flames burning inside and outside, warming them both.

Kathy sniffed as the coffee kettle began to steam. "Mmm, that smells wonderful."

"Clancy made it. He's been up taking shifts through the night with some of the other cowboys. It should be hot now. I'll get some cups." Patrick went to the wagon that was nearby and pulled out two tin mugs from the crate of dishes.

Kathy watched him return to the flickering light of the fire and thought how handsome he looked with his two-day old stubble and thick moustache that lifted at the edges as he smiled back at her. His broad shoulders were apparent through his heavy wool coat as he bent down and lifted off the kettle with his leather-gloved hand and poured them each a mug of steaming coffee.

"Here ya go." He turned to hand her one, noticing the sparkle in her eyes as the firelight danced in her dark pools of green.

Kathy thanked him and accepted the hot mug with a smile. She lifted it to her mouth and blew, then sipped some, feeling it warm her all the way down. Patrick took his place beside her and together they drank their coffee as they watched the camp start to come to life. Little by little, sleepy campers emerged from their tents and began rummaging around for kettles, pots and pans, and food to bring to their fires so they could start preparing breakfast.

"Good morning, Cassie. How did you sleep last night?" Kathy asked as Cassie joined her and Patrick beside the fire. Kathy slipped her arm around Cassie's waist and gave her a little squeeze, concerned about her daughter-in-law sleeping on the ground in her advancing condition.

"I slept a little." Cassie smiled up at Ed as he came to stand between her and his mother, wrapping his arms over their shoulders and giving them each a hug. "And thanks to Ed, I was warm all night." Cassie shivered in the frosty autumn air, remembering what would have been a long cold night without him.

Ed gave his wife a smile and then his mother as he stood between the two loveliest women he knew. "It's what I said I would do; 'keep you warm, when you are cold,' I mean." He turned to his mother. "Good morning, Mother," and leaned over and kissed her on the cheek. "I imagine you had good dreams last night." He was so happy for her, he couldn't help himself.

"Oh, Ed!" Kathy shook her head at his teasing. She wasn't about to tell anyone she'd had a wonderful dream about her and Patrick. But her cheeks reddened just thinking about it.

Patrick looked up to see her blushing and smiled at the mother and son. The smile never left his face as he situated the logs he'd added to the fire and placed the metal grate over the bed of hot coals so they could begin cooking.

"Well, I know Patrick must have had good dreams. Look at that silly smile on his face," Ed teased with an impish grin.

Patrick laughed good-naturedly. "I would have— had I actually slept." He winked at Kathy, causing her face to redden further.

"Oh, you two." Kathy smiled bashfully and tried to wave them off as she took her daughter-in-law by the arm. "Cassie, I think we'd better get breakfast going before these two get any worse."

Cassie grinned. "I agree. These two could go on all day like this." Cassie and her mother-in-law chuckled at the teasing and excused themselves to go get the box of food from the wagon.

Joy soon joined the women as they began cooking breakfast over the fire. Together, Joy, Kathy, Cassie, and the other women in the camp fried, boiled, and baked over the fires under the cover of the dark sky. The smell of the mouth-watering food drew the group together, as the last pan was pulled off the fire. Dutch ovens full of fried potatoes and onions were set next to covered skillets of scrambled eggs, crispy fried bacon and fluffy pancakes. As soon as the group of friends and neighbors gathered and settled, the blessing was said, and the women began filling tin plates. As hungry men, women, and children passed through the line, they nodded their heads and muttered their thanks to the cooks. They took their heaping plates and found a spot around the campfires to eat their food before it got cold. The campsite slowly came to life as friends and neighbors filled their stomachs. Joy took the coffee kettle around, filling and refilling mugs, and slowly the cold and sore campers stopped their grumbling about the uncomfortable night. Soon a cheerful banter and laughter filled the air as the conversation shifted to the exciting work ahead of them.

Clancy was one of the last to come into camp to eat breakfast. Joy smiled as she saw him stiffly ambling into camp, his hat hiding his face as his head drooped. She had been waiting for him to return after watching over the cattle most of the night and her heart leapt at the sight of him.

"Good morning, Clancy," said Joy cheerfully as he approached.

He looked up at the sound of her voice and right away she noticed Clancy's stubble had grown overnight, and his eyes drooped in exhaustion.

"Good morning, Joy," he said in a gravelly voice, almost too weak to smile back at her. He was cold and sore from sitting in the saddle all night and was very hungry, not to mention bone tired.

Clancy looked like he'd had a long night and she felt a pang of sympathy for him. "Come with me," Joy said tenderly as she took his hand and led him over to the back of the wagon, away from the group. "I've been keeping your breakfast warm, for when you came in from watching the herd," she said and watched him hoist himself up on the end of the wagon bed. She uncovered the plate of warm food she had set aside and handed it to him with a fork. "I'll be right back. I'll go get you a cup of hot coffee to go with it."

Clancy half smiled and thanked her as he quickly ate the plentiful helping of eggs, bacon, potatoes, and a stack of pancakes drenched in syrup.

Joy brought back a cup of steaming coffee and sat it on the wagon bed beside him while he continued to eat. "Rough night?" she asked, looking at him with concern.

"Not really, just the usual long night in the saddle. It'll pass. I'm feeling much better already. Thanks for the breakfast and fresh coffee," he said, and picked up the cup and took a sip as the steam rose into the frosty air. Clancy took a deep breath in and released it. "Ahh, just how I like it. Just like old Cookie used to make. Puts you in a better mood almost immediately." He winked and smiled at Joy.

"Cookie?" she puzzled with a small smile.

Clancy smiled. "Yes, Cookie. That's what we called the camp cook on the cattle drives. He was in charge of the chuckwagon, and he always made sure the coffee was hot and strong. His coffee kept us going on the long cold nights."

Joy wondered why he hadn't gone on the Texas cattle drive this year. "Do you miss it?" she asked.

Clancy thought for a second as he took a long drink of his coffee. "You know, I thought I would. But having a steady job and then meeting you has been better than any cattle drive I've ever been on," he said smiling.

Joy smiled and put her hand on his as it rested on the wagon. "I'm glad you stayed. Cheyenne has turned out to be a wonderful place, all because of you," she said honestly. "Do you think you'll ever go back home?" she asked sadly, wondering if he would be leaving her next spring.

Clancy smiled and squeezed her hand. "No, Joy," and added slowly, as if he'd read her mind, "I would never leave you. As long as you want me to stay, I will stay."

In the darkness of the early morning, Joy moved closer to Clancy as he leaned forward and kissed her gently on the lips. Joy's soft lips pressed into his, not resisting, but welcoming his. He'd wanted to kiss her since the first day he'd met her, and now it was happening, and his mind was reeling. Reluctantly, Clancy withdrew and smiled down at her. Even in the shadows he could see her shining eyes.

Joy smiled shyly at him, trying to catch her breath and calm the trembling that had taken over her body with his kiss. She held his hand and looked down at it as she stroked it with her thumb. "I don't ever want you to leave me," she said softly, finally looking up at him, with tears pooling in her eyes.

"Oh, Joy," he said, giving her hand a squeeze. His heart was racing and ached for her. He'd wondered if he would ever hear those words from a woman.

"I've lost too many people in my life. I don't want to lose you too," Joy said as the tears spilled over. She didn't know how much she'd been holding inside all these years, until now. Joy and her sister, Beth, had tried to be strong for their mother, after Pa and her brothers never came home from the war. The three women worked hard, taking in sewing, and managing the farm the best they could. But without the men in the family, the farm life had taken its toll on them. They had survived well enough, pulling together, taking care of everything. But with Beth and now her mother, soon to be married, what was to become of her? When would it be her turn? Joy wanted to be taken care of, held, cherished, and never let go. Her heart ached for it like nothing she'd ever felt before.

Clancy jumped down from the wagon bed, and took her into his arms, and held her tightly, as she wrapped hers around his neck and cried, releasing all her grief and heartache.

"Shh, I'm not going anywhere. I'll be here for you. Wild horses couldn't drag me away," Clancy stroked her long blonde braid as she shook with sobs.

Joy rested her head on his sturdy shoulder and felt safe in the moment. It had been the first time she'd truly let anyone see how much sadness she carried. She lifted her head and looked at him, still frowning, with tears shining on her cheeks.

"Joy, you can count on me. When I commit, I commit. I ride for the brand, and darling, you've branded your name into my heart." Clancy's voice was strong with emotion. "I will honor you until the end of time." Clancy was a romantic soul and had spent nights alone thinking about all he wanted to tell her, and now it was all pouring out.

Joy was astonished by his heartfelt words that brought her tears of joy. She held him even tighter as she cried with relief and happiness. When she finally settled, she looked up at him, smiling and blinking away the last of the tears. "Clancy, you're simply amazing. You're perfect for me, in every way," she said in a soft, shaky voice.

Clancy leaned in and kissed her, this time more passionately. Her words were music to his ears, and his heart was soaring high like an eagle. She fit perfectly against him as he held her in his strong arms. Both were left feeling a little dizzy from their kiss. Clancy didn't want to let go, but he heard people approaching and released her slowly. They backed away from each other as Cassie and Ed, walking arm in arm, became visible in the dim light of the starry morning.

"Oh, there you are, Clancy. We were hoping you'd come in," Ed said with relief as they came closer. "Did you have a chance to eat?" Then noted the empty plate and cup on the end of the wagon bed and Joy's bashful look.

"Yes, Joy was good enough to see that I got plenty." Smiling, Clancy winked at Joy so only she could see.

Joy hoped her reddened cheeks remained hidden in the shadows. *Oh goodness, what if they suspect we were kissing,* she thought. "I was just going to go get Clancy some more hot coffee," she said, and quickly grabbed his cup and started to go when Clancy offered to join her.

"Ok, we'll see you two in a while then," Ed said as Joy and Clancy scurried away, stifling their laughter. Ed shook his head in wonder. "Those two are like two little love birds. They remind me of us, not that long ago," Ed said smiling and gave Cassie a squeeze, remembering their stolen kisses.

Cassie turned and hugged him tightly. "What do you mean, 'not that long ago'? We're the same love birds we've always been," she said, pulling his head down to kiss him.

Ed delighted in her soft warm lips. She held her kiss a bit longer before releasing him, to smile up at him lovingly. "I stand corrected," he said in amusement. "We are every bit as in love as the day we met, and even more now, sweetheart. Although it is harder to get close to you. This cute little belly of yours is growing," he said smiling, looking down at her belly that seemed to grow overnight.

Cassie's smile broadened as she stroked his stubbled cheek, her eyes shining. She adored him immensely. "Just as my love grows for you, my dear."

"Oh, my sweet Cass. Every day I fall more in love with you," he said soberly and kissed her so she would know it.

***

Wispy clouds drifted across the pale blue sky as the day dawned, and a mist rose up from the frosty ground around the bellowing herd. The horses were saddled, branding irons were heated fiery red, and lassos and gumption were gathered for the day's work ahead.

Teams of ranchers and cowboys were organized to separate the different herds. Once the Crowley herd was cut from the rest, they branded them with the Circle H, marking them as part of the Havoc herd. Each yearling was counted and totaled. It had been a good year; the Havoc herd had almost doubled. Ed picked out the ones to be taken to the train station, selecting about thirty from the hundred-or-so two-year-olds that they had, along with twenty older dry cows, who didn't have calves. This year the herd had fared well and would bring them a good profit.

Branding was a team effort. With each man assigned a role to perform, the crew worked quickly. Clancy was exceptionally good at all the duties, especially roping. That morning he began the day assigned as one of the ropers. He'd ride into the herd to find the next cow to brand, then would quickly separate it from the herd. He had the ability to handle his horse in a way to cut the cow off from escaping back into the herd. Clancy and his horse moved as if they were of one mind. A second cowhand would rope the head as Clancy's rope held the hind legs, stretching the cow out, then Ed and Patrick, the wrestlers, would quickly flip it on its side. Once down, the two on horseback kept the ropes tight, so George could sear the brand into the cow's hide. The whole process was accomplished in a mere minute or two. Just as rapidly as it was done, the ropes were removed, and the cow was released. By mid-morning the crisp autumn day had the men sweating from the exertion.

The men would work a job until the crew needed a break, and they'd rotate. Everyone looked forward to roping, but not all were proficient at it.

Joy watched from a safe distance as the men worked. She stood in awe of the skill and endurance of the ropers and wrestlers, as they branded hundreds of cattle that day. There was a communal feeling, a sense of achievement, and a festiveness about the round-up that was exciting to be a part of. Good-natured joking and encouragement were heard throughout the camp and around the circle of branding teams. Everywhere Joy looked were hard-working cattlemen and women. She especially watched Clancy, who took an occasional opportunity to tip his hat to her. As the day wore on, she worked her way closer to the action and was soon regretting it. The smell of searing hide wafted her way and assaulted her nostrils. She quickly covered her nose with her gloved hand trying to block the stench of burnt hair and cow hide. It was something she wasn't prepared for and wondered how the men could stand the smell so close up. Clancy saw her wrinkle her nose and chuckled to himself.

After a hearty dinner, the men returned to their work of branding. This time George's herd was worked on. Only a few needed branding, those being born after the spring roundup. Then George selected his group of two-year-olds and barren heifers to be taken to market.

When they finished with each neighbor's branding, and separated out the ones to be sold, they released the rest of the herd. All those able to ride on horseback were organized to drive the cattle into town to the train station's stockyard. A few men, including

Patrick, offered to stay behind to help break camp. Cassie and some of the older women stayed as well, to prepare for supper, while Joy joined the group of riders and helped push the chosen cattle the eight or so miles back into the train station's stockyard.

The cattle drive consisted of over 300 grown cattle, consisting of a few bulls, some barren heifers, dry cows, and mostly two-year-old steers. The price per head was up to sixty-four dollars that year, minus the four dollars to ship them East by train. The money earned would be enough to see the ranchers through the year with some to set aside.

Chapter 15

Rogue Bull

The cattle drive was moving along well until they were about half-way to the stockyard, when one of the stubborn black bulls decided to break away from the herd and headed back toward the range. George kicked his horse and took off after the huge beast, whistling and sending his dog ahead of him. George came around on the far side of the bull "whooping" and slapping his thigh, trying to turn him back towards the herd as the dog was barking and nipping at the bull's heels. Suddenly, without warning, instead of turning back towards the herd, the bull charged right into George's horse, throwing his massive head into the horse's ribs, sending George and his mount toppling to the ground in a mess of flailing legs and dust.

George felt the world flip as he was slammed to the ground with such great force that it took his breath away. As he tried to suck in air he choked and coughed. His eyes blurred and he squeezed them closed and opened them again trying to see. His horse was stunned as well, as he lay on top of George's leg.

Clancy was not far behind George when the bull made the charge and was thrown and pinned under his horse. The bull ran a ways further, then slid to a stop, shaking his horns as clouds of dust billowed around him. The bull turned to charge George and his horse again, who were still struggling to get up. George's dog was ferociously barking in front of the bull, protecting George, as the bull pawed the ground and put his head down, preparing to charge again. Snorting wildly, the bull stared at its target with raging black eyes. Clancy saw George struggling to get up. *Get up!* screamed Clancy in his mind. But George didn't move. Something was wrong. Clancy let out a "whoop," spurring his horse, and took his lasso and swung it in the air above his head, galloping towards the bull. *Dear Lord! Make my aim sure!* he insistently prayed.

The rest of the group watched in horror, too far away to get to George in time to help him. George's horse got to his feet and bolted away in fear as the bull charged towards George. Clancy only had one shot to lasso the bull before it reached the man on the ground. He threw his lasso hard and saw it land over the bull's horns. In one fluid motion he yanked the lasso tight, cinching it around the base of the horns, and quickly wrapped the rope around his saddle horn as he pulled his horse to a sliding halt. The lasso snapped tight and pulled the bull's head sideways, flipping the bull's legs out from under him, throwing him to the ground only yards from George. The bull never knew what happened. One second he was charging and the next he was down on the ground, eating dust.

The bull struggled to get to his feet, and before he could, Clancy had dismounted and grabbed the rope, looping it around the bull's front and back hooves, hog-tying it in place. The bull snorted and blew as it struggled to get up but was unable to get free. George's dog barked and growled at the bull, pacing around him, keeping watch. Confused, the bull finally lay still, breathing hard, trying to figure out what to do next. Clancy made sure the bull wasn't going to move and looked over as George lay back on the ground, overcome with relief at not being trampled or gored to death.

Ed rode up to George and jumped down off his horse to see if he was all right. Ed looked at Clancy who tipped his head to confirm that he had the bull managed. "Are you all right?" Ed asked, kneeling beside George, who was blinking and staring blankly off in the distance.

"I think my leg is broke," George said through gritted teeth. The pain was excruciating in his left leg below the knee.

Ed looked down at George's legs, and sure enough, the left one was clearly broken, not laying at a normal angle. "Don't move. I'll get help and we'll take you to the doctor. Do you hurt anywhere else?" he asked, making a quick assessment of George's head and body.

"No, I don't think so, just my leg," George said, shaking in pain.

Ed took off his overcoat and placed it over George to keep him warm.

Joy rode up and jumped down from her horse. "What can I do to help?" she asked Ed, as she kneeled beside George.

"Stay with him and keep him calm while I go get help," Ed said, mounting his horse and spurring him into a full gallop towards town.

Three of Clancy's fellow cowboys came to help with the bull, putting more ropes around the bull's horns and keeping his one leg hobbled so he could be taken to the stockyard safely. They let the bull get up and rejoin the rest of the herd before they headed out. There was no more that they could do for George, and the animals needed to get moving if they were going to make it on time to be loaded on the evening train. Clancy sent George's dog with them and waved them off as they began to move the herd again.

Clancy came over to kneel beside George. "You're going to be Ok, George. Just hold on and we'll get you to town. Doc will be able to get you some pain medicine and set your leg," he said, patting George on the shoulder.

George looked at Clancy and through gritted teeth, muttered, "You saved my life. I thought I was a goner for sure." Then closed his eyes and tried to block out the pain. "Thank you," he whispered with a grimace.

"You're welcome. I just happened to be in the right place when it all happened. With God's help I was able to lasso that bull just in the nick of time. Thank God that He was watching over you," Clancy said, feeling great awe at the perfectly timed events. One second later and George would have been trampled or gored to death and that really shook him up. Before Clancy could think about it any further, he focused on what needed to be done next. "Joy, keep him calm and I'll get something to brace his leg with so we can move him when Ed gets back with Doc." Clancy turned and went to look for two straight sticks to brace the leg. It took a few minutes to find the right size and length he needed. Grabbing some rawhide out of his saddle bag, he went running back to George.

"Ok, George, I'm going to take a closer look, I'll have to cut your pants, so hold still so I don't hurt you," Clancy said. He had seen this done while on cattle drives when a cowboy broke his leg. He took out his knife and carefully cut the bottom of George's pants and long johns up to his thigh, revealing the break just below the knee. Luckily the bone hadn't broken through the skin. The skin was discoloring quickly, and the leg was swelling as it rested at an unnatural angle. Clancy gave George a piece of rawhide to bite on while he straightened the leg. "Ok, hang on George, this is going to smart somethin' fierce," Clancy said, and waited until George nodded his head while biting on the rawhide, signaling his readiness.

"Joy, I need you to help hold the sticks in place as soon as I get his leg straightened. Then I'll secure it with the rawhide." Clancy took a deep breath. "All right, here goes." Clancy braced himself for the pain he knew George would feel.

Quickly and carefully Clancy pulled George's leg straight, putting the bone back in place as best he could. George let out a loud groan as he clenched his teeth on the leather until he finally passed out from the pain. Joy gasped and cringed at the sound of the bone slipping back into place. She tried hard not to be sick or cry out in hysterics, it was so gruesome. It hurt her to see George in so much pain.

"Ok Joy, hold them right here," Clancy instructed. Placing the sticks along the leg, he slipped the rawhide underneath, wrapping it around twice, and secured it, placing one above and one below the break as Joy held them steady.

George's muscles relaxed with his leg being realigned. With his eyes still closed he began to breathe more evenly. His eyes partly opened as he came to. "Thank you," was all he could muster before he closed his eyes again. The exhaustion from pain was taking over.

A wagon was coming towards them fast, signaled by the dust billowing in the distance. It was Ed with the doctor.

"George, the Doc is almost here," Clancy said in a calm reassuring voice. Looking over at Joy he noticed how pale she looked around the mouth.

"Joy, can you get my canteen?" Clancy asked, trying to get her away from the scene.

Joy blinked a few times before she registered the request. "Sure," she said numbly, and got up to go to Clancy's horse. She handed the canteen to Clancy, who gave George a drink of water and handed it back to her as Ed pulled the wagon up beside them. The doctor and two other men jumped down from the back of the rig carrying a stretcher. While the doctor started his examination the others got the stretcher ready and waited for Doc to determine if it was safe to move George. With the doctor's "go-ahead," all the men carefully lifted him onto the stretcher and carried him to the wagon. George moaned and grimaced, trying not to cry out with the pain.

"Good job on splinting the leg, Clancy," Doc said, as they lifted George into the wagon and set him on a mattress that had been placed in back.

Ed climbed into the wagon bed to ride with George and let one of the other men drive the team. They had a few bumpy miles to go before George would be able to rest in the doctor's office. He would do what he could to help ease the jarring of the rig and he used his coat as a pillow to elevate the leg.

"Mabel," George muttered weakly as he reached out toward the campsite.

"Joy and I will go back to camp and get Mabel and bring her to town," Clancy told George, as he gave his outstretched hand a parting squeeze before the driver slapped the reins of the team and the wagon pulled away.

"Here's your canteen," Joy said, staring in the distance toward the wagon as it sped toward town, leaving a dust trail behind it. Her legs began to shake, and her knees suddenly felt weak as the world began to spin and darkness closed in around her vision.

Clancy caught her as she started to sink to the ground.

"Take some deep breaths, Joy," she heard Clancy say. Forcing herself to obey, she took a deep breath and then another, opening her eyes to see Clancy holding her as she lay on the dry prairie grass.

"What happened?" she asked in a daze.

"You fainted, my dear," he said, smoothing her blonde hair away from her face as she lifted her head.

"Oh—I guess I must have," Joy said, looking up at him, trying to clear her mind. "It was so scary seeing George, with his leg a mess and in so much pain. I've never seen anything so awful in all my life," Joy said, sitting up with his help. She put her hand to her head that started spinning again.

"I'm sorry you had to go through that, but I really needed your help." Clancy hated that she had been so traumatized.

The dizziness eased a little. "Thank you for catching me," she said, smiling up at him as he kneeled beside her.

"I'll catch you any time." Clancy smiled and kissed her on the forehead. "Can you stand?"

"Yes, I think so."

Clancy took her hand and put her arm over his shoulders, then wrapped his arm around her waist and easily helped her stand. "We should get to camp and tell them about George as soon as possible. But only if you are sure you're OK," he said, feeling an urgency to get the word to George's wife.

"I'll be all right," she said, holding onto Clancy's

arm.

Clancy steadied her. "I think you should ride with me." He looked her in the eyes and his heart ached to protect her from anything ever hurting her. Watching her pass out had scared him more than seeing George's broken leg. "I don't want you to fall off and have to take you to the doctor too," he said, forcing the worry from his face with a small smile.

Joy smiled weakly back at him as she nodded in agreement, "All right, let's just get going. Poor Mabel will want to be with him," Joy said, imagining if it had been Clancy that was injured.

With her arm over his shoulders, Clancy led her to his horse. Clancy put his hands around her waist and helped Joy up into his saddle. Quickly he tied her horse to his. Holding the saddle horn, he swung up behind Joy and took the reins from her, then gently kicked his horse into a trot back to camp with Midnight trailing behind.

Joy's head began to clear with the cool air rushing by as they rode in the lowering sunlight on that late autumn afternoon. Clancy's strong arms held her tight, making her feel safe and secure.

They made it back to camp in good time. Mabel came running when she saw the two of them on one horse and began crying when she heard the news.

"Oh, my poor George," she wept. "Thank heavens he's alive. It could have been so much worse. Thank you, Clancy, for saving his life," she said, hugging him.

With the wagon hitched, Cassie, Joy, and Clancy

climbed into the rig to bring Mabel back to town to be with George.

Kathy and Patrick decided to break camp. They knew the others would be hours before returning. The rest of the neighbors packed up as well, feeling the desire to be home with their loved ones. It took some time to gather up everything and repack the wagons. Patrick was able to get the big things loaded and drove the Havoc's wagon back to their home with Kathy. Back at the Havoc ranch, Kathy and Patrick unloaded the bedding and gear, then headed to the Hartford's to unload their things and heat up supper. They presumed that would be where everyone would end up, once George was taken care of.

***

Mabel and the others arrived at the doctor's office just as George's leg had been set and braced.

"George!" Mabel called out, racing into the doctor's office.

"We're back here, Mabel," called Ed, from the examination room.

Mabel entered, seeing George on the examination table with his leg wrapped and his eyes closed, and rushed to his side.

"Oh, George, my dear George," she cried, kissing his hand and cheeks, covering them in tears.

Doctor Ward put his hand on her shoulder. "I've given him some pain medicine. He'll be sleeping for a while," he said compassionately.

"Will he be all right, Doc?" she asked as tears ran

down her cheeks.

"I've set the break. It was a bad one, but should heal with time. I think you should take him home now while the pain medicine is working."

Mabel nodded her head, as her mind filled with worry.

"I'll come out to your place in the morning to check on him. Till then, keep the leg elevated and if you can find some ice, that'll help with the pain and swelling."

"We've got ice," said Ed standing nearby with his arm around Cassie. Ed felt relieved to be with her after such an unsettling day, relieved that he was able to convince her not to be riding in her pregnancy.

"He needs to stay off of it for six weeks at least, maybe longer to heal properly." As Doc got a bottle from the medicine cabinet he added, "You can give him some of this for the pain. Mix a teaspoon of powder in a glass of water and only give it when his pain is really bad," he said, handing Mabel the bottle.

"Aunt Mabel, we should get him home. Ed and Clancy can help carry him into the house," Cassie said, hugging her aunt as tears were gathering in her eyes. She loved her Uncle George so much. She couldn't imagine how horrible it would have been if Clancy hadn't stopped the bull.

Clancy stood at the end of the table watching the women crying, wanting to assist somehow. He thought of what this would mean for the Hartford ranch without George able to work it. That's when he had an idea. "I'd be happy to come out to the place and help carry him inside. And I can even help with the chores and things," he said, pausing to let Mrs. Hartford consider his offer. When she didn't immediately refuse, he went on, "I could help out for as long as needed. I would just need to let my boss know I'll be taking a couple of months off. I'm sure he'll understand." Clancy felt bad for this family. He knew how long it would take George to get back to fully caring for the ranch and wanted to help out.

Mabel stared at him in awe as she wiped tears away. She hadn't had time to think of how they would manage the ranch without George working. She was very grateful for the offer.

"Thank you Clancy, that would be very kind of you." Mabel felt a weight lift from her shoulders. Then she suggested, "You could stay in the spare bedroom while you're helping out. And we'll happily pay you for your services."

Clancy smiled at Mabel as she gripped George's hand in hers and kissed it.

"We can work out the details later," Clancy said, pleased she was considering his offer.

"Mabel, I can come over and help too," Ed said with relief, grateful for Clancy and his generosity. It would have been very difficult to run his ranch and George's by himself.

"Thank you, Ed, but I think with Clancy's help we should be all right," Mabel said, reaching out and squeezing each of their hands.

"Aunt Mabel, I think you're going to have your hands full taking care of Uncle George. I can come and help with cooking and cleaning," Cassie offered, understanding full well what it entailed to take care of someone. She'd seen it many times when she and her mother helped care for those who were ill or injured. The extra care of an incapacitated family member was a real strain on the rest of the family. It took everyone pitching in to lighten the burden.

Doctor Ward stepped back to check George's pulse. "I don't think that's a good idea, Cassie. I don't want you to be doing more than you already are this late in your pregnancy," he said.

Joy blurted out, "I can help! I can work half days at the shop and help out at the ranch the rest of the day. I know Bart and Bea would be fine with it." Joy loved Cassie like a sister and would do anything to help keep her and the baby healthy.

"And I could take her home in the evening after supper," suggested Clancy, helping to sell the idea.

Mabel was quietly thinking for a moment before she answered, "Yes, I guess that would work. Thank you, Joy. Thank you, Clancy." Looking around at all her loved ones and friends, she smiled with relief. "Now, let's get George home and we can work out the details there. Thank you for all your help, Doctor Ward," she said, warmly shaking his hand.

***

Once the men had carefully loaded George in the back of Mabel's wagon, they drove slowly home as the sun was setting in the sky. Leaving the others, Clancy rode over to his boss's house to talk to him and pack his belongings in a bag to take to the Hartford's ranch. Clancy hurried back to make it to the Hartford's in time to help carry George into the house.

Patrick had his arm around Kathy's shoulders as they walked out of the Hartford's house and met the wagon in the yard.

"How's George?" Kathy asked Joy, who sat beside the pale middle-aged man who had just hours ago been a picture of health.

Joy climbed out of the back and hugged her. "He's going to be OK, Ma, but he'll need a lot of help, and so will Mabel."

Kathy looked up at Patrick with concern in her eyes. She couldn't imagine how horrible she would feel if Patrick had been hurt. *Poor George and Mabel,* she thought.

Ed climbed out of the wagon bed. "We'll need your help, Sheriff O'Malley. If you can hold the end of the stretcher, the three of us can carry him in. Clancy and I can take the head and you take the feet," suggested Ed as they pulled the stretcher with George on it down to the end of the wagon.

George moaned with the movement, still in a semi-conscious, medication-induced stupor.

Mabel had climbed down from the front of the wagon and was standing by. "George dear, we're home now. They have to carry you into the house. Hold on just a little longer," she said as she took his hand. He turned his head toward her voice and groaned, then relaxed again.

"We'd better get moving. I think the medicine is

wearing off," said Clancy.

Cassie hurried inside, opened the bedroom door, and pulled back the covers on Aunt Mabel's bed. The men carefully carried George in and gently lifted him into bed. Once they left, Cassie and Mabel helped him out of his dusty clothes and into his nightshirt. Kathy brought in a bowl of water and a cloth and Mabel sponged his face and hands, then propped his broken leg on a pillow and tucked the blankets around him. The crease between his eyebrows smoothed and his breathing evened. He appeared to relax and fall asleep peacefully now that he was home and in bed.

Kathy came back into the bedroom. "Supper is ready if you would like to eat now. Patrick and I packed up camp, as did the others, and everything is already put away. So, you don't need to worry about that," she told Mabel as she walked to where Mabel sat on the edge of the bed, holding George's hand. Kathy squeezed Mabel's shoulder, hoping to reassure her.

Mabel smiled up at Kathy. "That was very thoughtful of you both. I think we could all do with something to eat. Would you mind bringing mine in here? I want to be here when George wakes," Mabel said.

"I can do that. I'll be right back." A few minutes later Kathy was back with soup and biscuits and a cup of coffee. "As soon as George wakes up let me know so I can bring him some too," Kathy said as she left the room and softly closed the door.

The others were chatting excitedly about the day and were dishing up supper when Kathy returned.

Mabel was thankful for the privacy. She kneeled at George's bedside and began to quietly weep, holding George's hand in hers. "Oh, dear Lord, please bless this dear man of mine. I love him so much; he is everything to me. Please help him heal quickly without complications, and bless him with strength to endure the pain. I am so grateful that his life was spared today and for the good people who helped him. Bless them for their efforts. I praise Thee dear Lord and Thy protective hand. In the name of Jesus Christ. Amen," she prayed with deep heartfelt emotion. As she ended her plea, she heard George whisper "amen." She opened her eyes as George pulled her hand to his lips and kissed it.

"George, you're awake," she said smiling with tears rolling down her cheeks. "I was so scared when I heard you'd been hurt. I was afraid I might lose you."

In a shaky, weak voice George responded, "Mabel, darling, I'm going to be fine. It was a miracle I wasn't hurt worse." He tried to smile at her. "God was watching over us and sent Clancy to help me. My prayers were heard."

"Thank God," Mabel said as tears trailed down her cheeks and crossed the edge of the smile that was beginning to form from hearing his voice.

George closed his eyes and fell back to sleep.

Mabel stood, kissed him on his forehead, then took her food out to join the others.

"How is he?" Cassie asked as Mabel came into the kitchen.

"George woke up for a minute and is sleeping

again. He seems to be a little better. I think he'll be good for a while," Mabel said, taking a place at the table as Kathy and Cassie gave her reassuring smiles.

"I'll go get some ice from the icehouse; that should help with the pain and swelling," Ed said as he finished eating. "Then Cass, I think we should get you and Ma and Joy back home." It had been an exhausting two days for all of them.

Ed left as Joy and Kathy began clearing the table after everyone finished eating.

Joy began heating water for the dishes and said, "Ma, I've offered to help here with things for a while."

"Oh, you have," Kathy said as she scraped the plates Patrick brought to her.

"I can work half days at the shop and then ride out here to help with meals and chores, then ride home each night. Mabel will be too busy caring for George to do everything she needs to do," Joy explained.

"And I'm going to stay on and help here full-time with the ranch while George is healing," Clancy informed Kathy as he brought dishes to the sink. "So, I can take her home at night, so you don't worry about her riding home alone in the dark."

Mabel chimed in, "Kathy, I'll let you have the final say. I don't want to take Joy away from her job and money you both need. But I can pay her wages. It would only be for a short time; I'm sure George will be up and around in a few weeks," Mabel hoped.

"Of course I'll agree, Mabel. If she wants to do it, then I think she should. We will all help as much as possible," Kathy said with a smile, wiping the dishes dry.

"Thank you, Ma," Joy said giving her mother a hug. She smiled at Clancy as she thought of all the time they would get to spend together on the ranch and the time alone every evening on their way back to town.

"Thank you all for your help today. I know George appreciates it as much as I do. God bless good family and friends," Mabel said, getting teary-eyed.

Cassie gave Mabel a hug and whispered in her ear. "God bless you and George. I love you both so much." Cassie felt so blessed to have her aunt and uncle in her life and didn't want to imagine what it would have been like without them.

Patrick stretched and yawned, then politely thanked everyone for their company and excused himself. "I need to get back to town," he said.

"I'll walk you out," said Kathy as she wiped her hands on her apron.

Patrick said goodbye to everyone and went to the door and put on his coat and hat, then helped Kathy with her coat, and they walked outside together.

It was getting colder now that the sun was down, and they walked closely together to his horse. Patrick put his arms around Kathy's waist and hugged her as she put her arms around his neck. "Goodnight, Kathy dear," he whispered in her ear. "I love you."

"I love you too, Patrick, sleep well, darling," she said, stepping back slowly, reluctant to let him go.

"I'll see you tomorrow, and the day after that and the day after that," Patrick said, smiling at her. "And soon to never be parted again." Pulling her back, he kissed her one last time before he climbed on his horse and rode away.

Chapter 16

Thanksgiving 1869

As November arrived, the first signs of winter began to appear in Cheyenne. With each passing week, it seemed that winter was making an effort to stay. For days the homestead would enjoy calm sunny blue skies and then one morning they'd awake to icy winds and flurries of snow that swirled and drifted across the homestead and prairie. That's how it was on that last week in November 1869, when Thanksgiving came. Outside the Havoc's cottage on that dark early morn, a bitter winter wind howled, finding any crack it could to sneak through, trying to reach those slumbering inside.

Cassie awoke shivering as the tormented wind whistled through the eaves and rattled the windows. Even with the thick blankets and woolen nightclothes, the chill in the air reached her skin. In seconds Ed was there, wrapping his arm around her large round stomach, pressing his chest against her back, warming her with his body and loving embrace.

Ed softly whispered in her ear, "Happy Thanksgiving, love."

"Happy Thanksgiving, darling," she whispered back, snuggling closer to him, seeking his warmth and comfort. "Do you know what I'm thankful for?" she asked sleepily.

"Hmm, what?" he asked, kissing her ear, and taking a deep breath of her sweet scent.

Cassie smiled at Ed's tender kiss. "This amazing man named Edward. Maybe you've heard of him? He's gentle and loving, strong and brave. He knows exactly what to do and say, and I love him with all my heart," she said, putting her arm over his and rubbing his hand as it rested against her.

"Wow, that's a lucky man. Well, I guess anyone who could win your affections deserves everything he gets," Ed said, kissing her neck.

Cassie lightly chuckled as his moustache tickled her neck. His kisses were warming her as well.

"You're the most wonderful woman, Cass," he said placing another kiss on her neck. "I thank heaven every day that you came to Cheyenne and rescued me."

Cassie slowly turned over in bed to face him, placing a hand on his cheek. "You say the sweetest things," she said dreamily.

"And you make my heart sing with *your* sweet words. My heart is in tune with you, that's how I know what you want and need. I try every day to be deserving of your love," Ed said, pulling her close as he caressed her back.

Cassie was touched by his words and kissed him passionately. "Oh, you'll get what you deserve," she said smiling, and kissed him again.

***

George and Mabel were in the kitchen having coffee when Clancy came in from doing the morning chores. He set down the bucket of fresh, still warm milk on the bench by the door and removed his gloves, hat, and coat, shaking a dusting of snow from off them before hanging them up.

"Good morning, Clancy," said Mabel, as she went to get another cup from the cupboard for him. "Happy Thanksgiving."

"Happy Thanksgiving," he said as he walked through the kitchen with the milk pail and set it in the sink to be strained. "It's a bitter cold day today." He blew on his hands to try to warm them. "There's about four inches of new snow out there and the wind's really kicking it up," he said as he washed his hands in the dish pan of warm soapy water. "Mmm. The coffee smells great," he said, as Mabel filled him a cup of coffee and handed it to him after he'd dried his hands.

"What time are you going to go get Kathy and Joy?" asked George as he finished his morning Bible reading.

"I told Joy I would be there at nine o'clock. The shop is closed today and she wants to be here as early as possible, to help with the cooking," Clancy said, as he took a sip of his coffee and sat down at the table to wait for breakfast.

"It's hard to believe that Kathy and Patrick will

be married this Saturday. It's so exciting. They both thought love was a thing of the past and now look how happy they are together," said Mabel with a smile as she sliced potatoes into a hot skillet, while the eggs and bacon sizzled.

"I'm sure Patrick is glad the elections are over, and he's officially Sheriff now. His job is secure, so they can relax and enjoy the wedding and honeymoon," George said with a smile.

"You know who else looks happy together?" Mabel asked, smiling at Clancy who grinned back at her. "You and Joy. And we are so happy for you, too. You're so good for each other," Mabel said as she came over to set the table with the stack of plates and utensils in her hands.

Clancy blushed slightly and smiled over his coffee at George, who gave him a wink. "I agree, Aunt Mabel," he said, still trying to get used to calling her that. It was at her insistence that he call her Aunt Mabel; she felt it too formal to call them Mr. and Mrs. Hartford after how close they had become. Clancy felt like family to them, she'd said. "I want to ask Joy to marry me, and I'd like to do it soon. Since you've hired me permanent-like, as your ranch foreman, I now feel I can finally provide for her," Clancy said with a grin on his face. "There's just one more thing to work out before I ask her. I just need to secure us a place to live."

George had already been contemplating Clancy and Joy's living situation if they should happen to marry. He closed his Bible and looked at Clancy seriously. "You know, as soon as you get married, you could both live here. We'll include it as part of your room and board. We've enjoyed having you both here so much. It would be hard for us to have you leave now. We don't know what we would have done without you. So, it makes perfect sense for you to just live here. Unless you don't feel it would be good as newlyweds to live with us old folks," reasoned George with a teasing smile. "We'd understand completely if you don't," he added with a straight face. "Of course, it's your decision. But know that we would be thrilled to have you both here as part of our family," he said warmly.

Clancy thought for a moment, touched by their offer and their kindness. "Thank you, I guess that would work. Seems like it would be about what it's like now, except we would all be sleeping under the same roof," Clancy reasoned, and blushed a little as he realized what he'd just said. He quickly went on, hoping they didn't notice. "Besides, I think Joy really likes it here, at least that's what she's told me. I know she enjoys your company, and on days when I'm on the range for long hours, I'm sure she'll appreciate it even more. But I'll ask her, just to make sure," he said, smiling as he thought of marrying Joy and living here on the beautiful ranch, raising youngsters.

Mabel spoke up, "You two talk about it and what-ever you decide will be fine with us. But know for sure, we love you both and consider you family," she said as she put the food on the table. She was so thankful for Clancy; he was able to run the ranch on his own. She didn't know what they would have done without him. Having the two young folks on the ranch would really liven things up around the place. Clancy's stories and jokes kept them constantly entertained. When Cassie moved out, there had been a void, which Joy and Clancy had filled. Now they couldn't imagine life without them around.

With Joy working half days at the Men's Shop and then coming out to the ranch to help with the meals and housekeeping, she and Mabel had grown very close. Mabel felt as though Joy was like a daughter, just like Cassie had become. Joy was cheerful, bubbly, and talkative, especially when Clancy was around. She practically glowed in his presence, as he did in hers. Even the gloomiest days seemed to brighten as the two couples spent time together.

George and Mabel had enjoyed watching the love grow between Joy and Clancy. Their company helped distract George from the monotony as he spent time recovering. He wasn't used to sitting around in the house all day. As his pain began to improve, so did his desire to do more than he should. He still needed more help than he liked, and Mabel did her best to keep him resting, but he was constantly trying to do things for himself. The crutches the doctor gave him helped with walking, but he was still not supposed to put any weight on the leg.

Once Mabel caught him trying to go outside to the outhouse by himself and had made it down the steps before she got to him. She pleaded with him not to do that again. He could have fallen on the slick steps and hurt himself further. He realized she was right, since he had almost done that exact thing. It was really testing his patience, waiting for the six weeks to be over so he could start using his leg again. At first, he could only lay in bed due to the pain, but then being in bed became unbearable. He tried for days sitting in his parlor chair reading, and then tried to find things to do to keep his mind and hands busy. But soon he began feeling like a caged animal.

One day, Clancy brought in a leather harness for George to repair. And while he worked at the kitchen table, Clancy had a wonderful idea; he suggested George use the extra leather to make a gun holster. Clancy showed George his "California" gun holster, also known as "The Slim Jim," that he had gotten in Texas on one of his cattle drives. George was very impressed with the workmanship and became inspired to make a similar one. With his leather tools and some new stamps, he was able to create a beautiful variation with a floral rosette pattern in the corner and stamped edges. He even made the holster belt with loops for extra cartridges. Mabel was happy to have him working on something he felt passionate about again, even if it meant giving up her kitchen table for large parts of the day.

Joy and Clancy found lots of time to talk and work together over those weeks. Joy could imagine herself being married to Clancy. She cooked with him specifically in mind, finding out his favorite foods and meals. Joy even did his laundry, which he felt bad about. But he was always quick to lend her a hand with carrying heavy things. They were a good team. Every night after supper, Clancy hitched up the horses and placed a hot rock in the blankets at the foot of the surrey, and drove Joy home, all bundled up together. They enjoyed the alone time even if it was cold. It gave them a chance to talk about the day and an excuse to snuggle, Clancy's strong arm around her, pulling her close to him as she listened to him talk about the ranch and cattle, and she talked about the sewing she was doing at the shop. Sometimes she would get him to tell her another story about his experiences on the cattle drives. Each day she looked forward to seeing him and never wanted it to end. But she knew eventually it would. George would get better, and Mabel would no longer need Joy to come out. Joy envied her mother; she wished Clancy would ask her to marry him. Then she would never have to spend a day apart from him. Joy wondered what he was waiting for. She was sure she had made herself understood that she loved him. She had told him on numerous occasions. And lately it had been every night after their goodnight kiss, she would tell him that she loved him. She knew he loved her, he told her at least every night and sometimes more often.

**

Later that morning Clancy drove into town to pick up Kathy, Patrick, and Joy in the sled. It was perfect conditions for using the sled; the four inches of new snow was now hard packed from the wind. That year, the family and friends were all meeting at the Hartford's for Thanksgiving dinner. Clancy had been invited by his Aunt and Uncle Holden for Thanksgiving dinner but had politely declined so he could spend it with Joy and her family. Once Mabel had heard that he had been invited to the Holden's, she felt bad and invited them to come as well. They declined the invitation for dinner but said they would all come out for pie in the afternoon, that way they could all visit with each other.

As Clancy drove to town his mind raced with thoughts about how he was going to ask Joy to marry him. He had been waiting for the perfect moment, and with his new job as the ranch foreman, he felt ready to propose. The sound of the horses' hooves crunching through the snow seemed to echo his pounding heart.

Clancy pulled up to the shop front and saw Joy in the upstairs window and waved. His heart skipped a beat as he thought of what was to come. She waved back and turned away to get her coat and things. With shaking hands he jumped out of the sled and tied the horses to the hitching rail and met Joy as she was coming down the back stairs of the apartment.

"Happy Thanksgiving," Clancy said, giving Joy a quick hug and kiss on the cheek. He thought she looked lovely with her hair down in blonde ringlets pulled up on the sides and secured with a bow in the back. Her knitted blue hat covered the top of her head and her ears and tied under her chin. She wore a long grey wool coat and mittens and a green dress. He liked the green in the dress, it matched the color of her eyes.

"Happy Thanksgiving, Clancy," Joy said with a big smile. "How was the drive this morning?" she asked, as he helped her climb in front and covered her with the thick blankets. She immediately felt the sting of the wind on her cheeks and nose. Lifting her scarf around her head, she tied it around her neck and tucked the ends down into her coat.

"Beautiful, with the fresh snow. But that cold wind goes right through you, so bundle up good," he said, smiling at her as she finished securing her scarf, and put her hands under the blankets.

Kathy and Sheriff O'Malley came out to the sled with baskets of food, which Clancy quickly took from Kathy. "Happy Thanksgiving," Clancy said as Kathy and Patrick climbed into the back seat of the sled.

"Happy Thanksgiving," they both said cheerfully. Patrick tucked the blankets around them, as Clancy helped put the food on the floor of the sled as Kathy and Patrick snuggled together with Patrick's arm around Kathy's shoulders.

Clancy untied the horses, then climbed in and pulled the blankets around his legs and got the horses going to the Hartford's ranch. As he drove, Kathy and Patrick began talking excitedly about the wedding plans. Again, Joy was wishing she was the one getting married, but she was still happy for her mother and Patrick. They both deserved to have someone to love. So for a moment she allowed herself to daydream of one day getting married.

As they drove on, the couples quieted, keeping

their faces covered as much as possible from the biting wind in the bright white morning. Clancy's mind was racing with anticipation almost as fast as the horses pulled the sleigh, all the while wondering when he would find the right time to ask Joy for her hand in marriage and how he would say it.

"Oh, guess what, Joy? The Hartford's have hired me as their ranch foreman. Permanently," Clancy announced, breaking the silence.

"Oh, Clancy. That's wonderful news," Joy said with excitement. She knew he'd been hoping to become a ranch foreman one day, if not on the Hartford ranch, then another in Cheyenne. Now his dream was coming true. She gave his arm a squeeze under the blankets to let him know how proud she was of him.

***

When they arrived, they could see Ed and Cassie's rig in the yard. As they came to a stop, Mabel came out, her shawl wrapped around her as she stood on the porch to greet them.

"Welcome everyone!" Mabel bubbled, as the last of her guests arrived. She was overjoyed to have so many friends and family at her home, and greeted each one with a hug as they came up the porch steps.

George was also in high spirits. As he sat in his parlor chair in front of the roaring fire with his leg up on the footstool, he invited Clancy and Sheriff O'Malley to come and sit with him and Ed so he could show them his newest holster creation.

Kathy had brought her favorite recipe of

cornbread as well as three pies. With the abundant supply of pumpkins and apples from Cassie's cellar, Kathy was able to create two pumpkin pies and one apple. She had been impressed with Cassie's home-making skills and her hard work, shown by the plentiful cellar that would keep her and Ed supplied for the winter. She appreciated her for her many talents but mostly for how deeply Cassie loved Ed and made him happy again.

With the pies carefully placed, Kathy's arms were free to give the women in the kitchen a hug.

"Happy Thanksgiving," Kathy said. "I see you've made the creamed corn and mashed sweet potatoes that you were talking about," she said admiring the dishes of bright yellow corn and orange potatoes still steaming on top of the stove.

"Yes, and I even brought a bottle of my dill pickles you like," Cassie said to Kathy with a smile.

Joy removed her coat and hat and joined the women in the kitchen "I can't wait to enjoy your pickles, Cassie. Someday when I get my own garden, I want to bottle pickles just like you," said Joy admiring the bottle of sour pickles Cassie had put up that fall.

Kathy, Mabel, Cassie, and Joy continued to chat in the kitchen as they finished preparing the dishes they would be serving. And as they cooked, they talked about Kathy's wedding, work at the shop, and Cassie's pregnancy along with the things women talk about when they get together.

The men sat beside the fire talking about guns, holsters, cattle, local government and the things

Western men talk about as they wait for the biggest meal of the year.

Every so often, one of the men would venture into the kitchen and see how close they were coming to eating time. Their mouths had been watering and stomachs growling for an hour and were nearly crazed with the delicious smells. And every time, one of the women would teasingly scold them, and shoo them out of the kitchen, to let them finish cooking. Reminding them that they would call them when it was ready.

Finally, in what seemed like another hour, the turkey was done. The mashed potatoes, stuffing, giblet gravy, sweet potatoes, creamed corn, cornbread, biscuits, and dill pickles were set on the table that was covered in a pretty white tablecloth. Every space on the table was either holding a dish of food, or an empty plate that waited to be filled.

The house was full of delicious smells and cheerful company. There was an excitement in the air as everyone took their seats and held hands for the blessing. George sat at the head of the table with Mabel to his left, and the rest of their beloved family took their seats. They all bowed their heads as George said a wonderful blessing of thanksgiving for friends and family, for a bounteous harvest, and mostly for the Savior's life and sacrifice. There were a few tears by the end of the prayer as they each thought of their own reason for thanks that year.

Before they began eating the feast, Mabel spoke up. "I have a wonderful idea. I would like to start a new tradition. I think it would be nice to go around the table and say what we are each thankful for," she said with a smile and looked to her husband. "George, would you like to go first?" she asked, patting his hand.

"Sure, dear," George said, taking a second to collect his thoughts and emotions before he started. "I have so many things to be thankful for." He cleared his throat and shook his head as he tried to keep his voice steady. "This month has been a challenging one, and my heart is very full of gratitude for my blessings. Most importantly, as I mentioned in the prayer, is my Savior, Jesus Christ. Next and just as importantly, I'm thankful for my lovely wife and best friend Mabel," his voice wavered as he said her name and squeezed her hand as he paused. Then he looked over at Cassie and continued, "Cassie, I'm so thankful you came to live here with us. You bring us so much joy and happiness, just like the daughter we never had. And I'm thankful for Clancy saving my life so that I can see your baby when it's born," he said, nodding to Clancy. "And of course, I'm thankful for all of you dear friends who are really like family to me," he said smiling, and then motioned for Mabel to go next. "Your turn, dear," he said encouraging her as she wiped a tear away.

"I could say the exact same thing as you did, George," she said, looking around the table. "I really do feel so grateful for the good life I have been blessed with. The knowledge of my Savior, and a loving husband who means everything to me." She paused and looked at Cassie. "Cassie, you coming here has been a God send; even though it has been a hard year for us, we still feel blessed to have each other. And now look at how our family is growing. We are truly blessed to have you all in our lives," she said, smiling as a tear rolled down her cheek.

Cassie's tears had begun during the prayer and continued as she thought of her parents and brothers and sisters she had lost. Ed put his arm around her, trying to comfort her.

"I'll go next," Cassie said, sniffing. "Or else I won't be able to if I wait." She took a deep breath and looked around the table. "I'm so thankful for all of you. When I came here, I thought I had nothing left. I was wrong, I have even more, and I'm so grateful. I found love here, love from Aunt Mabel and Uncle George, my second parents who care for me as a daughter. I found love of a good friend, a kindred spirit, my Madeline, so much like a sister. And most miraculously I found true love and healing through Edward, my hero. I'll forever be grateful for him loving me and our baby," she said, looking at Ed, smiling as he gave her a quick kiss.

Clancy took Joy's hand under the table and gave it a squeeze. He so wanted that with Joy, so much it made his heart ache.

"OK, my turn," Ed said as his throat began to tighten with emotion. "Cass, I'm going to always be grateful for you coming into my life. Every day I thank the Lord for the love you give me and the blessing you are to me. I'm also thankful you'll be making me a father soon. That leads to my parents, who I'm thankful adopted me and taught me everything I know, and still teach me," he said looking at his ma, smiling and reaching out and squeezing her hand. And then looking at Joy he continued, "And I'm thankful for my wonderful brothers and sisters, some of whom aren't here or with us anymore. And of course, all you wonderful friends," he said, with a little waver in his voice as he looked down. Cassie put her head on his shoulder and patted his hand that was resting on his knee. Ed looked back up at his mother who was wiping her tears away.

Then Kathy began, "Thank you, Edward. I'm also thankful for my family, for Ed marrying Cassie, a lovely woman that makes him so happy and will soon be making me a grandma," Kathy said, smiling at Cassie through her tears. "For Joy and Beth, for being so helpful through these past years, staying strong and cheerful even though I know it was hard. I'm thankful for those who are gone now, who gave me so many good memories. And now I'm very thankful for Patrick, for seeing something special in me, and loving me. I'm grateful the Lord saw fit to bless me again with a wonderful companion to love and spend the rest of my life with," Kathy said as Patrick hugged her.

Patrick released her and started next. "Kathy, you are what I'm most thankful for. I never knew I could be so happy. You are what I've always wanted; even though I wasn't searching, I found you. I'm thankful I get to share my life with you, darling, I love you," he said and hugged her small frame again and kissed the top of her head. Kathy's tears of joy rolled down her cheeks as she embraced him.

Joy cleared her throat as she felt it was her turn. "I'm thankful for my family, especially for my ma. She has been my support and friend my whole life, and the only consolation of having her getting married is that I get another pa. I'm very thankful for you, Patrick, for bringing so much happiness to my mother again. She really is a rare gem," Joy said as a tear spilled over, thinking about how much her mother meant to her. "I'm also thankful for Cassie, for her friendship and for bringing my brother happiness and love. And for the Hartford's; you are wonderful people, just like family. And last but not least, I'm thankful for Clancy, for being my best friend, and for being the wonderful man whom I love," she added, looking down shyly.

Clancy looked down at his hand that she was holding. "Umm," he cleared his throat trying to get the words to come. "Since I came to Cheyenne, I have discovered I have so much to be thankful for. I'm grateful for what my parents taught me; even though my family is far away, I feel like they are right here with me, you are all part of that. I am grateful for the good job George and Mabel have given me. And I'm especially thankful for Joy's love and friendship." Suddenly, overwhelmed with love, he got up from his seat, and got down on one knee, and took Joy's hand, looking deep into her eyes. "I love you so much, and I would be forever grateful, Joy, if you would be my wife. Will you marry me, Joy?" he asked sincerely.

Joy sat with a shocked look on her face and then smiled as new tears filled her eyes. Her heart pounded wildly and overflowed with joy. "Yes, oh yes!" she exclaimed as she wrapped her arms around his neck. "I love you so much, Clancy," she whispered, as tears of joy rolled down her cheeks.

"I love you too, Joy," he whispered as he held her, and his heart swelled almost out of his chest for the love he felt for her. Clancy couldn't believe it. She was going to be his wife.

Everyone around the table sat stunned as they watched Clancy and Joy, and then smiles spread and clapping and congratulations erupted. No one even minded that Thanksgiving dinner was getting cold.

It was a wonderful surprise, even to Clancy, he thought with delight. It had just seemed like the right time. They stood and embraced again. Everyone left their chairs and gathered around the happy couple. The men patted Clancy on the back and shook his hand, wishing him congratulations and good job. He was beaming as he smiled ear to ear. All the women hugged and kissed Joy, some shedding happy tears with her and some squeals too.

Finally, with all the congratulations given, they sat down and began to dish up the food, talking excitedly around the table as Joy and Clancy continued to hold hands.

Joy couldn't believe it. She was really engaged, finally he had asked her. And in the most shocking way. She had never suspected he would do something like that. Joy was so excited. It was almost too good to be true.

As they ate, someone asked when they would be getting married. Clancy hadn't even had a chance to think about that and looked to Joy.

"When would you like to get married?" he asked with a smile, and she shrugged her shoulders. If he had his way, it would have been immediately, but he knew women needed time to plan these things.

"I don't care when. Anytime would suit me perfectly," she said honestly. Joy had never had grand notions of her wedding day, like most women. She wasn't one for frivolous things, Joy was too practical for any of that.

Kathy looked at Patrick and whispered something to him. He smiled and nodded his head.

"Joy, Clancy, would you two be opposed to getting married on Saturday with us? A double wedding would be quite convenient, really. We'll already all be there. The Pastor, the church, and everything is already planned. Unless you want your own wedding day, we would understand," Kathy said smiling.

A new excitement spread through Joy. She looked at Clancy who grinned broadly. "What do you think?" she asked excitedly.

"I'm great with Saturday if you are," he said, not quite believing his luck. Engaged and married in two days.

Joy looked back at her ma. "I guess we'll be getting married on Saturday!" she exclaimed.

"Oh, how wonderful!" Mabel remarked with

exhilaration. "A double wedding. That's such good luck," she said happily.

Joy had a sudden thought. "Oh, what will I wear?" she wondered out loud. Then thought for a second. "I guess I can wear my Sunday dress if you don't mind, Clancy," she said, suddenly realizing how much she needed to do to get ready by Saturday.

Cassie spoke up, "Joy, you can borrow my wedding dress if you want, it should fit perfectly," she said with a smile.

Joy was excited again. "Yes, that would be wonderful. I guess it will all work out just fine," Joy said, smiling with relief.

The rest of their Thanksgiving feast was spent talking about the plans for the two weddings.

"Joy and I will wash the dishes," offered Clancy as they began cleaning the food and dirty dishes from off the table. He really wanted to talk to Joy alone.

Joy looked at him with surprise and saw him wink at her. "Yes, you all go sit down and rest, we'll finish up," Joy said smiling. "I know you are all tired from making all this food, so go sit down and rest," she encouraged.

They all relented as soon as they'd finished putting the food away. Relieved to rest, Cassie, Kathy, and Mabel went and sat down with the men around the fire. Cassie took the rocking chair and put her feet up on a stool Ed brought her. He was so concerned about her health now that she was seven months along.

"Thank you, darling," said Cassie as he sat down

beside her in one of the kitchen chairs.

Ed kissed her on the cheek. "Anything for you, Cass," he said, taking her hand. Lately he had been feeling very protective of her, even more than usual. It scared him to think how fragile she was, and some nights he lay there thinking, *What if something happens to her? What if she loses the baby or heaven forbid, dies?* He couldn't stand it if anything was to happen to her or the baby.

Cassie looked at him as he stared seriously into the fire, seeming to be hundreds of miles away. "Edward, why so solemn?" she asked in a whisper, feeling a little concerned. She caught him like this more and more lately. Cassie wondered if something was wrong, if he wasn't happy. She couldn't figure it out. Ed seemed so happy at times and looked so concerned at others.

Ed broke out of his trance and looked at Cassie and smiled. "Oh, it's nothing Cass. Just thinking about life," he said, trying to reassure her.

Cassie decided she would try and get him to talk about it once they got home. She was getting worried. He'd never kept things from her and now she felt he was.

Chapter 17

Double Wedding

In the kitchen, Joy washed the dishes as Clancy dried them. "So, are you surprised?" he whispered with a grin.

Joy handed him a plate. "I couldn't have been more surprised. I had no idea you were planning that," she whispered back, smiling at him as they stood shoulder to shoulder.

"Me either," he said softly with a chuckle. "I mean, I wanted to ask you today. I just had no idea when the time would be right. But then I heard you say you loved me right in front of everyone and I couldn't hold back," he said, leaning close to her so only she could hear, and then kissed her on the cheek before anyone could see.

Joy blushed and looked over her shoulder to see if anyone was watching them. They all seemed busy visiting and no one looked over. She looked up at Clancy with her green eyes twinkling. "You know, I wondered if you would ever get around to asking me," she said with relief. "I didn't think I could stand to wait any longer, I've wanted to be your wife for so long. And look. Now, we get to be married on Saturday, and I couldn't be happier," she said sweetly.

Clancy said loudly, "I think I need another towel. I'll go and get one in the pantry," he said, winking at her and motioning with his head to follow him. "I'm not sure where they are. Maybe you can show me?" he asked casually.

Joy smiled and blushed as her heart began pounding. "Sure, I'll show you, so you know where to find them next time," she said, following him into the back room off the kitchen.

Once alone in the back room, Clancy turned around and took Joy into his arms and kissed her. Her knees were shaking when he finally released her lips.

Clancy looked deep into her eyes and smoothed a stray blonde hair away from her cheek. "You don't know how long I've wanted you to be my wife. Since the day we met, I've felt the strongest desire to be with you for always. I was more convinced the more I got to know you. I love everything about you, Joy. I wanted to make sure I was able to provide you with a good life. And as soon as that happened, I knew it was time," he said softly as his strong arms held her steady.

Joy stared into his eyes, her arms around his neck, running her fingers through his soft blond hair. "I never want to be apart from you. I felt it too and have dreamed of being your wife for the longest time. Thank the dear Lord for the Hartford's giving you the job permanently," she said, smiling as she memorized the look on his handsome face.

"I was wondering where you would want to live. The Hartford's offered to let us live here with them as part of my pay, being room and board. What do you think?" Clancy asked, searching her expression for any reluctance.

Joy looked down momentarily to think about it and then smiled back up at him. "I think it's a suitable arrangement. I've felt completely at home with them and would rather live here than anywhere else. I just wonder if you would be comfortable with it as newlyweds?" she asked, feeling a little embarrassed mentioning it.

Clancy took a second to think and then answered, "I think for the time being it's our best option, seeing as how we are getting married in two days. Later we can maybe buy our own homestead or buy this one when the Hartford's get older. I see many possibilities," he said with eyes twinkling. All his dreams were coming true, and all in one day it seemed. He had a thought. "If you like, we can go on a honeymoon for a night or two at the hotel." His brow furrowed as he realized an issue. "The only problem is, I need to take care of the livestock since George is still laid up."

"Maybe you can ask Ed to help out for a day or two," she wondered out loud.

"Yes, that could work. If he says yes," he said, and wondered if maybe one of his buddies would as well. He could call in a favor.

"I think we better get back out there before someone comes looking for us," Joy said as she began to sense it getting quieter out in the other room. "I think a night or two would be just fine. I'm sure they will be understanding of that and I'm sure Ed will be able to manage it for a day or two," she said, smiling as he released her slowly. "After that, I am perfectly fine with living here. I'm sure we can find time to be alone," she said, smiling at him as she took his hand and walked to the door.

"Oh, the towel!" Clancy said and started to laugh softly. "Where are they? We can't leave empty-handed," he said with a big grin as he looked around the room for towels.

Joy began to laugh quietly as well. "Right there on the shelf in the corner," she said pointing to them, then turned to go back.

When they returned to the kitchen, they got a few questioning glances and smiles, but everyone was kind enough not to call further attention to them, knowing they needed time alone to talk.

Seeming to be in the clear, Clancy and Joy turned their backs to everyone and started laughing quietly like two kids up to mischief, as they began washing the dishes again.

**

The afternoon sped by as the family and friends relaxed and visited. Each enjoyed the time together sharing stories of past Thanksgivings and were busy making new memories.

Ed could tell Cassie was getting sleepy as her eyes drooped and closed every so often. Lately, he'd noticed Cassie looking exhausted by the middle of the day, and today was no different. He shook her gently when her eyes stayed closed and her head tilted forward as she sat in the rocking chair. She slowly opened her eyes. "You should go lay down and take a nap in Aunt Mabel's room," he said softly.

She tried to protest but then Aunt Mabel overheard and insisted as well.

"Bless your heart Cassie, you look like you need a little rest. You go right into my room and lay down," said Mabel. "We'll wake you up when the Holden's get here," she said kindly.

Cassie smiled weakly as Ed helped pull her out of the rocker, her belly making it harder for her to get up these days. He led her into the bedroom, put a pillow behind her back and pulled a spare blanket over her and kissed her on the forehead. "Go to sleep, my beautiful wife," he said, smoothing her hair with his hand, adoring her beautiful face as it relaxed, and her eyes closed. He would never tire of her angelic face. One last kiss and he left her quietly and shut the door.

An hour later the Holden's arrived. Mr. and Mrs. Holden, their daughters, Christy, Heather, May, Bea, and Bart all came together. Ed went out to greet them as he heard the sleigh with jingling bells. The sun was lowering, and it was cold and windy, but the sky was clear blue, and the sun sparkled off the snow during their drive in the countryside.

"Welcome!" Ed exclaimed, greeting them as they threw off the blankets and he assisted them out. "Glad you could all come out to celebrate today," he said cheerfully. He thought it was such a nice thing, to have a national holiday, to celebrate a day of giving thanks. Most businesses had closed for the day, and the town, he imagined, was quiet for once.

"Happy Thanksgiving!" they said, as they finished getting out of the sled and started for the house.

"Great to see you too," said Bart, shaking Ed's hand. "How is everyone today?" he asked, as he gathered the food from the sleigh and handed some to Ed.

"Everyone is in good health. Cass is a little tired, but that's normal for someone in her condition. How is Bea feeling?" he asked, watching her walk in with her mother and sisters.

Bart followed Ed's glance. "She's doing better, now the morning sickness is gone, I think," Bart said smiling. He loved the thought of being a father.

Cassie came out of the bedroom as soon as she heard the commotion in the front room. "Bea!" she exclaimed as soon as she saw Bea coming through the door. She went to her and gave her a big hug and whispered, "There is big news, I can't wait for you to hear. But I'll let Clancy and Joy tell it as soon as everyone gets into the house," she said quietly, helping her good friend out of her coat and hanging it up on the coat rack. "Welcome, Mrs. Holden, Heather, May and Christy. Happy Thanksgiving," Cassie said as they took off their coats and scarves and things.

Mr. Holden, Bart and Ed came inside carrying the delicious-smelling pies after putting the horses in the corral.

Mabel greeted Mr. Holden and took the pie he

was carrying. "Happy Thanksgiving, so glad you could all come out."

"Wouldn't miss this for the world," said Mr. Holden as he tipped his hat to her before he took it off and went to hang up his hat and coat.

"Ed, let's put the pies over here with the others," directed Mabel as Ed and Bart came in with three more pies.

Bart and Ed set the pies down on the counter with the others. Nine pies would be more than enough for the group. Smiles and loud jovial chatter filled the home, as did the smell of warm pies.

Ed loudly cleared his throat, and when that didn't work, spoke loudly, "Excuse me! Everyone! Clancy and Joy have an announcement to make," he said, getting everyone's attention.

Clancy and Joy took hands and stood in front of the fireplace. "We're getting married on Saturday!" Clancy blurted out.

All the Holden's were shocked and looked back and forth at the two grinning broadly, then cheered for the couple's good news.

"Congratulations, Clancy!" exclaimed Bart, as he shook Clancy's hand and squeezed his arm. "It's about time, good friend," he said chuckling.

"Well, I had some things to get in order first. But the deed is done!" Clancy announced proudly, as he chuckled with his friend.

Bart shook Joy's hand. "Congratulations, both of you. We're very happy for you. So, this Saturday, huh? That doesn't give you much time, does it?" he asked smiling.

"It's fine with me. I don't need a big fancy wedding. As long as we are both there, that's all that matters," said Joy as she wrapped her arm around Clancy's waist, and he put his arm around her shoulders. She looked up at him with adoring eyes.

"So right you are," agreed Bart, as he reached out for Bea as she came up to Joy. Her beautiful light red hair was up, and her cheeks were rosy from the cold drive. She had on her dark blue dress that she had worn on their first date. Bart loved her in that color, it made her eyes look so blue.

"Congratulations, Joy. Clancy is a very lucky fellow," Bea said smiling. "I was starting to get concerned that he would be a bachelor forever," Bea teased, as she smiled at her cousin. "I'm glad you got him to settle down. You really are good for him."

Joy smiled at Clancy, who chuckled good-naturedly and shrugged, feigning innocence. "Oh, are there some stories I haven't heard? He seemed pretty settled down when I met him," she said, wondering what Bea meant.

"Haven't you heard about how Bart and Clancy became friends?" Bea asked smiling at her cousin and then Bart. She loved the story and thought it was a little funny now that they were all good friends.

"Maybe we should let Clancy tell her some other time," Bart whispered as Mr. Holden came towards them.

Bea decided that was best. "You're right, I'll let Clancy tell you the whole thing another time," she said quietly, not wanting to make things awkward. Maybe not everyone would think their saloon fight and spending the night together in a jail cell as funny as she did.

Mr. Holden came up to Clancy and shook his hand. "Well nephew, your parents will be proud. I figure they will hear it after the fact. And as your closest relative I would like to give you an early wedding present. I would be happy to set you up with a new suit for your wedding," he said, smiling proudly at his closest nephew.

"Thank you, Uncle. That's very generous of you, but it's not really necessary. Joy will be wearing Cassie's wedding dress and that's all I think was a concern," said Clancy feeling overwhelmed by the offer.

"Nonsense, my brother would be disappointed if I didn't make sure you were properly outfitted for your wedding, no matter how short of notice. We will make sure you are as finely dressed as your bride," he said, not taking no for an answer.

Clancy was humbled by the offer. "Well, then thank you Uncle. I appreciate it very much, and I'm sure Joy does too," he said, smiling at her as she nodded in agreement.

"Very well, come into the shop tomorrow as early as possible and we will get you fitted with something we have on hand. And if you think of anything else, we can help with, let us know. We would like to help out in any way," he said shaking Joy's hand. "Joy, you will let us know, won't you?" he asked one of his favorite seamstresses.

"Yes Mr. Holden, if I think of anything, I'll let you know," Joy said graciously, feeling thankful for such a nice employer.

Kathy joined them and gave Joy's hand a squeeze. "We're having a double wedding, so everything should be already in place, Mr. Holden," she said kindly.

"Hmm, then I have an idea. I would like to make your bouquets. We have plenty of silk flowers; we can make you each one. It'll be our wedding gift to you two wonderful ladies," he said happily. He loved weddings and especially of those he considered family. They both had worked so hard in the Men's Shop since almost the day they'd arrived, it was the least he could do for them.

"Let's have pie, everyone!" announced Mabel to the group. "Come and dish up," she said as she set out plates and forks with glasses for milk and mugs for coffee she had brewing.

Mabel and Mrs. Holden had cut the pies and began dishing up May who was first to ask for a piece. "Ma, I'll have some of that peach pie, please." She was not shy and loved the smell of the peach pie and wanted to try that one first. May held out her plate with a huge smile. She loved these big family get-togethers. There was always good food and lots of exciting people to talk to. May couldn't wait to be old enough to get to work in her Papa's shop and get to visit with the girls that worked there.

Uncle George asked Cassie to bring him a little slice of the pumpkin pie and some of the peach as he sat with his leg up. He loved her peach pie and was looking forward to it.

"My goodness, Cassie, this peach pie is amazing. I feel like it is summertime. Mmm, my new favorite," said Uncle George with his first bite.

As they sat around eating pie, Ed brought out his guitar and began playing some familiar tunes. As they finished eating, Clancy and Bart joined in singing and then Bea and Cassie, until everyone was singing along with Ed's guitar. He played song after song. Some of their favorites like *Buffalo Gal* and *Yellow Rose of Texas* were sung twice. And then the most favorite of them all was sung by Ed, Bart, and Clancy, *Be My Wife*.

(Verse 1)

After all these years, suddenly you were here.
When I first saw you, on that summer's day.
There was no stopping, once you came my way.
Our hearts pulled us together, come what may.
Like two broken pieces, bound together to stay.

(chorus)

To have and to hold, forever and ever,
These happy moments, we spend together,
I will love you, all my life,
If you will just, be my wife.

(Verse 2)

I wanted to rescue you, but you rescued me.
I knelt at your feet, and you looked at me so sweet.
We were meant to be. Can't you see?
I wanted you to be mine,
Not for just a day, but for all time.

(chorus)
To have and to hold, forever and ever
These happy days, we'll spend together,
I will love you, all my life,
If you will just, be my wife.
(Verse 3)
You don't have to be afraid, I'm here, I'll stay.
So, lay your head on my shoulder,
And I'll dry your tears and quiet all your fears.
When you're having a bad day,
I'll make you laugh and kiss your blues away.
(chorus)
To have and to hold, forever and ever
These happy months we spend together,
I will love you, all my life,
If you will just, be my wife.
(Verse 4)
I know you are the woman for me,
And I'm the man you want me to be.
Maybe we should start a family?
I'll be your king if you'll be my queen.
And together, we'll reign in majesty.
(chorus)
To have and to hold, forever and ever
These happy years, we'll spend together,
I will love you, all my life,
If you will just, be my wife.
(Verse 5)
So, let me stay by your side, if I may.
And hold your hand when we're old and grey.
I'll keep you warm when you are cold.

And hold you tight and keep you safe.
And together we'll fly, when that joyous day arrives.
(chorus)
To have and to hold, forever and ever
This happy life, we'll spend together,
I will love you, all my life,
Because today, I made you my wife.
(Verse 6)
Today, God gave you to me, to love, honor and
cherish,
We'll fly like angels to the stars.
Happiness and joy will be ours.
Together we'll travel throughout time,
Now that you've chosen to be mine.
(chorus)
To have and to hold, forever and ever
A glorious eternity, we'll spend together,
I will love you, all my life,
Because today, I made you my wife.

The song had a special meaning to each couple. Each were in a different phase of their lives, as time passed, their love changed and grew. Joy had tears in her eyes, as did all the women. On the couch, Kathy snuggled closer to Patrick and he pulled her to him, hearing the words for the first time. Cassie smiled at Ed as she remembered the first time he sang that song to her on their wedding day and felt all of those feelings again. Bea watched Bart as he sang to her and thought of their wedding day as well and rubbed her belly when they came to the verse about starting a family. Aunt Mabel and Uncle George held each other's hands and looked at each other, each thinking about their many years together, and especially now, as they were becoming old and grey, as were Mr. and Mrs. Holden, who held hands as they sat side by side. The teenage girls were thinking of their future as brides one day and hoped it wouldn't be that far off. And May wondered why the women all had tears in their eyes. Clancy took Joy's hand and kissed it as the song came to a close. Just a few more days and he would make her his wife to love for the rest of his life.

***

Saturday came quickly. Kathy and Joy looked beautiful in their wedding dresses and Patrick and Clancy were dashing in their suits. As promised, silk bouquets were provided by Mr. Holden.

The ceremony was beautifully done, and the couples were pronounced husband and wife. The Pastor announced the new couples to the congregation of guests, "Mr. and Mrs. Patrick O'Malley and Mr. and Mrs. Clancy Holden." They left the church in horse drawn sleighs which took them to their reception at the Hartford's and then to their separate honeymoons at the hotels back in town.

***

Later that night as Cassie and Ed lay in bed, they talked about the beautiful wedding day, and Cassie suddenly remembered the date, November 27th; it was Ed's birthday.

Cassie sat upright in bed and looked at him. "Ed! It was your birthday today! Why didn't you say something? I didn't even get you a present. I feel terrible," Cassie said, feeling the tears coming. She felt horrible for forgetting his birthday.

Ed pulled her down to him and kissed her on the lips. "It's OK, you are my birthday present. I have everything I want right here. You couldn't have given me anything more than you already do every day," he said and kissed her again, blew out the lights and held his birthday present close to him.

Chapter 18

Christmas Preparations

Father Winter decided to settle in Cheyenne, and welcomed the month of December with a two-day storm that blanketed the town and prairie in pristine white. Every rooftop and fencepost now wore a fluffy white cap, and every branch hung low with a heavy coat of white frosting.

Cassie marveled at the many moods of winter in Wyoming. One day it was quiet and peaceful, with flakes floating down from the flat grey sky, making Ed laugh as she playfully tried to catch the snowflakes in her outstretched tongue and mittened hands. She laughed and rejoiced in the white heaven their homestead had become. Then one night, its mood changed. A furious beast of a storm came howling around the small cottage, blowing and sweeping the snow across the yard, sneaking through the smallest cracks in the cottage and barn, pushing and piling against anything standing in its way.

Cassie tightly gripped her knitted scarf in one hand and crossed the yard, carefully carrying the egg basket in the other as she squinted through the blowing snow that whipped her skirts around her. The icy wind stung her cheeks and nose, easily penetrating her heavy wool coat that didn't quite cover her belly, sending her shivering back to the warmth of the cottage as rapidly as her legs could move. A few days later, she awoke at sunrise to a deafening silence and hurried to look out the kitchen window to investigate. The storm was gone, leaving behind a brilliant blue sky and sparkling white drifts, pretending as if winter hadn't just tried to kill them. She shook her head in disbelief. Winter in Wyoming was sure different than any she had experienced in Missouri. She thought of how difficult winter made life on the ranch for both man and beast, worrying about the poor cattle out on the range. Ed reassured her that they knew how to survive on the prairie, finding grass where the snow had been blown clean away and protection in the hollows and trees. But for Ed it wasn't as easy. She watched as he carefully crossed the hard packed drifts between the barn and the cottage, carrying in the full milk bucket. Seeing her at the window, Ed smiled and waved cheerfully as she waved back. She didn't know how he kept on working outside in the cold, chopping wood, feeding and watering the animals, and all the other chores he had to do, despite the harsh weather. Thankfully most of her chores could be done inside the cottage. The thought of venturing out made her shiver, and she pulled her shawl close around her and headed back to the warm stove to put breakfast on the table.

With the days becoming shorter and the snow

deeper, Cassie found herself spending more and more time in her favorite chair in front of the warm fire, knitting, crocheting, and stitching as fast as her fingers could fly, all the while daydreaming of her baby to come. When the weather permitted, she would bundle up and accompany Ed on a trip into town. Each sleigh ride was an adventure as they crossed the prairie's ever-changing landscape of blowing and drifting snow. Surprisingly, despite the cold and wind, there were many people in town, warmly bundled and hurrying about, traveling by any means possible in order to gather up the necessary food and supplies for the days and weeks ahead. Just like Ed and Cassie, the citizens of Cheyenne never knew when they would have to hunker down and wait out another long storm.

Christmas was fast approaching, and Cassie could feel the growing excitement inside herself as she saw children standing in front of shop windows, awestruck and wide-eyed, dreaming of gifts from Santa Claus. She imagined their parents slipping inside the shops to make secret purchases to hide away until Christmas morning, just as she planned to do for Ed as soon as she found an opportunity.

Ed pulled on the horse's reins, bringing the sleigh to a sliding stop in front of the one-room post office, and helped Cassie step down onto the snow packed road. He knew how much she enjoyed mailing her carefully written letters and smiled as she returned joyfully, waving a letter in her mittened hand. Feeling much too excited to wait to read it at home, Cassie ripped open the letter and began reading it aloud to

Ed as he drove to the mercantile. The letter was from Madeline, who told them the latest news about her family, and all their Christmas plans, then mentioned how relieved she was to hear that Cassie's pregnancy was progressing well. Madeline was happy to hear how much Cassie loved being a wife and homemaker on the ranch and closed her letter, rejoicing in the birth of their Savior, and wished Cassie and Ed a Merry Christmas.

After their stop at the mercantile and dry goods store, they pulled up to the Men's Clothing Shop, and with Ed's help, carried in the clothing Cassie had completed over the past week. They were happily welcomed by Bart and Bea and the other seamstresses, and took a few minutes exchanging quick pleasantries before Cassie was given her next sewing assignment, along with the necessary bolts of fabric and notions to finish the article of clothing.

Back into the sleigh, and covered with heavy blankets tucked in around them, Ed and Cassie headed home, loaded with all their food and supplies and, just as important, uplifted spirits. Cassie smiled; it had been a good day. They had seen their friends and received a letter and enough food and supplies to sustain them for a while, and that set her mind at ease. On the drive home, with the sun reflecting off the brilliant white snow, and Major pulling the sleigh easily across the frozen ground, Cassie shaded her eyes and reread the letter from Madeline, then put it away and began making plans for when they returned home. She bubbled with excitement, anxious to finish Ed's

Christmas present, having purchased the last bit of red wool she needed to finish the socks and scarf she was making for him. Once home, as soon as he went out to the barn to work with the livestock, she frantically worked on her presents and quickly hid them away as soon as she heard him coming back. Holding in her giggles, she pretended to be busy doing something else as he entered the house, never wanting him to know what she was up to, hoping to surprise him on Christmas morning.

With only a few more days until Christmas, Cassie began to feel anxious about having everything ready in time. She looked around the cottage; she still had presents that needed to be wrapped, and there were the chores and all the baking that still needed done. Her list of chores along with all the extra preparations made her wonder how she could accomplish it all in time. Trying to calm her nerves, she sat down and made a list of all she had to do, then got to work. She wanted everything to be perfect for their first Christmas together as husband and wife, knowing next year she would have a baby in the house, and everything would be different then.

As Cassie worked on her list, her mind wandered back to their visit at the Hartford ranch earlier that week. Joining Joy and Aunt Mabel in the kitchen for tea and cookies, Cassie and the two women sat at the table and began planning the menu for the Christmas holiday. Uncle George and Ed congregated in front of the crackling fire sitting in the parlor chairs, with George propping his foot up on a stool as they discussed the ranch and his latest leatherwork. Cassie smiled to see Uncle George in such good spirits. She knew it hadn't been easy for him to be laid up in the house while others did the work he wanted to be doing himself. But the doctor said his leg was healing nicely and finally gave him permission to put some weight on it. George had a bit of stiffness and limped when he walked, and eventually relented to using a cane. Still not able to ride, or safely venture far outside, George kept busy with his leatherworking. When Clancy came inside from chores, the men joined the women at the kitchen table, and Joy brought over a hot pot of coffee, filled the men's cups, and set on a new plate of applesauce cookies. Clancy sat down, warming his hands around his mug as he relayed what he'd overheard while in town earlier that day. It seemed George's reputation as a fine leatherworker was growing, and the shops were having a hard time keeping his goods in stock. Cassie was proud of what Uncle George was accomplishing despite his injury. His new-found talent was a blessing as well as a good business.

Although George wished he could work outside, Clancy could not escape the bitter cold and snow, as he was responsible for taking care of all that needed done outside on the ranch. He did welcome the times he would see Ed out on the prairie, and they would take a minute to catch up about everything going on. Having a friend like Ed so nearby was a blessing when he needed help. Ed had even stepped in to care for the livestock for the two days Clancy was on his honeymoon. Cassie knew the favor would be returned as the two worked well together; even closer than neighbors, they were family.

Cassie noticed Joy and Aunt Mabel got along very well, seeming to enjoy sharing in the cooking and household chores as if they were mother and daughter. Joy spent most of her days at home on the ranch now, ever since Clancy had surprised her with a sewing machine as a late wedding present, and did her sewing for the Men's Shop at home between chores. On occasion Joy would come along with Cassie and Ed for a trip into town and the two young women would spend the whole time chatting and laughing, much to Ed's mock displeasure. Cassie knew Ed was just teasing and was actually pleased with their friendship, as he frequently was the one who offered to take Joy into town with them so the two young women could visit along the way. Cassie felt blessed to have such a dear sister-in-law and friend, as they had become very close, sharing in their experiences as young wives. Not only was she grateful for her close family, but for her dear friends, Bart and Bea. Nearly every Friday evening, weather permitting, they got together to have supper at the Hartford's or the Havoc's, with Joy and Clancy joining them as well. Afterwards, they would sing and play music or games, or just sit and visit until late in the evening. The three young couples were as close as family, and Cassie counted them as rich blessings, more than she could have ever imagined. And with Aunt Mabel and Uncle George just down the road and Sunday supper with Kathy and Patrick all gathering at the Hartford's or Havoc's ranches, there was always family close by to help out and especially to help keep the winter blues away.

As Christmas Eve fell on a Friday that year, the Dress Shop and Men's Shop closed early at noon. Mr. Holden and Bart took the opportunity to show their appreciation to their staff by presenting each employee with an envelope containing a Christmas bonus, and wished them all a cheerful "Merry Christmas" as they departed for the holiday.

Bea, who was always full of holiday spirit, stood by and offered warm hugs to each employee, saying goodbye and wishing them a joyous Christmas celebration.

Kathy, Joy, and Cassie expressed their gratitude and returned the sentiment, saying their goodbye's and wishing a merry Christmas to all. The three women then bundled up and headed home to get ready for their Christmas Eve supper with the Hartford family.

Meanwhile, Bart and Bea were the last ones to leave the shop. They quickly locked up and made their way home to prepare for their own Christmas Eve gathering at Bea's parents'.

***

Cassie was putting the last pan of rolls in the oven for Christmas Eve supper when Ed came in from chores to wash up and change before they left.

"I'll be ready in a minute," Ed said, kissing the little dust of flour she'd gotten on her cheek. "You taste almost as good as the rolls smell," he said as he hurried to the bedroom to change for the party.

Cassie smiled and wiped her face with a dishtowel and turned and began cleaning up the table. In her rush, as she reached across the table, her protruding stomach knocked off the pitcher of milk. With a crash, the pitcher hit the floor and milk splattered everywhere and ran out across the floorboards. As soon as it happened she felt the last of her patience snap and began to cry in frustration at the sight of the mess. To make matters worse, as she attempted to bend down to mop up the milk, she ended up soaking the front of her dress in it.

Ed, hearing the crash from inside the bedroom, came rushing into the kitchen and found Cassie kneeling on the floor in a puddle of milk, with tears streaming down her face. "Are you all right?" he asked with concern, unsure of what happened.

"I'm fine! I'm just clumsy," she said between frustrated sobs, futilely trying to wipe up the mess with the now milk-saturated towel.

Ed wrapped his arms around her and held her close. "Cass, darling. It's going to be all right. I'll take care of it," he said soothingly as he lifted her up and held her until she started to settle.

She sniffed and wiped her eyes with the corner of her apron. "I'm sorry Ed, I know it's silly to cry over spilled milk, but I just feel so huge and awkward. And I'm so emotional," she said in frustration. "I don't even recognize myself. Look at me, I'm a mess," she said, motioning to her dripping wet skirt. Her emotions had been all over the place lately, making her feel miserable, on top of never feeling comfortable no matter what she did or what she wore. Cassie tried to keep a positive attitude, but her moods were affecting her behavior and she feared Ed would not be able to stand her much longer. And that thought brought on a new set of tears.

Ed held her close. "It's okay Cass, I understand. Just remember I love you and I am here for you. You don't have to go through this alone," he gently said, and wiped her tears away with a gentle thumb.

Cassie's heart swelled with love for Ed. He knew just what she needed and how to comfort her.

Ed guided her to a nearby chair and quickly went to work. When he finished, he kneeled in front of her and took her hands in his. "Cass, to me you're not a mess. You're a beautiful woman who is growing a baby inside of her. That takes a lot of energy and a long time and is a true miracle. To think that this tiny being will soon be a part of our lives is amazing. God gave women the gift of carrying life, and to me, that makes you an angel. I am so proud of you for being so patient and enduring through it all." He spoke with kindness and admiration, kissing her hands gently. Ed knew how much she was struggling with her pregnancy. He saw how difficult it was for her to bend over and do everyday tasks and how she was having trouble getting comfortable at night. She was becoming increasingly tired and more frustrated, which led to her being impatient and emotional. He did everything he could to help her and make her feel more comfortable.

Cassie's eyes began to fill with tears once again, but this time they were tears of gratitude and love for Ed. "Thank you, Ed darling. You do help me, so much," she said, wiping away her tears and giving him a small smile. "I'll be all right in a minute."

"Here, you go get changed and I'll take out the rolls when they are done," Ed said, as he helped her stand up out of the chair, then turned her around and unbuttoned her dress so she could change for the evening ahead. Before she left he slipped his arms around her belly and kissed her neck. "I adore you, Cass, and that includes all the things that come with this baby," he said softly. "Every day you look more and more beautiful to me," he said, as he gently rubbed her stomach.

Cassie turned and wrapped her arms around his neck. "I love you, Edward," she said and kissed him. "I really am the luckiest woman to have you as my husband," she said smiling, then headed off to the bedroom to change into the one dress that she hoped still fit.

Cassie returned to the kitchen with a clean dress on and her hair freshly brushed and pulled up in a bun. "Would you mind buttoning me up?" she asked humbly and turned around, head tilted forward allowing him access to her back and neckline.

Ed smiled and put down the towel and began buttoning. "Anything for you."

"Thank you for cleaning up for me." She'd noticed the rolls cooling on the counter and the kitchen all wiped down and everything put away. "I'm so sorry for how I've been acting, I'm sure it has been difficult for you, having to deal with all the extra you are helping me with, and on top of that—putting up with my moods," she said, looking at the floor.

Ed finished buttoning her dress and turned her around, looking deeply into her eyes. "Cass, I love every single moment of my life with you, even this baby and what it's doing to you. I will never resent any of it, as it's part of what brought you to me. I claimed you as mine, and this baby is part of you, making it mine too. When I lost Mary and our baby, I thought I would never be happy again," he spoke with such emotion that his voice caught in his throat for a moment. "Now I have you, and the baby is coming soon. You're all that matters to me," he confessed before looking away, lost in his thoughts.

"Thank you, Ed. You mean everything to me," she said, leaning in for a tender kiss. Ed's love and support gave her the strength to face each day with hope and joy even in the midst of her emotional struggles.

Tears gathered in his eyes as he confessed his deepest thoughts. "About a month ago, you asked me why I was acting so somber. It was because I was worrying about you and the baby. Around that time you were about as far along as Mary was when the Indians attacked. And I am sorry but somehow that was all I could think about for a time. Over and over again my mind raced to, 'What if something happens to Cass and the baby. How can I ever live without her?' You are the most precious thing in my life. I would die for you, Cass, just to keep you safe. I'm not ever going to stop worrying about you or stop loving you," he said, taking her face in his hands and kissing her softly as a tear rolled down his cheek.

Cassie smiled through tears of joy as he kissed and hugged her tightly. "Oh Ed, I love you so much. My darling Edward." She had not heard him talk of Mary since that day at the lake. Her heart ached to think about how he must be feeling and how worried he must be.

As Ed held her close, he whispered, "I want this Christmas to be the best one yet, Cassie. I want to create new traditions. I know how much you must be missing your family and want to make it as special as possible for you." He remembered the last few years, spending Christmas alone and trying to forget the pain of losing his wife, Mary, and the terrible Christmases he had experienced during the war. But now he had Cassie, the love of his life, to celebrate Christmas with.

Cassie gazed up at Ed, her heart brimming with love and gratitude. "Ed, you're an incredible blessing to me in my life," she expressed, her emotions running deep. She knew with him by her side, anything was possible—even experiencing a joyful Christmas despite her jumbled feelings. A smile adorned her face as she embraced him tightly, confident that this year would be a unique and cherished one—one she would never forget.

Chapter 19

Christmas Eve at the Hartford's

In town, Kathy and Patrick packed up the Christmas cookies she'd made for the Christmas Eve supper, and climbed into the buggy to drive out to the Hartford's. Kathy was grateful that she had managed to finish all of her Christmas preparations earlier in the day, so she could relax and enjoy the holiday.

Patrick bundled the blankets around Kathy, giving her a tender kiss before settling in beside her. He made sure the blankets were secure around his legs and clucked to the horse to get going. The sun was already setting as they set out on their trip out of town. It was clear and calm, and the horse knew the way even if darkness should fall before they arrived.

"I'm so excited for Christmas this year," said Kathy as they drove across the snow-packed road, looking grey in the dusky sky. "It's been a long time since I've felt that way," she said, looking up at her handsome husband with love in her eyes. It had only been a month since their wedding, and she still felt like a giddy school girl around him.

Their cozy apartment was just the right size for the two of them. The lace curtains, rag rugs, and warm quilt on the bed were nice, but wouldn't feel like home without him. Kathy loved being a wife again. She found joy in taking care of their small space. Even cooking for Patrick was a pleasure, fixing his favorite meals, knowing how much he appreciated it. After dinner, she enjoyed the time they spent relaxing in front of the pot-bellied stove, reading together or talking and getting to know each other even more. For Kathy, everything felt like home with Patrick by her side. She squeezed his hand, feeling grateful for everything they had together. "I love being a newly-wed again," she said with a contented sigh.

Patrick leaned in to give her a quick kiss on the cheek. "I feel the same way," he said, then leaned over and kissed her again.

Kathy snuggled closer to him, enjoying the warmth of his body next to hers. She couldn't believe how lucky she was to have found Patrick and how much he loved her in return.

As they continued on their way to the Hartford's, Kathy couldn't help but anticipate what was to come. "I'm sure this will be the best Christmas I've had in years. I have you here with me and that will make it the best," Kathy said, smiling with eyes twinkling in the dim light.

"Well, I'm sure this will be the best Christmas I've ever had—because of you," he said, smiling at her. He truly had never been this happy. He loved the smell of her silky chocolate colored hair and the softness of her skin and how she fit perfectly against him as they curled up at night. He hoped they had forever together, for that is what he wanted. It felt like they were young love-struck kids, not an old married couple, as some assumed. He leaned over and kissed her again and smiled broadly.

They drove on in silence for a time, both deep in thought until Kathy asked, "What do you want for Christmas, Patrick?"

"Oh, let me see," he said playfully, pausing to pretend to think about it. An impish grin spread across his face as he decided to tease her. "I think I will tell you tonight when we get home," he said, wagging his bushy grey eyebrows and winking at her.

Kathy blushed and she squeezed his arm. "Oh, Patrick, you tease," she said, laughing as he joined in with her. She was so in love, and it was wonderful. And then she decided to tease him back. "I hope it isn't too expensive, since I don't have much money," she said rolling her lips together, trying not to break a smile.

"Oh, what I want doesn't cost money. And only you can give it to me," he said, making her blush even further.

At that point, all she could do was laugh. "Well, it is Christmas." She laughed even more as he pulled her closer to him and patted her round hip. "I do love you, Patrick O'Malley," she said, as he looked at her with eyes full of love, and she tipped her head up, welcoming his kiss.

"And I love you, Kathy O'Malley," he said with

deep emotion, both feeling a little breathless from their passionate kiss.

***

Joy was in the kitchen fixing supper for the guests, when Clancy came in from chores. He removed his coat and hat and went to the sink to wash up.

"Smells delicious, Joy." Clancy looked over at the pot of potato soup. It had plenty of bacon, potatoes, and onions, with a thick white sauce, just the way he liked it. It bubbled as she added a few more spices, stirred it with the large wooden spoon, then covered the pot to simmer.

"Thanks, Clancy dear," Joy said as he came over and gave her a hug. "Are you done with the chores?" she asked, smiling up at him from within his arms.

"I have finished with everything that needs to be done today. I'll go get changed and be right out to help you with the rest of supper," he said, and gave her a quick kiss.

"Aunt and Uncle went to change as well. The soup has about thirty minutes left to cook and by then I think everyone will be here. Give me just a minute to put the rice pudding in the oven and then I'll be right in." Joy added the raisins, eggs, milk, nutmeg, and sugar mixture to the cooked rice and set it in the oven to bake. Taking off her apron and hanging it up, she headed to the bedroom to change.

Clancy had already changed into his clean shirt and pants and was putting his boots back on when Joy joined him. "What can I do to help?" he asked, pushing on his other boot and standing up.

"You can set the table, please." Joy turned and unbuttoned her dress and stepped out of it as Clancy came up behind her and took her around the waist.

"First, I need a little incentive." He kissed her neck and Joy giggled quietly.

"Clancy. We have guests coming soon. I need to get changed," she said half-heartedly, trying to break free. He held her tighter with one arm and tickled her with his free hand. She struggled a little harder as she giggled.

"Shh, or you'll be heard," he said, laughing softly. Clancy loved to tease her and hear her laugh.

"OK, OK, what will it take to get you to go set the table and let me get dressed?" Joy asked, laughing quietly. She knew she wasn't getting anywhere unless she played along.

Clancy loosened his grip and turned her around to face him. "I think a kiss will do the trick." He smiled as he leaned forward and puckered his lips.

Joy happily obliged and wrapped her arms around his neck and gave him a sweet long kiss. "There now, satisfied?" she asked, smiling as much from his playfulness as the way his lips brought her so much joy.

"Yes—for now," he teased. "We may have to continue this later," he said with a wink and a smile, and get her go.

Joy smiled after him as he headed off to set the table. Oh, how she loved his spontaneity and playfulness. She sat down at the dressing table mirror and undid her hair. She brushed her long blonde hair smooth, pulled the sides back with two combs, and then twisted it up into a bun held with pins. She dressed in her white blouse with ruffles down the front and her plaid blue and green wool skirt, wanting to look as festive as possible for Christmas Eve. Joy placed the cameo against her high-collared neckline and tied it in back with the black ribbon that held it in place. Joy studied her reflection and was pleased with the results. As she stepped out of the room, she saw that Clancy had set the kitchen table with a white tablecloth, a lamp in the center, and the dishes all arranged. She was grateful for his help and appreciated how nice the table looked.

"You look lovely, Joy," said Clancy in awe, wondering how he had gotten so lucky.

Her cheeks pinked at his compliment, as his eyes appreciated the full view.

"Thank you, Clancy. And thank you for setting the table," Joy said as she put on her apron and checked on the rice pudding. "Will you do me a favor and take the rice pudding out? I think it is finished. I'm going to get the buttermilk out of the pantry," she said, and hurried to the door leading to the pantry.

Mabel and George emerged from the bedroom where they had been changing and wrapping presents when they heard Clancy announce that the guests had arrived.

Cassie and Edward were the first to pull up to the house, nestled in the thick snowy trees, looking so warm and inviting with candles flickering in the front windows. Ed helped Cassie out of the sleigh and guided her across the crunchy snow as he carried the basket of warm rolls. She was dressed in her dark green velvet dress that matched her sparkling eyes, and a pretty green velvet bonnet with white lace edges and a big green bow tied under her chin. Her thick charcoal wool coat was only buttoned at the top button due to her big belly. Ed thought she looked stunning in the moonlight as it rose on the horizon, radiating the festive spirit of Christmas Eve.

They were greeted at the door with open arms and hugs and kisses. "Merry Christmas Cassie and Ed!" Joy and Aunt Mabel exclaimed. Aunt Mabel took the basket from Ed and quickly closed the door as the wind began to pick up.

Clancy and Uncle George warmly greeted them, wishing them Merry Christmas, shaking Ed's hand, and giving Cassie a big hug. Cassie took off her coat, hat, and gloves, revealing her beautiful green velvet dress while Ed left his outerwear on and excused himself to go back outside to take care of the horses, unhitching them and putting them in the barn with some hay.

"Come and warm yourself by the fire. Supper is nearly ready, and we will eat as soon as Ma and Patrick get here," said Joy. "I'll put the rolls in the warming box to keep warm," she said, inhaling the yeasty smell of the warm bread. "Mm, they smell heavenly, Cassie."

"Thank you, Joy, everything smells delicious." Cassie breathed in the mouth-watering aroma as she headed to the fireplace. The crackling of the wood and the warm glow of the flames made her feel cozy and at home as she warmed her hands in front of the fire. She couldn't help but admire the beautiful Christmas tree that stood in the corner, draped in white and red strings of popcorn and cranberries. Little red ribbons were tied to the tips of some branches, with ginger-bread men on others, and scattered here and there she saw a red cardinal, a tiny glass bell, and a pair of tiny red mittens. And at the very top, nearly touching the ceiling, a silver star that shined in the reflected lamplight. The tree smelled of delicious pine, cinnamon, cranberries, and gingerbread, which reminded Cassie of the Christmas mornings she'd had as a little girl in Missouri. She reminisced about the excitement she felt on Christmas Eve, sneaking around, hiding the presents she made for her family, and placing them under the tree to be opened the next morning. The memories brought a lump in her throat, and tears filled her eyes as she thought of her family, the carols they sang, her father reading the Christmas story from St. Luke, her mother baking Christmas cookies, and all the happy times they had shared over the years. Cassie quickly wiped her tears away and turned to greet Kathy and Patrick as they walked through the front door.

"Merry Christmas, everyone!" Kathy and Patrick exclaimed.

Ed followed them inside, kissed his mother and shook Patrick's hand, and then offered to go back outside to unhitch their horse.

"It looks like everyone's here," said Mabel. "Let's

get supper on the table and eat, I would hate to have any of this get cold," she said, taking the basket of cookies from Patrick and setting them near the stove.

A few minutes later Ed returned from settling the animals in the barn and everyone was called to the table. Everyone gathered around and took a seat. The supper was a beautiful Christmas Eve spread, with warm and savory potato soup and buttery rolls, and bottled apple preserves. There was lovely conversation around the table about the exciting day that awaited them tomorrow.

As the family finished their supper, they gathered around the roaring fireplace. The flames danced and crackled and popped, casting a warm glow across the room. The hearth was adorned with pine boughs and holly berries, adding to the festive ambiance.

George, Mabel, and Joy sat together on the couch, while Clancy pulled up a kitchen chair and sat beside them. Ed made sure that Cassie and his mother were comfortable in the parlor chairs, while he and Patrick took up additional chairs and circled around the fireplace. They were all close together, creating a cozy atmosphere.

George began the evening with a family prayer, giving thanks for the birth of Jesus and for their loved ones, both present and absent. The mention of those who couldn't be there brought a few tears to some of their eyes. Cassie reached out and squeezed Ed's hand, while Clancy put his arm around Joy's waist as he thought of his family back home. Patrick and Kathy held each other's hands tightly, finding solace in each other's presence. George and Mabel felt the presence of those who had passed before, making the holy night feel even more special.

After the prayer Uncle George read the Christmas story of Jesus' birth from the Bible. Cassie gazed into the fire, lost in thought about the miracle of the Savior's birth. She rubbed her round stomach as she thought of how Mary must have felt, giving birth in a barn surrounded by animals. She thought about Joseph's unwavering love and care for Mary and the baby Jesus, raising him as his own son, despite knowing he wasn't biologically his. Cassie looked at Ed and smiled, feeling overwhelmed with love for him. Ed seemed to sense her emotions and put his arm around her, giving her a gentle squeeze. As her eyes filled with tears, Ed smiled at her, and she knew he loved her just as much as Joseph loved Mary and Jesus.

As the story came to a close, Ed rose from his seat and retrieved his guitar. "Ma, would you play us *Silent Night*?" he asked, handing the guitar to his mother.

Everyone looked at Kathy in surprise, except for Joy and Ed, who both smiled. It had been a while since she had played, but she reluctantly took the guitar. Patrick looked at her in awe as she began to strum the first few chords.

"Kathy, you didn't tell me you could play the guitar," Patrick said, impressed.

Kathy smiled humbly.

"Ma taught me when I was little. She's really quite

good," Ed said, sitting back down beside Cassie and smiling at his mother. "It's been a family tradition for Ma to play *Silent Night* on Christmas Eve. Or did you forget about that?" he asked his mother with a mischievous grin.

"No son, I didn't forget," Kathy replied weakly, her eyes glistening with tears.

She began to sing, and Patrick was astonished at how beautiful her voice was. She was a little shaky at first and then gained confidence as she continued singing.

Cassie unconsciously placed her hand on her stomach as Kathy sang, "Round yon virgin, mother, and child. Holy infant so tender and mild. Sleep in heavenly peace, sleep in heavenly peace." Her voice carried the sweet melody as the group joined in, harmonizing together as they sang the last two verses.

When the song ended, they all clapped and wiped away a few tears. Kathy smiled and handed the guitar back to Ed. "Now you play for us. How about *Away in a Manger*?" she asked.

"Sure, I can do that if you all sing with me," Ed said, taking the guitar in his arms, and played the introduction. They all began to sing, their voices blending together perfectly. The sound of their singing echoed off the walls, creating a magical atmosphere that filled the room with warmth and love.

"Away in a manger, no crib for his bed,
The little Lord Jesus laid down his sweet head.
The stars in the heavens looked down where he lay,

The little Lord Jesus, asleep on the hay.

The cattle are lowing; the poor baby wakes,
But little Lord Jesus, no crying he makes.
I love thee, Lord Jesus; look down from the sky
And stay by my cradle till morning is nigh.

Be near me, Lord Jesus; I ask thee to stay
Close by me forever, and love me, I pray.
Bless all the dear children in thy tender care,
And fit us for heaven to live with thee there."

As they sang the lullaby, their voices soft and sweet, they thought of the baby Jesus in the stable stall, lying in a manger of hay surrounded by the cattle. They sang a few more Christmas favorites before stopping to gather around the table once again, enjoying rice pudding with Christmas cookies, and milk.

Cassie was filled with happiness and love, surrounded by all the people she adored. When it was time to leave to go home, she hugged them all tightly and kissed her aunt and uncle, wishing them a Merry Christmas. They bundled up and stepped outside into the bitter cold wind. Clouds had gathered while they had been inside and heavy snowflakes began to fall, blowing in sideways.

Cassie held tightly to Ed's hand as they made their way to the sleigh, the snow crunching under their feet. She could feel the icy wind cutting through her coat and her teeth began to chatter. The snow was already piling up on the road as they drove off, waving goodbye and wishing a Merry Christmas to those standing in the doorway of the ranch house, the windows glowing yellow against the snow. The lantern Ed had lit helped him navigate as he carefully and slowly drove through the treacherous conditions the short distance to home.

Despite the weather, Cassie still felt content and warm inside. She was grateful for the love and warmth of her family and friends and for the miracle of Christmas that brought them all together. As they rode home, the snow continued to fall, covering everything in a pristine blanket of white. Cassie gazed out from under the blankets around them as the snow continued, and thought about the beauty and wonder of the holiday season.

"Is it safe to travel back to town in this?" Mabel asked Patrick and Kathy when they loaded into their buggy.

Patrick seemed confident that they would make it home safely, reasoning that the snow had just started, and the drive was only a few miles. They lit a lantern and placed it on the buggy to light the way. Kathy and Patrick, tucked into their blankets, waved goodbye to the others, taking off quickly to try to beat the worst of the storm.

Mabel prayed that they would all get to their homes safely. She didn't want this wonderful night to end in tragedy. She loved these people so much and for the first time in their marriage, their home was full of family.

George put his arm around her shoulders and

pulled her inside. "Come inside, Ma. They will be fine. The Lord will watch over them," he said, reassuring her.

Ed and Cassie worked their way home in the blizzard, heading into the wind the whole way until the trees down their lane gave them some protection. They were relieved they finally made it home safely but worried about Kathy and Patrick. Ed reassured Cassie that Patrick wouldn't let anything happen to his mother, and that he was sure they would be fine, even though he was a little concerned.

As they settled in for the night, Cassie couldn't help but think about how blessed she was and all she had to be thankful for. She was grateful for her family and friends, and for the warmth and safety of their little cottage, and especially how blessed she was to have Ed to love and care for her through all the days of her life. Her heart swelled with the blessing their marriage was and prayed they would have many, many years together. As she prayed, she asked that Kathy and Patrick would make it home safely. The snow continued to fall heavily outside, but inside, as Cassie closed her prayer, she felt at peace, surrounded by the love and warmth of her home and memories of a truly magical Christmas Eve.

***

Patrick and Kathy had a rougher time getting home than they had anticipated, struggling through the heavy snow and wind. At one point, Patrick had grown extremely concerned, but eventually he spotted the lights from the city through the storm and relaxed. Finally they arrived home safely and stoked the pot-bellied stove before cuddling together in their warm, cozy bed.

"You sing and play beautifully, my dear," Patrick said holding her close. "I wish I had known you could play. I would have bought you a guitar for Christmas," he said, honestly wishing he could hear more of her singing and playing.

"Thank you, sweetheart. But there will be many more Christmases. You can get me one next year," Kathy replied, snuggling up to him. "This year, I got what I wanted for Christmas already—you," she said, giving him a loving squeeze.

Patrick pulled her closer, feeling the warmth of her body against his. "That's just what I was thinking," he said. "And I love it," he added, kissing her tenderly.

As they lay together in the warmth of their bed, listening to the wind howling outside, they both felt a deep sense of contentment and gratitude for the love they shared. They knew that no matter what challenges lay ahead, that their love would sustain them through even the toughest of times. With that in mind, they drifted off to sleep, dreaming of the bright future that awaited them.

***

Cassie changed into her nightdress and climbed into bed. By lamplight, she opened her Bible to St. Luke, reading the Christmas story one more time before she went to sleep.

Ed came into the cottage, covered in snow after putting the sleigh and horses away in the barn. "It's really coming down now. I'm not sure how long this will last, but it looks like it might be a bad one," he said from the kitchen. He took off his outerwear and boots before adding a few more big logs to the fire, then came into the bedroom to get undressed. "Brr, it's really cold, too," he said, slipping off his clothes and jumping under the covers to get warm.

Cassie laid her Bible down on the bedside table and blew out the lamp as Ed snuggled up against her. "Brr, you're cold!" she exclaimed as his cold feet touched her warm ones and she pulled them away. She giggled as he tried to put them on her again.

After some time, Cassie was finally able to get Ed warm. As they whispered their goodnights in the dark, they thought of their love that would stand the test of time, knowing no matter the storms they would face, their love would remain strong through it all.

As they slept, the wind howled outside and the snow continued to pile up, but inside, Cassie and Ed remained warm and safe in each other's loving embrace.

Chapter 20

Unexpected Christmas

That night, the blizzard raged on while Cassie peacefully slept in her warm bed beside Ed and began to dream. It was a lovely dream; one she didn't want to wake up from. In her dream, she was sitting on the porch on a warm summer's day watching a little Indian boy and a small girl playing in the thick grass and trees that surrounded the cottage. They were squealing and laughing as they ran, chasing a butterfly through the green grass and vibrant flowers. The little girl toddled through waist-high grass, clapping and giggling, as she reached up to try and catch the butterfly as it fluttered from one flower to another, then flew over her head. Suddenly, her little dark braids flew up as she fell backwards, tumbling to the ground, disappearing among the tall grass. Cassie leaned forward to see if she was all right and breathed a sigh of relief, seeing the little girl's smiling face as she sat upright. The little boy hurried to her side as she raised her arms to him. He lifted her and placed her on her feet, all the while warmly smiling as he uttered sweet words of encouragement.

Taking her by the hand, he steadied her as they resumed their game, chasing after the butterfly as the sun shone brightly between the leaves of the trees. Cassie laughed with the two children as they darted through the wildflowers, giggling each time they nearly caught the flying, yellow-winged insect. Cassie's heart swelled with happiness and love for the children, wanting to join them in their chase, but the light in her dream faded as darkness closed in around her vision. Suddenly, she was pulled from her wonderful dream by a strange noise, leaving her feeling disoriented and perplexed.

Still half asleep, she wondered what the strange sound was that had wakened her. She listened harder. There it was again, loud and beating. She finally realized that someone was banging at their front door. Cassie forced her heavy eyelids open and sat up straight in bed, her heart suddenly racing. "Ed! Wake up!" She shook him as she heard the startling noise again. "Someone's pounding on the door!" she urgently whispered. Her eyes darted back and forth, unable to see anything in the pitch dark, and sensing something was terribly wrong. Who could be knocking at this hour?

Ed came up out of a dead sleep and sprang into action. He tried to discern the source of the pounding noise as he pulled on his pants and boots, then slipped on his shirt, not bothering to button it up over his long underwear.

Cassie's eyes adjusted to the darkness just enough to see as she frantically got out of bed, not even noticing the biting cold as her feet touched the floorboards. Locating her robe by feel, she shoved her arms through the sleeves and secured it around her pregnant stomach as she stepped into her slippers.

"Stay here," he whispered, leaving her in the unlit bedroom and grabbing his loaded shotgun by the front door. Ed's instincts told him there was cause for alarm. Something felt off.

Ed moved quietly through the dark cottage, as he listened for any sound of movement. The only light came from the small fire he had stoked in the fireplace hours ago. The hairs on the back of his neck stood on end, and his heart pounded in his chest as he approached the front door.

"Who is it?" he demanded, shouting through the thick wood of the locked door.

There was no answer. Then banging again, louder, and more insistent this time. Cassie stood in the doorway of the bedroom and felt a cold chill run down her spine as she began to tremble.

"Cass, go back into the bedroom and close the door," Ed whispered insistently, as he cocked his rifle.

Cassie obeyed, as her fear increased. *Please God, protect us!*

Ed hunched over, peeking out the kitchen window, but he couldn't see anything in the darkness of the storm. His heart was pounding so loudly in his ears, he could hardly hear the wind that raged outside. Ed looked back, ensuring the bedroom door was closed with Cassie safely hidden behind it.

Slowly, he turned the key, unlocking the front

door. In one swift motion he swung the door wide open as he stepped back, lifting his rifle, ready to shoot if need be. He could barely see through the thick flurry of white, but he could make out a dark shadowed figure looming in front of him.

Ed felt a surge of fear as he cautiously took a step toward the figure, his gun trained on it, ready to fire at the first sign of movement. He nearly jumped out of his skin when he heard a deep, gravelly voice coming from the snow-laden beast.

"Help…"

It isn't a beast. It's a man! Or is it? Ed's mind reeled with questions, as he backed up and the large dark figure stepped into the doorway. Ed squinted, willing his eyes to see who was there, but to no avail.

The thickly accented word came again, "Help…" The ominous being took one step into the cottage.

Finally, illuminated by the flickering fire in the fireplace, Ed saw a dark-skinned face with black shining eyes, staring back at him. Before him stood, protected under a thick furry hide, a tall man carrying a dark-haired woman in his arms, her face hidden against his neck. Snow blew in around them as he halted just inside the open doorway, with snow piled on the hide, giving it the appearance of a large snowy beast. He spoke again, in halting English, "Woman. Need doctor."

Ed realized it was an Indian man, cloaked in a buffalo robe. He still had his gun aimed at the man, hesitating. He didn't know what he should do, weighing the possibilities as many thoughts crossed his mind. His most important concern was for Cassie's safety.

Freezing wind and snow continued to blow through the cottage door. Realizing he couldn't leave the door open forever, Ed reluctantly lowered his gun, keeping it pointed at the man as he side-stepped to close the door. Ed motioned with his rifle for him to move further into the room by the fireplace.

"Bring her inside. I'll do what I can to help." Ed's voice sounded strange to his own ears, strained and off key, like overtightened strings on a guitar.

As the man entered the cottage, Ed couldn't help but feel a sense of unease. He didn't know what he was getting himself into, but he knew that he had to do what he could to help this woman.

Cassie listened against the bedroom door and heard an unfamiliar voice and wondered who was there and what was being said. Overcome with worry for Ed, she quietly opened the bedroom door and peered out. She froze. The sight of the dark-faced man made her blood run cold. She began to tremble in fright as her heart raced like a runaway locomotive. It had been a long time since she'd seen an Indian close up, but not long enough. Terror filled her mind as memories of another horrific night came flooding back, and with it the anguish of all she had lost and endured.

While Cassie stood immobilized, the Indian man continued to move further into her home as he carried a woman to the fireplace and laid her down in front of it. She was coughing and wheezing. Without warning, a small child emerged from behind the man's large robe and went to sit beside the woman. Cassie silently gasped as she covered her open mouth and her eyes widened in astonishment.

Ed knew that he needed to help the woman, but he also couldn't shake the feeling of unease that lingered in the back of his mind. Taking a deep breath, he moved closer to the man and spoke in a calm, measured voice, "I'll do what I can to help." He saw the woman shiver as she wrapped her arms around herself as she lay on the cold floor. "But first, we need to get her warmed up."

Cassie saw the child, and assumed the woman was his mother. Almost immediately her fears abated. She sympathized with the woman lying on the floor, and watched as the man took off the heavy buffalo robe and placed it over his woman.

The man pleaded with Ed, "Woman. Sick. Need doctor," as his hands signed the words.

Cassie pulled her robe more tightly around her pregnant frame, and timidly came out of the bedroom, startling Ed and the stranger. Their heads jerked around in unison, both men wide-eyed with alarm, staring back at her.

"Cass, get back in the bedroom; it's not safe out here," Ed demanded in a stern voice, a tone he had never used with her before.

Cassie stood there, on the brink of tears, knowing in her heart Ed was only trying to protect her. But Cassie was confident she would be safe. Her fears had dissipated, and she felt a certain peace and calmness come over her. "Ed, she needs my help. She's sick. We should do something," she beseeched him.

"No Cass, not you! You stay away! You don't know what she has." His brow furrowed and his eyes were wild with fright, as he posed the question, "What if you get sick?"

Cassie could see he was more than upset. Ed looked terrified. Here was the man who had vowed to protect her, even unto death, and she knew he would do so if they should attack. Cassie understood Ed's concern for her but tried to reason with him anyways.

"If she's contagious, then the little boy and the man would have it too. They look well enough," she attempted to reassure him as she stood outside the bedroom door, hugging herself tightly in the freezing cold room.

The Indian man turned to Ed and implored, "Water."

Cassie looked at Ed with brows furrowed. "I won't touch them, please just help them, please," she begged.

"All right, I'll give them some water, but you are to stay clear away from them. I won't have you getting sick. You hear me? You stay over there," he said pointing across the room, and eased up his grip on the gun as he went to the kitchen.

Ed slowly laid down his rifle on the table and got a cup of water and took it to the Indian man.

The man took it and kneeled down. He carefully lifted the woman's head and held the cup to her lips so she could drink. She swallowed, then choked and coughed in a deep, ragged-sounding coughing fit. Cassie watched, feeling anxious to help, worried that the woman wouldn't be able to catch her breath again. Finally, the woman's cough calmed, and she laid back in exhaustion, breathing more evenly. Then moments later, she let out a painful groan that sent sympathy pains through Cassie.

The Indian man stood and motioned with his hands, as he said frowning, "Baby. Soon. Need doctor."

Cassie gave Ed a concerned look. "Do you think he means his wife is pregnant as well as sick?"

Ed shrugged his shoulders. "I don't know." Then bitterly added, "And honestly, I don't care." He was angry about having Indians in his home, possibly infecting his expectant wife, endangering Cassie and their baby.

Cassie spoke up, addressing the Indian man. "Your woman is going to have a baby, like me?" she asked as she put her hands on her belly to show she was pregnant.

He affirmed with a nod. "Baby," then signed as he shook his head in a negative response. "No good. Need medicine. Need doctor." The Indian man used halted, broken English mixed with words Cassie and Ed didn't understand.

Cassie turned to Ed and pleaded with him, "We need to do something, Ed. We have to help her."

"We can't go for the doctor. The storm is too bad; I'd never make it." Ed added under his breath, "And who knows if he would help an Indian anyways?"

Cassie watched the woman as she held her stomach and moaned and turned to implore Ed again. "We need to help her! Maybe I can make her some tea or a mustard pack to put on her chest for the cough." She clasped her hands to her chest, begging Ed, frantic to help the poor woman before it was too late. "Something—please, Ed. We need to try."

Ed heard the desperation in Cassie's voice and his heart began to soften. He gazed at the sick woman and then at the man, his face drawn as the man's eyes implored Ed to show mercy. Ed's fierce anger was beginning to subside, but he continued to feel cautious. Relenting, he nodded his head to Cassie, and she rushed to the stove to get the fire going and put on water to boil. She pulled out a towel and put together the remedy her ma had taught her for chest congestion. Cassie could only try to do her best since there was no hope for a doctor in this blizzard. And she knew Ed was right, there was no way of knowing if he would have helped the Indians anyways. She and Ed were their only hope, and Cassie would do everything she knew how.

The Indian woman moaned again, and Cassie felt her pain along with an ache in her heart. The man kneeled beside the woman and took her hand and said something in their native language that seemed to soothe her, and she nodded. He looked up at Cassie as Ed brought the compress to the man and Ed pointed to his chest, indicating to place it on the woman's chest. The Indian man opened her leather shirt and laid the compress on her chest. She moaned again. The man looked at Cassie and spoke. She didn't understand the words but felt she knew what he was saying.

"Ed, I think she's in labor. The moaning seems to be coming every few minutes. I think she's having contractions." Cassie inched closer as she watched the scared faces of the distressed couple.

Ed studied the sick woman lying on the floor in front of the fire and his heart ached for her. Something happened inside him as he gave up his fear. It was his nightmare, the one he had experienced over and over after he'd lost his pregnant wife, Mary. Ed knew what it was like to feel desperate for help, to be afraid for his wife and child's safety. He recalled the pain of his own similar experience, his own suffering, as he looked at the struggling woman. Through this Indian couple, he saw himself and his wife, Mary, and their baby. In an instant he knew what he must to do.

Quickly, Ed ran to the spare bedroom and pulled off the mattress and blankets and brought them into the front room. He helped the man lift his sick wife onto the makeshift bed. The small child moved out of the way, now warm, shedding his thick fur coat while keeping constant watch on his mother.

"Cassie, boil water and get some string, scissors, and towels. We'll do what we can to help her." Ed's voice held a sense of urgency.

Cassie was relieved to see Ed's change of heart and snapped into action. She lit the lamp in the kitchen and darted around, gathering the supplies they needed.

"You stay over there, Cass. I don't want you getting sick. I'll do what I can." Ed took the things she'd gathered and set them on the small table nearby.

Cassie paced the floor halfway across the room as the Indian woman moaned and coughed uncontrollably for an hour or so. It was so late that the little child finally succumbed to exhaustion and fell asleep, curled near his mother on a blanket. Cassie felt heartbroken at the sight. She wringed her hands as she watched and prayed. She wanted to help and knew how. She had watched her ma as a midwife so many times. If only Ed would let her.

"How many months is she?" Cassie broke the silence between the woman's soft moans and bouts of coughing.

The Indian man looked puzzled, then appeared to understand Cassie's question and answered with deep sorrow, "Six moons."

Immediately, Cassie knew the baby would not survive. The tears began to form and burn her eyes. "Ed, she's too early." Tears began to run down her face as she whispered the words, "The baby won't make it."

Ed's face was drawn. "I know—the baby is too small."

The Indian woman looked up at Cassie, as a tear rolled down her copper cheek; the woman knew as well.

It broke Cassie's heart to watch the woman's suffering. Unable to stand it any longer, Cassie ran to the woman's side and knelt down beside her before Ed could stop her.

"Cass, NO!" Ed shouted, grabbing Cassie's wrist before she could touch her.

Cassie looked up into Ed's eyes and pleaded with him in a soft gentle voice, "Ed, it will be all right. And if not, then so be it. I couldn't live with myself, if I sat by and did nothing to help." A tear rolled down her cheek as she silently stood her ground, not taking her eyes off his.

Her words struck hard, and Ed slowly released her. Cassie turned to the Indian woman and tenderly wiped away the tears from her soft brown cheeks. Stroking her dark hair away from her face, she tried to soothe her. The woman looked at Cassie with just a hint of a smile, then closed her black diamond eyes and relaxed, letting out a long breath.

"If anything happens to you," Ed murmured with great sadness, "I'll never forgive myself." His moustache pulled down at the corners as his frown deepened.

"Ed, it's my choice. Besides, I don't think you could live with yourself either, if we didn't do all we could to help," she gently reasoned. "Wouldn't you want them to help me if I was in her place? You would. Right?" Cassie nodded ever so slightly as she watched him struggle with his internal battle of doing what he knew they should and wanting to protect her.

Ed looked away as a tear rolled down his cheek and ran his hand over his face, brushing the tears away. The thought of losing Cassie was too great. But he knew she was right; he would want someone to help her, at any cost. He quietly consented, "Do what you can to help her." And prayed with all his heart that Cassie would be safe.

"Good. Now darling, will you get me a cold wet cloth for her forehead? She's burning up. And another cup of water." She threw out instructions as she pulled back the buffalo hide to cool the woman down. Cassie laid her hand on the woman's pregnant stomach and felt how small she was; as a contraction came, she moaned again. "She's definitely in labor. And I'm afraid she'll deliver soon." Cassie became more concerned when she saw blood on the woman's leggings. She looked up at the husband and saw he'd noticed the blood as well. He kneeled on the other side and took his wife's hand and spoke comforting words to her as she blinked sadly up at him.

Cassie had to look away and wipe her tears before she could look back at her patient. *I have to be strong for her,* she thought. If she could only take one thing from her mother's medical training, it would be to act in confidence and reassurance when caring for the sick. Fear increased pain and there was no good in that. The woman needed to trust that Cassie could help her and that she was not afraid. So, she did as she had seen her mother do many times before. Cassie put on a brave face and tried to reassure the woman. "Sh, it's going to be OK," she soothed with a tender smile. "You'll soon feel better and be able to rest," she added with deep compassion.

Cassie took the cool cloth from Ed and placed it on the woman's forehead, saying more soothing words she knew the woman didn't know, but possibly could understand her meaning.

The woman relaxed between the contractions and Cassie helped her remove the leggings under her buckskin dress. With one final moan the lifeless infant was born. Cassie gently wrapped the tiny baby girl's body in a towel and laid her on her mother's chest. The tiny body was perfectly formed, but much too small and fragile to live outside her mother's body.

The Indian man, kneeling beside his wife, leaned over and kissed the infant and his wife's foreheads. He spoke softly to them in words Ed and Cassie didn't know but felt deeply. Cassie wiped her tears on the back of her sleeve. She tied and cut the cord and tucked away the afterbirth in a towel. There was too much bleeding, despite all Cassie could do to stop it. Finally, she stood and washed her hands in the hot water and dried them. Cassie then quietly went to Ed as he stood off in a corner of the room. He took her in his arms and held her as she softly cried. Ed cried for the Indian couple as well, as his body shook with sobs. It was too familiar, and it all came flooding back to him. Ed knew what this Indian man was feeling. Cassie held him and felt his body break down under the weight of sadness he felt. Together they grieved with the man in the room.

It was only minutes later that the Indian woman took her last breath. The Indian man groaned in agony as his woman's spirit left this world. He bowed down over her lifeless body and lifted her by the shoulders to hold her closer and wailed. He rocked with her for a while, speaking words of endearment and sorrow in his native tongue. Reverently laying her down, he took out his knife and deliberately cut off a section of his braided hair and gently laid it on her chest as he chanted. Cassie and Ed's hearts were breaking for them as they watched and cried. In time, the Indian man pulled the blankets over his loved one's bodies and slowly stood with what looked like the weight of the world on his shoulders.

"Woman, baby. Go to Great Spirit. I go now. Take woman. Sacred burial grounds. Reservation no good. No doctor. No food." The man turned back to his woman and infant's bodies. He wrapped the blankets around them and woke the small boy. He began talking to him quietly. The boy whimpered and the man held him by the arms and said something sternly, then took his small arm and led him over to Cassie. Taking Cassie's hand, he placed the little boy's hand in hers and covered their hands with his. "You take boy. No mother. Boy need mother." The Indian man motioned to her. "I come—grass grow tall."

Cassie nodded her head as she held the boy's small hand, and tears ran down her cheeks.

Realizing the man was leaving soon, Ed snapped into action. He quickly filled a sack full of food and handed it to the Indian man, then motioned for him to wait. Ed put on his coat and hat and squeezed Cassie's hand. "I'll be right back." He departed into the darkness toward the barn through the gentle falling snow, the fury of the storm having finally subsided.

The Indian put on the buffalo robe and went back to the bodies and gently picked them up. He carried them to the door and Cassie opened it for him. The little boy clung to her robe and cried quietly as his father faded into the darkness with his mother and baby sister.

Ed saw the man leave the house and motioned for him to come into the barn. Together they fashioned a travois over one of the Crowley horses. The Indian man reverently laid the bodies on the wooden frame and lashings, securing them into place.

"Thank!" He signed and clasped arms with Ed in a hearty grip.

"You're welcome. Good luck." Ed watched as the Indian turned and left, leading the horse with his precious cargo, fading into the dark winter night.

Cassie had closed the door behind the man and looked down at the little boy and his tear-streaked cheeks. His big dark eyes blinked up at her, trying hard not to cry. Her heart broke for him. She kneeled down and took him in her arms and hugged him tightly, whispering comforting words to him. He whimpered and sniffed. In time he settled and blinked back the tears. "Come." She stood and took him to the table and sat him on a chair. In her nightdress she prepared him some food and placed it in front of him.

"Go ahead, eat," she gently encouraged. He sat and looked at her and then the food, unsure of what to do. She decided he needed further encouragement and poured herself some milk and took a drink, showing him it was good. Seeing her, he took the cup in both hands and quickly gulped the milk and grabbed the bread and took large mouthfuls. As fast as he was eating, she wondered how long it had been since he'd had any food. Cassie poured him some more milk and he finished that, as well as another piece of bread. When he'd had his fill, she took him to sit with her in front of the fire and held him on her lap in the soft chair. Cassie stroked his small dark head as he lay against her as he fell asleep, holding onto her long braid, possibly reminding him of his mother.

Cassie sat in front of the fireplace, holding the sleeping little boy, lost in thought. She couldn't shake the image of the Indian man leaving in the night with the bodies of his loved ones. Her heart ached for him and the little boy he had entrusted to her care.

As she sat there, gently rocking the boy, Ed returned, his face grim and reddened from the cold. He brought in some more firewood and knelt by the hearth, warming his hands, staring into the flames.

Ed noticed the look on her face and placed a hand on her shoulder. "You did the right thing, Cass."

Cassie nodded, feeling slightly comforted. She looked down at the little boy in her arms and pulled him closer as he nestled into her. She wondered what the future held for him, for all of them.

"We'll take care of him for now," Ed said, as if reading her thoughts. "Until we figure out what to do."

Cassie felt a small glimmer of hope at his words. They would take care of the boy, for now. And that was all she could ask for.

"Let's put him in the other bed and try to get some

sleep. It'll be morning soon." Ed gently picked up the little boy and carried him into the spare bedroom.

Cassie followed and turned down the covers as Ed laid him carefully down. She tucked the blankets around the little boy and kissed his small head.

Together they blew out the lamps and went to bed. As they held and comforted each other, they slowly dropped off to sleep. It had been a long, hard night.

Chapter 21

Christmas Morning

Ed awoke a few hours later, knowing he needed to get up to start the chores. He silently climbed out of bed, hoping to let Cassie sleep as long as possible. She lay still and breathed evenly as he snuck out of the bedroom. In the front room, he gathered the blood-stained mattress and took it outside to burn later and went to the barn to start the chores. As he milked the cow, he replayed over and over in his mind everything that had happened last night. Cassie had been amazing. And she had been right. He hoped they had done enough. Ed couldn't help but sympathize with the poor man. He knew the Indian man had a long sad road ahead of him. *And what of this child?* Ed wondered as he continued to sit on the milk stool, even after the pail was full. In the solitude of the barn, Ed finally allowed his emotions to surface. He covered his face with his hands and wept as he remembered the same thing happening to him only a few years ago. While his mind was engaged in memories from his past, his heart ached, and he continued to weep. He wept for worry that Cassie may have the same thing happen to her, and prayed that she would be protected. His thoughts returned to the Indian man holding his wife and daughter as he mourned. Once again Ed felt the piercing in his heart that he had experienced when he held his own dead wife and daughter. It took some time before he could calm himself and wiped away his tears. In a daze, he stood and took the pail to the work bench and went about finishing his chores. His body moved out of habit as he absently pitched hay, watered the animals, and poured feed into the feed trough, still thinking about the Indian family.

Cassie awoke to weeping, coming from the other room. As quickly as she could, she got out of bed and put on her robe and slippers and went to the frightened little boy. She found the little boy sitting up in bed crying, looking around the spare bedroom in fear. Taking the child into her arms, she sat down on the bedside and rocked him. "Sh, it's going to be all right. I'm here. I'll take care of you, little one." She repeated the soothing words as she stroked his long black hair until he finally relaxed and fell back to sleep. Cassie carefully laid him down and tucked him under the thick quilts and went to get dressed. It was time to start breakfast.

Ed came into the cottage to find Cassie stoking the fire in the kitchen stove. "Merry Christmas, darling," he said quietly, coming up behind her, wrapping his arms around her waist and kissing her cheek.

"Oh! It's Christmas morning!" Surprised, she gleefully turned around to return his kiss. "Oh Ed,

I'd completely forgotten! I've been so busy thinking about last night that I didn't even remember it was Christmas day." She paused as she frowned, wondering about last night and felt the deep sadness all over again. "Do you suppose we did enough?" She looked up into his eyes as her tears gathered.

Ed held her gaze as he kept her safely in his arms. "Yes Cass, we did all we could have." A smile lifted the corners of his mouth as his heart swelled with love for her. "I'm so proud of you. You were right, I know that. I shouldn't have tried to stop you from helping her." He brushed a stray hair away from her cheek as he confessed his fears to her. "I'm so afraid of losing you." He looked back toward the fireplace and frowned. "Seeing that woman on the floor reminded me of what happened to my Mary, when she lost our baby and died." Tears ran down his cheeks into his moustache that quivered with emotion. "You did exactly what I would have wanted if it had been you." A sob escaped as he smiled at her. "Oh, Cass, I love you."

Cassie pulled him close and rested her head on his chest and cried. "I love you so much, Edward. I know how much you care for me. I know you were only trying to protect me. I just wish we could have saved the woman and her child."

"Cass, there is no way they would have lived, but take comfort that you helped ease her suffering and brought some peace to them." Releasing his tight hold, he looked at her and wiped away her tears. "I felt so bad for the man, I gave him one of the Crowley horses and helped him make a travois to carry the bodies back to the sacred burial grounds. I hope he's all right. It's a horrible feeling to lose someone you love." Ed dropped his gaze as he thought of all the years of heartache after Mary and his baby died. "But I am living proof that a heart can be mended. With your love, Cass, it has been possible." He looked deeply into her eyes, smiling through his tears.

"As you have healed mine, my darling." She held his face, wiping away his tears with her thumbs as her heart burned with love for him.

He pulled her close and hugged her tightly as he stroked her silky hair. "Oh, my Cass."

Cassie settled against his body and closed her eyes as she thought of Christmas Eve, the Christmas story, and the carols they had sung. "Ed, I've come to realize something this Christmas. I didn't realize there was something bitter buried deep down inside of me, until it was gone. I feel light and free. The bitter and angry feelings I had for the Indians who hurt me, and my family are gone. Am I making any sense?" she asked, looking up at him, still not sure she understood it herself.

"Yes, I think I understand."

"Well I don't understand it myself."

"Don't you see what has happened?" Ed wondered if she realized she had faced her fears and overcome them.

"I'm not sure." She was still puzzled why she would suddenly feel this way. "I really thought I had already forgiven them. I was sure I had let go of my hatred a long time ago."

"I'm sure to some extent you had. But you have gone further, my dear. You have done as Christ taught us. You have loved your enemies. Cass, you were willing to risk your life to help them. How can you despise those you have served and loved?" he asked of her, as much as he asked it of himself. He thought for a moment as he realized the bitterness was gone from his heart as well. His anger toward those who had caused the loss of his wife and child was gone, and he felt light and free.

"That must be it," Cassie said with astonishment. "But how?" she wondered out loud, as she felt the change in her heart. Maybe in some subconscious recesses of her mind, she had still despised those who had taken her family away and harmed her. Cassie thought she had overcome it a long time ago. But now she felt it was gone; peace was there instead.

"I feel the same way, Cass. I feel like a burden has been lifted. Just now I realize it. I've become so used to carrying around a bit of resentment for those who took my wife and daughter, I didn't even notice it was still there. And suddenly, it's gone. I feel lighter, freer. Thank you, Cass, for helping me through it." He hugged her again. His heart was so full today.

"Oh Ed, I'm so happy. What a blessing this is. It's a miracle." She laid her head on his chest, soaking up his affections. "This is a Christmas I will never forget," she said softly.

"Me either, darling." Ed stroked her long hair, as he rested his head on hers.

They stayed that way, relishing the feeling, until they heard a faint cry as the small boy began to wake. Ed and Cassie went to him. Cassie sat on the edge of the bed and stroked the boy's face as he lay there, looking up at her with tears running into his hair.

"It's OK, little one. We're here. You're safe. We will take care of you and love you," Cassie said, as tears ran down her cheeks.

He sat up slowly and spoke in his native language.

Cassie took him into her arms and cuddled him. "It will be all right, little one," she said reassuringly.

"Let's get him something to eat. I'll bet he's starving," said Ed, as he tried to lead the little boy from the room. But the boy would not leave Cassie's side, clinging to her harder.

"Come on little one, let's get you some food to eat," Cassie said as she stood and took his hand and led him into the kitchen. "Maybe he would like some milk," she said to Ed.

"I'll get it," Ed said and turned to pour the milk into a cup for the boy. Ed handed the child the cup, which he took and drank down in steady gulps and wiped his mouth with his buckskin sleeve when he was done. Ed smiled at the little Indian boy. "He sure is hungry."

"I'll make breakfast. What do you think he likes?" she asked.

Ed smiled at Cassie. "At this point I think anything would taste great to him."

"You're right. I guess we don't have anything he's used to on hand," she said, laughing softly. "Unless you have some venison or pemican handy."

Ed laughed with her. "Not at the moment."

"Well, then. I guess eggs and pancakes will have to be good enough for his first Christmas breakfast," she said smiling.

"I'm sure that will be wonderful," said Ed, kissing her on the cheek.

Together they all ate breakfast as the sun slowly rose on that clear morning. The storm had blown itself out and left a thick white layer of snow on everything.

"What do you think his name is?" Cassie asked, thinking she couldn't call him 'little one' forever.

"I don't know. Maybe he will tell us," Ed said, looking at the boy. "What is your name?" he asked, enunciating each word as he pointed to the boy. Pointing to himself, he said, "Ed." The little boy tilted his head as he looked at him, confused. Ed tried again, pointing to the boy and then to himself and saying his name. When he said nothing, he then pointed to Cassie and said, "Cass."

The boy looked at Cassie and smiled. "Cass," he said with a thick accent and making the "S" sound very long.

"Yes, very good. That is Cass. I'm Ed," he said, pointing to himself again.

The little boy smiled, liking the game. "Ed," he said, making the "D" accented.

"Good." Ed pointed to the boy and tried to get him to say his name, but he just sat there, looking puzzled.

"Well, we'll figure it out somehow," Cassie said, as she watched the boy study them as they ate their pancakes with their forks.

He picked up the fork by his plate and gripped it awkwardly and attempted to stab the fork into the pancake. Making a few attempts with Cassie trying to help, he finally gave up and picked up a whole pancake and bit off large bites as syrup dripped over his fingers. He smiled as he chewed the buttery, fried bread, then licked the syrup off his fingers.

Ed smiled broadly at the boy and his innocence. "You're right, we just need to give him time," Ed said, as he ate his own breakfast.

"You know, just before I fell asleep, I was reading the Christmas story in Luke..." said Cassie and paused as the boy pointed frantically to himself.

"Luka," he said smiling and pointing to himself excitedly. "Luka!"

"Your name is Luka?" Cassie asked with wonder.

He smiled wider and nodded as he repeated, "Luka," and took another bite of his pancake, using his hands to break off a smaller piece.

"Luka, huh. How old do you think he is?" Ed asked Cassie.

"Hm, he may be three or four years old," Cassie guessed. "It's hard to tell, but that would be my estimate," she said, thinking there was so much they didn't know about him.

"I wonder what reservation they're from?" asked Ed, thinking about the man and woman, trying to remember if there was anything that would be a clue as to which tribe they belonged to.

"I don't know. Are there any reservations nearby?"

"None for hundreds of miles." Ed took a long drink of his coffee, feeling it warm him clear to his toes. "He must have been pretty desperate to leave in the winter with a pregnant wife and small child." He thought how cold and miserable they must have been to travel on foot for hundreds of miles.

"He said he was coming back in the spring, right?" Cassie dished the little boy another pancake and received a wide smile in return.

"That's what I understood him to be saying. I guess we will find out then." Suddenly he remembered something. Ed finished his last bite of bacon and eggs, and washed it down with the rest of his coffee. "That was delicious, Cass." He pushed himself back from the table and rubbed his stomach as he stood up. "I have something I need to go get. I'll be right back." Ed pulled on his coat and hat, and tipped it to her with a grin as he left to go out to the snow-covered barn.

Cassie smiled after Ed and turned back to the little boy.

"Well, Luka. It's time to clean up breakfast, so we can open Christmas presents." Cassie awkwardly pushed herself up from the table and began clearing off the dishes and motioned for him to bring his dish to the sink.

Luka jumped down from his chair and grabbed his plate and licked the rest of the syrup from it before handing it to her to wash. Cassie chuckled. Her little helper caught on quickly and within minutes, they had the dishes done and together went to sit in front of the crackling fire while the sun began to brighten the room.

It wasn't long before the front door swung open, and Ed stepped into the cottage. Cassie turned to watch him enter, his arms overloaded with a large object covered in a canvas tarp. With a kick of his heel, he closed the door and carried the present over and set it down in front of the fireplace. Cassie's eyes widened at the size of the present and hugged Luka as he sat on her lap in the parlor chair.

"Oh, Ed. What have you done?" Her eyes sparkled with delight. She couldn't begin to imagine what was under the tarp.

Luka studied Cassie's excited expression and then the man smiling proudly at her and wondered what was happening.

"Merry Christmas, Cass!" Ed leaned over and lifted off the canvas to reveal his present.

A beautiful cradle sat in front of her. "Oh, my goodness. It's beautiful. Oh Ed, I love it!"

Luka moved off her lap as Cassie scooted off the chair and kneeled beside the cradle. Tenderly, she ran her fingers over the smooth dark wood, polished to a shine, and imagined rocking her baby to sleep in it.

"I'm glad you like it." Ed smiling down at her, delighted that she liked it. She looked up, adoring him as he leaned over and gave her a kiss.

Luka watched them closely and joined Cassie beside the cradle and began rocking it back and forth.

"It's for the baby, Luka." Cassie pointed to her

stomach and then to the cradle. It was clear he didn't understand, so she pretended she was holding a baby and placed it carefully in the cradle. They watched as his eyes sparkled as he began to understand. "Baby," Cassie repeated.

"Bae-bee," he slowly enunciating each syllable, then smiled.

"Good, Luka. You said 'baby,'" Ed praised, rubbing the little boy's head.

"Bae-bee, bae-bee." He pointed to Cassie's stomach.

Cassie smiled and hugged him. "You are so smart, Luka." She put her hands on her stomach lovingly and repeated, "Yes, baby."

"Bae-bee. Bae-bee," he said over and over, looking back and forth from Ed to Cassie as they nodded and repeated the word.

Cassie suddenly remembered her gifts. "Oh, Ed. I have your presents hidden as well. I'll go get them. One minute and I'll be right back," she said putting her index finger up, and went to the bedroom to bring out her gifts from the trunk she'd hidden them in. "Merry Christmas, Ed!" Cassie took her present out from behind her back and proudly handed Ed the guitar case she'd purchased for him.

"Oh Cass, how nice. It's just perfect!" Ed took the case and placed it on the rug in front of the chairs.

His smile was all the proof she needed to see he was pleased with her gift. His mouth dropped open as he undid the latches, and opened the hard leather case, revealing the red velvet lining. He stood up and gave Cassie a big hug and a kiss.

"Thank you, dear. I love it!" In three long strides, he retrieved his guitar that was standing up against the wall in the corner and returned to place it reverently into its new resting place. The smooth curved instrument looked beautiful nestled inside the dark red velvet. Overjoyed, he closed the charcoal-colored case, secured the latches, and picked it up by the handle. "It's perfect!"

"And here is your other present." Cassie grinned and handed him a package wrapped in colored paper, tied with red ribbon.

Ed set down the guitar case and sat down in the other parlor chair to open his second present. With a grin, he untied the ribbon and folded back the paper wrapping to reveal a grey and red scarf with matching socks. "Very nice, Cass." He wrapped the scarf around his neck and pulled off his boots and socks and pulled on the new thick socks. He curled and extended his toes inside the soft wool. "Very warm and comfortable; thank you, dear." Ed stood and gave her another kiss.

"You're welcome. I'm glad you like them," Cassie said with pleasure.

Luka watched with curiosity, wondering what was happening. Cassie looked at Ed and then at Luka, feeling bad that she didn't have a gift for Luka for Christmas. If only she had time, she could have made him something. Suddenly she had an idea and went to the windowsill in the kitchen. She came back and handed her gift to Luka.

It was the clear glass bluebird, one of the only things that had survived in the fire. "Luka, this is called a Bluebird of Happiness. It's to bring you happiness when you put it in the window sill so the sun can shine through it. There's a poem that goes like this, 'Those we love don't go away, they walk beside us every day. Unseen, unheard, but always near, so loved, so missed, so very dear.' This will help you remember that your mother is near you and will always love you," Cassie said, as she handed the glass bluebird to him.

Luka took the clear blue figurine in his hands and turned it over and over, looking at it from every angle, then lifted it to his lips and kissed it. He smiled up at Cassie with wide dark adoring eyes. He held it to his chest with both hands, then came to Cassie and wrapped his arms around her neck and hugged her.

"Merry Christmas, Luka," Cassie said, with glistening eyes.

Ed was smiling, his eyes shining. "Merry Christmas, sweetheart," he said with a catch in his voice.

"Merry Christmas, darling," Cassie said with a smile, as a happy tear rolled down her cheek.

Chapter 22

Luka

It was a beautiful Christmas morning on the Havoc ranch as Cassie, Ed, and Luka bundled up for the sleigh ride to George and Mabel's house for Christmas dinner. Cassie and Luka stepped out of the cottage into the frosty air and were met with a glorious view from the porch. The yard, trees, barn, and corral, even the chicken coop and fence posts, had a fresh coat of pristine white. Mounds of snow covered everything, turning their modest ranch into a magical winter wonderland. Only Ed's footprints from the cottage to the barn broke the smooth layer of virgin snow that Father Winter left as a Christmas present the night before. Cassie and Luka descended the porch steps as Ed opened the barn's double doors. Seconds later, Ed snapped the reins over the team and emerged from the barn with the two bays pulling the sleigh behind them. Luka's eyes widened at the sight of the sleigh. To Luka, it appeared that Ed was sitting in a big black box with the sides cut out, being pulled by horses as it floated above the deep snow. His eyes questioned Cassie, and then he pointed, rattling off a string of words she could only guess at. His mouth fell open in awe as the riding box approached. She gave his little gloved hand a squeeze and explained to him that it was a sleigh. Ed pulled back on the reins, bringing it to a sliding stop in front of the steps, and jumped out to help Cassie and Luka into the sleigh. Luka eagerly climbed in beside Cassie and sat on the cushioned seat. His head swung this way and that, trying to see how this wagon without wheels worked. Ed winked at Cassie as he tucked a heavy buffalo hide over their legs to keep them warm and got the horses going with a flick of the reins. As they took off down the lane, the sleighbells that adorned the harnesses began jingling with each horse's footfall. Luka's eyes sparkled with excitement as he pointed at the joyful sounding bells. Cassie and Ed chuckled at his enthusiasm and wondered if this was his first time hearing such a merry sound. Through the trees they glided down the lane, barely making tracks in the deep snow. Once they turned onto the main road, Luka climbed over Cassie's legs and leaned over the side of the sleigh to investigate the runners that squeaked as they slid across the hard packed snow. Cassie held onto him as best she could as she shared a warm smile with Ed, marveling at the young boy's wonder for the new world around him. Even the team seemed to sense the excitement, nickering and snorting as they tossed their heads, sending out small clouds of frosty breath into the air as they pranced. The ice-cold air bit their noses and cheeks as the horses picked up speed, kicking up clouds of snow as they easily pulled the sleigh of precious cargo. The sun illuminated crystals of ice that sparkled like diamonds across the white prairie. Cassie lifted her scarf over her mouth and nose and did the same for Luka as she tucked him back under the robe. Tipping her head back in the sunshine, she delighted in the bright blue sky that stretched far into the horizon and breathed in a deep breath of clean smelling snow and sighed contentedly. On one side of the road, they slid past branches and fence posts adorned with mounds of white, and on the other side spread the open prairie of snow-drifted hills and valleys, creating a picturesque scene, reminiscent of a Christmas postcard.

As the sleigh pulled into the yard of the snow-capped ranch house, Uncle George and Aunt Mabel stepped out on the porch, eager to welcome Cassie and Ed to their home on Christmas morning.

"Merry Christmas!" George and Mabel exclaimed in unison, smiling and waving as the sleigh came to a stop in front of the porch. Suddenly, seeing a small Indian child sitting between Ed and Cassie, they froze in place and their jaws dropped as their minds tried to make sense of it all.

Ed's voice was full of holiday cheer as he wished them a "Merry Christmas!" stepping out of the sleigh. Offering George and Mabel a reassuring smile, he helped Cassie down and took Luka in his arms as they climbed the steps together.

Mabel clamped her mouth shut as she tried to regain her composure and asked, "Land sakes, what have we here?" She stood wide-eyed, in disbelief.

Cassie stepped forward warmly embracing each of them. "Merry Christmas, Aunt Mabel and Uncle George," her calm voice and warm smile doing little to break their shock. "We'll explain everything in a moment." She tried to sound reassuring as she followed Ed inside to get warm.

Hearing Ed and Cassie arrive, Patrick and Kathy arose from their chairs by the warm crackling fire and went to greet them. "Merry Christmas!" they joyously sang out, as Ed and Cassie entered.

All seemed to go quiet as they were struck by the sight of Luka.

Kathy broke the silence, and asked, her voice full of concern, "What's going on, Ed? Whose child is this?" She was unable to fathom that her son would be involved with Indians, let alone holding an Indian child as if it was his own.

"Merry Christmas, Ma." Ed greeted her with a warm smile on his face as he went and gave her a hug with his free arm and a quick kiss on the cheek. He set the boy down and Luka turned to Cassie and wrapped his arms around her, burying his face in her skirt as he clung to her shyly.

George and Mabel closed the door behind them as they all stood surrounding Ed, Cassie, and the little Indian boy.

With no immediate explanation provided, George took charge of the questioning. "Cassie, what's this all about? Where did he come from?" George asked with seriousness, echoing the curiosity that everyone shared.

"Let's sit down and we'll explain." Ed led them to gather around the fireplace where the warmth of the flickering flames filled the room with a magical glow.

Cassie held Luka on her lap, while Ed settled beside her and began to explain the events of their night. The others sat in awe, intently listening, glancing intermittently at Cassie and the Indian boy and then back to Ed as he continued the amazing story.

Luka sat quietly, unaware of what was being said, and looked all around the room; that is, until he set eyes on the Christmas tree in the corner. Initially, he looked puzzled at the site of an indoor tree, then became excited as he noticed the beautiful ornaments. Luka pointed to the tree, then looked at Cassie, as if to ask if he could go see it. Cassie smiled, nodding her head, understanding his unspoken request. For a moment everyone's eyes followed them before returning their attention back to Ed.

Luka's eyes were full of wonder, as he gazed up at the towering tree and pointed excitedly at the little red bird hanging on a pine bough above him. Cassie carefully plucked it from the needled branch and handed it to him, allowing him to take a closer look. Luka tenderly stroked its red feathery wings and tail, then kissed it and smiled up at Cassie while cradling it in his small brown hands.

"Bird," Cassie whispered quietly, not wanting to disturb Ed telling of all that had happened.

"Burr-duh. Huuchuuh," Luka responded, his smile widening as he extended the bird towards Cassie.

"Yes, very good. Bird—Huuchuuh," Cassie affirmed with a smile and hung the red bird back on the branch. They continued their journey around the tree, removing different ornaments and naming them first in English and then in Luka's Indian language. Luka eagerly attempted to repeat every word Cassie uttered and she in turn echoed his words. Luka seemed to delight in the game they were playing.

Nearby, Ed continued to recount every detail he could recall about what had transpired, diligently addressing their questions as they sought for further insight.

Patrick shook his head in disbelief. "I can't believe they travel all that way during winter, especially in the midst of that storm last night. It was such a bad one. I began to wonder if we would make it home last night. And what a relief it was when we finally did. Going any further would have been dreadful. We could hardly see. If it hadn't been for the city lights guiding us, we could have easily lost our way," he added, looking at Kathy, who nodded in agreement.

Mabel put her hand over her heart, deeply saddened. "And that poor woman. Sick and in labor too. He must have been very desperate to seek help," she empathized, recalling her own experiences with miscarriages. Each one had been very traumatic for her and George, even under the best conditions and with a doctor present. She couldn't imagine how horrible it must have been for the woman in a strange place, unable to understand the language and no doctor to help her. It broke her heart.

Kathy looked over at Cassie, her concern evident as she voiced her worries, "Do you think she was contagious with something?" Kathy asked, worried about Cassie or Ed falling ill and fearing the worst.

"I worried about that at first," Ed said, his voice filled with reassurance. "But Cass didn't think so. The man and boy didn't seem to be sick, which gave her peace of mind that she wasn't contagious. We suspect that she got sick from the cold in her weakened condition. But I guess we'll find out soon enough if she was." Ed's gaze swept around the room at his family and loved ones as the weight of the possibility of bringing them some unknown sickness fell heavily upon him. "I'm sorry. We weren't thinking. Maybe it wasn't a good idea for us to come here today."

"Nonsense! We'll be fine," George interjected with certainty. "We will put our trust in the Lord." George had a steadfast belief that the Lord would bless those in His service. "You have done a good thing, helping them. Each of us would have all done the same thing. Right?" George posed the question of the others who nodded in agreement.

"Yes, we would have," affirmed Kathy, looking lovingly at Patrick as she squeezed his hand.

"I just wonder where they came from?" Patrick questioned, looking at the boy's buckskin tunic and leggings, searching for any tribal markings.

Ed rubbed his chin as he thought out loud, "The nearest reservation is around Wind River Valley, where the Eastern Shoshone tribe is located. I remember last July, the government and Chief

Washakie, along with other Shoshone and Bannock chiefs, signed the Fort Bridger Treaty. That's when the Eastern Shoshone tribes agreed to settle on the land around the Wind River. In exchange, the government promised to provide them with food, clothes, farming equipment and seeds, as well as provide them with a doctor, teachers, and others to help them get settled. The treaty even outlined plans for the government to build a mill, a blacksmith, and schools. Judging by the situation we find ourselves in, it seems unlikely that the government has fulfilled their promises," Ed added. "Now look at what's happened."

George sighed, his voice filled with concern, "No wonder they were fleeing; this little boy appears on the verge of starvation," he remarked. "Good grief, it's been well over a year ago since they were placed on the reservation. That's ample time for the supplies and resources to reach them. I'm afraid if this isn't resolved soon we'll start seeing more situations like this and perhaps even a full-blown war," he added, his gaze alternating between the boy and Cassie.

Joy shivered, recalling the Indian uprisings in Kansas and the attack on Ed's wife, as well as the violence that befell Cassie's family in Missouri. She reached out and clutched Clancy's hand for reassurance. "That frightens me," she quietly admitted, her voice filled with apprehension.

Clancy looked at Joy and tried to give her a reassuring smile. "We'll be safe. Don't you worry, Joy. The reservation is hundreds of miles away," he said, calming her some, then turning to Ed, asked, "Surely you won't keep him until his father returns?" Clancy's gaze lingered on the boy with the long black braids.

Cassie overheard and turned to look at Ed and then Clancy, determination evident in her voice, "I don't think we can do anything else. His father put him in my care, and I feel like it's what I would want, if it was my child," Cassie asserted protectively, squeezing the little boy's hand as she smiled down at him.

Patrick understood Cassie's feelings but had to consider his duty as Sheriff. "I should report this to the mayor. He can notify the Commissioner of Indian Affairs and let him do an investigation. At least let them know that the conditions are so dire they're fleeing. And maybe they can get the child back to the reservation with his people," Patrick suggested, thinking logically.

Cassie heart raced as she imagined what that would mean for the boy. "Oh no. Please don't do that," Cassie begged Patrick. "I don't want Luka to have to go back there. He wouldn't be safe. We can take care of him until his father returns. We don't even know if that's the reservation they came from. His father won't know where to find him. He said he would be back here in the spring," Cassie explained, her gaze moving between Luka and Patrick as tears gathered in her eyes. "Please."

"Patrick, I know as Sheriff you feel responsible to handle this, but I think waiting a little while won't make a difference. Please just give us some time to figure out what is best for the boy," Ed implored, his voice filled with urgency.

Patrick could see the deep attachment that Cassie and Ed had to the boy. "OK, OK," he relented, putting his hand up to stop their begging. "I guess it wouldn't matter to wait a little while. Maybe I'll just do some snooping around and see if there've been other instances. The last thing we want is more Indians coming here. You got lucky, I think. These people were looking for help." Patrick felt protective of his new family and the city he had stewardship over.

Cassie spoke up, her voice thoughtful, "I guess I'd never thought about it until now, how the Indians must feel. At least not in such a personal way. The settlers have pushed them further and further off their hunting grounds as they migrated into the area. And others are killing their food for sport, as I witnessed on my way here to Cheyenne. Now the government has confined them to reservations in an attempt to try to control them, but they have no resources, it seems. What do we expect them to do? What if it was us? What would you do to save your family?" Cassie posed the question to the group, inviting them to empathize with their plight. She still carried the pain of what had happened to her own family, but she recognized the complex nature of their circumstances. "Ed and I have every reason in the world to despise them. But how can we hate those who are just trying to survive?" Cassie asked, trying to help them see what she and Ed had come to realize.

Clancy had his own opinion on the matter, wanting to make his position clear. "Don't get me wrong, Cassie. We understand where you're coming from. It isn't right what's been done to them," he expressed, rising from his seat, and making his way to the fire-place to add a few more logs to the fire. "But we will not stand by while anyone threatens the safety of our families. We can't undo what has already been done. We must try to keep our families safe while doing what we can to help. And if that means caring for this little boy, then I'm behind you. But I won't stand by and allow Indian warriors anywhere near my family. Thousands of miles of open prairie free for anyone, and yet they claimed it as their own, considering it *all* to be theirs," Clancy said with a touch of irritation. "We have as much right as they do to settle this land. It's what has been done since the beginning of time. Civilizations are built or preserved by the strongest armies conquering the weaker ones. It's what we did to earn our freedom from the tyrannic rule of the British monarch."

"Look." George slowly stood with the support of his cane and turned to speak to his loved ones. "We understand that there are good and evil people in this world, Clancy. There are those who seek to harm oth-ers for their wicked purposes, and then there are the rest of us who just want to live in harmony with our fellow man. And we could debate this all day and still not solve the problem of humanity," he declared, as the family patriarch. "Today is Christmas, a time to celebrate the birth of our Lord, who brought salvation to *all* mankind," he said with finality. A smile spread across his face as a thought crossed his mind. "I think we should open our Christmas presents now!" he declared, his grin spreading as he looked around the room, excited for the surprises that awaited them.

Everyone nodded in agreement, feeling a sense of relief wash over them. They were eager to let the subject fade away and redirect their thoughts to something more uplifting.

George hobbled over to Ed and leaned down to whisper something to him as the others wondered what they were up to. Ed then made his way to George and Mabel's bedroom, emerging moments later carrying a large object concealed by a blanket that he cheerfully placed in front of Cassie.

George and Mabel stood on either side of the cloth-covered gift as Ed moved aside.

"Mabel and I wanted to give you this," George announced, a warm smile covering his face as he removed the blanket and revealed a beautiful rocking chair. "Merry Christmas, Cassie," he declared, joy and love resonating in his voice.

"Oh, Uncle George, it's absolutely beautiful. Thank you both so much!" Cassie exclaimed in delight, as she rose from her seat. Her fingertips lightly traced the intricately carved crest above the spindled back and graceful curved arms of the smooth, polished wood.

"Take a seat and see how it feels," Mabel suggested, her face beaming.

Cassie turned and lowered herself in the comfortable rocking chair and immediately set it to rocking with her feet, enjoying the gentle back-and-forth motion. Luka stood beside her and watched.

She opened her arms and he climbed onto her lap. Giggles filled the room as the chair tipped back and forth. Delighted, Cassie couldn't help but join in; his laughter brought a smile to everyone's face.

"Well, we can tell someone likes it," Mabel chuckled as she affectionately tousled his dark hair.

"I love it too. Thank you so much." Cassie beamed, smiling as she gave Mabel's hand a squeeze, then looked to her husband standing by. "Ed, can you go get the presents we brought?"

"Sure, darling," Ed said, and went to put his outerwear on, to go out to the sleigh.

"I'll come with you and help," smiled Clancy, and grabbed his coat and hat and followed him out, closing the door behind them.

"Let's see, I think there's something here for you, Joy," Kathy said, getting up and retrieving a gift from under the Christmas tree. "It's from Patrick and me," she added, passing the large flat rectangular box to Joy.

Joy carefully untied the ribbon and lifted the lid, revealing a beautiful riding skirt and fitted jacket. "Oh Ma, Patrick! It's beautiful. My very own riding outfit," she exclaimed with delight, as she carefully lifted the jacket out of the box and stood to hold it in front of her. The supple, light brown suede felt soft and warm, and the tailoring was impeccable. "I love it. Thank you both so much," she whispered, moved by the thoughtful gift, and went on to give each of them a heartfelt hug.

"Next, this one," Mabel announced, motioning

for Patrick to help her. "Joy, this is from George and me," she explained while Patrick retrieved a large item hidden behind the tree covered in a white potato sack. Placing it on the floor before her, Joy eagerly pulled back the sack to reveal a new saddle. "Uncle George! Did you make this?" she asked in amazement, her gaze fixed on the beautifully crafted dark leather. "It's beautiful." Joy reverently ran her hand over the smooth seat and saddle horn, tracing along the stamped rosettes and stitching on the sides. The scent of fresh rich leather filled the air. "Oh, thank you so much, I love it," she declared, unable to contain her gratitude she walked over to George and wrapped her arms around his neck and gave him a big hug and kiss on the cheek. Then she turned to hug Mabel with equal joy and affection.

George blushed from her show of appreciation and tried to explain, "I thought you could use one." Unable to hold back the excitement, he cracked a mischievous grin. "Especially now."

Joy gave him a puzzled look. "Uncle George, what do you mean?"

"Why don't you go look out the window and see for yourself." George pointed to the front window as his smile spread across his face.

Joy and the others eagerly went to the window. As they scanned the yard, they spotted Clancy standing beside a chestnut mare. Clancy's face was beaming with excitement as he waved at Joy through the window.

Without hesitation, Joy ran to the door, flung it

open and darted outside. "Oh, my goodness. She's beautiful!" Joy threw her arms around Clancy's neck, nearly knocking him over.

Clancy chuckled as he recovered and steadied himself, keeping an arm around her waist. "I thought you should have your very own horse if you're going to be living on a cattle ranch," Clancy explained, overjoyed with her exuberant reaction.

"Oh Clancy, I love her." Joy gently caressed the horse's muzzle, noticing the white star on the horse's forehead. "I still can't believe it. You bought me my own horse!"

"And you can name her whatever you want. She's yours." Clancy smiled broadly.

"I think I'll call her Star. Look at how the star on her head shines, just like the Star of Bethlehem on Christmas Day. It suits her perfectly. Star." Joy continued to affectionately stroke the horse's forehead and the space between the ears. The horse lowered her head, appreciating the attention. "I can't wait to ride her." Joy stepped to the horse's neck and ran her fingers through the bright copper mane. "Ma and Patrick gave me a riding outfit and Uncle George and Aunt Mabel gave me a saddle. It all makes sense now." Joy smiled over at Clancy as she put the puzzle pieces together. "You must have all conspired together for this," Joy deduced with glee, her green eyes sparkling.

"Yes, we've been working on it for the past month. It's been hard keeping it a secret. At one point we thought you would discover the surprise. It was tricky since I had to make sure you were in town when they brought her out and had to hide her in the barn for the past two days, but it was worth it just to see the look on your face," Clancy revealed and embraced her warmly. "Goodness, you're freezing. You didn't even put your coat on. You'd better get into the house before you catch a cold," he urged, placing a tender kiss on her rosy cheek. "Merry Christmas, darling. I love you."

"Oh Clancy, I love you so much. Thank you for such a thoughtful present. I adore her," Joy's voice was filled with love and affection. She wrapped her arms around Clancy and gave him another enthusiastic kiss. Releasing him, she quickly ran into the house where the others were watching from the window.

"You did good, Clancy," Ed praised with a nod and a smile as Clancy passed him, leading the horse back to the corral. With his arms loaded, Ed carried the remaining presents from the sleigh into the house.

As soon as Clancy returned from the barn they resumed unwrapping their presents. Most of the gifts were ones they'd handmade for each other. Cassie had crocheted various items, gifting the men grey wool scarfs, and the women red mittens, and colorful hot pads. In turn, Kathy gave Cassie a beautiful baby blanket that she had knitted out of yellow yarn.

Then it was Patrick's turn to present his gift to Kathy. "Merry Christmas, sweetheart." A warm smile spread across his face as he handed her a small ribbon-tied box.

Kathy carefully untied the ribbon and lifted the lid and gasped in surprise at the stunning cameo pin nestled on a bed of blue velvet. The oval medallion showcased a raised ivory stone intricately etched in the form of a woman's face, set against a backdrop of light pink agate, and encircled with a delicate gold framework. Kathy's eyes widened and began to well up with tears. "Oh Patrick, it's incredibly beautiful," she whispered as she gently traced the profile of the lovely maiden with her cascading curls and soulful gaze. "You shouldn't have. It's too much," Kathy's soft voice was filled with gratitude as she attempted to contain her emotions.

"Kathy, you're worth every penny. It's perfect for you." Patrick took it from her and pinned it on the neck of her dark blue dress. "There, it's as beautiful as you are," he said lovingly as he smiled at her shedding joyful tears.

"Oh, Patrick, you're the best." Kathy, overwhelmed with affection, embraced him tightly and kissed him.

"Oh Ma, it is so beautiful. He's right, it's perfect for you. It's the prettiest one I've ever seen, just like you, Ma," Joy gushed, hugging her mother, causing Kathy to cry more happy tears.

Joy was next and took a soft wrapped package and handed it to Cassie. "This is for you, Cassie, and for the baby," she said with a pleased smile.

Cassie unwrapped the gift revealing a pale-yellow hat and matching booties that Joy had crocheted. "They're lovely Joy, and so soft. Thank you. The baby will look adorable in these," Cassie said, and hugged her.

Kathy slipped away and returned from Mabel's

room, carrying a present that she handed to Patrick. "Merry Christmas, sweetheart," Kathy said smiling.

Patrick settled into a parlor chair and eagerly unwrapped the gift, his eyes widening in astonishment as he discovered a new gun holster and belt. "Oh my goodness, what's this?" he asked, clearly delighted, and taken aback.

"I asked George to make you a custom gun holster and belt. I thought you needed a new one," Kathy explained, her satisfied smile widening at his excitement.

"I think it's wonderful. Very exquisite craftsmanship." He was admiring the intricate details when his eyes fell upon his initials on the loop. "And personalized, how unique. I love them. Thank you both!" Patrick stood up, hugging Kathy and giving her a kiss. He went to George and shook his hand gratefully. "Thank you, George. It really is the best I've seen." Patrick slid the belt through the loop of the holster and buckled it around his waist. "And a perfect fit too." Patrick moved the belt low on his hips, noting it stayed in place.

"It's a new style we've been working on at the saddle shop. We're thinking of calling it the 'Cheyenne,'" said George. "Maybe it will become famous one day," he smiled impishly as he shrugged. "You never know."

Luka watched wide-eyed at all the activity, as he rocked in Cassie's new rocking chair.

"There's one last present," announced George.

Cassie and the others looked around, noting there were no more presents under the tree and all looked back at George, puzzled.

"Ed, in the furthest stall of the barn, you'll find your present. Why don't you go get it and bring it in." George glanced at Mabel, Joy, and Clancy with a knowing smile playing on his lips as they grinned back at him. It was clear they all shared the secret.

Ed put on his coat and hat and went outside. A few minutes later he returned from the barn, holding something in his arms. He had a huge smile and walked up to Luka and knelt down in front of the rocking chair. "Look Luka, look what we got for Christmas. A new puppy." Ed revealed the warm ball of fur, as Luka stopped rocking and his eyes got wide.

"Sadee'a!" Luka squealed with delight. He slid off the rocking chair to pet the little black and white puppy that wiggled in Ed's arms. "Sadee'a," Luka repeated, and kissed the puppy's silky soft head. The puppy whimpered and licked Luka on the nose, making him giggle.

There were "oohs" and "ahs" all around the group as they watched the puppy and Luka get to know each other. Ed carefully placed the pup on the floor and it wagged its small tail and sniffed at Luka's moccasins. Luka smiled and sat down cross-legged. The puppy playfully climbed over his legs, curled up and lay her head down and soon fell asleep as Luka pet her soft fur.

"Luka, do you like the puppy?" Ed asked, his smile reflecting the joy and excitement that filled the room.

Luka looked up at Ed when he heard his name and smiled. "Sadee'a," Luka repeated, his hand gently rubbing the puppy's head.

"This is the best Christmas ever," Ed exclaimed, smiling and looking around at his family. "I would have never guessed your dog had her puppies already," he said to George.

"She gave birth to them about eight weeks ago, not long after the roundup. It's been quite a challenge keeping them a secret. She's the smartest one out of the litter as far as I can tell," George explained, pointing towards the puppy. "They're all weaned now so I can start finding new homes for them. And if you want her, this little one is yours," George added, settling comfortably into his chair.

"What do you say, Cass?" Ed asked, looking over at her as she now sat in the rocking chair, her hands resting on her round stomach, rocking as she watched Luka and the puppy.

Cassie gazed up at Ed, her eyes sparkling. "I don't know how I can say no. Just look at how happy they are together." She looked back at the two youngsters rolling on the floor and laughed as the puppy playfully climbed onto Luka's chest, showering his face with affectionate puppy kisses. "Besides, I know you've been wanting a dog to help you with the cattle. So, my answer is yes," Cassie declared, her smile widening with delight.

"Wonderful!" Ed crouched down beside Luka as he sat up, to tell him the good news. "Luka, we get to take the puppy home. Sadee'a is coming home." Ed's smile spread across his face as Luka's eyes lit up upon hearing the two words he understood: Luka and Sadee'a.

"Sadee'a," Luka said again with a smile.

"What shall we name her?" Ed asked as he crouched down and smoothed the little boy's hair. "How about Sadie," Ed suggested to Luka, who smiled. "Close enough to Sadee'a. Since the pup's a girl, it would be a fitting name. How about it, Cass?" Ed looked to Cassie for approval.

"Sadie, yes, I like it." Cassie gave Ed a playful wink, knowing he was really thinking of Luka.

"Sadie," Luka repeated the name, his smile growing as he confirmed it with Cassie and Ed.

Chapter 23

My Joy is Full

As the family gathered around the table for their Christmas dinner, they excitedly shared stories about the wonderful Christmas presents they'd received and the efforts they'd gone through to create their surprises. Laughter filled the room as they animatedly recounted their close calls and the hurried measures taken to keep their surprises under wraps.

Luka sat in awe at all the food before them as they bowed their heads for the blessing. As they dished up, they wondered if he'd ever seen so much food all at once, and joked, that possibly neither had they. The table was loaded with the wonderful feast of roasted ham and mashed potatoes, baked beans, creamed corn, cooked carrots, rolls, and of course, Cassie's dill pickles. They filled their plates and watched Luka do so as well, reaching for the rolls more than once. Everything tasted delicious and smelled amazing. There was not a person there who didn't feel as if this was one of their best dinners yet.

***

With dinner over and cleaned up, Joy and Clancy decided to go horseback riding.

Joy excused herself to go change into her new riding clothes while Clancy put the new saddle on Star. Beautifully outfitted and bubbling with excitement, Joy hurried out to meet Clancy with her new horse, thinking this had been the most wonderful Christmas ever.

Together they rode down the lane, relishing in the sunny Christmas day. Reaching the main road, they left it behind and traveled over the small hills on the prairie, enjoying the crisp clean smell of fresh snow that kicked up with each of the horses' steps. The chestnut mare was a well-trained horse and Joy felt comfortable riding through the thick snow as Clancy broke a path for them. As they headed back along the road, Joy brought up the Indian and wondered if there was any possibility he was still around.

Clancy kept a keen eye out for any tracks as they passed Ed and Cassie's homestead, but the snow and wind had completely erased any trace of the Indian and his travois. Joy felt a sense of relief, hoping he had found safety and was far away from their home. She couldn't help but imagine the fear she would have experienced if they'd come to her home, even if they had just been seeking shelter.

***

Later that afternoon, Bart and Bea joined the festivities and were greeted by Ed as they arrived. As they entered, they were taken aback, just like everyone else, upon seeing Luka. Cassie guided Bea to the couch, inviting her to sit beside her so she could share the incredible story of how the Indian boy had become part of their family. Meanwhile, Bart politely declined a seat, allowing the women and expectant mothers take the comfortable chairs, and instead stood back, captivated by the accounts of the intense journey that Cassie and Ed had endured.

Bart couldn't help but be amazed at how composed everyone was in the presence of an Indian, especially Cassie. He had expected her to be deeply disturbed at the sight of an Indian, even if it was just a child. Something had certainly transformed within her. He vividly recalled the aftermath of the attack when he saw Cassie at the funeral, a mere shell of the vibrant woman he once knew and proposed to. Gaunt, broken, and distant, she seemed lost in her own world. Today, however, she emanated joy, love, and inner peace. Bart was genuinely happy for her, realizing everything had worked out as it should have. As he observed Cassie holding the Indian child in her arms, a radiant smile gracing her face, Bart contemplated the profound changes that had taken place since Cassie left him. Their lives had been marked by numerous transformative events in the past eight months. They had both matured and grown in ways they could have never foreseen. Cassie, once the woman he believed he wanted, possessed a fun-loving spirit, exuding optimism, and finding joy in life's simplest pleasures. On the other hand, Bea with her light red hair contrasting Cassie's, radiated a different kind of beauty—prim, poised, and thoughtful in all her actions. It was Bea who truly resonated with Bart's heart, fulfilling his deepest wants and needs.

He couldn't erase the memory of the day he arrived in Cheyenne, only to witness Cassie sharing a kiss with Ed. At the time, he believed he'd lost his chance at happiness. However, he now realized how mistaken he'd been. Losing what he thought was love, ultimately led him to discover his true path and heart's desire—Bea, his one true love, his soulmate.

Bea was his equal in every way. She not only supported his talents and abilities, but also inspired him to be authentic and true to himself. With her, he felt the best version of himself, and he knew he brought out the best in her too. He cherished her unique gifts and admired her personality like no one else had ever before. They complimented each other perfectly, just as Ed and Cassie did. He could see that. Bart could clearly see the natural connection they all shared as if they were family. He was grateful for the way God had orchestrated their lives to intertwine in the most beautiful way, and he held deep appreciation for that.

A contented smile spread across Bart's face as his attention shifted to Clancy, who sat beside Joy by the warm fire. Seeing the happiness radiating from Clancy filled Bart with joy, reminiscent of the night they spent together in jail, discussing life and love. They never expected to become such close friends, nor did they anticipate the incredible blessings that awaited them in finding the women of their dreams. Bart cherished his life now, finding great fulfillment in running his own business, second only to marrying Bea. The anticipation of becoming a father and starting a family of his own filled him with pure excitement and delight.

Bart marveled at the incredible fortune of being surrounded by such wonderful people. Being far from his own family, he never imagined feeling so at home, and he was truly grateful for the path that had led him to this moment. Bart realized he wouldn't change a single thing if given the chance. Through his experiences he'd learned valuable lessons about himself and love, which he would have never encountered had he remained in Missouri working for his father.

With his heart brimming with love and gratitude, Bart moved to sit beside Bea on the edge of the couch. He gently held her slender hand and placed a tender kiss on it, savoring the immense love he felt for her.

"Hasn't this been a wonderful Christmas?" Bart asked Bea.

"It most certainly has," Bea simply declared, but her eyes spoke volumes as she smiled lovingly back at her husband.

Cassie beamed at Bart and Bea, overwhelmed by a deep sense of gratitude for the close bond they shared. To her, they were more than friends; they were cherished family members. With a warm smile, Cassie interjected, "I must say, this is one of the most memorable Christmases I've ever had. Though I miss my family dearly, being surrounded by all of you makes me feel as if they're right here with me in this very room. You are my family now, and that's what makes this Christmas so incredibly special," her voice trembled with emotion as she looked around the room, her eyes filled with love for each and every person gathered there.

Ed came and stood beside Cassie, and she took his hand and looked up at him. "I hope you had a good Christmas, Ed," Cassie said wishfully.

"I believe this is the best Christmas I've ever had." Feeling his heart swelling, Ed smiled down at Cassie. "You're the best present I've ever had, and to spend it with my family and friends makes it even better." He looked around the room at all the loved ones who were present.

At about that time, George slowly stood and announced it was time for their Christmas devotional and gathered them around, waving Mabel and Kathy over from the kitchen as Patrick brought over some kitchen chairs for them to sit on. George opened with a prayer and then led them in a few of their favorite Christmas hymns.

Luka listened intently as they sang of Jesus' birth. Then Ed did the reading of the Christmas story and some scriptures about the early years of Jesus' youth. They watched Luka as he seemed to be trying to understand what was being said. Cassie wondered if he felt the presence of the Holy Spirit, as she did, as the scriptures were read, and hymns were sung. Deep in her heart she felt the confirmation from the Holy Spirit of the truthfulness of the message. A sense of peace and overwhelming joy enveloped her as she celebrated Christmas Day, honoring the birth of her

Savior, in the midst of her beloved family and friends.

During the reading of the scriptures, Bea beamed down at Luka, as he sat beside her and in awe, he reached up to touch her beautiful red hair. Bea smiled and leaned closer so he could observe it better. Bea was drawn to him; as a natural born teacher she loved little children, and wanted to take him under her wing to love and protect as Christ would. He appeared to be a meek and obedient child, gentle and respectful, as he sat still listening and watching all the strange new things around him.

It broke Bea's heart as she had listened to the story of how he came to be there. This poor little boy just lost his mother, baby sister, and father all in one night. His resilience amazed her, after all he'd been through, and wondered about what he'd already suffered in his first few years of life. Bea kept thinking of the poor Indian woman, pregnant and ill, coming to a foreign place begging for help from a person who couldn't understand her language. She felt sympathy for the woman that made Bea think about her own pregnancy. To lose her baby in childbirth was one of her biggest fears. She rested her hands on her stomach as she thought of her long-awaited dream. All she ever wanted was to have a family. She had waited so long and was so close to having her dream fulfilled and began to fear it might not happen. Bea could understand why Cassie was so taken with Luka. It was in their motherly nature that made them want to nurture him. She took his little brown hand and held it, admiring how small and soft it was. He looked down at her slender pale fingers and touched them with equal admiration.

As soon as the devotional ended, Kathy and Mabel went to the kitchen to heat the beef stew and make the biscuits.

"Thank you for having us here for Christmas, Mabel. It's been wonderful. It's been years since I've felt this much excitement and joy about Christmas," Kathy said, pulling the large pot of stew forward to the hottest part of the stove, then looked over her shoulder at Patrick sitting on the floor playing with Luka and the puppy. Ed and Cassie were arm in arm sitting on the couch, laughing and talking to Bart and Bea. Joy was sitting on Clancy's lap in one of the parlor chairs close to the fire, watching the happy trio. George had fallen asleep in the other parlor chair and was softly snoring. It made Kathy smile at the homey scene.

"You're most welcome," Mabel said and paused her kneading of the biscuit dough to look over to see what Kathy was smiling at. She noted her home was different this Christmas. The roaring fire in the fireplace, with family and friends sitting close by. The decorated Christmas tree in the corner, and pine boughs over the hearth, making it feel warm and Christmassy in the lamplight as darkness settled in. The sound of talking and laughter filled the home. Yes, it was a wonderful Christmas. "I feel the same way. Before Cassie came, Christmas was quiet and lonely here. This has been the most exciting Christmas we've ever had. I feel very blessed to have so many family and friends here with us this year. And just think, next year there will be at least two more to add to the bunch. My cup runneth over." Mabel praised God and shared a joyful smile with Kathy.

"Oh, what fun that'll be. I can't wait to be a grandma. Just look at Patrick," Kathy said glancing back at him giving Luka a horsy ride, crawling around the floor with Luka on his back, bucking and bouncing to make the boy giggle. "He's such a natural around children. He'll be a wonderful grandpa." Kathy's eyes filled with adoration as she watched him playing with Luka.

Mabel agreed. "And I'm with you, I can't wait to be a grand aunt. George and I love Cassie and Ed so much, and now Joy and Clancy. They're like our own family. I imagine we'll be seeing many small children around here in the next few years. This house will be bursting at the seams in no time." Mabel imagined little children laughing and playing as she placed the rolled-out and cut biscuit dough onto the pan to bake, delighting in the idea.

"I can't think of anything more wonderful," Kathy said, stirring the thick stew of meat and vegetables as it began to boil. "Do you think Luka will still be here then?" Kathy asked, tasting the stew's broth and adding a little more salt.

"I'm not sure. It's possible the little boy will be with us for only a short time, but it feels like he's already part of the family. I would hate for him to go back to live in those dire circumstances." Mabel glanced over at the leather-clad boy, now laying on the rug in front of the fire while Patrick took a rest. "I guess we'll see in time." The puppy climbed on top of Luka's back and licked his ears and neck, making him giggle. "I will miss his delightful laugh if he does leave. What a bright spirit he has, so much like his name," Mabel said joyously. "Every time he laughs, he fills the room with light." She placed the pan of biscuits into the oven and closed the heavy door to bake.

"Do you think that's what Luka's name means?" Kathy wondered out loud as she stirred the bubbling stew and slid it to the back of the stove to simmer and placed the lid back on.

"I know Luke means light in Latin. It's very close to Luka. Maybe that's why his parents named him that. He brings them light," supposed Mabel. "He's such a cheerful boy with such a bubbly laugh. It's contagious." Mabel laughed as Luka giggled again.

"I've certainly noticed a change in Ed and Cassie," Kathy remarked, standing shoulder to shoulder with Mabel at the stove while she poured them each a cup of coffee. "Their countenances seem brighter. Maybe it's the Christmas spirit, or perhaps something else entirely. But they both appear at peace, and it brings me joy to see them like this. Especially Ed, considering all he's been through these past few years. I don't think I've ever seen him look so happy."

Together they took their steaming cups of coffee and sat down at the table to wait for the biscuits to bake.

"I understand what you mean. Since you didn't know Cassie before, let me tell you, she's positively glowing now compared to when she first arrived here. Oh, she's always been a beautiful woman, but back then, she seemed so thin and frail, with dark circles and a deep sadness in her eyes. It was as if her heart and spirit were broken. But then Ed came into her life. He's been a Godsend for her. The transformation began the very first day they met. She had a sparkle in her eyes that now shines from her whole countenance. A deep happiness and peace have come over her, even when she speaks of her family. It's something only true love and God can do," Mabel replied, looking fondly at Cassie and Ed as they chatted with Bart and Bea by the fireplace.

"Yes, I see the change in both of them, and I feel it in myself too. After my husband and sons passed away, I thought I could be strong and settled for a life of contentment. I was merely surviving, not truly embracing life to the fullest. But when I met Patrick, he showed me how much more there was to experience and enjoy. He makes me feel young and alive again. Now, I'm genuinely excited about living. Before Patrick, I was merely existing. I'll forever be grateful to God for giving me such a wonderful man to love and share my life with," Kathy said, her eyes glistening with tears of joy.

Mabel reached over and put her hand on top of Kathy's. "I'm so happy for you both. You're wonderful people and it's amazing that you found each other," Mabel said, smiling as she reflected on their strong friendship.

"I've even been blessed with two more sons and

another daughter," Kathy said smiling as she looked over at Joy and Clancy. "I couldn't have asked for better men for my daughters or a better woman for Ed. Beth writes how blessed she is to have such a loving and supportive husband. From her letters it is clear she is very happy. And it's evident that Clancy is one of the best. I see how devoted he is to Joy, and her to him. Look how in love they are. Joy has become her joyful self again since we came here. She reminds me so much of Cassie, so full of love and happiness. Joy was only ten years old when the war started. She's always been an angel of a daughter. I believe we appropriately named her. She was cheerful and happy, never complaining, and such a peacemaker in our family. But after four years, when her father and brothers didn't come home, I could tell she had changed. She was full of pain and sorrow. Even when I tried to get her to talk about it, she wouldn't open up. I think she was trying to be brave for me," Kathy said as she sipped her coffee, thinking back to that painful time in her life. "I rarely saw her grieve for them or complain about having to work so hard to keep the farm running. As a mother, I worried that such a loss and burden at her age would affect her the rest of her life. It's hard enough as an adult, when all the men you love leave and never come home," her voice waivered as she wiped a tear away. "But fourteen years old is such a pivotal time in a girl's life. I had hoped one day she would let down her guard and trust her heart to someone. And then she met Clancy, and her joy began to come back. Clancy has been what she needed, strong and brave but sweet and gentle; he's totally committed to her. It comforts my heart to know she hasn't lost her faith in God after all that has happened. Through those challenging years, it would have been easy to be bitter and angry at Him. Maybe that's why God blessed her with such a good man." She smiled contentedly as she gazed at Joy and Clancy cuddling in front of the fire. "So, I thank the Lord for bringing us here, so we could both find love again." Kathy allowed the tears of joy to run down her cheeks, unchecked in the kitchen's soft lamplight.

"I'm grateful to the Lord for enriching our home with increased love and happiness. To be surrounded by Joy and Clancy's bright and lighthearted spirits, makes us feel young again. They have replaced the void we felt after Cassie got married, with full hearts. And look, our family continues to grow. You, Joy, Patrick, and the others, are as close to us as family. These have been the happiest months in our marriage, even with all the challenging things we've been through recently, and we have you all to thank for it. You've all been a great blessing to us." Mabel felt happy tears slip down her cheeks past the corners of her smile.

"And we're fortunate to have you too, Mabel. Your unwavering faith and commitment to God, along with George's, provide strength to all of us. We witnessed the care and patience you both displayed while George was recuperating; it couldn't have been easy, but your love for each other shone through. You are exemplary in your marriage and faithful companionship. As dear friends, you're as close to us as our own family," Kathy said, gently squeezing Mabel's hand. She glanced at the stove, the sweet aroma of cooked bread filling the air. "I believe the biscuits are done. Shall we call the others for supper?" Kathy wiped away her tears, smiling, and stood up to set the table, while Mabel went to take out the biscuits.

***

After enjoying the warm soup and biscuits, the happy couples bundled up and began their farewells. Hugs and gratitude for the wonderful Christmas presents and company were exchanged before they set off to their sleighs.

Kathy and Patrick waved cheerfully as they drove away down the snow-packed lane toward town, cocooned in cozy blankets and Christmas joy.

Bart and Bea started singing a carol as they left, their voices carrying a Christmas melody into the fading night.

Cassie and Ed followed last, bidding everyone a final Merry Christmas while standing on the porch bathed in the warm, yellow glow of light.

Luka sat snugly between them, cradling the puppy on his lap as they journeyed home. Soon, both Luka and the puppy dozed off, undisturbed even as the sleigh pulled up in front of the cottage, enveloping them in darkness. The only sounds were the horses' soft puffs and hooves stamping on the ground, creating a peaceful ambiance under the rising winter moon in the east. Luka's head rested against Cassie, his breathing slow and steady in deep slumber. Ed gently carried both Luka and the puppy into the house, while Cassie waited for him to return and assist her.

Ed gently placed Luka in his bed and covered him and the puppy with the quilts. The puppy whimpered for a moment before settling again, snuggling closer to Luka. Ed's heart filled with warmth looking at the sleeping boy, who seemed like a little angel in slumber. He thanked God for the blessings they had received that day, feeling complete peace and overflowing joy when he thought of Cassie and their baby. A tear rolled down his cheek as he stood there, expressing gratitude to God for Cassie and the love they shared, even for the innocent child who had come into their lives.

While waiting for Ed's return, Cassie's mind drifted back to the night before, and offered a prayer for Luka's father, asking for protection and comfort for both of them. Gazing up at the night sky adorned with twinkling stars and a radiant Milky Way, Cassie felt wonder at the vastness of the universe. Tears filled her eyes as she contemplated God's blessings upon her. The immensity of the universe and an overwhelming sense of love enveloped her. Whispering her gratitude, she looked heavenward and smiled. "My joy is full."

Chapter 24

Cassie's Miracle

One day while Luka was napping, Cassie sat down at the little table in front of the window and composed a letter.

January 4, 1870
My Dearest Madeline,
Thank you for the lovely Christmas card and gift you sent me. I treasure the beautiful lace collar even more knowing you crocheted it for me, not to mention how perfectly it complements nearly every dress I wear.

I hope you received the Christmas card I sent you. I pray that you and your family are all well and had a good Christmas.

I regret having taken so long to write back to you. So much has happened, and I want to share it with you now. Therefore, I apologize in advance; this letter may be quite lengthy.

To begin, I should fill you in on a few joyful happenings here in Cheyenne. I believe a few letters back, I told you about Ed's mother,

Kathy, and his sister, Joy, moving here to work at the Men's Clothing Shop with Bart and Bea. Well, incredible news; we've had a double wedding! At the end of November, Kathy and Joy were both married.

Kathy, shortly after arriving in Cheyenne, met none other than our wonderful new sheriff, Patrick O'Malley. It didn't take long for them to became friends and fall in love. (There must be something special about sheriffs in Cheyenne.) It was a miracle of love. Patrick, a long-time man of the law and sworn bachelor, quickly realized the widow Kathy was the one for him. Although Kathy took a little convincing to believe that a soon-to-be grandmother could fall in love and marry again, Patrick helped her see that love can happen at any age, and now the two of them are happily married. It's beautiful to witness that even later in life, two people can find love again.

And then Joy, Ed's youngest sister, fell in love with Clancy Holden, a local cowboy who also happens to be Bea's cousin. Clancy was one of the experienced cowboys that helped us during the fall roundup and even helped save Uncle George's life. Uncle George is fine now, but sustained a badly broken leg after a bull charged him, knocking him and his horse to the ground. That same day, Clancy volunteered to help Uncle

George with the ranch chores and Joy volunteered to help Aunt Mabel in the house while Uncle George recovered. It seems that all the time Clancy and Joy spent working together helped them form a quick bond, and they were soon courting. They got engaged on Thanksgiving and decided to be married on the same day as Kathy and Patrick, saving time on planning another wedding. The double wedding was held a few days later. We are so blessed to have added two more family members who are as dear to me as my own brother and father were.

These past two months have been filled with many joyful moments, but if I'm being completely honest, they have also been very challenging. I'm sure my pregnancy is a lot like most women's. At times, I am excited and happy that the baby is growing and will soon be here, and other times when I'm feeling uncomfortable, I become discouraged and easily frustrated with myself. I never realized until now how hard pregnancy is. When my mother was pregnant, I was too young to notice if she was tired or discouraged or even suffered from swollen feet or an aching back. Women don't mention these kinds of personal things in public, and I had no idea how difficult this would be. I find it is easy to feel sorry for myself but thank heavens for Ed; he doesn't let me stay sad for long. He knows just what to say and do to make me feel loved and supported. What a blessing he has been to help me through this trying time. I am grateful for his demonstration of increased love and patience as he helps ease my burdens and calms my worries.

Christmas was a day Ed and I will never forget. Somehow it has changed us both. Maybe if I explain what happened over Christmas, you will understand what I mean.

It was late in the night, Christmas Eve, during a bad snowstorm, when we awoke to someone banging on our door. You can imagine our shock when an Indian man, woman, and child came to our home seeking refuge. The family appeared to have left the reservation due to the poor conditions there and came looking for help when the woman became ill. Cautious, yet feeling obligated, Ed let them inside while the storm continued to rage on. Ed was terrified and wouldn't let me go near the woman, fearing I would get sick or worse. I admit, at first I was terrified as well, but once I saw the poor woman and child, my fears abated, and peace came over me. Then and there, I knew I had to help the sick woman who also appeared to be in pre-term labor. It took some time to convince Ed to let me assist her, but eventually he realized he would want the same for me if I was in her situation. I did what I could, using what I had learned from my mother practicing as a nurse and midwife. Sadly, the poor woman delivered. The tiny baby girl was perfectly formed but was born much too early to survive. Despite my best efforts to keep the mother alive, she joined her daughter in heaven that night. Our hearts broke as we watched the man mourn the loss of his wife and child. It's still hard to think of without shedding tears. I believe Ed was greatly affected as well, understanding what the man was feeling as his first wife and baby died so similarly.

Soon after the death of his wife and child, the Indian man prepared to take their bodies back to the sacred burial grounds. Before leaving, he placed the care of his son in our hands. We had a hard time understanding what little English he could speak, but the father seemed to be saying he would be back for the boy in the spring. We felt so bad for the little boy, having just lost his mother and baby sister, and then his father leaving him with strangers. Although he still misses his parents and cries at times, I am able to comfort him, and he seems to be thriving here. I love him and am pleased that he has taken a special liking to me. Perhaps I remind him of his mother. His name is Luka, but we call him Luke to help attract less attention in town. We don't want him to be taken away from us while we are waiting for his father to return. I must mention how smart Luke is for his age, being only about three or four years old. He is learning English much quicker than we are learning his language. Luke is a blessing in our lives and has filled our home with an abundance of love and laughter. A miracle has happened. As horrible as that tragic Christmas night was, in some miraculous way, by helping the Indian couple and caring for their child, Ed and I have found a change come over us. Our hearts are healed despite the tragedies that were inflicted upon us by the acts of others. I wondered how it was so. I had supposed that I had already forgiven those who harmed me and destroyed my home and family that night in May. But it wasn't until Christmas that I realized I had still been carrying around some deeply hidden bitterness, because once it was gone, I felt nothing but peace and love. Our hearts have been healed, and Ed and I believe it is nothing short of a miracle—the miracle of forgiveness. Only through the Savior Jesus Christ could this be possible.

I'm at peace and full of love for this Indian child and the baby I am carrying. No longer does my pregnancy feel like a burden. I want you to know what a miracle this experience has been for us, truly a blessing from God.

I will close now and write to you again soon. It won't be much longer, and I'll have

*great news to share with you about the baby.
Just another four or five weeks to go. God
bless you and your family. I love and miss you
and think of you often.*
    Your Kindred Spirit,
    Cassie

***

The month of January passed quickly with Luka
around. His energy was high, and he was constantly curious and eager to learn. Whenever he pointed
at something, Cassie or Ed would tell him what it
was. And when he wasn't talking, he could be found
exploring or playing with the puppy.

Over those four weeks, the puppy grew rapidly,
and with Luka and the puppy around, Cassie had little time to dwell on her own discomfort. The cold and
wind and occasional heavy snowstorm kept them
indoors most of time. Luka's inquisitiveness and
helpfulness made him an active participant in both
household chores and barn duties with Ed. Although
some tasks were too big for him, Luka remained
undeterred and always eager to try.

Ed also spent time training the puppy, teaching
Luka to use commands as well. Sadie, being a bor-
der collie, had a strong instinct to herd, which she
often displayed when following Luka. Her barking
and playful running encouraged him to head back to
the house when he wandered off too far. Cassie and
Ed delighted in watching their playful interactions,
making them great playmates and best friends.

Frequently, the sound of Luka's giggles woke them up, as the puppy showered him with wet kisses. The two were inseparable. While Luka embraced the customs and culture of living on a ranch, Sadie learned how to be a skilled cow dog.

The first Sunday they took Luka to church, they got many quizzical looks. Despite dressing him in "white man" clothes and cutting his hair, he stood out among the others. To reduce attention, they even decided to call him Luke, worried that someone might report him to the authorities, and take him back to one of the reservations.

With the looks came questions, which Ed seemed to subdue with a vague explanation about where Luka came from, calming the gossiping down some. Ed explained to Reverend Gather after church that his mountain man friend had just lost his wife and couldn't care for the boy and left him with them to care for in his absence. Most people in the West understood that mountain men frequently married Indian women and accepted his explanation. That earned Luka some sympathy. It was as close to the truth as they could come without outright telling anyone that he had come from a reservation. And since no one dared ask them directly, they left it at that. Besides, they reasoned, they couldn't have told them anyways; they really didn't know where he came from.

Ed and Cassie could tell Luke missed his parents. Sometimes Luke would cry for his mother and Cassie would hold and rock him until he settled. At night when Cassie would braid her hair, he would fall asleep holding her braid as she rocked him in her rocking chair. Cassie guessed it was similar to what his mother used to do. Once in a while, he awoke in the night crying and each time Cassie came and sat by him, stroking his hair, and singing softly to him until he fell back to sleep. Some days he would look outside as if searching for his father, but was quickly distracted by the puppy.

In the evening Ed would get down on the floor and play and wrestle with Luke, joined by Sadie, making Cassie laugh until her sides hurt. One of Luke's favorite activities was to sit on the porch swing and swing back and forth or climb on the porch railing. He was very active even for a boy of his age. They still didn't really know how old he was, but figured he was closer to four years old, the more they got to know him. He was learning to speak English quickly and his motor skills were quite good. And as the weeks passed, he put on weight, which made him appear even older than they had at first thought.

Cassie borrowed a children's primer from Bea and began reading to Luke at night. Each time, he would point to the pictures and listen for words he knew and repeat them. He was a very bright boy. He loved to sit on Cassie's lap, even though the space was becoming smaller and smaller as her belly grew. She would rock him in the rocker as they read, and Cassie found it a welcome distraction during that last month of her pregnancy. His goodnight hugs and kisses were endearing and stole Cassie's heart. Frequently he took her by his little hand to show her a new discovery he'd made, and she would share in his wonder. Luke was a ray of sunshine in their home that long grey winter month.

Luke was also very tender towards Cassie. Many times he would feel the baby kick him when he was sitting close to Cassie, and he would smile and say "baby" as he put his hand softly on her stomach and feel the soft kicking.

One evening late in January, Ed, Cassie, and Luke were gathered around the cheery fire that crackled and popped in the fireplace. Luke climbed onto Cassie's lap, and she began reading Luke *The Story of the Three Bears*. "Once upon a time, there were three bears who lived in a house in the forest. There was a Papa Bear, a Mama Bear, and a Baby Bear."

Luke stopped Cassie's reading and pointed to her. "Mama?" he asked, with a slight tilt of his head. Then, pointing to her stomach he asked, "Baby mama?"

Cassie smiled and nodded her head. "Yes Luke, I'll be the baby's mama."

He pointed to himself and said, "Luke." And then he pointed to Cassie with a questioning look. "Luke mama?" he asked.

Cassie found herself at a loss for words. He looked up at her with his big dark eyes and she followed her instincts. "Yes, Luke's mama," she said, and he hugged her tight around the neck. Didn't he understand his mother was dead? What words could she use to help him understand? Had she made the right decision? She didn't know, but it felt right at the moment.

Ed observed the heartwarming interaction

between Cassie and Luke, and when Cassie looked at him, he smiled in return. She playfully teased him, asking if they should call him "Papa" now.

"You can call me whatever you want; I'll answer to just about anything," he teased, eliciting a laugh from Cassie. "By the way, you're a wonderful mama," he added, feeling a surge of pride for Cassie. She had embraced her role as Luke's adoptive mother with such sweetness and love. It reminded him of his own adoption and the loving relationship he had with his mother all those years ago. Cassie resembled his mother in her patience and affection. She spent hours teaching, reading, and singing to Luke, just as his mother did for him. She had helped him build confidence and reassured him when he felt afraid. His mother was the first one he truly bonded with, trusted, and loved.

"And you're a wonderful papa," Cassie said sweetly.

Luke looked up at Cassie and repeated the word, "Mama." Then he gazed at Ed and pointed, saying, "Papa."

Cassie smiled as Ed shrugged his shoulders and said, "Yes Luke, Papa." Ed figured he would soon be a papa himself, so why not just let the father-son bond begin now?

Later that night, they put Luke to bed and blew out the lamps. It'd been a long day and they were both tired, especially Cassie. She had spent a lot of time cleaning that day, feeling the need to get things ready for the baby's arrival. As she settled in bed next to

Ed, she asked him to rub her aching back. His strong yet gentle hands kneaded her muscles as she tried to relax.

"You really are a wonderful mother, Cass. I was thinking of how much you remind me of my ma when I was adopted. You're so good with Luke. No wonder he wants to call you Mama. You give him so much love and attention. His mother in heaven is grateful, I'm sure," he said, wrapping his arm around her stomach and snuggling up to her. Cassie fell asleep, softly snoring within minutes. He found it cute that she had started snoring recently.

***

Cassie awoke a short time later, startled by a pain in her lower back. Carefully easing out of bed, she felt a gush as she stood up. *My water broke!* she thought in surprise. *I'm in labor,* she silently realized, and smiled. *No sense waking Ed right now, I'll just walk around and let nature take its course.* Cassie slipped on her robe and went to the pantry to get a towel, mopping up the floor. She changed out of her wet nightdress and into her old one. It felt somewhat ironic to her that she was in the same nightdress that had brought her to this point. *Oh well, no sense ruining my new one. This one will serve its purpose to the end,* she reasoned thoughtfully.

Cassie went to the kitchen and boiled some water for tea, stoked the fire, and sat in the front room reading and rocking, trying to pass time as the pains came and went. The puppy came out of the small bedroom and laid at Cassie's feet in front of the fire, as if to protect her. Sadie walked the floor with Cassie for hours until the pains became so intense that Cassie felt she should wake Ed. She didn't know how much longer it would be, but she was wanting his support now. Cassie sent the puppy to lay beside Luke and closed the door, not wanting to wake him, unsure of how loud her cries might become.

Cassie went into her bedroom, lit the lamp, and walked to Ed's side of the bed, gently shaking him. "Ed, honey. I'm in labor," she said softly.

Ed awoke and gasped at the words. "Cass, are you sure?" he asked with concern as he sat up in bed, trying to clear his head from his deep sleep.

"My water broke a while ago. I'm sure," Cassie said smiling. Then another contraction came, and she had to lean over and concentrate on breathing, as the pains intensified in her lower back and stomach. She couldn't walk through the contractions now.

Ed jumped out of bed and quickly put on his clothes. "Cass, what do you need me to do?" he asked, his voice filled with fear. "Maybe I should go get Aunt Mabel," he wondered aloud.

"No! Don't leave me!" She grimaced as she grabbed his arm and squeezed, trying to breathe through the pain. "I don't think there's much time." She gasped, trying to catch her breath after the strong contraction. "Go get the water boiling, and the scissors and twine, and a few extra towels." Cassie felt another contraction starting to build. "UHH!" she groaned involuntarily.

Ed was torn; he wanted to stay beside her and hold her hand, but she waved him off as she eased to her knees at the side of the bed. Frantically she sent him off as she began to feel pressure in her pelvis. "Go, hurry!" Cassie knew she was close. The urge to push was building. Remembering all her mother had taught her, she tried to remain calm and pant through the contractions. Momentarily, she thought of sleeping Luke and bit back her scream, not wanting to awaken him, and instead gritted her teeth and clenched the covers with her fists.

Ed felt panicked. His mind was going in a million directions. He hurried to get the water boiling and gathered the things she'd asked for. *What if I should go get help? But I can't leave her,* he reasoned in his head. *Dear God, please help her be safe,* he pleaded as he prayed in his heart. He could hear Cassie's moans from the kitchen. She sounded like she was in great pain, and he ran to her side.

"Help me into bed; I have to push." Cassie grimaced in pain. Despite the cold in the room, she was sweating, and her cheeks were flushed. Ed helped ease her into bed and propped her up with pillows behind her back. He rushed out to the kitchen, brought in the boiled water, set it on a bedside table with the other things, then placed the towels under her and sat on the bedside.

"What can I do now?" Ed felt scared and helpless.

Cassie looked up at him with pleading eyes. "Don't leave me. I'm scared; I don't know if I can do this." Shaking with pain and fear, she firmly gripped his hand as if he was her lifeline.

Ed listened to his heart and knew what she needed of him. "Cass, you can do this. You were made for this. Come on now, I don't know anyone stronger than you," Ed smiled reassuringly. "I love you, and we can do this together." He leaned forward, kissing her on the forehead.

Cassie tried to smile, as his confidence and reassurance eased her fears and gave her strength to keep going. Cassie nodded her acceptance.

"Here it comes again," Cassie said as the contraction and urge to push came stronger than ever. "I have to push," she said with gritted teeth, and filled her lungs with air.

"Then push, darling! Push hard!" Ed cheered her on.

Cassie pulled her knees up to her chest and pushed with all her might until the contraction eased up. She relaxed and he wiped the sweat from her forehead. "Good job, Cass. That was great. You can do this," Ed said, feeling a sense of peace come over him.

Another contraction started building again. Cassie held her breath and tried to push as hard as she could. "UHH!" she nearly screamed with the pain. The baby was crowning, the baby's head was nearly out. Cassie tried to pant but was shaking and unable to focus from the pain.

"Cass, Cass, look darling, the baby is almost here!" said Ed excitedly, as he was about to witness the miracle of birth.

Cassie's eyes pleaded with him and God as she

tried to endure the pain.

"One more time, honey. Push really hard, slow and steady," he said, preparing the towel.

Cassie looked up at Ed's joyful face and pushed with all her might. "UHH!" she groaned through the end of the contraction as the baby's head emerged. The pain was overwhelming, and she longed for it to be over. Fortunately, she didn't have to wait long. The next contraction required little effort, and with great relief, the baby's body was born.

Ed took the baby into the towel, wiping the face, and rubbing the baby until it cried. Cassie lay back, panting from the exertion, her eyes closed as she heard the baby cry for the first time. A wave of relief washed over her, and tears of joy streamed down her cheeks.

"Open your eyes, darling. Meet your daughter," Ed said as he handed Cassie the newborn baby girl.

Cassie opened her eyes and her arms as Ed placed the baby across her chest. "Oh Ed. She's so beautiful," Cassie said joyfully through her sobs as she stroked the baby's soft cheek. "Shh, sweetheart, it's okay, Mama's here."

The little baby girl settled for a moment and opened her big dark eyes to gaze at Cassie's face. The baby frowned and let out a broken-hearted cry that Cassie soothed with tender kisses.

"Aww, I know, honey. It was hard for Mama too. But now you're here, safe and sound," Cassie whispered, trying to comfort her.

Ed tied off the cord and used the sterilized scissors

to cut it. He wrapped up the afterbirth and set it aside, quickly cleaning up the bed.

"Oh Cass, she's so beautiful. She looks so much like you, especially with all that dark hair," he said, beaming at them while quickly wiping a tear away. "I'm so incredibly proud of you, darling. You did such a great job. I love you so much," he said, kissing her tenderly.

They stopped kissing when the baby started crying again, and they both laughed. Ed leaned down to kiss the baby's forehead. "She wanted her own kiss too," he said smiling as he wiped away another tear.

"I couldn't have done it without you, sweetheart." Cassie smiled up at him; seeing how emotional he was made her heart swell with love for him. "I love you so much, Ed," she said, taking his hand. "You can hold her if you want. Here, go see your papa." Cassie gently helped Ed take the baby from her arms.

"Oh, my goodness, you're the prettiest little thing next to your mama," Ed said as he looked down into the baby's pretty dark grey eyes, her long dark lashes fluttering as she tried to see who was standing above her. "I love you, little one," Ed whispered, tears running down his cheeks. His heart overflowed with love for her. Ed looked at Cassie lying in bed, looking so beautiful with her flushed cheeks and sparkling green eyes. "Oh Cass, I love you so much. You've made me so happy." Ed sank down on the bedside facing Cassie, and leaned over and kissed her.

Cassie sat up and looked at the baby in Ed's arms. "She loves you too, Papa. Almost as much as I love you," she said as more tears of joy ran down her cheeks.

Ed handed the baby back to Cassie as the baby rooted around. "I think she's wanting to eat now," he said smiling, and helped Cassie get comfortable so she could feed the baby. He thought it was the sweetest thing to see Cassie feeding her. He marveled at the miracle of birth. It was amazing to him that a woman could do such a hard and wonderful thing. He'd seen childbirth go badly twice before, and to him it was a miracle—a perfect little being had been created and born alive and well.

"What shall we name her?" Cassie asked, gazing at the tiny face and cradling the little body as she nursed.

"Maybe we should call her Cassie's Miracle," Ed said emotionally, his arm enveloping Cassie as he pressed a gentle kiss on her forehead. "Because she truly is a blessing, your miracle," he added, his voice wavering as he leaned his head against Cassie's.

As Cassie gazed at the precious little baby in her arms, she couldn't help but agree. "She is my treasured little blessing, a true miracle," Cassie's voice quivering with emotion. After taking a calming breath, she proposed, "But perhaps Megan would be a more fitting choice." A warm smile graced her face as she looked at Ed. "Ever since I read *Little Women* I've adored the name Meg. What do you think?" Cassie asked, her heart melting as the baby's tiny fingers wrapped around hers.

"I love it. Anything you want I would give you,

darling. You are my hero. And I love you so much, Cass," Ed said as his heart swelled to overflowing.

"I love you, Ed. You're the best thing that ever happened to me. You are such a blessing in my life. Thank you for being there for me when I needed love and sticking by me through it all. I will love you forever and ever more," Cassie vowed. Fresh tears of joy spilled onto her cheeks as she looked into Ed's glistening eyes and thanking the Almighty for all her blessings.

"Honey, you were the one who was there for me. I'm whole and full of love because of you. I'll be yours forever," Ed said passionately, and gently leaned forward, kissing her, long and sweet.

The End.

9 781957 506746